THE SONS
OF GODWINE

Part Two of
The Last Great Saxon Earls

BOOKS BY MERCEDES ROCHELLE

Heir to a Prophecy

The Last Great Saxon Earls Series
Godwine Kingmaker
The Sons of Godwine

THE SONS
OF GODWINE

Part Two of
The Last Great Saxon Earls

Mercedes Rochelle

ANGLO-SAXON
ENGLAND

Map by Gregg Sollisch

1

ENGLAND AND THE
CONTINENT BEFORE
THE NORMAN CONQUEST

N

Edinburgh
SCOTLAND
•Bamburgh
•Alnwick

•Durham

NORTHUMBRIA

York
•Stamford Bridge

R. Ouse

North
Sea

•Rhuddlan

Harlech •

MERCIA

EAST
ANGLIA

•Ely

WALES

•Hereford

Gloucester•

•Oxford

•Bristol

R. Thames London

WESSEX

•Winchester

•Dover

FLANDERS

Hastings
Pevensey

St. Valery

PONTHIEU

English Channel

Bayeux

Rouen

VEXIN

NORMANDY

•Paris

Val-es-Dunes

R. Dives

R. Seine

St. Brieue •

•St. Michel

Dinan• •Dol

BRITTANY

MAINE

ANJOU

miles: 0   50   100   150   200

Map by Gregg Sollisch

CAST OF CHARACTERS

AELFGAR, EARL OF MERCIA, born 1030: Son of Leofric and Godgifu (Lady Godiva). Earl of East Anglia in 1051 and again in 1053. Probably died late 1062.

BALDWIN V, COUNT OF FLANDERS born 1012: Reigned 1035-1067. Half-brother of Judith of Flanders, father of Matilda duchess of Normandy.

COPSIG: Yorkshire Thegn who became Tostig's right-hand man in Northumbria.

COSPATRIC SON OF MALDRED: Member of the younger branch of Uthred earl of Northumberland (Bernicia) who was killed on the order of Canute in 1016. Cousin of King Malcolm III.

EALDRED, Archbishop of York from 1060-1069, Bishop of Hereford 1056-1060. Ealdred crowned Harold Godwineson king in 1066.

EALDGYTH OF MERCIA: Daughter of Earl Aelfgar and sister of Edwin and Morcar.

EDITH SWANNECK: Also known as Edith the Fair. Wealthy East Anglian noble woman; almost nothing is known about her background. She married Harold Godwineson shortly after he became earl of East Anglia.

EDITHA GODWINESON born c.1025: Eldest daughter of Earl Godwine, married to King Edward the Confessor in 1045 and crowned queen.

EDWIN, EARL OF MERCIA born c.1028: Eldest son of Aelfgar Earl of Mercia and grandson of Leofric Earl of Mercia. Edwin became earl in 1062. He died in 1071.

GOSPATRICK SON OF UHTRED: Member of the senior branch of Uthred earl of Northumberland (Bernicia) who was killed on the order of Canute in 1016. Ruler in Cumbria during Siward's reign.

GRUFFYDD AP LLEWELYN, Prince of Wales, born 1007:
Prince of Wales 1055. Married to Ealdgyth, sister of
Edwin and Morcar.

GYRTH GODWINESON born c.1032: Fourth son of Earl
Godwine. Gyrth became earl of East Anglia between 1055-
57.

GYTHA THORKELSDOTTIR born c.997: Wife of Earl
Godwine and mother of Harold Godwineson. She was born
in Denmark and given in marriage to Godwine during
Canute's reign.

HAKON SWEGNSSON born c.1047: Illegitimate son of Swegn
Godwineson, taken to Normandy as hostage along with
Wulfnoth and released to Harold in 1064.

HAROLD GODWINESON born c.1022: Second son of Earl
Godwine. Harold became Earl of East Anglia in 1045.
After Godwine's death in 1053, Harold became second
Earl of Wessex. King of England 1066.

JUDITH OF FLANDERS born 1030-35: Wife of Tostig
Godwineson and daughter of Baldwin IV Count of
Flanders (half-sister to Baldwin V). Aunt to Matilda
duchess of Normandy. Married around 1051 to Tostig.

LEOFWINE GODWINESON born c.1035: Fifth son of Earl
Godwine. Leofwine became earl of Kent, Essex,
Middlesex, Hertford, Surrey and probably
Buckinghamshire between 1055-57.

MALCOLM III, KING OF SCOTLAND b.1031: Also known
as Malcolm Canmore (great chief). Defeated Macbeth at
the Battle of Dunsinane. Reigned 1058-1093.

MATILDA OF FLANDERS, born c.1031: Wife of William the
Conqueror and daughter of Baldwin V Count of Flanders.
Niece of Judith of Flanders.

MORCAR, EARL OF NORTHUMBRIA born c.1044:
Younger son of Aelfgar Earl of Mercia and grandson of Leofric Earl of Mercia.

STIGAND, Archbishop of Canterbury (1052) and Winchester (1047).

SVEIN II ESTRIDSSON, KING OF DENMARK born c.1019: son of Jarl Ulf and Estrid Svendsdatter (sister of King Canute). King from 1047-1074. Took his mother's surname to emphasize his Danish royalty (she was daughter of Sweyn Forkbeard).

SWEGN GODWINESON born c.1020: Eldest son of Earl Godwine. In 1043 became earl of territory including Gloucestershire, Herefordshire, Oxfordshire. Outlawed for kidnapping Eadgifu, Abbess of Leominster and had a son by her named Hakon. Exiled for life and declared *nithing* for killing his cousin Beorn. Died while on pilgrimage in 1052.

TOSTIG GODWINESON born c.1026: Third son of Earl Godwine. Tostig became Earl of Northumbria in 1055.

WILLIAM THE CONQUEROR, Duke of Normandy and King of England, born 1028: duke from 1035; king from 1066. Died 1087

WULFNOTH GODWINESON born c.1040: Sixth and youngest son of Earl Godwine. Spent most of his life as as a hostage to William the Conqueror.

PROLOGUE:

Queen Editha Writes

It is near the end of my life now, but I do not lie to say I am glad of it. Truly, what do I have left to live for? Four of my brothers died in battle six years ago, and Wulfnoth languishes a hostage in Normandy. My mother was forced to flee the country. I am left all alone.

Even after all this time, grief threatens to overwhelm me when I think about my family...so powerful, so vigorous, yet all destroyed in a few short years. But still, we left our mark on history; never again will the world see our equal.

I can say this now without vanity, having seen what the Normans did to our country. And to think that at one time I actually admired them. That was before...when I prospered, secure in the knowledge that my father was on hand to keep them under control. How was I supposed to know my own husband would turn against my family?

Back then, the Normans were only visitors, willing to share their knowledge and culture with our court. They were always polite to me, and I found their conversation fresh and exciting. Even after Duke William became King, he treated me with respect—for a while, at least. But William showed his true colors soon enough; he took my lands away, and exiled me to this dreary castle in Winchester, where my predecessor Emma lived out the end of her life. How ironic that I swore I would never follow in her footsteps.

But I'm not here to write about myself. On the contrary, I am afraid the Normans are determined to blacken the glory of my family and justify their hated presence here. This I must not allow. My brothers and I have had our disagreements along the way but we are all heirs to our beloved father and our story must be told.

When I arranged for the good monks of St. Bertin to compose a history, I originally intended it to tell the story of my father, and I persuaded all my brothers to write down their memories. Once Harold became King, I realized our whole family needed to be part of the story—especially since poor Tostig's reputation had suffered so much after the rebellion. As if they understood the seriousness of the situation, much of their remembrances were given me during those brief, worrisome days before they were killed.

But once William became King, I knew my project would be suppressed and I changed the commission to a Life of my husband King Edward. And so it stands. But I preserved my real story, and intend to pass it on to my last surviving brother Wulfnoth, who can prepare it for a future chronicler not hostile to our house. Harold, Tostig, Gyrth, Leofwine, and Wulfnoth...all are very dear to me. They are the best witnesses to the momentous events that signaled the end of our age.

Chapter 1

HAROLD REMEMBERS

I don't remember much about my childhood, probably because it was uneventful. Or at least I thought so. How was I to know we were among the wealthiest, most powerful families in all of England? I didn't realize that father had climbed up from obscurity to the top ranks of our kingdom through sheer cunning and wisdom. How King Canute the Great had taken him in and favored him over all of our countrymen, and how father had to make some difficult choices along the way. Some called him betrayer of our people, while others saw him as our best advocate.

By the time I was born all that uncertainty was behind him. As a child I do remember a lot of activity in our household, for back then Canute had a palace in Bosham, too. He was always coming in and out, trailing a pack of courtiers who usually found themselves waiting for something to do. So they played with me and my brother Swegn, letting us climb onto their backs and beg to be carried around. We learned to handle their swords and axes until we finally got blades of our own. We were never bored, though we did fight amongst ourselves, especially when Tostig got big enough to defend himself.

I never understood why Tostig was always picking a fight with me. It seemed like no matter what I did, he flew into a temper and came at me with his fists. I was bigger than him, so he didn't hurt me much, but I found his rages very tiresome. As he got older, we came to a sort of understanding; after all, we didn't want to let father down. He had enough problems with Swegn.

My older brother Swegn was an odd child, fretful and spoiled, for father gave him anything he wanted and sheltered him from mother's impatience. He was miserable, the rotten apple in our family, yet still father loved him best. The rest of us never understood. Our parents frequently fought about him, and Swegn seemed to revel in the attention. He was always getting into trouble, until the day he died. His troubles just got bigger as he got older.

Everything changed when Canute's little daughter drowned in the mill race and the king no longer wanted to come here. Father started spending more and more time in Winchester, and mother stayed gladly at home, for Bosham was—and still is—the most beautiful place in England.

She had much to do. No matter how long he was away, father still managed to get her with child again and again. There were eleven of us all told, not counting the stillborns, and I was the second. The second son. And mother's favorite, to tell the truth. I don't really understand why mother didn't care for Swegn, but I couldn't help but be influenced by her attitude. When she shouted at my big brother, I would try to hit him. Of course, this infuriated father, but he wasn't around all that often so it didn't matter.

After me there was Tostig, then Edith who was everyone's favorite. I was already ten years old when Gyrth came along, then three years later came Leofwine. By the time Wulfnoth was born I was eighteen. I lost track of the birth dates of my other siblings: Alfgar, Edgiva, Elgiva, and Gunhilda; to be honest, they were too young to be of much interest to me.

And then there was my nephew Hakon, ill-begotten from that shameful liaison between Swegn and the Abbess of Leominster, the ungrateful girl my parents took in as a ward. After Swegn's exile, father took the child into our household, so there

8

was another addition to our family. He was close to Wulfnoth in age, so those two were raised together.

Father made sure we had proper military training and he brought in the best warriors both Danish and Saxon. We learned our letters and spoke three languages, though I admit Edith was a much better student than I was. I loved the swordplay and horseback riding, and then discovered hawking. Before long I had established the largest mews in all of Wessex. I was proud of my birds and took one everywhere with me. Falconry is still my greatest passion.

Even today I look back on Bosham as my safe place. I had no troubles, no responsibilities, no worries. Oh, it seems so long ago!

TOSTIG REMEMBERS

I used to wonder why Harold and I didn't get along when we were young; in fact, I wasted a lot of time worrying about it. After all, we had a common enemy in our brother Swegn. Swegn came first with our father, no matter what we did to gain his attention. Swegn, Swegn, Swegn. I got so tired of hearing his name all the time, I wanted to scream. It felt like I was always biting back on my anger, and there were times I didn't know where to turn.

Swegn knew he was protected, and you can be sure he took advantage of us. He'd steal my things, though in a clever way so I couldn't prove it. Sometimes I would fight back when he insulted me, though he'd always run to father. "Don't *peck* on Swegn" father would shout at me. "Stop bothering him." And if I didn't, I knew what would happen. A backhanded slap would follow, even if I was right and Swegn was wrong.

And it seemed that Harold was always a witness, snickering behind his hand. That made it even worse. I was so mad at him for not standing behind me. It was as though he didn't care how much I got scolded, just as long as it wasn't him getting into trouble.

Oh, yes. Swegn was the favorite with our father—not Harold. But it never bothered Harold that father didn't love him best, because he had mother to turn to. She showered him with attention, and ignored Swegn instead. Although I could tell that Harold was not quite satisfied with his place, he was a lot better off than the rest of us. It seems my parents were both alike in that way: they each favored one son, and one son only. So I naturally turned to Harold, and I can truly say I worshipped him—when I was young, that is. I followed him everywhere, trying to walk like him, talk like him, be like him. And where did it get me? Nowhere.

I think he saw my behavior as competition, which it wasn't, really, at all. I was just imitating him; I thought he was godlike. His physical perfection was as natural as his easy manner. He had splendid arms and shoulders, sinewy legs, and not an ounce of fat anywhere on his body. He was never nervous, never at a loss for words. But what I remember most was that Harold was so clever with his hands...so strong. He could do anything he wanted, anything at all. Everything came easy to Harold, not like me. I had to struggle to keep up with him. I was always having trouble expressing myself, and I'd just get frustrated and angry, especially when he laughed at me.

So when he should have appreciated my efforts, instead he did his best to defeat me. He laughed at my clumsy attempts at writing; I was no good at it, and I knew it. He made fun of my speech, my eating habits, my poor archery skills. And when I lashed out at him in anger, Harold beat me into the ground, just for fun.

Ah, yes. Harold taught me not to admire him. So instead, I decided to best him. I trained in secret, learning how to use my

10

fists, then my sword. Afterwards, when he least expected it, I would attack him, trying to get on top. But I could never win with Harold; he would use some trick or other to get under my defenses, then straddle me on the floor, leering down at me with those perfectly straight teeth. I hated him. I think I wanted to kill him.

So instead of joining together and teaching Swegn a lesson, we spent most of our time fighting with each other. It became a challenge, even a pleasure, to see how I could sting him. Oh, he was quick, all right, but now and then I managed to sneak something past him, catch him making a mistake. Then I would exploit my advantage for all it was worth. I never felt guilty about it, because he deserved everything he got.

It was Harold's vanity that usually brought him trouble. Mother made him so full of himself, he thought he could do no wrong. So he usually opened his big mouth, interrupting our parents when he wasn't spoken to, or saying something clay-brained just to hear himself talk. This usually got an unpleasant reaction out of father, who I don't think really liked him very much.

I remember the time my father came home after King Canute died. His face was so changed I hardly recognized him. We always knew father loved the king, but I never realized how much until then. It was as if he had lost a brother. Well, a brother he loved. For a couple of days we tiptoed around the house, trying not to make too much noise; but Harold, outspoken as ever, thought he had the right to intrude on our father's grief.

"I don't understand, father," he said. "You always said that the Saxons should have a say in their own government. Now that the king is dead, isn't this our chance to take what is due us?"

My father raised his head from his hands, looking at Harold so angrily even my brother stepped back a pace. "Get away from me," he warned. "You don't know what you're saying."

Even then, Harold didn't have the sense to stop. "But Canute was an invader; he imposed Danish rule on the Saxons."

Father leaped to his feet, eyes flashing. He even knocked the bench over, so violent was his reaction. "He is more Saxon than most of us," he almost shouted, but his voice broke instead. "In his heart. He loved our country! Why do you think he spent all his time here? Now get out, both of you, and leave me alone!"

There you are. Once again, I got into trouble because of Harold's insolence. But this was the first time our father ever told us to go away. I was so angry I took extra revenge, goading Harold until he burst into tears. This shocked me into silence; never had I seen my brother cry. He didn't have the strength to strike back; he just sat down on the floor and bawled like a baby. We were just boys then, remember.

I'm embarrassed to admit it, but I felt sorry for him, almost as if it was a shame to see him lose his confidence. But when I apologized and put my arms around him, he shrugged me off like I was his worst enemy. That was it. That was the last time I ever felt any concern about his feelings.

It wasn't until later I discovered the real reason for my father's reaction. Although he loved the king greatly and would have defended him with his life, what bothered him most was having to live with the dilemma of abandoning the Saxons to join the Danes in the first place. To us Godwines, the end justifies the means, and he found it necessary to fight in battle against the Saxons so he could gain Canute's confidence.

This brought him the scorn of his people, and especially his parents. Harold never knew this; nor did he ever know that father brought me home to meet our grandfather. It was our little secret, father's and mine. He and my grandfather Wulfnoth hadn't spoken for thirty years, but they made up in the end.

Anyway, even though we often fought, I can still say that Harold and I understood each other—where it counted. If he really needed help, my brother knew he could depend on me. I never let him down.

GYRTH REMEMBERS

I don't remember anything about King Canute; I was only three years old when he died, and ten when King Edward took the throne. But I do remember those early years when I was growing up. There was always something happening in our household and my father was away much of the time, trying to appease Canute's sons. I think he had a difficult time of it, but he tried to keep his troubles from the rest of us.

My brother Harold is ten years older than me, so he didn't really give me much attention. Neither did Tostig. I spent most of my time with Leofwine, so it was the two of us and the two of them, growing up.

Well, not exactly. I can't remember many days when Harold and Tostig were not fighting. It's really too bad, because I loved the both of them and it made me cry when they started shouting at each other.

Sometimes when I cried, Harold stopped and picked me up. I think he was a little ashamed of himself, and he tried to play with me. He would ask me what I was doing, but when I started to show him he quickly got bored and turned away. Tostig might come along later when Harold wasn't around; he would bring a sweet for me and Leofwine and made us promise not to tell.

As I got older, once in a while Harold would take me riding with him. He taught me how to use my legs to stay in the saddle and once he even brought a falcon along. I still remember how thrilled I was when he released that bird and it shot like an arrow toward its prey, taking it down in an instant. My brother cooed

13

and clucked at that lucky falcon all the way home. He was amazingly gentle and I think his bird loved him. How could it not? I was almost jealous.

I was so disappointed when they made Harold the Earl of East Anglia. I was fourteen then, and off he went to live in his own house far away from us. I knew I would never have the chance to get to know him as an adult; he still thought of me as a child and he seemed so far above me I dared not approach him. I waved as he rode away from Bosham with his little retinue, and as if he sensed it he turned and waved back to me. I treasured that moment, even though Tostig gave a little snort and mumbled something about being finally rid of him.

I understood why Harold was mother's favorite. He should have been the oldest. He was a worthy successor, not Swegn. Harold was strong where Swegn was weak. Harold always seemed clean and he smelled so fresh. Swegn always looked like he had been rolling in the dirt. When Harold smiled, it felt like the sun came out. Swegn rarely smiled, and his face was creased from so much frowning. There just wasn't any comparison between them.

I don't think Swegn was ever nice to Leofwine and me. I can't say he was particularly mean to us, but he always acted like we were a nuisance if we got in his way. We simply learned to avoid him. When he got in trouble, Swegn had a way of acting the repentant which always seemed to work with father. He'd done it over and over, and father always forgave him no matter what our mother said. And she objected plenty of times. Harold agreed with her since he was usually a witness, and this would infuriate my father even further. They would have such terrible arguments over Swegn, and the rest of us could only sit back and watch helplessly. We never understood why Swegn usually escaped punishment. Why was he father's favorite?

When he left home for Herefordshire no one missed him. Except for father, of course. This was before all the trouble

14

began...before his exile. When Swegn abducted Eadgifu and father brought her home, shamed and heavy with child, the tension between my parents was almost unbearable until the babe was born. My father named him Hakon, and he sent Eadgifu immediately back to where she came from. Things settled down after that. Tostig took an odd liking to the child and tried to talk us into paying attention to him. But I guess it was like Harold and me only in reverse. What use had I for a baby?

HAROLD REMEMBERS

Going back, I was only thirteen when Canute died, and his passing turned our household upside down. Father was never really the same after that, as though he had lost his best friend. I suppose he did, after all. He was always the king's favorite, but his position changed when Canute's sons took over. They were not at all like their father, nor did they possess any of his better qualities. Both Harold Harefoot and Harthacnut were vulgar, selfish men and they drove father to distraction.

When King Edward came to the throne, for a while it seemed things were going to improve for my family. The king needed father to gain the crown with the least opposition, and he owed us many favors. First, he gave Swegn an earldom. Then, in the fourth year of his reign, in 1045 he married my sister Editha. I don't think she was a very willing bride, but she was always a dutiful daughter and never would have thought to resist the will of our parents.

Harold was right. Edward was 22 years older than me and his exile had not been kind to him. But father so wanted me to be

15

queen and mother of the heir. Even if I had wanted to, I couldn't gainsay him. The early years of my marriage were hard, but Edward and I learned to love each other... Editha

That same year, Edward made me Earl of East Anglia, a singular honor. I was twenty-four years old at the time, but I felt well prepared. When we were young father had taken both Swegn and me with him when he visited his shires; we witnessed many charters and observed the process of law giving. The hardest part was leaving home.

I remember that day. My whole family—aside from Swegn who had already been gone for two years—was lined up outside the door, looking for all the world like bereaved kin. I wasn't dying! Mother was wiping her eyes, holding Gunhilda on her hip. Gyrth and Leofwine were holding hands, poor boys. Father was uncharacteristically silent, shifting his weight from one foot to the other. Finally he stepped forward and held my stirrup while I mounted.

"Do not hesitate to summon me if you need reinforcements," he said for the fourth time that day.

"I shall be fine," I assured him. But suddenly I didn't feel as confident as when I started. I looked at the harbor, then at the church tower, then back at father. This had always been so secure to me...so safe. I looked to my other side and saw my little group of thirty freshly recruited troops, mounted and waiting patiently next to the supply wagon. Their leader, Torr and I practically grew up together. In fact, they were all my age, ready for some new experience, and they belonged to me.

I smiled. This was going to be an adventure, for certes.

East Anglia did not have an earl since 1021, when King Canute removed Earl Thorkell from his post. There were no further threats from the Norsemen during Canute's reign, and he must have felt comfortable ruling the earldom from the throne. Not so with Edward; Magnus of Norway was threatening invasion, and King Edward appointed me Earl to defend those borders. Growing up in Bosham was the best training I could have had for commanding a naval force, and father made sure I learned my lessons well.

But first I needed to get settled. My destination was Cambridge, where father owned the Castle overlooking the River Cam and gave it over to my use. From north to south, Cambridge was almost in the middle of East Anglia. For once I was glad of my Danish ancestry, as this town was heavily settled by the Norsemen, and had been a large trading, military and administrative center for centuries. They even had their own mint. It was perfect for me.

Cambridge was governed by the local Reeve named Eadric of Laxfield, one of the wealthiest men in the country and powerful in East Anglia. His wealth rivaled my own family, and I knew he was used to being in charge. He probably thought of himself as a dominant chieftain. Well, it was time he got used to the new King's methods. Wessex was on the throne now, and I was Eadric's new master.

Eadric had already been alerted to my coming, so I expected him to greet me. As we approached the town, many of the farmers dropped their tools and came forward, regarding me curiously and raising an occasional hand in welcome. I stopped now and them and asked the name of a bolder sort, which I immediately committed to memory; I learned early on that people responded well when remembered by name. As we came closer to the town walls, our arrival was announced by two blasts on a horn. No problem there, but no Eadric either.

When we passed through the gates, I felt uneasy. The townspeople went about their business as usual, which made sense; soldiers were commonplace and no one knew my personal

17

banner as yet. I was used to London and this was a much smaller town, but I could see it was prosperous, nonetheless. Shopkeepers hawked their wares and waved their hands around; dogs darted between the legs of our horses. I almost stopped at bakery when the hearty aroma of fresh bread hit my nostrils, as I realized I hadn't eaten for several hours. I could hear the clang on the blacksmith's anvil and saw the thick smoke from his forge.

The main street led directly to the Council House, larger and more ornate than its neighbors. I could see the Castle on the hill, near the Great Bridge. There was much activity crossing over to the other bank, which had its own large settlement.

But what drew my concern was the solid row of warriors standing before the Council House, bristling with weapons. They parted as I dismounted, giving me and my followers enough room to mount the steps, but nothing more. Everyone stared at me and I decided to ignore them all. I motioned for my men to follow and I went inside, blinking as my eyes adjusted to the gloom.

I had entered a large chamber lit by windows in either end of the building and a row of torches along both walls. At the far end stood a large platform, with a high seat flanked by other chairs. I approached halfway into the room and stopped, holding up a hand for my followers to halt. The high seat was occupied.

It had to be Eadric. So this was to be my first challenge. Now I understood why father kept offering reinforcements.

I don't know how long I stood there, but it was long enough for Eadric to realize he was taking a risk in defying me. He rose slowly from the high seat and stepped to the side, bowing briefly. It wasn't much of an acknowledgement, but it was enough for the moment.

I strode forward as confidently as I could manage, knowing I was taller than most men and broader at the shoulders. My men were close behind me but paused as I mounted the platform to the high seat. I nodded to Eadric and sat. I could hear him take in a breath.

I counted to ten before facing him. I saw that his men who had been outside had crowded through the door behind us. Some of them had a hand on their sword hilt.

"Reeve Eadric," I began in a reasonable voice. "I have heard glowing reports of your governance, and hope you will consent to continue in your high office." Of course, I had heard nothing of the kind, but he didn't need to know that. His lips were pursed and hard face expressionless, but I fancied I saw his jaw relax.

"Please," I asserted. "Introduce me to your officers." I nodded at my own men, jerking my head toward the side of the hall. They understood and stepped aside. I sat back in the high seat, keeping my spine straight like I had learned from my father.

Eadric gestured to his men then put both hands behind his back. I wondered if he was clenching his fists. Slowly his men came forward and stood uncertainly before the platform.

"Your name?" I asked the closest, pointing to him then to the steps. He paused, shrugged his shoulders, then knelt on one knee.

"Stanwine, my Lord." He looked up at me, not quite as hostile. "Thegn Stanwine."

"Thegn Stanwine," I repeated, memorizing his face. "Your family has been here for generations?"

"Why yes." He seemed surprised, though he shouldn't have. It was an easy guess.

"My thanks, Thegn Stanwine. And your name, friend?" I looked at the next man and Stanwine backed away."

"Thegn Gerhard." The second man came forward a little less reluctantly and we repeated the same ritual. I could feel Eadric fret at my side, and after the sixth introduction I turned to him.

"I see these men are all thegns," I said.

He let out his breath in a huff. "That is because they all belong to the Guild of Cambridge Thegns," he said, as if

19

explaining to a child. "As do I. If any one of us stands in need of help, the others are sure to come forward."

Was that a threat? I chose to ignore it. "Very admirable," I conceded. I turned back to the clump of Cambridge Thegns until I had learned the name of every one. Finally I stood. "Now Reeve Eadric, we have come a long way and would rest a bit. Could you see my men to their barracks?" I turned to my followers. "Torr, bring six men to attend me. The rest can go with Reeve Eadric."

Eadric bowed, turning on his heel and stalking away. At his nod, Stanwine awaited my pleasure.

"Earl Harold," he said formally. "We have freshened the rooms in your Castle, and we have found local servants for you. I trust everything will be to your liking."

"Lead on, Thegn Stanwine."

Looking dignified, the man led us to Castle Hill. My new home was a solid timber structure with a great view of the surrounding area. There was no palisade but I imagined the city walls had always sufficed for protection. Together we walked around the outside of the building. I asked him questions about the structures across the river, then complimented him on the tidiness of my stables and outbuildings. At first his answers were curt, but soon he was volunteering information. Good. At that point I was content to let him go.

I soon discovered the Castle was large enough to house my full contingent, and before the week's end I had moved my men into my private garrison. I felt much safer that way. During that same week I had several meetings with Eadric, but did not make any progress with him. He was jealous of his position and refused to share information. For the moment I left him alone; the management of this complex shire was largely his domain. But he would need to learn that I outranked him. This stand-off could not last forever, and I kept my own counsel, hoping he wouldn't mistake my quiet watchfulness for weakness.

I soon started walking through the city with a small escort. Every day I picked a different direction and wandered through the winding streets, casually asking questions and purchasing small items from the local merchants. Recognizing that my patronage could make their fortune, the locals fell over themselves trying to cultivate my business. No one missed my notice, from the smallest individual to the largest guild. This was my town now, and I intended to win it over. I knew my behavior irritated Eadric, but what could he could do about it?

At the end of my second week, I felt ready to begin my progress through my new earldom. It was time to curry favor with the mostly-Danish chieftains. Eadric had avoided me for the most part, but I thought it proper to send him a message announcing my proposed tour. I even invited him to join my retinue, but he declined the honor. I was not disappointed, but I should have been suspicious. I only had to learn that lesson once!

I determined to pay a visit to the nearby St. Bene't Church with its splendid stone tower. I planned to make an offering before leaving the city. Taking a handful of followers with me, I approached the main doors, only to be blocked by a small crowd of well-dressed worshippers. We tarried patiently as they passed slowly into the church, chatting with each other just as though they were going to some kind of celebration. Inside, the tower was not large enough to support a large congregation, so my men stayed near the rear wall. I moved forward, slipping between the others who seemed content to stand around waiting for something. Once I approached the altar, I saw who they were waiting for.

She was kneeling on a little ornamental pray stool. From my position I could only see her back, covered by a long veil, but the richness of her garments betrayed her social status. Curious, I edged over to the side so I could see her better. One look at that lovely profile and I nearly forgot why I had come. Her head was slightly forward and her lips were pressed against her forefingers, eyes closed. She was the picture of perfection.

Then she looked at me. And smiled.

Somehow I found the courage to approach this vision. Was she real? Of course I had to wait for her to finish her prayers, while some of her companions eyed me jealously and tried to nudge me aside. Not a chance! As the lady stood up and backed away, crossing herself, I bumped them right back, making excuses and smiling at my would-be rivals, until I accidently on purpose brushed into the object of my interest. She was not the least bit startled and smiled a bit as I bowed slightly.

"My apologies, my lady. I am Earl Harold Godwineson."

I heard some murmuring behind me. She curtsied very prettily.

"Our new Earl?" she whispered. I had forgotten we were in a House of God and realized my voice had carried a bit too far. I lowered my pitch for her ears alone.

"Why, yes. Every day I find better reasons to appreciate East Anglia."

She had the good grace to blush. I was charmed.

"What might be your name, my lady?"

"I am called Eddeva. Eddeva Pulcra."

"Eddeva Pulcra."

"My husband's name, may he rest in peace." She crossed herself and I hastily did the same.

What a graceful bearing she had. Eddeva of the swan's neck. "To me, you are Edith Swanneck," I murmured.

A slow smile spread across her face. "I like that," she said.

We were passing outside and I paused at the top of the stone staircase, admiring the beautiful day. "It is a rare sunny afternoon," I ventured. "Will you walk with me?"

She nodded, and our two sets of companions followed behind us as we walked toward the river; her men were joined by three maids. A well-trod path passed under a bower of willow trees; the others fell back, allowing us a little privacy.

"You live nearby?" I ventured, hoping I wasn't too forward.

22

"Yes." She pointed across the river. "Across the fen at Hinton."

"Hinton? Hinton Manor?" She had caught me by surprise. "Why, that is one of my destinations. You are the mistress of Hinton?"

"And many other manors as well." She reached down and picked a flower from the riverside. Sniffing, she offered the blossom to me. "As you were planning to visit me, let me extend the first invitation."

I was speechless. She was a great heiress and I was hopelessly smitten. Who wouldn't be?

"When should I come?" I was already delaying my progress in my mind.

"Well, why not the day after tomorrow? And bring your retinue, of course." She turned, gesturing to our followers who didn't seem willing to mix. I smiled at my men, feeling foolish and elated. But my smile froze on my face when I saw Eadric of Laxfield sitting astride his black horse behind them in the distance. I knew he was glaring at me.

While I watched, he kicked his mount and approached us. I took a quick glance at Edith but her face betrayed no emotion, one way or the other. We watched him come nearer and I noted that all the others stepped aside, making way for him. The stallion made as if to bite Torr, but Eadric pulled his head back.

"Well met, my Lady Eddeva. My Lord Harold." His hungry gaze seemed to devour her. I shifted my weight, annoyed.

His horse rolled its eyes at me, putting back his ears. It snorted when he jerked its reins.

"My Lady, I have some packages for you, from your goldsmith."

She nodded. "I thank you, Lord Eadric. Shall I send my man for them?"

"Oh, do not bother. I will deliver them myself on the morrow." He glanced at me, frowning.

23

"As you wish. I thank you, Lord Eadric. And now I must go." She nodded at me. "My Lord Harold."

Eadric and I watched as she returned the way we had just come. Her maids gathered around her and the men followed close behind. Eadric cleared his throat.

"I suggest you keep your distance from the lady."

"What?" For once, I was not interested in keeping the peace.

"Leave her to me."

"And what do you mean by that?"

"My Lord Harold, I have known Lady Eddeva for all of her life. She is under my protection."

"That is all well and good," I retorted. "Are you her guardian?"

"Not exactly. I am a friend of the family."

"I am happy to hear that. However, I think she is free to pick her other friends as well."

Giving me a sullen look, he jerked his horse's reins and rode away from me.

I rode my favorite horse and brought ten of my hearth troops to visit Edith. We crossed the Great Bridge and took the old Roman road through the fens; countless years ago, someone had built a strong berm which rose safely above the marshy ground. My men were complaining and slapping mosquitos all the way, but I didn't even notice. Yes, I admit it; I was too excited to care. Soon enough, we crossed into a dense forest, then the road led through a tidy little hamlet, which I duly noted belonged to the manor of Hinton. We passed little watercourses that teemed with eels and fish; we saw mills and poultry enclosures, a little wooden church and a burial ground.

I stopped a ceorl who was leading an ox. "Where does the Lady Eddeva live?"

He pointed along the road. "Ahead, just around the bend," he answered.

"Well, come on!" I called to my men, and kicked my mount forward.

We found her palace soon enough; Edith's house was a lovely timber residence with a thatched roof and many wings. It was surrounded by a low stone wall and nestled among tidy outbuildings. As we passed through the gate a handful of grooms ran up to tend our horses; I think they were waiting for us.

Edith clearly knew how to impress her guests. She personally met us at the door and beckoned her servants, who each came forward with a bowl of scented water and a cloth for us to wipe our dusty faces and hands. Actually, we weren't all that dusty since we had only ridden about four miles. But I was charmed, nonetheless.

I sat next to her at head table, and my men joined her own substantial household for a feast much more extravagant than any they ever experienced at my hands. Wine flowed freely, and course followed elegant course. We had little game birds wrapped in bacon, salmon and fruit tarts, baked lampreys, pheasant stuffed with spiced apples...no wonder she needed two days to prepare for us! Unfortunately, I tasted very little of the food because all my attention was focused on the lady.

Edith Swanneck. It was the perfect name for her. Although she was wearing a veil, because she was at home she let her long blond braids peek out, interwoven with silk threads. Her skin was flawless, and her long fingers broke bread with the most delicate movements, like a bird. She smiled at me with a little twinkle in her eye, then lowered long lashes as though she suddenly remembered to be modest.

Her conversation was easy, even for a soldier like myself. "So you will be touring East Anglia?"

I gulped down a bite. "Yes. I must determine how many men we can raise for the king, how large a fleet we can command, and how many goods are produced by the local landowners."

"Ah, then you should start with me. At last count, between myself and my father, we hold some 280 hides in five shires."

"Your father? What is his name?"

"Ulfcytel of Burgh. He is a hardy soldier and a good man."

"Well then, I can visit him on my way to see the king. I believe Burgh is close to Ipswich, where I planned to stop."

She sipped her wine then touched a piece of cloth to her mouth.

"So you will not be going to London directly?"

"Nay, I plan to travel to the coast first, then swing around. I would be at Burgh in a fortnight or so, I would think."

"You would be welcome, most assuredly. I will send word."

I was quite satisfied by her interest. We spoke more about little things—her sheep, the wool, the crops. She took me outside and showed me her extensive herb gardens, though I soon lost track of all the names.

"Here is Chamomile," she said, opening a scissors hanging from a ribbon on her belt. She clipped a sweet-smelling flower and held it under my nose. I obediently took a sniff. "It is said that never a man should lose his life from infection after Chamomile was prepared in his food."

"And here is Fennel," she added, breaking off a long feathery twig. "It conveys longevity, strength, and courage."

I couldn't help capturing her hand and bringing it to my lips. "And what do you use for a love spell?"

She smiled. "Oh, Verbena, most definitely." Pulling her hand away, she walked me over to a swath of spiky, tiny lilac colored blossoms. She picked one and held it close to her breast. "But it does not work unless the recipient is already inclined."

26

"Ah, that should not be a problem," I started, then whirled around as someone cleared his throat behind me. I was usually happy to see Torr, but right now I wished him on the other side Cambridge.

"My Lord," he said apologetically. "I fear it is getting late and we need to return home."

I looked at the sun, already turning the sky pink.

"Oh dear," the Lady said. "I haven't been paying attention. Come, your men must be waiting for you."

She took my hand and pulled me toward the house. Was she glad to be interrupted?

But Edith was right. The servants were cleaning the hall and outside my men were mostly mounted. Apparently we were lingering longer than I thought. One of my men was holding my horse, and Torr gave me an embarrassed smile as he swung into his own saddle. I turned to Edith.

"My most gracious friend," I started. It was all I dared say in front of the others. "We are charmed and flattered by all your attention. I can't think of a feast I ever enjoyed more."

I could see a slight flush at the base of her slender neck.

"I trust there will be others," she murmured in response. "Fare thee well for now."

There was nothing left to say. As I was leaving, I turned back quickly. "Don't forget to write to your father!"

She nodded and raised a hand. That was a meeting I would not miss.

Two days later I started my progress with some of my men and ten new volunteers from Cambridge. I was interested in creating my own personal force as soon as possible, and saw this as an opportunity to get started. As I had told Edith, we headed east for the coast and I began assessing our naval strength. Although King Edward was interested in reducing the size of our national fleet and the taxes that went with it, I determined that my earldom was a prime target for possible attacks from old *Scania*. My father had always felt that a strong navy made for a strong defense, and I agreed wholeheartedly. Fortunately, many of my people were of Danish stock, so they were with me on this.

Everywhere I went, I was greeted most graciously, fed well and comfortably lodged. Not everyone was as threatened as Eadric of Laxfield, and once again I wondered if there was more to his resistance than I could readily see. My trip was very useful, but I admit I was anxious to get home and conduct my own personal campaign to capture the heart of Edith Swanneck. I thought of little else whenever my duties gave me a pause.

Finally I could wait no longer. I directed our path toward Burgh, where I hoped Edith's father was expecting us. He was indeed a wealthy man, and owned no fewer than eight manors in the immediate vicinity. His roads and bridges were well-maintained, and I could see he was an asset to any earldom. As we approached his timber castle, we were greeted by a small entourage who rode out, banners flapping, to escort us to their thegn's residence. I saw where Edith learned her ceremonies.

As we entered the gates, Ulfcytel came forward, cloaked in an embroidered mantle with cords and tassels hanging below the shoulders. He raised up the welcoming cup with two hands. I gave him my best smile as I accepted the cup, and as I took a sip my eyes slipped over to the door. There she was! My beautiful Edith Swanneck had delivered the message herself!

Ulfcytel grinned widely at my reaction, and he shouted his greetings to my retinue as they gladly relinquished their horses to his grooms. He put an arm around my shoulders and brought me up to his daughter. It was all very informal yet she still curtsied as I approached. I bowed back.

"Well met," I beamed. "Such a surprise to see you!"

Edith exchanged glances with her father. "We are most honored to receive you," she replied, "and I wanted to be sure father was well prepared."

And so he was. We stayed for a week and never wanted for anything. Ulfcytel had arranged a feast the first day, a stag hunt the second day, and the third day Ulfcytel surprised me with a gift of a falcon, which thrilled me more than I can express. We hunted that very afternoon and many of our catches showed up on his table afterwards. Edith accompanied us when we flew the falcons, for she was raised to the hunt and followed my activities with enthusiasm.

As we were returning to her father's castle, we were so engaged in conversation we fell behind the rest of the party, who discreetly left us alone. I admit it: I was ready to take advantage of the earliest opportunity to woo her. By now, I didn't care whether I made a fool of myself or not. I had to know.

"Edith," I began, pushing my horse a little closer until my knee brushed against hers. I couldn't help but wonder how she managed to ride so gracefully with all that skirt material. "I don't know how else to begin but to come out straight with it. I mean to ask your father's permission to marry you."

She made a little gasp. Was I too forward? "With your acceptance, of course," I added hastily.

I had to look at her. To my great relief, she was smiling.

"Did you doubt it? I had feared you would not ask."

It was my turn to let out a breath. We did understand each other.

"I had feared you would not accept."

She laughed heartily and my heart sang. But there was one other thing I had to know. "I was concerned about Eadric of Laxfield," I ventured.

"What?" Her voice turned cold.

"He said you were under his protection."

She made a dismissive gesture. "He overreaches himself. Never mind Eadric of Laxfield." We rode in silence for a few minutes; I could see that she was thinking. "I read the law," she protested. "I am under the protection of the Church and the State." She bit her lip, then shook her head.

"No, it is not fair to you," she went on. "Let me explain. My husband Asser died eleven months ago. Eadric is waiting impatiently for one year to pass, as he hopes to marry me at the soonest."

Ah, I was beginning to understand. As a widow, she enjoyed more freedom than an unmarried daughter. But according to Canute's law if she married before a year had passed she would forfeit any lands she inherited from her husband. This law applied even if she remarried against her will, which would discourage any would-be abductors.

But the thought of Eadric trying to force marriage on Edith was enough to make me think of murder.

"Luckily, my father is close enough to keep any unwelcome suitors at bay," she added.

I took a deep breath. "I assume that includes Eadric, then."

She didn't answer. Was she just being prudent?

"Then I must make sure your father considers me suitable," I added, making my own conclusions.

"I support your intent," she said readily. "I foresee he will find you quite acceptable."

That was reassuring enough. But still...

"Your husband?"

"Ah, he was a very nice man, but much older than me. I married him to please my father." She rode a minute in silence then seemed to come to a decision. "You see, Harold, my husband was in the Guild of Cambridge Thegns. I believe you have been introduced to some of them..."

I nodded, remembering my first day.

"My husband was out with Reeve Eadric the day he died. They were collecting taxes, and his horse shied, throwing him onto a stone wall. Poor man. He was gone in a few minutes, but lived long enough to ask Eadric to watch over me."

Did she believe that? I frowned.

"I know what you are thinking," she sighed. "No one else was present. I don't know. Or did he even speak before he died? His head had been split open by a sharp stone. But I saw no reason to question Eadric. Until now."

It was my turn to be deep in thought. "Do you think he would try to force you?"

"To marry him? I would hope not!"

"But if he thinks he has the right..."

I could see the doubt on her face. That was enough.

"How long could you stay with your father?"

"No, Harold. I am safe enough until my year is up. I think Eadric values my inheritance more than my person."

I wasn't so sure, but she was adamant.

"Then I will make certain I have returned before then."

And so we had agreed. That very night I met with her father and discovered he was well informed about our plans. Ulfcytel was a bluff, uncomplicated man and took his daughter's decision in stride. After all, there were benefits to being father-in-law to the Earl of East Anglia. We quickly agreed on her dowry and the handgeld I would present to her family. Already he was thinking about the wedding celebrations and the influential guests he would invite. That took away some of my discomfort about cutting my progress short; those farthest away could attend the wedding, and I would be able to meet all of them.

Later that night as the men were still drinking, Edith and I found a semblance of privacy in a window alcove. We could hear the laughter as I put a finger under her chin and brought her lips to meet my own. She tasted so sweet! Soon my arms were around her and I drew her close to me, savoring the feel of her soft skin against my cheek.

"My dear lady," I murmured. "I pledge my heart to you for the rest of my days."

"I will hold you to that," she whispered, and I saw her smile in the shadow. "Come, my love, before we are missed."

She tried to pull away but I grabbed her hand, drawing her back. "How can I let you go?"

"You never shall. Even when you are not with me, I will be in your thoughts."

She was so right. When I finally rode away to see the king, her face was still before me. So this is what it felt like to love a woman!

I was anxious to see the king and get back to Cambridge, for I was still uncomfortable about Edith's safety. But by the time I reached London, I saw I needn't have worried. To my surprise, I saw Eadric at a distance, conferring with someone who looked like the Mayor. What was he doing in London? I must find out.

But first, I needed to see my father who I knew was in residence at his Southwark house. He would be anxious to know how I was progressing in my earldom.

Father lived in a sizeable fortified palace near London Bridge. I clattered through his gate with my men, and we raised such a happy clamor he was out the door in no time. He gathered me into a big bear hug, not his usual greeting. But I could see he was genuinely glad to see me. His broad smile and proud eyes made my heart swell. For once I wasn't in Swegn's shadow! I could meet father on equal terms, and I felt I had acquitted myself well my first few months as Earl.

He was greedy for tidings and I forced myself to speak about business, answering his questions and laying out my plans. But as soon as I could gracefully do so, I told him my great news.

"Father, I plan to marry," I started slowly, thinking of Edith's face.

He took a quick breath. "So soon?"

"She is a great heiress, father. And beautiful. Her father holds much influence with the other thegns."

"I had hoped for you to wed a noble lady," he said finally. I was disappointed by his reaction.

"That's not important to me," I tried to assure him. "I love this woman."

"Ah. A love match." His tone was infuriating.

"I have decided. Her father has already given his blessing."

He sat forward, putting his cup on the table with decision. "Well then, that's final. But you must promise one thing."

I think I blinked at him, surprised.

"Harold, you must marry her in the Danish manner. Like Canute and his first wife."

I frowned, considering. It was a common-law marriage, perfectly acceptable. But I knew what he was referring to. Once Canute married for the state, his first wife was easily put aside in favor of Queen Emma.

"I don't know how Edith would feel about that."

"Harold, it doesn't matter. Who knows what will happen in the future? You may need a dynastic tie, and you can't let your emotions get in the way of your prospects."

I was on the verge of objecting, but the substance of his words pierced my stubborn resistance. As usual, my father was thinking way ahead of today, or even tomorrow. What kind of future did he envision for me?

"Of course, it may never happen," I mumbled, and he was quick to agree.

"Then you are none the worse for doing so. What is her ancestry?"

"Edith is of Danish blood."

"Well then, there should be no problem. Is it settled then?"

33

There was no denying him when father made up his mind. "Of course," I acknowledged, hoping I could be as persuasive as him.

"Then we shall see the king on the morrow."

I slept little that night, between worrying about what Eadric was doing in London, and trying to decide how I should present our common-law wedding to Edith. After all, she was a major donor to St. Bene't Church, where I first met her. I wondered if I could recruit her father to my side.

Luckily, my father was an early riser and we were on our way to Westminster Palace just after the sun rose. As usual, we didn't have to wait to be introduced to the king, but I was surprised to see that Eadric had preceded us. He was equally surprised to see me, and I fancied I saw a look of panic cross his face.

"Ah, Harold," Edward said, holding out a hand to me. "Your visit is very timely, and you can help us sort out this problem."

This was unexpected, and I didn't know what was amiss. Father took a seat beside and slightly behind the king and nodded. He was always ready for anything and sat back, his chin on folded hands.

"Sire," I said quietly, bending a knee. "What is this problem?"

Eadric stood back, arms crossed over his chest.

"I have received reports that Eadric has not been releasing my full portion of the taxes he has collected. Is this true?"

I cleared my throat. I could almost feel Eadric's eyes on my back. "I have just started my progress through East Anglia. So far I have not seen anything amiss."

"Hmm." Edward shifted in his throne. "I must see an accounting."

"Most certainly, Sire." I stood, bowing slightly.

"It has been two years since my coronation. It is time my northern subjects understood that the Danish ways are no longer serviceable."

I cringed despite myself. But Eadric had obviously been stung by that statement. He stepped forward, forgetting himself. "The laws of Canute have served us in the Danelaw for 35 years," he objected. "It is those laws I abide by."

"It is those laws that permit a royally appointed Reeve to stuff his coffers at his own discretion!"

Ah, now I was beginning to understand. Edward must have discovered that Eadric was the wealthiest landowner in East Anglia.

"And as long as we are on the subject," Edward continued, "I refuse my permission for you to marry Eddeva Pulcra. I would not have such a concentration of wealth in one household."

"Eddeva Pulcra!" I blurted, unable to control my emotions. I whirled around, hands drawn into fists. Luckily, father had quickly strode to my side and put a restraining hand on my arm.

"What is this?" Edward asked, quick to grasp the situation.

Eadric was staring at me, eyes nearly bulging from his face. "I warned you to stay away from her," he growled. Then he turned to the king, bowing. "Sire, I need time to put forward my suit more formally."

"No. No, you do not. The lady has promised to marry me and we have the blessing of her father."

If I hadn't been so nervous about Edward, I would have enjoyed the look of distress on Eadric's face. He took a step toward me, raising his fist.

"You are a scoundrel and an upstart." He was nearly shouting now.

Father let go of my arm and nearly struck the man himself. It was my turn to put out a restraining hand.

"Silence!" Edward stood, and I could see he was shaking. "How dare you speak thus to my Earl in my court! You go too far, Reeve Eadric!"

"Your Earl has little authority in my City," Eadric retorted. "His presence is unwelcome and noxious." He turned to me, pulling up to his full height. "You are a meddler and you bear false witness. I advise you to stay away!"

"Nay!" the king shouted in anger. "It is your turn to stay away. You are outlawed, Reeve Eadric of Laxfield. I give you five days to leave the country!"

I was appalled. Eadric thought I had secretly accused him of wrongdoing. I was about to object, but once again father delayed me.

"Think on this," he whispered in my ear. "There is time to reverse his sentence, if you so desire."

The king's pronouncement took all the fight out of Eadric. The man glared at me before turning on his heel and leaving the room, taking his thegns with him.

Edward sat heavily on his throne. "Just who *is* this Eddeva Pulcra?" he asked wearily.

I stepped forward and knelt before him. "She is the daughter of a thegn in East Anglia and the widow of Thegn Asser Pulcra these last eleven months. I would make her my common-law wife, with your permission."

The King scratched his beard, frowning. "Yes, yes. She has been very good about submitting my heriot tax... and a most substantial portion it was, too. However, I do not approve of these Danish marriages. I feel it against the law of the Church."

I sighed. Between my father and the king, I would have no peace. But father came to my rescue.

"Sire, it is customary in the Danelaw. All traditional rites will be observed."

Edward shook his head. "Oh, very well. I will not deny this request, Earl Harold. But you must undertake an accounting of

36

your earldom. I need more revenue if you want to build up a naval force."

There was much more business along those lines, but I admit my mind was elsewhere. Much as I disliked Eadric, it would not serve my purposes to be saddled with his undoing. I must get to the source of this problem. But, as my father so cleverly pointed out, it would not hurt to have him out of the country until Edith was safely my wife.

When I was alone, the first thing I did was write to her; if Eadric was hell-bent on getting to her first, there was no way any messenger of mine could overtake him. But I had to try, if only to ease my mind. Alas, I wasn't sure whether she was still at her father's estate or on her way back to Cambridge, so I had to send two messengers.

But a letter wasn't enough. The following day I made my excuses and left town with my men as quickly as I could. Eadric still had enough time to cause trouble. I had to make a choice, and I concluded she might try for home as soon as I was gone.

It took two days of hard riding before I reached Cambridge, and I headed straight for Hinton. It was well that I did, because I saw Eadric's horse tied up before Edith's manor house. I hoped he hadn't been there long.

I recognized Thegns Stanwine and Gerhard in his entourage; they were standing with the horses and eyeing the doorway uncomfortably. I decided it was best to act relaxed; they would be answering to me soon, and I didn't want to show any weakness in their presence.

I dismounted and moved to Torr, speaking in a low voice.

"I don't really expect trouble," I said with my back to Eadric's guard. I pretended to adjust his stirrup. "But keep good vigil."

He nodded and I walked casually toward Stanwine. The man started to turn away from me then thought better of it.

"My Lord Harold," he said, glancing at some of the others. "What brings you here?"

"I owe the Lady Edith a visit," I said carelessly. "Are you here with Reeve Eadric?"

"Yes, he is inside." He coughed. "I suppose you know he is preparing for exile."

"I believe he has two days." I was sure he would tell Eadric I was counting. "I imagine he is here to bid farewell to the Lady."

At that moment, the man in question burst in anger from the door. He halted at the sight of me.

"You are the cause of all this," he spat at me.

"I would not be so sure of that, if I were you," I answered smoothly.

Edith appeared in the doorway. "That is exactly what I told Eadric," she said loudly.

He gave her an angry look. "It seems you did not deserve all the care I lavished on you after your husband's death."

"Eadric of Laxfield, I wish you well and promise to forget the things you said today in haste," she responded. "Harold, I am glad to see you. Please enter."

She held a hand out toward me and I was not loth to respond. I tried to brush past Eadric but he grabbed my arm. I stopped, pushing his hand away.

"You probably won't believe me, but I will do an accounting for the king. If you can be cleared of wrongdoing I swear I will do so."

He clenched his teeth for a moment. "You will find nothing to complain of."

"Then you have nothing to worry about."

For a moment he looked uncertain, then strode through his group of retainers, gesturing for them to follow. I continued on my way and entered the house, pulling the door shut.

She leaned heavily against the wall. I saw she was shaking.

"What did he say?"

She took an unsteady breath. "He came to see if you had told the truth. He accused me of disloyalty...as if I owed him a debt of gratitude. I feared he might harm me..."

That was enough to send me outside again, but she slipped between me and the door.

"No, Harold. It is finished. When he heard you arrive he forgot all about me."

"He is a dangerous man. Has he ever acted like this before?"

She shook her head. "He was always in control. Right now he is lost, and can't accept what has happened. I told him you had no time to go to the king, but he thinks you sent a messenger with an accusation, to get him out of the way. I know it wasn't you, but I am almost glad he is gone."

I took her into my arms, tucking her head under my chin. "No, love. It wasn't me. But who was it?"

She shrugged her shoulders. Was it the lady herself?

I was intrigued but decided to store that question away for the future. I had more important things to worry about now.

But first, I wanted to make sure Eadric was on his way. I checked on my men and satisfied myself that all was well. Then I went in search of Edith, who was instructing her maids to bring us food and drink. She was ever the perfect chatelaine.

"The King gave his blessing for our betrothal," I started nervously. She smiled sweetly. "Though Eadric asked him for your hand first." Her smile faded.

"The King denied him," I mused, "saying he did not want such a concentration of wealth in one household. I had no idea Eadric would be so forward." I took her chin in my hand and kissed her softly. "You are so precious to me, I don't know what I would have done had it gone otherwise."

Edith shook her head as though to rid herself of such a thought. "I could never have married that man," she assured me. "Never." She sat in thought for a moment.

"My goldsmith... Do you remember, Harold, the first day we met? Eadric had a package to deliver to me from my goldsmith. I thought it odd at the time that the man did not come himself, and I later learned Eadric insisted he take the package for me. He dismissed my goldsmith who wrote to me on his way to London. He was most distraught. You see, my goldsmith is also the mint master in Cambridge, and has many dealings with Eadric. They have an uneasy relationship, and I wonder sometimes..."

She adjusted her veil and I saw she was ordering her thoughts. "I fear...I fear I wrote back to him in some anger. What was Eadric doing? What gave him the right to interfere with my goldsmith?"

"I think I begin to see," I said. "Perhaps your goldsmith spoke to the king."

"But what could he have said? I never intended for Eadric to lose everything."

"Ah, Edith. What does your goldsmith know that you don't know? I would meet this man of yours, in time. For now, let us rejoice in our good fortune. I have much less to fear from your suitor now that he must leave the country. And if Edward's concerns are groundless, he can easily reinstate Eadric in all his offices. After you are safely my wife."

She poured us a drink of mead. "It will be a long two months."

"I would post some of my men here, to protect you."

She paused before sipping. "Is that necessary?"

"I am afraid so. I would not take any chances."

"All right. For you, I would agree to anything."

There was my chance! "Edith..."

She put her cup down and snuggled into my shoulder. I hated to spoil the moment, but I was never one for delaying the unpleasant.

"About our wedding. I would marry *more Danico,* in the Danish manner." I stopped, holding my breath.

"Hmm." She sat up, looking sideways at me. "Is that important to you?"

I hesitated. It wouldn't help to say my father insisted on it.

"Yes, it is."

"Then that is what we shall do. My father would favor such a marriage."

That was all. I couldn't believe my good fortune. Perhaps she didn't see the disadvantages of common-law marriage. Or perhaps she was wise enough to accept the consequences. I didn't ask. And I don't think I'll ever know.

Eadric of Laxfield only took a handful of men with him; most of the Guild of Cambridge Thegns were family men and many had estates to care for. At first, they stayed away from me so I resumed my daily jaunts around the city, greeting everyone by name and solving little problems here and there. I established myself in the Council House and started to review Eadric's duties; I knew he had many assistants, some of whom accompanied him into exile. But not all of them.

The first person to come to me willingly was Thegn Stanwine. That was a good sign; of all the Reeve's followers, he was friendliest to me. He came alone and knelt before me, bowing his head.

"That is not necessary, Stanwine." I touched him on the arm and he stood.

"Earl Harold. I am here to ask for your support during the exile of my lord Eadric. In return, I promise I will aid you wherever I can."

I tried not to let my relief show on my face. "I accept." I hope I sounded gracious. "And my first charge to you is to make all of Eadric's followers understand that I extend my protection to all of them. I do not intend to reverse his policies, unless the situation demands it. I want a smooth transition. I want to clear his name and bring Eadric back. He is too valuable for us to lose."

Stanwine made no attempt to hide his own relief. He practically ran from the room, and for the next few days I was overwhelmed with eager deputies, aides and petitioners who soon filled my coffers with gifts and my offices with workers. I was never happier than when I was buried in work, and I had no shortage of things that needed finishing. Taxes waited to be collected, the fyrd needed to be organized, estates needed to be managed. And I had a wedding to arrange!

The two months leading up to our hand-fasting were the busiest weeks of my life. Constant messengers rode back and forth between my beloved and myself, for she had an enormous clientele and many plans to work out. Luckily, Ulfcytel had insisted he host the ceremony and celebrations, so I only had to worry about inviting my own family and father's influential friends. I had few of my own, as yet.

Our handfasting day was set for Friday, the old *Friggas-day* in honor of the goddess of marriage. If we were going to wed in the Danish manner, we would certainly do it with all correct rituals. I arrived a few days in advance and discovered that Edith had gotten there ahead of me. I found her in the kitchen building, counting supplies, and gathered her into a close embrace almost before she saw me. Her smile was so glowing it melted my heart and I kissed her, ignoring the whispered comments of the servants.

"No trouble, then?" I asked.

"None. I have brought your hearth troops with me, and they are a hungry bunch, indeed!"

I kissed her fingertips. "The next few days will be the hardest for me. I long to have you all to myself."

She laughed, a soft and sensuous sound. I felt myself stiffening.

"Now go, Harold. I have much to do." She turned me around and pushed my back. "You will have me soon enough."

I laughed, then turned at the sound of my name. Torr was beckoning to me, for my family had just arrived with their entourage in three wagons.

I hadn't seen mother since I left Bosham and it was to her I went first, lifting her off the ground and twirling her around. I think I was her favorite and she had always spoiled me. For a moment it seemed she and I were the only people in the world and I turned my ear as she whispered endearments. Then my little sisters started clamoring for attention and father came around from the back of the wagon, holding out his arms. Even Tostig, fidgeting with the ropes, looked magnanimous. Leofwine and Gyrth were already wandering off, looking for amusement. My life was different now, but for a moment I caught myself wishing I was back in the sheltering arms of my family.

However, that spell broke as Edith came forward, smiling sweetly and offering the welcoming cup to my mother. She would be my family now, and it suddenly occurred to me I never even considered the possibility my parents might dislike her. As my mother took the cup from her, she gave me such a strange look that I shuddered. Did I imagine jealousy in her eyes?

Father was a little restrained, as well. He greeted Edith with all outward forms of courtesy, but I knew that his usual charm was dampened. Luckily, Edith didn't know any better.

Ulfcytel was right behind her, and we were suddenly surrounded by servants, taking down packages and clothing and causing plenty of confusion before leading my family to their guest quarters. I took Edith's hand and we watched them move away from us, taking their noise with them.

She turned to me. "They are lovely, your family."

I smiled awkwardly, pushing a lock of hair away from her forehead. "You are lovely, my dear. They will all come to adore you."

43

She looked surprised. "Why wouldn't they? For your sake."

Someone was tugging at my tunic. I turned, and little Wulfnoth stepped back, sucking on his thumb.

"You've grown," I laughed, picking him up and putting him on my shoulders. "Oof, you are getting heavy!" We turned to Edith who clapped her hands.

"Is this Wulfnoth?" she teased.

My little brother grabbed two handfuls of hair. He needed balance. The three of us walked around the inside of Ulfcytel's bailey, happy for a moment's quiet. But more people were arriving all the time, and we were soon welcoming new guests at the gate. Everyone know Edith, and I was proud of the way she held herself, like a great princess greeting her subjects. She always seemed to know what to say, and she was so beautiful in an unconscious sort of way. She would be a great helpmeet.

Then I spotted him. Beorn, my cousin. He had joined our household after Harthacnut died, and we had taken to each other at once. I think I loved him more than my own brothers. He was so handsome and strong, with thick black hair and the most piercing eyes. He could beat me at wrestling any time he wanted. It was with great satisfaction that we became earls at the same time, myself in East Anglia and he Earl of the Middle-Angles. Our borders touched the whole length of our earldoms, and he made a good buffer between me and Swegn.

Accompanied by a large retinue, Beorn saw me and made straight for my Edith, sweeping her off her feet and threatening to save her before it was too late. Of course she loved it and I was helpless to intervene, stuck as I was with my little brother on my shoulders. Beorn gently put her down and grabbed Wulfnoth instead, tossing him into the air like a little ball. He loved the attention, too. Then it was my turn, and my cousin took me into such a hug he nearly knocked the breath out of my chest. He put me at arm's length and grinned.

"I am so happy for you, Harold. Does your beautiful lady have a sister?"

"No she does not, but we'll find you a willing bride," I laughed.

He looked around approvingly. "I see many suitable prospects already."

He was ready to chase a pretty girl when I held him back for a moment. "I have so much to talk with you about. Make some time for me!"

"Who is the busy one here?" He laughed. "Yes, it has been an interesting year. I would know how you fare in your new office. Where is your mother?"

Edith and I watched him as he went looking for my parents. "She practically raised him," I told her. "He was mother's favorite, back in Denmark. Before she married my father." I paused, thinking, because my parents' early history was a little confused. "That makes him a few years older than me...six, I think."

"Well, I am glad he came," Edith assured me. "Looks like the only one missing is Swegn."

I let out a huff. "He can stay away as far as I am concerned. He won't be missed."

She gave me an odd look. I hadn't told Edith much about my older brother, for I preferred not to think about him. "There's time enough for that when we're all settled and have nothing else to do," I assured her, taking her hand and kissing it. Luckily, someone called her name and Swegn was forgotten.

The day before our celebration, Edith was removed from of my sight. Along with my mother and other women in her entourage, she was escorted to the bath house. Tubs of hot water sat next to heated stones that let off steam when water was sprinkled on them. My turn was to be the next morning, and I admit I waited impatiently for the ceremonies to be over.

The next morning started with the sword-giving ritual. In front of my brothers and Ulfcytel, my father came forward bearing

45

an exquisite sword. He slowly pulled the blade from its scabbard and held up for the admiration of the others. I recognized it; this weapon was given him by King Canute. He presented the sword to me hilt first.

"I bid you remember your family," he intoned, "and our place in this world. We were raised up by King Canute of blessed memory and owe our service to the monarchs of this great country. I give you Canute's sword so that through you and your heirs, our name shall resound down the ages."

I took the sword from him and he strapped the scabbard belt around my waist. I was almost sorry I would have to give it away, but the ritual demanded that my wife would hold it for our future son.

But first I had to face another tradition. I must brook the ministrations of my father and the other married men who would accompany me to the bathhouse. I removed my clothes and sword and gave them into the care of a servant who would dress me in my wedding attire.

The tubs were quite large—big enough for two people to sit in. It did feel good to have warm water against my skin, and soon I was happily leaning forward while a servant scrubbed my back. The others were settling into their own tubs, while father shared mine. Then the mugs were passed around and filled with mead.

"Well, son," father started, settling his shoulders against the warm wood. "It is time for us experienced men to give you some valuable advice. Eh?" He turned around to the others, who cheerfully agreed. "First, and most important of all, to preserve happiness in your household, let the wife think she is always speaking the truth."

Uproarious laughter filled the room, from everyone but myself. "As the All-father said," he continued more soberly, "Fairly must he speak and offer gifts, he who wants to win a woman's love; praise the figure of the fair maiden; he wins who flatters." This statement was met with murmured agreement and everyone took a little drink.

"Keep your promises," another called out, "and you will never go wrong."

And more of this kind of advice kept coming forth; I could see the old-timers were enjoying themselves mightily. I think this ritual was more for their sake than mine; I had enough experience with women to know what not to do!

Eventually the bath water was cooling and we were ready to move on to the handfasting ceremony. I held still while my brothers took turns trying to dress me, inexperienced though they were in such things. Finally it was time. My family preceded me to the great hall, where Ulfcytel and his kin were waiting. I was ready, and my father walked by my side, carrying a large sum of gold, part of the bride-price we had already agreed upon. He handed it to Edith's father, who in turn gestured for a servant to bring forward the bride's dowry.

The gifts were duly exchanged, then we all moved outside. The ceremony was to take place in the grove sacred to the Gods, a short distance outside the wooden walls. As we were walking down the path, I looked to our left and my heart took a little jump. There she was, in a silky flowing dress the color of the sky, a wedding crown on her head sparkling with jewels. She and her women were preceded by a young cousin who held aloft a sword that was destined to become mine, in place of the one I would relinquish.

By now, even I had been caught up in the Norse ritual. There was a hush over our little crowd as we moved into the sacred grove and took our places near a primitive altar built from stones. Ulfcytel had invited a godi—a temple priest—to officiate, and he began with a most impressive invocation to the gods.

"Lords of the sky, Ladies of the sacred earth. Spirits and the ancestors, we dwell together. My folk are all here?"

"Yes," we cried, all together.

47

"Then the host is gathered." He held up a long blade and waited as his acolytes brought forward a sow. The youngest boy held out a golden bowl.

"Freyja, goddess of love, sexuality, beauty and fertility, I call upon you this day and ask you to attend this rite. Our praise goes up to you on the wings of eagles; our voices on the wind. Hear us Freyja, we pray to thee as we offer up this sacrifice of life. Accept it and open our hearts and give to us of your peace and life. *So sind Sie!*"

"So be it!" we added.

At that, the godi took the blade and cut the throat of the sow so skillfully it barely knew what had happened. However, the boy was ready with the bowl and caught the blood as it gushed forth. The sow dropped to her knees and wavered a moment before falling to the ground. We knew this animal would form part of our wedding feast, but the blood had another function. Once the bowl was full, the godi placed it upon the altar and dipped a bundle of fir-twigs into the liquid. He turned toward us and quickly flicked the twigs, so that a fine mist covered us and our guests.

"Freyja," he chanted, "hallow these waters and give to us of your power and inspiration and vitality."

Then he turned to us. "And now, groom and bride, are you ready to proceed?"

"We are," we answered as one.

"Then let those of family and friend come forward and stand behind groom at this time. Let those of family and friend come forward and stand behind bride at this time." Obedient, they complied.

Groom, do you have your ancestral sword?

"I do." I pulled the gorgeous sword from its scabbard and placed her wedding ring on the blade. I felt a momentary bliss when I presented it to Edith and watched her pick up the ring, placing it on her fourth finger. Then I turned the sword around and presented it to her, hilt-first. "I give you this sword to hold in trust

48

for our son," I intoned, "so that he may in turn pass it on to his own sons."

I unbuckled the sword belt and handed it to Edith's cousin. He, in turn, drew the sword he was carrying and handed it to the bride.

"You cannot go forth without a sword!" She cried, putting a ring on its point and holding it out to me. I picked up the ring placed it on my own finger, then smiled as she awkwardly turned the blade around. Grasping the hilt of the new sword, I couldn't help but admire it. The balance was perfect and it truly rivaled the sword I had just given away. "I give you this weapon knowing you will keep me and ours safe from harm," she said, transferring her protection from her father to myself.

Tostig strapped the new scabbard about my waist. I smiled at him briefly.

"And now," the godi said, "I call on Freyja and the Lords of the Sky to smile down on us this happy marriage and observe the oaths which bind them together forever and a day."

There were more oaths of the same sort, then we set off on our bride-running, where both parties raced to the feast hall. It was all very unnecessary, for the groom had to get there first. Otherwise, how would I have been able to block the doorway with my sword, and carry my beloved over the threshold? But of course, it was all in good fun and it would certainly have been bad luck if she had tripped going into the house. By then, I was so elated you could have made me do just about anything and I would have agreed.

The feast hall was hung with wreaths of flowers and wands of hawthorn for good luck. Edith and I sat at the head table flanked by our parents, and the feasting started almost immediately. There was another custom we must perform, and she was quick to get up again and bring forth the loving cup filled with mead. She stood across the table from me and handed it over. I still remember the verse she chanted:

49

Ale I bring thee, thou oak-of-battle,
With strength blended and brightest honor;
'Tis mixed with magic and mighty songs,
With goodly spells, wish-speeding runes.[1]

I took the cup from her hands and made the sign of the Hammer over it, consecrating the mead to Thor. "Odin," I called before taking a drink, so as not to be disrespectful. Then, as she returned to her seat, I passed the cup back to her and she toasted Freyja before taking her sip.

I handed the cup to my mother and she smiled sweetly at me before drinking and passing it on. She looked ravishing, as though it was her own wedding. For a moment I wondered what it had been like, with mother as a blushing bride, but there was too much activity for me to dwell on such outlandish thoughts. Of course she must have had a great ceremony. Look how much she loved father.

It seemed to take forever before it was time for our bedding. I kept glancing sideways at Edith when I thought she wasn't looking. I couldn't believe my good fortune and I suppose I thought she might disappear like a woodland fairy. But no, she was solid flesh and blood and I flattered myself she was anxious as I was, though truth to tell she was the perfect chatelaine, as ever. She frequently got up and went around the tables, and I felt obliged to join her though I really wanted her all to myself. I could see she had many well-wishers, and that made it easier for me to tolerate their remarks with good grace.

But time passes for us all and finally we were ready to be escorted to our bridal chamber. Edith went first, for she needed to be dressed by her maids and put into bed. By now, the wine had

---

[1] *Hollander, Poetic Edda, p. 109*

been flowing freely and there was much ribaldry at my expense. Father and Ulfcytel made a great show of leading me to the bedroom by torchlight, and I won't dwell on the foolish things everyone said.

Once we opened the door, I forgot about the others. Edith was sitting up in bed, propped against the headboard. She wore her bridal crown, and her long hair had been let down so that she was almost sitting on the loose curls. For a moment, my companions were silenced by her beauty.

"Harold is the lucky one tonight!" Tostig chortled. I hoped he wouldn't get any cruder than that.

"There's something strange happening in his tunic," someone else injected.

I turned to father. "Please," I begged. "Bring the godi." He laughed, then turned around, telling the others to find the high priest. I didn't think I could take much more of this.

Luckily, the man was nearby and he looked so dignified that humor fled the room. He nodded to me. I knew what I had to do and crossed over to the bed. I removed Edith's bridal crown as a symbol of our physical union and the godi gave another of his invocations. I got under the covers with my beloved lady, and after congratulating us the others slowly left the room, wishing us well. My father was last and paused at the door, giving us the strangest look.

"May you both be happy in your new life, and I wish you many children." The words were heartfelt, but he almost looked jealous. I couldn't understand it.

"Thank you, father," Edith said. He smiled crookedly and left us alone.

I turned to her, suddenly abashed. "You are so beautiful, I am almost afraid to touch you."

She nestled into my shoulder and I put my arm around her. She touched the base of my throat with her finger.

51

"I'm not afraid to touch you," she whispered. "In fact, I hope you touch me all over so I can return the favor."

Shyness is not my natural state and I gleefully abandoned it. Before the night was over, we had managed to learn much about each other.

As I remember, dawn came too quickly for me. We had one more ceremony to perform and I had to leave her to the ministrations of her maids. Already my witnesses were gathering in the great hall, anticipating the feasting that would go on continuously for the rest of the week. I walked to a side table and my cousin Beorn handed me some bread and cheese; this was good enough while waiting for my bride to appear. Father came over with the rest of my morning-gifts, including the most spectacular necklace I could find. He placed the items on the table in a spot set aside for that purpose. I admired the spun-glass beads that felt so cool in my hands.

"Are you happy, son?"

"Most happy. I thank you for helping my suit with the king."

"Ah, yours won't be the only happy wedding this year. King Edward has agreed to marry your sister."

I couldn't have been more surprised. She hadn't mentioned a word to me. Well, to tell true, I didn't yet have a chance to speak with anybody at length.

"She must be excited."

Father shrugged his shoulders. "She is a good and obedient daughter. Edward will take care of her, and our house will be greatly honored."

I looked across the room. There she was, standing with mother. She didn't look too happy from this distance. I resolved to speak with her at the soonest.

"Ah, here she comes," father said. I turned as Edith crossed into the room with her maids. She was wearing a finely pleated, long white veil pinned to a little cloth band tied around her forehead. Her ladies escorted her to the front of the hall and I joined them, still holding the necklace.

"My bride," I spoke loudly, making sure everyone could hear me. "I have brought the rest of your morning gifts, which I present to you with loving hands." I fastened the necklace and waved my hand toward the table, stacked with linens, household goods and gold. "I also give over to you five hides of land, upon which rests the church of Waltham, previously owned by Tovi the Proud. I pledge that I will rebuild the church and endow it with a new college of canons."

I knew that would please Edith, because we both had a fondness for that place. And indeed I was correct; she broke into tears of happiness and everyone clapped their hands in support of my gift. I pulled a ring of keys from my pouch and presented it to her.

"As you are now the mistress of my estate," I said, a little softer, "I have a manor at Nazeing, a short ride from Waltham which shall be yours as well. I present you with the keys to my house. Keep them safe for me." For a moment the room was silent.

Someone sneezed and the spell was broken. Taking a collective sigh, people felt free to move about. Many came up to us and gave us little gifts; others gathered to share gossip. There were a good many thegns in my earldom I had yet to meet, but tomorrow was soon enough.

Harold did indeed talk with me about my upcoming wedding to Edward. He was so sympathetic I allowed myself to cry for the first time. We both knew this was not likely to be a love match. I envied Harold's happiness but did not begrudge him. Mine was a great honor, and I was prepared to make my family proud... Editha

Chapter 2

HAROLD REMEMBERS

Edith and I had spent the first half of our honeymoon visiting my estates in the south, many along the coast. On the way back to Cambridge we determined to visit her new possessions around Waltham Abbey. Our little entourage followed us at a short distance as we took a leisurely ride through the countryside, stopping at every village along the way to speak with the residents and learn their concerns. Once they discovered I was their new Earl their reticence passed, and I watched as they called to each other, summoning friends and family to meet the "great folk", as I heard them say.

When we reached the abbey, the priests were all in a flutter to prepare a suitable repast for us. While we were waiting, we visited the little church they said was a couple hundred years old. It was short and squat and made of stone, but I was most interested in the famous Holy Cross.

Edith ran her hand along the back of a long wooden bench. "This Cross it said to cure the sick."

I took her hand and led her to the steps of the altar. We looked at the large black marble cross hanging on the far wall. "Indeed it does. I can attest to that myself."

She looked at me in surprise. We were learning so much about each other.

"This cross was brought to Waltham back in 1035." I loved this story and couldn't help tell it again. "It was said that a peasant on the lands of Tovi the Proud had a vision about a great relic. My father knew Tovi well; he was Canute's standard bearer. In fact it was at his wedding feast that King Harthacnut fell over and died—just as he was making a toast."

She shuddered a little. I gave a short laugh. "Nobody mourned his passing, except Queen Emma. Anyway, the cross was discovered on his Montacute estate in Somersetshire. Tovi, who had recently converted, vowed to deliver the cross to a great religious house. He loaded it on a wagon pulled by twelve white and twelve red oxen. Then he called out the name Westminster, and the oxen refused to move."

Curious about my story, Edith sat on the bench, patting the space beside her.

"Oxen are a stubborn breed, as you know," I continued, sitting down. "But Tovi wondered if God was trying to tell him something. Winchester, he called out, but still to no effect. Canterbury, Reading, he went on and on and those oxen refused to move. Then he remembered Waltham where he had a hunting lodge, and its little Saxon church even smaller than this one. As soon as he called out Waltham, the twenty-four oxen moved as one, and they pulled the wagon on their own all the way here. He sent 66 people to accompany the cross on its journey."

"Hmm," she exclaimed, adjusting her dress to make herself more comfortable. "I never heard the whole story before. But what has this to do with you?"

Well, I had started this conversation though I usually didn't like to talk about it.

"It happened when I was a child," I began slowly. "I fell one day and when I woke up the next morning I couldn't move my legs. As the day went on, the rest of my body was powerless. I was terrified." It was my turn to shudder at the memory.

"How awful for you."

55

"Mother and father didn't know what to do. She stayed by my bedside for days. Finally, father had the idea to bring me here for a pilgrimage."

I took a deep breath. "It was so painful. They put animal hides and blankets in the bed of a wagon, but every bump was agony. I couldn't move, but I could still feel plenty of discomfort.

"So when we reached Waltham, they put me on a litter and placed me in front of the altar. For two days we sat here while my parents took turns praying for a cure. And then it happened."

She took my hand. "What happened?"

"I sat up. I couldn't believe it. Slowly, my legs felt a like a weight had been removed from them. I stood, a little shaky, but I didn't fall. It really was a miracle. This is truly a holy place for me."

Edith sighed. A tear ran down her face. I wiped it with my finger.

"It's all right now," I said. "It never happened again."

She smiled through her tears. "And you made this place my bride-gift. I am so honored!"

"This just tells you how much you mean to me. We can rebuild this church together, and make it more glorious. We can establish a college of canons to look over the Holy Cross. This will be our special legacy."

"Oh, my dear..." She stopped. I knew she had something on her mind.

"Harold..."

I turned on the bench, giving her my full attention.

"Harold, as long as we are in this place of mercy, there is something I have to confess to you."

I blinked in surprise. What could she possibly have done wrong?

"Harold, about Eadric... Remember I told you I sent a letter to my goldsmith on his way to London?"

"Yes, I remember."

"Well, it wasn't the goldsmith who made an accusation to the king. It was me."

I remember my shock. I think my mouth fell open.

"You have to understand," she added hastily. "He seemed to think he owned me. On his visit the day after I met you, he told me to stay away from you. As though he thought he was my legal guardian and could command me..." She shuddered. "I was frightened. And angry. I wrote a letter to King Edward telling him Eadric had overstepped his authority, and I sent it with my goldsmith who would deliver it personally. Just because he's a reeve..."

I couldn't help myself. I burst into laughter then clapped my hand over my mouth. Taking her arm, I ran from the church and pulled her out the door. Once in the fresh air I picked her up and twirled her around.

"Overstepped his authority!" I whooped. "You imprudent, dear, wonderful girl! So the king thought you were talking about money!" I laughed even more heartily until I ran out of breath. "And in writing that silly letter, you taught Eadric a thing or two, didn't you? And removed our biggest obstacle. Edith, you are amazing."

Relieved, she let out a shaky laugh. She smoothed her skirt where I rumpled it. "I didn't mean for all that to happen. I just wanted him to leave me alone..."

"And I suppose Eadric didn't know about Edward's temper. I can see why he thought it was me who made the accusation."

That thought sobered me up. I took her hand again and we walked to the riverside. We watched a pair of swans swim back and forth under some overhanging tree limbs. They honked at us, scolding.

"Oh, Harold. I didn't want..."

"No matter. It's done now and he need never know. I will find a way to bring him home, I promise. And he may well be less antagonistic in the future."

57

Back in Cambridge, I went about examining Reeve Eadric's finances in earnest, and I soon discovered I really did need his help. Cambridge, deemed a *hundred* all by itself, was surrounded by 14 other *hundreds*, and as each *hundred* supports around one hundred homesteads, that's a lot of people just in this region. As Reeve, Eadric collected taxes, enforced the king's peace, presided over local courts, received fines, and I don't even know what else. He carefully recorded all these diverse activities, including the portions he was permitted to keep in exchange for his administrative duties. This Royal allowance went back to Canute's days.

I was sure he skimmed off his own personal share, but there was no way to determine how much. It was almost to be expected. He sent plenty of funds on to the king; of that I was sure. I was content. I had my own duties; I didn't want to take his on, too. I had to find a way to bring him back.

About a month after our return to Cambridge, a letter came from my father. This was not unusual except that the messenger tarried for a response. I brought it over to Edith as she sat by the window, taking advantage of the afternoon light to finish an embroidered piece. I sat on the bed.

"It's from father," I said. "Listen to this: 'Your brother Swegn has abducted Abbess Eadgifu from Leominster Abbey. I fear King Edward may outlaw him for this. I think you had better come to London.' Oh, Swegn, you addle-brain."

Edith straightened, pushing the needle into her fabric for safekeeping. "Why in God's name would your brother do that?"

"Oh, they were childhood friends. Eadgifu was a ward of my father's, and they sent her to Leominster when Swegn started paying too much attention to her."

She went back to her work. "Poor girl. I suppose no one asked about her feelings on the matter."

I was puzzled. "Why should they?"

"Why indeed. Now you know. Maybe she went with him willingly."

I was aghast. "An Abbess? To relinquish her post for such as Swegn?" I couldn't keep the scorn from my voice.

"How well do you know Swegn?" she shot back.

I had to pause for a moment. Although he was only two years older than me, my brother was nearly a stranger. He had always kept to himself, and I knew mother didn't care for him so I didn't care for him.

"I thought so," she nodded to herself. "Since he didn't show up at our handfasting."

I should have thought about that. Edith deserved to be told everything, and she had probably been waiting for me to explain his absence. "Swegn was not easy to be around," I admitted. "He was always angry about something. He kept getting in trouble, though father usually defended him no matter what it was."

"And the girl?"

"Ah. Yes, I see you are right. Eadgifu was his only companion."

"And they took her away from him. Poor Swegn."

That annoyed me. "Poor Swegn? King Edward made him Earl of Herefordshire. What does he have to be unhappy about?"

"Is an earldom all that matters?"

I didn't understand her question. What else was there?

By the time I reached London, my father was already there with the Archbishop of Canterbury. I made my way to his Southwark palace and was greeted by my brother Tostig, who looked as smug as he used to when he had just stolen my favorite toy. With some effort I hid my annoyance.

"Swegn?" I asked, looking about.

"Gone." He leaned toward my ear so nobody else would hear. "Father insisted he leave the country before King Edward heard the news. But it didn't matter. As soon as the king learned of Swegn's shame, he outlawed him anyway."

"Ah." I saw now why Tostig was so full of anticipation. He thought the vacant earldom would go to him.

"Well, Herefordshire borders on Mercia," I mused, knowing Tostig was very aware of this fact. "The king might give it over to Leofric."

My brother turned two shades of red. "It would be best for our family if you try to persuade him otherwise," he retorted.

"Me? As if I could persuade the king to do anything." I was enjoying myself at Tostig's expense, but that came to an end when father entered the room.

"Oh, there you are Harold. Good. Come, both of you. We must be ready for the Witenagemot."

It was father's way to have a family meeting whenever possible, before facing an assembly. He wanted us all to be in agreement before his enemies. And in front of his friends, of course. We dared not cross him.

"Harold," father said, sitting down at a table and accepting a pitcher of ale from a servant. We were off to the side while the servants set up the hall for supper. He filled the Archbishop's cup first. "I sent Swegn to Flanders until this crisis passes."

I looked the other way so father would not see my face. Swegn's very presence invoked a crisis.

"But first I hope to raise a fleet to help Denmark," he went on, "which is one purpose of tomorrow's Witan. The other, of course, is to see what the king will do with Swegn's vacant earldom."

Father's face took on a pained expression. "I hope it's only temporary. I had a long discussion with the king the other day. I believe I have persuaded him to keep the earldom in our family."

Tostig leaned an elbow on the table, looking confident.

"Until Swegn returns," I prodded.

"Yes, yes, of course. If Leofric gets a taste of the revenue, he would never let it go. Willingly."

The hall was getting noisy; I turned, watching the servants bang trestle tables together. Beorn was making his way over to our corner. I stood up, waving.

"Cousin," I called. "Well come." We made room for him and he sat beside me, giving a big grin.

"Big day tomorrow." He slapped me on the shoulder. "It must take a lot to drag you away from your new wife."

I laughed, but father was showing signs of impatience. "Beorn, have you heard from your brother?"

"Svein? Yes. The news is not good. King Magnus of Norway has joined forces with his uncle Harald Sigurdson."

"Who?" I asked. I didn't remember his name.

"Brother of King Olaf, from back in Canute's day. After Olaf was killed at the battle of Stiklestad, Harald fled the country. It is said he went east to Russia. I am told he even went to Constantinople, though I don't know how true that is."

"Harald Sigurdson," father repeated. "I thought he was dead."

"Oh no. Not only is he very much alive, he is so rich in gold no man can compare to him in wealth. When he returned from Constantinople, at first he and my brother became allies. But when Harald's nephew Magnus King of Norway learned of his return, I'm told he secretly sent to Harald with an offer. Together they made a bargain to divide the kingdom between them, and the treasure as well. Harald started a quarrel with my brother and went over to Magnus."

"I had heard something of the sort," father said, "but not the details. So this is why Svein has asked us for help."

"Together, Magnus and Harald, now called Hardrada—Hard Ruler, they say—drove Svein from Jutland. He is just barely

61

hanging onto his inheritance, for he is only in possession of Scania now."

"And he needs our help," father added. "I hope I can convince the Witan."

Alas, it was not meant to be. Swegn's behavior put father in a bad position and at the Witenagemot King Edward seemed anxious to test his own authority. At first, he gave father what he asked, probably to catch him off guard.

When the meeting began, the king came right to the point. "The first order of business," he said, "is to determine what to do with the vacant earldom, now that Swegn Godwineson has been banished." He could not forbear a triumphant glance at father.

"After giving the matter much thought, I have divided it three ways. Herefordshire will come under the control of my cousin, Ralf de Mantes. Oxfordshire will henceforth be annexed to Earl Beorn's territory. And Gloucestershire will be given to Earl Harold."

Beorn and I looked at each other. This was an unexpected surprise. I couldn't help but glance at Tostig who was looking down, biting his lip. I knew how disappointed he was. My second glance was across the room at Leofric of Mercia, who looked more angry than disappointed. Well, his son was only sixteen years old. He could wait.

Once again, Edward hurried on. "The next matter is the Danish question. Earl Godwine will present his argument." He leaned back, listening while some of his Norman friends whispered in his ear. Father stood.

"King Svein Estridson is presently in great need of our help. Magnus of Norway has been very successful with his incursions into Danish territory. Already he has overrun Jutland and Sjaelland, leaving Svein only Scania. I propose we send fifty ships to his aid, before Magnus has complete control over all of Denmark as well as Norway."

Leofric was the first to jump to his feet. "This is absurd! Why risk English blood over a foreign cause?" Many in the room stood up, voicing their agreement. I could see father was starting to sweat.

"If Magnus gains undisputed control of Denmark, he will surely turn his attention back to us. It is well known he made an agreement with Harthacnut that he would inherit the crown if Harthacnut died. This is not a foreign war, I say!"

Leofric was still on his feet. "And I say that Godwine wants to expend our men and riches to protect the throne of Denmark for his own nephew!"

I could see Earl Siward stand up, adding his voice to Leofric's. Father had few allies today.

After watching the chaos with evident satisfaction, Edward finally stood, hand out. "Then it is decided? We will not give aid to Svein? Who is in favor of this decision?"

Father tried one more time. "Remember," he shouted. "If my predictions are true and Magnus does attack, we do not have the means to defend ourselves against him."

That quieted the room down. Edward had already reduced the fleet to its smallest size yet and canceled the Danegeld. It was a popular move, but I don't think it was a wise one. That's why I needed to get busy in my own earldom.

But the decision was already made. Edward bade the scribes to record the Witan's decision. Leofric glared across the room at us as father sat heavily in his chair; I suppose his small victory didn't make up for his son's loss of an earldom.

However, I never saw father defeated before. It was painful to look at. But when I approached him his face brightened.

"Well, today wasn't a total loss. I am content that you and Beorn will watch over Swegn's earldom."

Watch over. He never gave up.

"Too bad about Herefordshire," he went on. "But we shall see what happens."

I didn't really care. Close to the border, Herefordshire took a lot of watching. Let Earl Ralph break his head against those stubborn Welshmen. Between Beorn and myself, we had enough to do, and I was well satisfied we could put together a formidable alliance.

Tostig was long gone by the time Beorn and I left the hall. My cousin put an arm around my shoulder, leading me toward the door.

"Come Harold, I know where we can find the best ale in town and the best whores in London. We have much to discuss. And to celebrate."

As always, I let Beorn take the lead. He was a shrewd man, full of energy and determination. Before we were into our second cup of ale, he was already pointing out the weak districts in our new earldoms.

"Your Swegn was lax, I noticed." With his finger he drew a rough outline of our earldoms on the damp table. "There is much lawlessness between the towns here, and here." He traced the Roman road which crossed through both our territories. "Those outlaws need employment. And we need to recruit more troops. That will be my first priority."

He turned around, reaching for a tavern wench. Running his hand down her arm, he easily drew her into his lap. I rarely saw a woman turn him down.

"But not today's priority," he assured me, taking an empty mug out of her hand and putting it on the table. I was about to say something when I felt someone massaging my shoulder. Maybe Beorn was right.

Before leaving, I needed to speak with King Edward. Of course, I planned to assure him I would take Gloucestershire firmly in hand. But I also needed Eadric of Laxfield back in his old post. The King agreed to receive me, but when I entered his chamber, I saw he was not alone. Aside from Edward, I was the only Englishman in the room. The rest of his advisors were French, or worse, Norman.

I approached Edward and bent my knee.

"Sire," I started, "I am grateful for your trust in granting me this new territory."

"Guard it well, Harold," he said, looking over his shoulder at something. I don't think he was giving me all his attention. I waited until he was ready.

"Yes?" he asked.

"Sire, I have done as you asked and investigated the tax situation in Cambridgeshire under Eadric of Laxfield's control. My conclusion is there was no wrongdoing, and Reeve Eadric has submitted to you the full accounting, less his portion."

"Hmm? Oh, Eadric. If I recall, I received a message accusing him of..." He paused.

"Overstepping his authority? I investigated that as well. He was administering with a heavy hand, which I intend to correct. He was not mismanaging the taxes. I would request you lift his banishment."

The King looked bored. "Very well. As you wish. Take care of the details."

Eadric took his time returning to Cambridge, and by then I was more than ready to turn control back to him. But first, we had to establish a new relationship. The day Stanwine came in to tell me Eadric had returned, I first bade him to summon the local merchants who were waiting for an audience. As the supplicants entered the room, I gestured for Stanwine to bring in Eadric. He was quick to do so, and when the prodigal Reeve entered my chamber, he had to wait for me to finish my business. I made sure to sit on my high chair so I could look down at everyone.

Having attained their requests satisfactorily, the merchants turned to leave and were startled to see Eadric standing quietly by the door. They greeted him somewhat reservedly, hazarding a look at me before they did so to gauge my reaction. I kept my face perfectly expressionless.

So did Eadric, to give him credit. He walked slowly toward me then knelt at my feet, looking at the floor. He was uncomfortable and I knew it.

"No need for that," I said after a moment, stepping down. I grasped him by the elbow and pulled him up. He raised his eyes to mine and I searched his face for hostility, finding none.

"I welcome you back," I assured him in all sincerity. "You have been sorely missed."

I could see he was still confused but strove to hide it. "Stanwine tells me you asked the king directly to restore my lands and my position."

"I promised you I would do so."

He cleared his throat. "Earl Harold, I was mistaken in my conduct toward you. I hope you forgive me."

I lowered my voice. "Edith and I both forgive you and hope you will be our friend."

He wiped an eye. "I am honored. I will serve you well."

"That is all I ask," I assured him. "I must raise a navy and need you here to resume your duties."

He exchanged glances with Stanwine. They were very close, and his friend had already asked leave to return his patronage to Eadric. Of course I agreed. They all worked for me, in the end.

Eadric proved as good as his word, and even gave Edith the deference she deserved as wife of his earl. For her part, Edith treated him like an old friend and we all began to relax around each other. And it was in good time, too; I was already building my new naval force and was away much of the time. Eadric made it his personal responsibility to overlook our household, and he finally found himself a welcome presence in our home.

There were rumors a Viking fleet had been spotted in the Channel, and Edward summoned his navy. Father had been proven right once again. But it was the other rumor that disturbed me; my brother Swegn had been seen with eight ships playing the pirate, though where he was headed remained a mystery.

While awaiting reinforcements at Maldon on the Blackwater River, I was inspecting the new warship supplied for the king's service. Someone shouted my name from the wharf and I turned in annoyance, which I quickly forgot when an exhausted rider practically fell from his horse.

"Earl Harold," he gasped, handing me a scroll. "Earl Beorn bids you accompany him to London."

I was surprised. My cousin must have known I was busy.

I broke the seal on the scroll. Beorn had hastily scripted a few words: "I received a timely warning. Your brother Swegn has secretly returned and petitions the king for his earldom back."

I couldn't suppress a groan. It was just like Swegn to disregard father's warning to wait. I looked at the messenger.

"You cannot ride any further. Where is Beorn?"

"He is headed for your estate at Nazeing and hopes to meet you there."

Efficient as ever. Nazeing was on my way to London. Too bad Edith was in Cambridge, for she would have loved to have seen Beorn.

"That is good. You have done well."

The man smiled as he adjusted the reins of his sweating horse. For a moment I watched him walk away, then called to Torr. He was lashing something up but dropped the rope and hastened over to me.

"A change of plans, my friend. We will take a small guard and ride in an hour."

Torr was the most reliable man that ever served me. Without a word he nodded and turned on his heel; I was sure I wouldn't have to give him another thought. All would be done as I wanted.

It was late in the day and we would have to travel all night before reaching Nazeing. Luckily, there was a full moon and a level road. As promised, Beorn was waiting for me and jumped up from his pallet when I entered the hall.

"I was hoping my messenger would find you," he said, relieved. "You need your sleep then we must ride hard for London before it's too late."

"Too late?" My mind was a bit muddled from the long ride.

"I have a man at court. Swegn seems to have convinced the king he has repented his disgraceful behavior. Edward only waits the approval of the Archbishop before consenting to give his earldom back."

"Sly devil. I wonder how he could convince the king?"

"I don't know, but I'll be cursed if I let that bastard steal back his earldom. We've worked so hard to improve things, and we can't just give it up." He removed my cloak and I remember mumbling a response before falling onto Beorn's pallet in a deep sleep.

After a few hours' rest, Beorn shook me awake.

"Splash some water on your face," he said, handing me a piece of bread with honey slathered over it. "We dare not waste any more time."

Beorn was usually so easy in his manner I took him seriously. Our little retinue roused themselves and we were on the road within the hour.

My cousin was right; we were almost too late. The men guarding the king's audience chamber stepped aside after announcing us. I was taken aback to see my brother Swegn sitting by Edward's side, deep in conversation about a point of religious doctrine. As if he knew the first thing about the Church!

The little worm! Forgetting myself, forgetting my father's dedication to Swegn, I strode forward. Beorn was right at my side as we knelt before the king.

"Sire," I said. I surprised even myself at the harshness of my voice. "I fear you may be harboring a viper at your side."

Swegn jerked forward, but was restrained by the king's warning grasp.

"Surely you are not referring to your brother," he said.

"I most certainly am."

Edward frowned. "I am of the opinion that Swegn repents the wrongs he has done. We are awaiting the Archbishop of Canterbury's advice."

I couldn't believe my brother's audacity. Swegn always seemed to wriggle out of trouble. "And if he is forgiven?"

"I intend to give back his earldom."

That was just too much. Beorn and I jumped to our feet.

"I do not believe his people want him back." I fought to keep my voice even, but it didn't matter. Edward stood up, glaring at us.

"It is not for the populace to decide."

Beorn said, "But Sire, we have ruled well there. Do we deserve to have our lands taken from us?"

"I would have you remember they are my lands, not yours." Edward's voice was icy.

I threw a warning look at Beorn. "I believe that Swegn has been leading the Viking raids on your shores." I was guessing, but judging from my brother's reaction, I had hit the mark.

"That is a lie!" he cried, fists upraised.

"See, Sire, how quickly he returns to his old temperament."

Biting his lip, Swegn lowered his arms. "Brother, you push me too far."

69

Edward had missed none of this. Shaken, he turned to Swegn. "Is there any truth in what he said?"

My brother shook his head. "Harold lies! I came to England with eight ships, it is true, but I have led no raids."

"Why did you need eight ships?" I asked loudly.

Swegn glared at me. "Protection against pirates."

"Protection." I forced a laugh. "Who will protect England against you?"

"That is enough!" Edward shouted, startling all of us. "You are forbidden to quarrel in my presence." He sat in his throne, exhausted. "Harold, Beorn, you refuse to give up Swegn's portion of your earldoms?"

We faced Edward squarely. "We refuse." I spoke for the both of us.

The King shook his head. "Such strife," he said. "I cannot have it. Swegn, the time has not yet come for your return. I give you four days to get your affairs in order, then you must leave again, and await my summons."

Swegn's glare shifted from me to Edward. "Sire, you do not mean this injustice!"

Edward's face hardened. "I have decided. It is not for you to question my judgment." Before his sentence was finished, Swegn strode from the room.

Beorn and I looked at each other, not certain what to do. Edward decided for us; he turned away and spoke to one of his churchmen. My cousin and I backed from the room, relieved to have forestalled disaster.

If only I knew...

"Harold," the king barked. I stopped. "I am off to Sandwich to inspect the fleet. Meet me there."

I nodded, at a loss for words. How was I going to break the news to father?

For now the king was finished with us. The day was still young, and we couldn't waste much time savoring our triumph

70

over Swegn. To tell true, we didn't feel very good about it. However, there was still much to do and we needed to refresh ourselves before moving on. We gathered our men at the nearby public house and planned our next step.

"I can guess where Swegn is going," Beorn mused, pouring a mug of ale. "We have to get there first."

I sighed. "Father will be furious."

"Do you know where he is?"

I thought for a moment. "He is supposed to take the first sweep along the southern coast. By now, I imagine he is closer to Pevensey. If we are lucky, Swegn doesn't have any idea where to start."

I looked sideways at Beorn. "You'll have to go without me."

He nodded slowly. "I know. You cannot disobey the king."

"I don't see any other way. I'm sorry, Beorn."

"No, I must. We owe your father an explanation."

There was nothing else to say. After much resistance he agreed to take three of my men with him. I stood with my housecarls and watched them disappear into the London crowd. It was the last time I saw him alive.

GYRTH REMEMBERS

After Swegn's outlawry, things never seemed quite the same for our family. When my reckless brother came back unbidden from exile and threw himself on the king's mercy, he almost got his earldom back. But it wasn't meant to be. Why should Harold and our cousin Beorn give up their territory to Swegn? What had he done to deserve it? The king was so easy to sway, and Swegn knew it. But then, so did Harold.

So when Harold and Beorn objected to Swegn's attempt to steal his earldom back, the king was understandably influenced. My brother and cousin were a strong pair; they had always taken each other's side, especially in a fight. I don't see how King Edward could have faced them down. Not in favor of Swegn. So he gave my troublesome brother four days to leave the country, and Swegn put tail between his legs and slunk off to Flanders. Or so it should have been.

But no, he went to my father instead, hoping to secure his help once more. His timing couldn't have been worse. Father was in Pevensey, hard-pressed to finish his preparations against the pirates—and I wonder if Swegn wasn't one of them.

Anticipating Swegn's movements, Beorn had gotten there first. I know. I was there running errands for father as he organized his campaign.

When Beorn was announced, father straightened from his table in surprise. Something was not right; my cousin shouldn't be here.

Father had long ago learned to wait for other people to speak first. He told me it was the strongest way to negotiate. For a moment he and Beorn looked at each other, then my cousin let out a big sigh.

"Uncle," he started, then faltered a bit. "There is something I have to tell you."

Father put aside his papers. "Go on," he urged. I could see how tired he was.

"It's about Swegn. He is back."

"Back! Back in England?"

"Yes, he went to the king."

Father let out a grunt of disgust. "I told him to wait."

"He was trying to wriggle back into the king's favor."

"Hmm." I could see my father was thinking hard. But he didn't have long to reflect. With a bang, Swegn burst into the room like he owned the place. He was full of anger, but when he saw Beorn his face fell.

I could tell father was annoyed but tried to hide it. He gave a little half-smile to my brother.

"You are always welcome, son. I hope you come in peace."

"Father," Swegn faltered, then glared at Beorn. "Will you leave us alone?"

"I think not." Beorn always stood his ground with Swegn.

"Father," Swegn began again in that annoying whine of his, "my brother and cousin seek to keep me from my earldom. Why do they need my lands, when they have their own?"

At that, Father's expression softened. "Swegn..."

"As I was making my peace with Edward, they came charging in and refused to cooperate. They turned him against me by their selfish bickering."

As usual, my father swung on Beorn. "You did not tell me that. Is it true?"

"Partly. He would have lost Edward's favor soon enough."

"How do you know that?" Swegn snarled.

"Because I know what kind of man you are."

"Stop, both of you!" Father shook his head. "We are supposed to stay together. If our family is divided, our enemies will tear us to pieces."

Shamed, the others stopped. But father wasn't finished. He glared at Beorn.

"I am ashamed of you, and Harold, too. You should never have humiliated Swegn before the king. You have ruined all that I worked for, these many months. I must start over again.

"What were you thinking of? Only your greed? If that's what was so important to you, I could have given you compensation out of my own earldom."

Poor Beorn. I'm sure Harold would have backed him up, if only he had been there. My cousin sighed. "Perhaps I can return to Edward, and change my position."

Father stared hard at him. "Do you mean that?"

"Yes, uncle. I would never willingly defy you."

Swegn was clearly incredulous. "What about Harold?"

Beorn said, "He has been commanded to meet the king at Sandwich, with his ships. But I think I can talk him into agreeing, as well."

Swegn looked at Beorn. "You would do this for me?"

"I do it for your father."

I don't know. I'm not sure Harold would have agreed to all this, but what could my cousin do in the face of my father's wrath?

It's such a shame circumstances weren't different. But because Beorn agreed to go with Swegn and see the king, he signed his own death warrant. Why they went to Bosham, the opposite direction from the king, I don't know. What I do know is that soon after they boarded his ship, Swegn turned on him and murdered our poor cousin. He made some excuse like Beorn drove him to it, but I didn't believe him. Neither did anyone else. Swegn was declared *Nithing* and driven back into exile, back to Flanders where Count Baldwin obligingly took him in. Again. Little did I know we would follow in a few short years.

LEOFWINE REMEMBERS

I remember that day when Swegn and Beorn boarded his ship in Bosham. I was too young to completely understand his exile and unexpected return, but I was old enough to be fascinated with the eight ships Swegn left at anchor.

At low tide you can see across the whole bay, or rather the whole bay is green with seaweed rather than blue with water. I had to walk a ways along the shore before I reached the boats, barely afloat. I removed my *hosen* and tucked them into my belt, took off my shoes and waded in, so I could touch the sides of the ships and study their construction. These were more like warships than the chunky merchant vessels I was used to seeing tied up at our docks. They were sleek and low, with elaborately carved rowlocks and since ours was a friendly port, they had removed the dragon heads from the prows.

Although I believe Swegn employed mostly Danish mercenaries, they were relaxed and friendly and even joked a little with me as I studied the ships. They didn't have benches but rather seemed to rely on their wooden trunks for seats, which they moved around at random to suit their needs. Since they had planned to stay for several days in one place, they erected tents that covered most of the deck and were lounging in the cool shade, drinking and playing board games, which they seemed to enjoy greatly.

Finally one of the Danes invited me up. Nothing loth, I scrambled aboard.

"What is your name?" the friendly Northman asked.

"Leofwine. I am Swegn's brother."

"Well, we won't hold it against you," he laughed, and the others joined in. This was the first time I had a suspicion they didn't hold my brother in much esteem. But they were friendly enough with me and even taught me some moves in their game, which I picked up very quickly.

But as the tide started in again, I decided to go back before I was stranded. They waved good-naturedly to me and went back to their drinking. Thoughtfully, I waded to shore and was nearing town when I saw Swegn and Beorn riding toward me, followed by three others. They were coming down the main road and seemed to be in a hurry. But they did pull rein when they recognized me.

"What are you doing here?" Swegn asked. I swear he seemed irritated that someone saw him.

"I was looking at the ships," I answered, pulling myself up. I wished I had put back on my shoes.

"What did they say to you?"

I looked questioningly at my big brother. "Nothing."

"Nothing," he retorted in that sing-songy voice he used when making fun of me. "Nothing. Come on, Beorn. We must be ready to sail when the tide is in."

He spurred his horse and Beorn followed without even looking at me. That was the last time I saw him. When I heard later that my cousin was slain on those very ships, I emptied my stomach. Those were evil days.

I understand that six of Swegn's ships deserted him after the murder, though two were captured near Hastings. The locals killed all of their crews and gave over their ships to King Edward. I always wondered if these were the men who played the board game with me? Or were they the two ships that accompanied Swegn to Flanders? I'll never know.

Within a year Swegn was back again. I still don't understand why, but Bishop Ealdred the peacemaker took it upon himself to visit him in Count Baldwin's court. For some reason he determined that my brother was sufficiently remorseful to come back. Against all odds, even though the king and Witan had declared him *nithing,* my brother Swegn was reinstalled in his earldom. I understand Bishop Ealdred was having trouble keeping the peace there and actually needed Swegn's help. Was this the region vacated by poor Beorn? I was too young to know. And Harold was quiet on the subject; I think he held himself partially responsible for Beorn's death.

HAROLD REMEMBERS

As promised, I returned to Maldon and proceeded with my ships to meet the king. At Sandwich our fleets were united and I took charge of Edward's flagship. Tostig was waiting for me there and I put him in command of the next biggest vessel. We sailed around the point and made our way toward Pevensey, where I expected to find father and the rest of the fleet. They had been held up by bad weather, but the clouds were lifting by the time I joined them.

Father was waving to us from the shore. He was giving instructions to his shipmasters as they made space for the rest of us. Luckily Pevensey boasted a long beach, for we were filling up the bay quickly.

I spotted my brother Gyrth who seemed anxious to join me. Edward's ship was so large we anchored some way into the bay and my brother jumped into a little skiff, bringing himself alongside. We threw down a rope ladder.

Climbing up, he gripped my hand a little too hard. I knew something was amiss.

"What has happened?" I asked him anxiously. He looked toward father who was conferring with Tostig.

"It's about Swegn," he said, turning back to me with a worried look.

I cursed. "That maggot. I hoped we could avoid him."

"Beorn got here first. But Swegn was right behind him."

I started pacing the deck. "How much does father know?"

"About King Edward? Enough, I dare say. He was furious at both of them—Swegn for coming back, Beorn for humiliating him in front of the king. He said you ruined everything he has been working for."

"That sounds like him," I said bitterly.

"Beorn felt so bad he offered to make things right with the king."

I stared at him in shock. "He did what?"

"He was uncomfortable about it," Gyrth said. "But he wanted to please father. He thought he could persuade you to accept."

77

"Never!" Despite myself, I was angry. I slammed the gunnel with my fist. Looking toward father, I swear he was staring at me.

"I wonder what Swegn thought," my brother muttered. I turned to him, suddenly realizing why Beorn was nowhere to be seen.

"You don't mean to tell me—"

"They went off together. To see the king."

I expelled my breath like he had just kicked me in the stomach. That's what it felt like.

"I dare say Beorn can take care of himself," Gyrth tried to reassure me. He didn't sound convincing.

I waited. I knew there was more.

"I just don't understand why they rode west," he finished.

Something was wrong, very wrong. I could feel it. I barely had time to compose myself when I saw father gesturing for me to come ashore. I remember I was breathing hard, gripping one of the ropes like a lifeline to my cousin. I needed to find them. Before it was too late.

Father's gesturing became more insistent. I took a deep breath. "Let's go, Gyrth. I know we have a mission." Silently he followed me as we climbed down to his skiff.

Father was fuming while we rowed back. I could see it in his bearing. He barely glanced at Gyrth before turning his back and shoving his way through the little crowd. They parted before us as we followed meekly. I wasn't used to seeing his choler and I admit to some uneasiness as we entered his little lodge and closed the door. It was just the three of us. He leaned against the table, his back to us.

"You told him," he said to Gyrth.

"Yes."

He turned around, arms crossed. His face was still smoldering.

"Why did you do it?" he asked me.

78

I admit it. For once, my irritation got the better of me.

"Isn't it obvious?" I retorted. "He had no right to his earldom."

"And you had no right to claim it for yourself!"

The words were left unspoken between us. Beorn and I were supposed to watch over his lands until the prodigal son came back. But I was having none of it.

"And you sent him off with Beorn!" I couldn't help it; my voice seethed with accusation.

"And what of it? Maybe your cousin will repair the damage."

"Then why did they ride west?"

Father's face fell. He didn't know. He looked at Gyrth in confusion. My brother nodded.

"West? I do not know."

I was about to add some rejoinder when the knock at the door interrupted our argument. A boatswain poked his head in.

"The fleet is ready, Earl Godwine."

Father grabbed his sword and buckled it on with Gyrth's help.

"Don't let me down this time," he snarled at me as he threw the door open.

That wasn't necessary! I was too shocked to respond; nor would it have mattered. He wouldn't have heard me anyway.

My vessels were a little disorganized yet, but as Father led the fleet west along the coast we fell in behind his last ships. We were forty-two in all and made an impressive array as we formed ourselves into a loose formation, close enough for visual communication.

By now the sky had cleared and visibility was good—good enough to see no enemy ships on the horizon.

For a full day we looked. But as it turned out, the danger had passed. The offending fleet must have been dispersed by the same storm that held father in port. We docked at Portsmouth and

I knew father would insist on taking another sweep of the Channel.

But I couldn't wait any longer; I had to know what happened with Swegn and Beorn. I presented myself to my father and asked to be relieved of my command. He knew why. Without looking up, he gestured to Tostig who bent obligingly, lending an ear.

"Take over Harold's ship," he said. "Your next in command can step up and take your place."

That was his answer. I was dismissed.

The harbors around Portsmouth are all connected, including Bosham, and I was able to engage a small fishing boat to take me home. I even took a set of oars to quicken our speed. I must have looked a fright, for none of the crew spoke to me.

Alas, it didn't matter. By the time I neared my destination, I saw Beorn's three companions—the three I sent to protect him— sitting atop an old stone wall, just waiting for me. Their long faces told me that the worst had happened.

I jumped into the shallow water and ran up to them, grabbing the nearest by the arm.

"Tell me!"

"Earl Harold," he started, almost embarrassed. "It all happened so quickly. One minute we were sailing east, then the next the two of them were fighting. With knives. Their men were holding us back when Beorn slipped and Swegn stabbed him in the heart. He died almost at once."

The man paused as I put my face in my hands.

No, no. This couldn't be happening.

I fell to one knee and they caught me before I went all the way down. I didn't care: it was all my fault. All my fault. I should never have sent him off alone.

"They turned the ships around and went westward," the man went on hurriedly, pulling me up. "They forced us to disembark then kept going west. I don't know where they were headed…" He shook his head. "We failed you, Earl Harold."

I'm afraid I didn't have any words of comfort for the man. "Are you sure he is dead?" My cousin. I couldn't accept it.

They all nodded slowly. "Of that there is no doubt," he said.

I turned and trudged away from the quay, waving them off. I needed to be alone. Without realizing it I headed for the church in Bosham, where Canute had buried his little daughter. Somehow I always found comfort there.

I knelt before the altar and wept shamelessly. Poor Beorn deserved more than such a fate at my brother's hands.

"I curse you, Swegn," I finally spat out, as though making a holy oath. "May God send you to the depths of hell. If I don't do it first."

I hated him. I had always hated him. I'm not ashamed to say that cursing my wretched brother made me feel better. Furthermore, I resolved that I would gather the housecarls, the thegns, and any other warriors I could find and call a *gemot* to denounce my brother.

I don't know how long I knelt there, but as I left the church, somewhat composed, Beorn's three companions were still waiting for me. I gestured for them to follow, for I dreaded what was to come and their presence gave me strength. I did not know if mother had heard the tragic news, and hoped I would be the one to break it to her. Or maybe "hope" was the wrong word; she was very fond of her nephew.

Mother was at home; her warm greeting told me she knew nothing. She threw her arms around my neck and drew me to her. I inhaled deeply, enjoying her lavender scent which always recalled fond childhood memories. Then she stopped, noticing my companions.

81

"So this is not a family visit," she said, not unkindly. "Come. Harold's friends are always welcome."

She sent the servants scrambling for food and wine. I wanted to get rid of my bad news right away but I restrained myself; after all, things were never going to be quite the same again.

Of course, this reflection made me quiet and I sipped my wine slowly, turning the cup in my hands.

"What is it, Harold?" Mother always knew.

"I have some bad news to tell you."

That was an awkward start. She waited, patiently.

"Swegn came back, unannounced."

She let out a sharp exhale, shaking her head. "I know. Against his father's wishes."

"It's worse than that. He went to the king, trying to get his earldom back. Beorn and I refused to concede our territories."

"How did you know..."

"Beorn had a man at court who told him. Together we went to the king. Swegn was already there, acting for all the world like a penitent." I couldn't keep the bitterness from my voice.

"Not a pretty sight, I imagine."

I looked at her gratefully. She always understood. "It didn't last long. As soon as we spoke up, he reverted back to his usual manner."

I hesitated at that point. My companions were eating quietly, afraid to speak up.

My mother put a hand on my arm. "What happened then?"

"Edward decided it was not the time to reinstate Swegn. He gave him four days to leave the country. Only, Swegn went to father instead."

She tightened her hand. I spoke quicker now.

"I had to command the king's ship, so Beorn went alone to father, hoping to get there first. I suppose he didn't succeed. I sent these three men with him. Pearce, Alfred, and Cedric." I turned to Pearce. "How did Beorn end up on a ship?"

He took a big gulp. "Your father was furious, and Beorn offered to go back to the king and make things right."

I stared at him in anger, though it wasn't his fault. "Why didn't they go to Sandwich where the king was?"

Mother was clearly confused. I covered her hand with my own.

"Swegn told him he was afraid his crews would desert if he left them alone too long. He persuaded Beorn to accompany him back to Bosham, and from here they could take the ships to Sandwich."

"And once on board..." I turned to Mother. "There was a knife fight. Swegn killed Beorn."

She clapped her hand to her mouth. Tears immediately started running down her face.

"My Beorn," she murmured. "Oh Harold, Leofwine saw them and told me how odd they acted. I was waiting for them to come. And then they were gone."

I think it was the first time I saw her cry. I held her in my arms and wished I could cry along with her.

I would say I acted out of anger when I boarded my ship and set sail for Hastings. If I had met Swegn on the way I don't know what I would have done. But apparently he was still busy plundering the poor villages somewhere. There were no ships in sight.

After we docked, I wasted no time sending out messages to Beorn's earldom as well as my own, announcing my cousin's murder and convoking a military *gemot*. King Edward was still at Sandwich and the *gemot* needed his presence to make it official.

The men of Hastings were furious when they heard of Beorn's murder; Swegn had no allies here. I joined them when they put together a fleet of fast-moving ships and set out to find his little flotilla. I don't know what we expected to encounter, but luck was with us and we spotted two low-riding ships on the horizon. Pearce put a hand over his brow to block the sun, but he shook his head.

"I cannot tell from this distance," he said.

"In all likelihood they don't belong in our waters." My anger had not died down and I needed to fight somebody. "Let us go after them. Maybe they still carry the body of Beorn."

The others didn't need to be told twice. They trimmed the sails and we shot forward, making straight for the vessels. Considering their reaction, we must have judged aright. The two boats turned and fled from us but we were faster, and we eventually caught up with them. The men of Hastings were *lithsmen,* trained to fight on ship as well as land, and their prowess was every bit as formidable as the pirates.

As we neared the enemy vessels, Pearce cried out triumphantly. "Yes, I recognize them. Those two ships were with Swegn." I was elated. Could I capture my brother and bring him to the king?

My men lined the sides of the ships; we were four to their two, and the blood lust was upon us. As we caught up with Swegn's boats, my men threw their grapnels and caught the gunwales with their iron hooks. Pulling the vessels close, we leaped on the two boats, swords and axes singing. Our opponents put up a good fight but they were so badly outnumbered they didn't stand a chance. I plunged my blade into the chest of a leader then looked around for Swegn. Two bodies splashed into the water followed by three more.

"Halt!" I called. "We need witnesses!" I twisted around to look; the unarmored bodies bobbed in the water, but my brother was not among them.

My sturdy sailors held three men by the arms; all the fight had gone out of them. The villains wouldn't look at me so I grabbed the nearest by the chin.

"Where is Swegn?" I growled at him.

The man jerked his face out of my grasp. He had some spirit in him, after all. "I don't know. We left him at Dartmouth."

"Dartmouth? Why there?"

"That's where he buried his cousin Beorn." He said that so carelessly! I clenched my teeth.

"Bind these men. And let us present these ships to the king," I snarled. "Edward will see that the men of Hastings know how to protect the coast." Stripping the dead pirates of any valuables, we pushed their corpses into the sea and threw buckets of water onto the decking to rinse off the blood.

It was late in the afternoon and though I was anxious to move on to Sandwich, I agreed to spend the night at Hastings. We ate well and drank to our day's work, though in my case I hoped the ale would help the pain go away. Of course it did not. I kept seeing Beorn's laughing face, kept remembering the times we drank together. Before my head fell senseless to the table, I think I was talking to him. Nobody bothered me, but I did get some worried looks the next morning. I wonder what I said?

The following day we manned the two pirate vessels, sailed past the cliffs of Dover and into the port of Sandwich. Leaving my companions to secure the boats, I immediately made my way to the palace. I couldn't wait another minute.

Edward was talking with his council but the guards let me in without delay. I strode forward then stopped in my tracks when I saw Father in attendance. He whirled around, mouth open in surprise. I was just as startled to see him, though I probably shouldn't have been. He had been on royal business after all. I went down on one knee before the king.

85

"I am glad you have come, Earl Harold," he said. "I received your messages and was distressed to hear the sorry news about Beorn's death. Please tell me all you know."

As I told the king about Swegn's odious behavior, he questioned me closely. For once, he actually gave me his undivided attention. I noticed out of the corner of my eye that father kept edging closer; he probably did not know the full story either. When I finished, father had turned pale and I thought he looked faint.

Edward noticed I was looking at father and he turned as well.

"Sit down, man," he said. Father found a chair, relieved.

"Yes, Harold, I agree with your proposal. I have sent out my own messages calling for a *gemot*. We shall not tolerate your brother's presence in my kingdom."

Father stood up again, aghast. I cringed, inwardly; I would have preferred to tell him in my own way.

"Sire," he started, taking a step forward.

"No, Earl Godwine. That man is *nithing*. Worthless in my eyes. He is dishonored."

For once I agreed with the king. But I could not look father in the eye. He would never understand.

"Sire," father said, ignoring me. "I have important issues that demand my attention. I beg your pardon." Bowing, he backed from the room.

Edward turned to me. "Now, Harold. I understand you come from Hastings..."

I told the king about our sea battle and the bravery of his subjects. Then I formally presented the two ships into his care. He graciously accepted, and this seemed like a good moment to bring up my other question.

"Sire, I would translate the remains of Beorn to Winchester. He deserves a better resting place than that backwater town of Dartmouth."

Edward considered this. One of his Bishops leaned forward and spoke in his ear.

"After all, he was an Earl. By your decree," I added.

I knew Edward was thinking of Beorn's Danish ancestry; it was something he preferred to forget. But it was true he gave my cousin precedence over other candidates. Finally he nodded. "Very well. I shall send ahead so they may prepare for you."

That was a great relief. I bowed, seeing my little audience was at an end. Edward had moved his attention to someone else so I was free to go.

I expected father to be waiting outside, but Tostig had tarried instead. He fell in beside me as I went looking for a hostel.

"How long have you been here, brother?" I asked.

"I stayed with father the whole time we searched for raiders. It seems you had better luck finding them than we did."

"Not good enough. Swegn got away."

He nodded, putting his head close to my ear. "What did you say in there? Father was terribly distressed."

Did he send Tostig to question me? Probably not; my brother was always sticking his nose into my business.

"Tostig, I am calling a *gemot* to declare Swegn an outlaw. Had I known father was with the king, I would have waited."

Tostig let out a whistle. "No wonder he was upset. But the bastard deserves it. I understand he seized Beorn, tied him up, threw him into a boat and murdered him."

"I don't think it quite happened that way, but it doesn't matter, does it? Our cousin is dead at Swegn's hand and I intend to see justice is done. Are you with me, Tostig?"

He didn't hesitate. "Of course I am with you. Swegn has gotten away with many deeds, but murder should not be one of them!"

We walked for a moment in silence. "What will father do after he has a chance to think it over?"

"Hmm." Tostig rubbed the back of his head. "I see why you want to stay in a hostel. For once I think you had better let me approach him."

For once, I agreed with him.

A week later Edward convoked a military *gemot* in a natural amphitheatre near Sandwich; so many people had come there was no room to hold the meeting indoors. I recognized many of the new arrivals; some took ship with Beorn, some were his household troops, others were thegns in his earldom.

During that week I talked with many of them in the streets, the alehouses, the docks; once they discovered I was determined to condemn my brother they opened up and told me more stories than I needed to know. Apparently Swegn had a genius for making enemies.

Finally the day of the *gemot* dawned, and I preceded almost everyone to the makeshift platform that was built for the king. I greeted as many as I could before Tostig showed up in the king's entourage, without father. That was not a good sign. I took my brother aside.

"He is not coming?"

"Of course not. Did you expect otherwise?"

"No. Not really. Did he have anything to say?"

Tostig looked troubled. "He said he would do what he could to bring Swegn back."

I let out a groan; I couldn't believe it. "He can't be serious."

"I don't think he had much conviction," Tostig added slowly. "It's as though he thinks he must defend Swegn because no one else will."

I believed him, for it had ever been this way. "Tostig, is he angry with me?"

I knew the answer was bad, because my brother forbore from sneering. "He wouldn't speak your name. He wouldn't talk about you at all."

I turned away so Tostig wouldn't see my face. "It's my fault Beorn is dead," I said so quietly he asked me to repeat myself. "It's all my fault," I said, turning to face him. "I never should have let him go alone."

I don't know whether Tostig understood what I was saying, but he had the good sense to leave me alone. It was just as well, because at that moment, the crowd was parting for King Edward, followed by his Bishops and Norman advisors.

I don't know whether Edward was motivated by his obvious dislike of our father or his affection for Beorn. But I detected in his face an intense concentration I never saw before. He mounted the steps looking for all the world like the worthy heir of the great Alfred that he was. People quieted down immediately while I took my place beside him as the only Earl in attendance.

"I have called this *gemot*," he said, trying to throw his voice, "to address the recent murder of Earl Beorn by the miscreant Swegn Godwineson. I ask all of you in attendance, my men of Mercia, Wessex and East Anglia, to sit in judgment."

He turned to me. "I ask Earl Harold to tell us what he knows of this detestable event."

I kept thinking of father, but in truth my anger was stronger than my filial duty.

"I come here directly from Bosham," I spoke, sure that my voice was stronger than Edward's, "where I learned of Beorn's death directly from his companions, who were too few to save him from Swegn and his paid assassins."

The warriors in the crowd jostled each other. They could hear me just fine. "All of you know that Swegn is my older brother. But he had been in exile for another grave offense and thought he could choose the time and place for his return. Beorn tried to reason with him, and paid for this mistake with his life."

89

I paused while the assembly raised their voices in outrage. But I wasn't finished yet. "Relying on his kinship, Beorn let Swegn persuade him to travel by boat to the king. How was he to know that my brother planned to slay him? And dump his body at Dartmouth? The good men of Hastings captured two of Swegn's ships, but it appears my brother has fled."

I was gratified by the response. But I had said enough. The King stepped forward, holding up his hands.

"According to Canute's law," he shouted as the assembly quieted down, "Swegn Godwineson should be declared *nithing*. He shall be driven off the king's estates with *nithing's* word, and shall be exiled from every land under my rule. Swegn Godwineson is cursed. He is an outlaw. What is your judgment?"

The men roared their agreement. As one, the *here* of England declared my brother a worthless wretch. Edward had some other business to finish as long as the assembly was called, and I moved to the back of the platform.

"Let me bring us back to the defense of my kingdom. Because recent events have demonstrated our need once again, I intend to establish an alliance of coastal ports. But primarily, I will start with five major Head Ports: Sandwich, Dover, Hastings, Hythe, and Romney. These towns will be under my especial care, and I grant to them *sake and soke*, the right to keep all legal fees assigned in court cases. I also grant them the right to collect my tolls."

This was a surprise to everyone, I think, except perhaps his Norman advisors. It even caught my attention for a moment.

"These ports will be relieved of *fyrd* service on land. In exchange, they will provide me with *ship fyrd* services, as well as 20 manned ships to guard the sea for fifteen days when I require their service. I will meet with the burghers of these Cinque Ports to work out the details."

This was the beginning of a mighty plan to protect our coastline. I was surprised Edward had not discussed the matter with me. I wondered whether he spoke to father about it, since these ports were in Wessex. Alas, this was not the time to ask.

When the *gemot* was adjourned to everyone's satisfaction, I was approached by many of Beorn's supporters. When they learned I intended to go to Dartmouth and recover his body, a large number of them decided to accompany me. I think my cousin would have appreciated his influence.

Dartmouth was a tiny hamlet with a natural port, tucked into the hills of Devon. The little church, if it could even be called that, was a stone hut with a sod roof. They had done the best they could with poor Beorn, and had buried him in a wood coffin under a mound of earth and stones. Together we took turns digging up the grave, then transferred his body onto a wagon. It was a long walk to Winchester, for we were forced to match our pace to the slow-moving *wain*. But in a way I was comforted by the presence of my cousin, and gained some solace from the time I spent walking by his side.

The old minster at Winchester was hundreds of years old, and Saint Swithin graced our capital with his everlasting presence. Edward's messengers had given the churchmen enough time to prepare a vault for Beorn, and they were waiting for us in their most ceremonial vestments. As the priests carried my cousin into the minster, chanting in their unintelligible Latin, I was impressed by the number of kings and important persons who were buried there. We walked past grave markers of Kings of Wessex going back to the 7th century: Kings Egbert, Eadred, Edwy, and even Alfred the Great. And there, next to Canute, was an open stone coffin waiting for my dear Beorn. His death may have been unworthy, but in his afterlife he had great companions.

Chapter 3

TOSTIG REMEMBERS

I accompanied Harold as he recovered Beorn and moved him to Winchester, but he never spoke a single word to me; I daresay he didn't even realize I was there, so wrapped up was he in his own guilt. And well he should have been; if he and Beorn had not been so selfish about Swegn's earldom, none of this would have happened. Did they really need to rush into the king's presence and humiliate Swegn to his face? Not that I want to defend my ruthless brother; but knowing Swegn, what other reaction could they expect?

And to make matters even worse, Harold just had to appear before the king and declare Swegn an outlaw, so that father was caught in the most embarrassing position ever. After all those years of telling us that the family must stay together, poor father's pride got slapped down in front of the king.

I heard it all from King Edward. I think he actually enjoyed seeing my father's discomfiture. I am glad the king seems to like my company, but I wonder sometimes if he forgets I am a son of Godwine. He is friendly to Harold and me, so I suppose that in our case, the sins of the father are not passed on to the sons. Or so it seems.

Still, I am a little hurt that when the king originally split Swegn's earldom, it went to Harold and Beorn and I saw nothing. I'm not sure why I was passed over. And to see Harold make such a disturbance over giving it back... how does he think I felt about that? They already had their own titles without Swegn's parcels. I had nothing. And who was helping father patrol the coast? The landless one. I didn't make a big objection; I didn't draw any attention to myself. Did it matter what I thought? Of course not.

And what about now? Now Beorn's earldom was vacant, and Swegn's portion too. Was Harold going to demand that as well?

But in the end, it didn't matter. Nothing happened. Then, in an astonishing turn-about, a few months later Bishop Ealdred went to Flanders and brought a repentant Swegn back to the country. It seems that Ealdred, who was attempting to defend Herefordshire against the unruly Welsh, couldn't manage alone. He found himself unable to withstand the depredations of their Prince, Gruffydd ap Llewelyn. He needed Swegn, who had allied with Gruffydd before his first exile and seemed able to reason with him.

In mid-Lent of the year 1050, Edward held his usual Witenagemot. All the great Earls were expected to come. We were graced with the presence of Leofric of Mercia and his reckless son Aelfgar. We also saw Siward of Northumbria and Earl Ralf the useless, nephew of King Edward. Harold was coming, a little delayed due to the birth of his second son. Father was already in residence at Southwark when Bishop Ealdred arrived with Swegn. So was I.

The Bishop came in first, followed by my brother. Then again, it wasn't the brother I knew. Before, Swegn could always be spotted—even from behind—by his swagger. He had always acted like he was the best, the smartest, the cleverest. But the person I was staring at now looked like he had the air knocked out of him one too many times. There was no swagger; in fact, if anything, his shoulders were a little stooped. He looked at father from under a bent brow, not straight-on as was his wont.

Ealdred stepped aside and Swegn threw himself to his knees before father. "Please forgive me," he practically sobbed. "I have done much wrong and am prepared to make amends."

I could see father struggling with himself. Even if Swegn hadn't killed Beorn—unforgivable under any circumstances—his rash behavior destroyed any progress father had made with the king. For all of us. He tried to make Swegn rise up from the floor but my brother stubbornly refused to move. It was embarrassing.

"You see, Earl Godwine," the Bishop said, placing a hand on Swegn's shoulder. "He is most repentant. I am inclined to believe he is finally ready to retake his place at the head of his earldom."

I wasn't so sure. I was more inclined to believe Swegn was putting on a very good performance. He wasn't fooling me, anyway.

But I didn't have a weakness for him like father did; I watched as his face softened. This time, Swegn responded to another attempt to raise him up; he threw his arms around father's neck and sobbed onto his shoulder. It was very convincing and as expected, father relented before this show of emotions.

"My son," he said, putting Swegn at arm's length. "You have come back to me."

Swegn wiped his runny nose. "Never again will I transgress. I will build a magnificent church for Beorn..." He stopped, puzzled.

"Beorn lies in Winchester Minster," father said gently. "Harold brought him there."

A pained expression crossed Swegn's face. "Harold."

"He loved Beorn like a brother," I interjected. Both of them ignored me.

"It happened after the *gemot*," father continued "Where you were declared *nithing*."

94

"I know." Swegn bowed his head again. "I hope King Edward will forgive me and lift my outlawry. With Bishop Ealdred's help." He looked trustingly at the prelate.

This was too much for me. I got up and left the room, though no one seemed to notice.

King Edward's Witenagemot was well attended, and father had done much work ahead of time concerning the king's Cinque Ports and the new provisions. Since the key towns were all in Wessex, this meant my father would naturally be warden of the ports. It was a great honor and we all hoped it would draw attention away from the Swegn business.

As we were waiting for the king, Harold showed up accompanied by an impressive retinue of housecarls. I almost envied him; he looked so confident and strong. He kept stopping to speak to so many people that we had to wait for him like the other supplicants. Finally he spotted us and his whole attitude changed; he and father had not spoken in all of these months.

Harold looked from father to Swegn and back again. I'm sure he wished himself somewhere else, but I never saw him run away from an unpleasant situation. Looking resigned, he came straight for father.

For once, our father spoke first. "How is the babe?"

"Healthy and noisy," he laughed briefly. "And the mother is well." His voice trailed off.

Silence. Harold and Swegn looked at each other.

"Brother," Swegn started. He still had the bearing of a penitent. "I have much to answer for. In this life and the next."

Like myself, Harold looked confused by Swegn's new behavior. I could see he didn't know what to say, for once. He took a deep breath.

"I was overcome with anguish when I went to the king..." Harold started.

"Say no more, Harold. What you did was well and good. I deserved every single chastisement. I was *nithing*. I hated myself. But now, I hope to come back to the world a new man."

Harold blinked. He found it as hard to believe as I did.

Swegn turned to father. "If I can forgive him, so can you."

Now he was a peacemaker! But father was relieved and he wordlessly took Harold into a hug. I was impressed; I never saw that before.

Edward saw it too. He was right behind us and had witnessed the whole scene. Bishop Ealdred was with him.

"My Godwine family all together," the king said, a little sardonically. "Well, Bishop, I see why you have brought him back. Our Swegn has well and truly repented. Herefordshire needs their earl, and I need peace on my western border."

He signaled for everyone to follow. "Come. We have much to discuss with our Witan."

Bishop Ealdred had his way. Swegn's outlawry was reversed and he was given his earldom back.

So much for a vacancy to fill. I would just have to be patient.

Although I had two natural children, listening to Harold talk about his family reminded me I should start thinking about my own future. I wasn't exactly landless—father had taken care of that—and I still hoped to come into an earldom. It was time I found a wife.

On one of King Edward's endless embassies to the continent, I took a side trip to visit Count Baldwin V and attended the marriage of his son to the widow of Hainault. It was all very rowdy, and I almost left early except that I noticed Baldwin's half-sister sitting quietly by the side of some bishop or other. She looked up and our eyes met...I swear, it was only for a moment but I knew she was the one.

Nobody would accuse me of being shy. I went up to the bishop, pretending we were well acquainted, and asked for an introduction to the lady at his side. I knew who she was though I had never seen her up close.

"This is Judith, sister of Count Baldwin," he said with his mouth half-full.

"May I sit?" I asked, and she made room for me on the bench. I sat with my back to the table.

"Lady Judith. How surprising that I haven't bet you before."

"Indeed. If I am not mistaken, you are Tostig Godwineson."

I was strangely flattered she knew my name.

"I know your brother, of course."

I made a face, despite myself. "You must mean Swegn."

"No, actually, I meant Harold. He passed through recently on his way to Rome. He spoke highly of you."

That was a surprise. Was she flattering me again?

"Swegn kept to himself," she continued. "We rarely spoke. He is a sad man." She reached for a fig and offered me one. She moved slowly and deliberately, and had a certain charm about her I couldn't describe. Why did I enjoy watching her hands? Judith is not the most beautiful woman I ever saw, but beauty is not what you think about when you are near her; you think about that half-smile and the crinkle around her eyes.

"Harold said you have more brothers at home," she went on, filling the sudden silence. "You must have quite a large family."

"There are eleven of us. Poor mother has been kept very busy."

She laughed, a tinkling sound. "I hope to meet her, some day."

I was beginning to hope so, too.

"You would love her. She reminds me of you." There. I could flatter, too. She gave me one of her half smiles.

We had a long conversation that evening, though I don't remember much of what we talked about. The Bishop gave his seat and I made myself comfortable at the table, though I refrained from drinking. It was all very pleasant and I quite enjoyed myself. I even relaxed, something I rarely do.

The next day I made a few discreet inquiries about her and was disappointed to discover she had no great fortune. On the other hand, her brother's court was one of the most interesting places I ever visited. He welcomed guests of all persuasions, and didn't bother to question whether they were an outlaw, passing through, or even planning an invasion. He particularly seemed to like sheltering exiles as Swegn knew all too well. He could be one useful kinsman. And I liked him.

I'm not one to waste my time. I liked the idea of choosing my own wife. Harold did it, and I could see how happy he was. As for Judith... well, I had advantages. Others have said I am a handsome man. I am almost as tall as Harold. My shoulders fill my tunic. My long blond hair is thick and glossy; my eyes are a deep sapphire blue. I sit a horse well. I speak three languages and know my classical history. Like her I am deeply religious. I was not a bad choice, and as far as I knew, no one else had put in a bid for her hand.

I sought Judith out, finding her in the chapel. It took some patience but I waited for her to finish her prayers, noticing with some satisfaction that the peristyle was sheltered and few people passed by. We could talk in private. I leaned against a pillar and watched, until she crossed herself and stood up gracefully. Turning, she paused, looking thoughtfully at me, and came forward without hesitation. I liked that.

"Would you walk with me?" I said in my most persuasive voice. I put her hand on my arm and we took a turn around the inner courtyard. At first I didn't know what to say, but she seemed happy to compare the flowers and talk about the wedding we had just attended. When she fell silent, I pulled her over to a bench and took both her hands.

"Judith," I began, feeling somewhat foolish. I knew this was rather sudden. But I had made up my mind and saw no reason to stray from my purpose. "I have something to ask you. I can offer you very little at the moment, but as you know, my father is a great earl and it is only a matter of time before I have my own earldom." Did I believe this? I'm not sure, myself. "I need a helpmeet and I would have you by my side."

She glanced down modestly then favored me with a smile. "What would your father say to such a match?"

A wise question, indeed. Harold had married a wealthy woman but she was not noble; Judith was noble but not wealthy. Would father be disappointed? Still, I had a feeling my father would enjoy tweaking King Edward's nose; Baldwin had been a thorn in the king's side for many years. Of course, I couldn't tell her that.

"He has no plans for me that I know of," I said truthfully.

"Then may I suggest you discover his feelings. If he has no objections and my brother has no objections, I would certainly have none."

Not the most passionate response, but satisfactory. I wrote my father that very night.

While we waited for an answer, Judith and I got to know each other better. We took mass together. We took little trips to local shrines with a suitable escort. Her brother encouraged us to sit together when feasting, so I suspected he was glad to find a spouse for her.

Father's response came in a fortnight. "You have my blessing," he wrote. "Though I feel you should wed Judith in Flanders so as not to antagonize the king. At the moment, he is not friendly to me and heeds his Norman advisors in everything. Come at your soonest with your bride, and we will have our own celebration at Bosham, surrounded by our closest friends."

He wrote another letter to Count Baldwin, more formal, negotiating terms for our wedding. Judith's dowry was respectable, and her brother granted her some estates in Flanders. The wedding was beautiful but sparsely attended, but neither Judith nor I minded. In fact, I was anxious to get back to England. As soon as it was acceptable, we boarded a ship to Bosham.

Our family greeted us at the dock as we tied up. There was father, looking worried, next to mother, beautiful as ever. Harold was openly curious about my wife, his arm placed possessively around his own fair Edith. As soon as I could, I leaped from the ship and helped my blushing bride to the shore.

"This is Judith, father. My sweeting...meet my father, and my brothers Harold, Leofwine, Gyrth, and little Wulfnoth. Where is Swegn?"

"On his way back from his earldom. He promised to come tonight. And how is Count Baldwin?"

"My brother sends his greetings," Judith said, "and his invitation to visit to Flanders, as soon as you can arrange it."

"I hope it will be soon," father laughed. "I would very much like to get away."

It wasn't until later I realized how prophetic his statement turned out to be.

Judith and I were at the head table next to our parents. Since I am the third son, this is the first time I ever sat in such a high position. But after all, this was my bride-ale and I intended to enjoy it. Judith was at her most charming and even Swegn, who came in late, was on his best behavior in front of her. Many cheers were given to us, and I was in the middle of taking a large swig of mead when a royal envoy demanded entrance into the hall.

Everything stopped as we watched the messenger, full of importance, stride up to head table. I stood up but he ignored me, turning to our father.

100

"King Edward of England summons Earl Godwine to appear before him at his palace of Gloucester, immediately."

It was father's turn to stand up. "What is the purpose of this summons?"

"There has been a disturbance at Dover."

"What sort of disturbance?"

The man looked hungrily at the laden tables. I wanted to hit him. "Count Eustace of Boulogne has been attacked by the townsmen, and driven thence."

No. I couldn't believe it. I turned to Judith as a slow murmuring in the room increased in volume. She was biting her lip, trying not to cry. I bent over and whispered into her ear.

"I will make this up to you." I tried to sound reassuring, but father had already started away and I was terribly distracted.

"Eat," he said, gesturing at the tables as he left the room. Most of our guests did so quietly, but my brothers and I wanted to help.

Harold got up and approached Judith, taking both her hands in his. "I am so sorry," he said quietly, sounding more sincere than I ever could. He beckoned Edith over. "My lady will keep you company while we sort things out." Edith went over to my seat and Harold put an arm around my shoulders, accompanying me out as we followed father. It was a rare gesture from him and I was surprised at how grateful I felt.

We all gathered around our father, talking at once. He was already slipping into a cloak as the servants were scurrying around packing some bags for him. Father's housecarls were in and out the door. When I reached for my own cloak he put his hands up in the air to stop me.

"I do not want to disturb the festivities. Go back; enjoy yourselves. I will deal with this matter, and return right away."

"Father," I insisted, "we are already disturbed. Let us go with you."

"No." His voice was decisive. "He has summoned only myself. I do not want to make things seem more important than they are."

"At least let me come." Swegn stepped forward. I don't know why he thought he could help.

"No, son. Your presence might make things worse." Father spoke true, but I almost felt sorry for Swegn; he looked so stricken. But father would not be persuaded.

"Do not worry. How bad can this be?"

Well, we were to find out soon enough.

Everyone knows about father's outlawry. There were those who thought Eustace of Boulogne planned the debacle at Dover ahead of time with King Edward, expressly to bring my father down. There were others who said my marriage to Judith antagonized Eustace, who saw our rapprochement with Flanders as a threat to Boulogne. If that's the case, it was almost worth all the trouble. Cursed Frenchman.

GYRTH REMEMBERS

Although father wanted us to continue without him, the spirit had gone out of Tostig's wedding celebrations and everyone settled down to a rather sullen wait. Even Tostig was subdued. And in good time our uneasiness was confirmed.

Two days afterwards, six men from Dover came into Bosham, having ridden so hard they looked like they were ready to fall from their saddles. They were bitterly disappointed my father was not present but soon accepted food and drink and managed to put a good face on it. My family eagerly gathered around the newcomers and clamored for information. The good men of Dover were so upset they couldn't hold back, and the whole story came out.

The King's brother-in-law, Eustace of Boulogne, stopped in Dover on his way back to the Continent after a visit to Edward. We don't know why, but he tried to force the townspeople to quarter his men for the night. If he had behaved like a guest, all would have been well. But instead, they acted like conquerors and knocked down doors, pushed people out of the way, grabbed food off the tables. Of course the townspeople defended their homes, and the situation soon turned violent. Twenty of our men from Dover were killed, but they took nineteen of the enemy with them.

At first we were all shocked into silence, then Harold and Tostig started pacing around the table, shouting their objections to the room. Swegn was surprisingly restrained but I could see he was in agreement. By the time my father returned they were in a righteous uproar. As soon as he walked into the house they surrounded him, demanding vengeance.

But father, as usual, took control and made the Dover men repeat their story. He listened carefully then told us that the king had demanded military chastisement. My brothers started up again but he silenced them with a single sentence.

"I defied him," he said sadly.

I remember the complete silence in the room. For once, my brothers were speechless. Only mother dared voice what we were just beginning to comprehend.

"Godwine...that makes you a traitor," she whispered.

He knew that already. I imagine he was thinking of it all the way home.

"If it makes me a traitor, so be it. I must do what is right."

As young as I was, I knew things would never be the same again. Even Harold was looking at the floor, not knowing what to do.

To my surprise, Swegn was the one who stepped forward "I am with you, father," he said, breaking the silence. For the first time in my life I was proud of him.

"So am I," said Harold, a little shamefacedly. Of course, the others followed and I believe my father was relieved. I wondered...did he think we wouldn't support him?

The next series of events is a little confusing, but I will put it in as much order as I can. As soon as my father decided on a course of action, he wasted no time. He sent Harold and Swegn off to raise a levy. The King was at Gloucester, and according to my father the Three Earls (himself as Earl of Wessex, Harold as Earl of East Anglia, and Swegn as Earl of Herefordshire) would be able to represent the southern half of the country at a military Gemot.

"We will be ready for either debate or for battle," he said to my brothers. Tostig went with them but Leofwine and I stayed in Bosham with our mother and sisters. As it turned out, King Edward had already summoned his northern earls, but my father got there first.

We knew about the early events as they were happening because less than a fortnight after father left, his captain Eirik returned with an urgent message.

Eirik was Danish so mother was comfortable with him. He had known father since Canute's days. But she was surprised when he knelt before her.

"Come, old friend," she laughed. "This is not necessary."

When he refused to get up her face fell. Something was not right.

"My lady," he started slowly. "I come from the Earl."

This was no mere message. She took a deep breath. "Is he hurt?"

"No, no." Eirik got up despite himself. "Everyone is fine. But your husband sends a message. The king is demanding an exchange of hostages. Specifically, he insists you send Wulfnoth and Hakon at the soonest."

My little brother and cousin were standing nearby; Wulfnoth clapped his hands in excitement.

"Did you hear, Hakon? We are going join father." For an eleven year-old, this was an adventure. I admit I was a little envious, but I didn't realize what being a hostage could mean. My mother burst into tears, and she took my squirming brother into her arms. But there was nothing to be done and she got the boys ready.

Wulfnoth and Hakon were squealing excitedly while mother pulled fresh tunics over their heads and brushed their hair. She put together two sacks full of clothing, and I helped cinch a belt around Wulfnoth's waist while he put his arms up, pretending to be important like our father putting his hauberk on. Eirik waited patiently for them to finish, and gently took the clothes out of mother's arms. Two horses stood ready for the boys, and Eirik picked each of them up and placed them in the saddles, handing them the reins. As they rode off, they were so excited they forgot to wave good-bye.

Alas, this is the last time I ever saw my little brother.

HAROLD REMEMBERS

That terrible day when we all realized we were on the wrong side of the king's law, I think I saw my father age before my eyes. Never had we been in this position before. Father had always enforced the king's will, even in the bad old days of Harthacnut. How could things have gone so wrong, so quickly?

After father broke the news to us, all that night messengers rode in with promises of support from Wessex thegns. King Edward had overstepped his authority; the Normans had to be punished; Eustace was a traitor, and other wild accusations. By morning, father had made up his mind.

"We will take a stand," he told us. "We cannot permit him to treat us like a conquered race. He is on the throne by our invitation, and he rules with our consent. We will be ready for either debate or for battle."

My brothers and I looked at each other. It felt like the ground was shifting beneath our feet.

"Swegn," father sighed, putting his hands my brother's shoulders. "At the risk of offending the king, I need you to raise a levy from your earldom."

I waited. Father stared a long time at Swegn as though willing him to be the son he needed. We all knew that Swegn was shakily settled into his earldom, and father was asking a lot from him. My brother looked at the floor; I think he felt shame that we doubted his resolution. Swegn was no coward, but neither was he steadfast.

I coughed, breaking the spell. "I will do the same, from East Anglia."

Father let out a breath, looking relieved. "I wish I could keep you out of this, Harold. But yes, a show of strength would help our cause. Tostig, I would have you by my side as well."

Tostig had no men to summon. But he was strong and I think father needed someone at his back.

The four of us were alone in the room. Father put his hands on his hips, looking from one to the other of us.

"I have raised fine sons, and I am proud of you," he said. This was rare praise and we cherished it. But at the same time he looked so exhausted, I wished there was something I could say to make it better. It felt to me like our cause was lost, but I would follow him regardless of the consequences.

We had no time to waste. Gathering our belongings, we summoned our men and saddled the horses. Swegn rode to the west and I, northeast to Nazeing. Father was to await his levy at Swegn's manor of Beverstone, south of Gloucester.

I passed through London on the way to my earldom. Some of father's thegns were residing at his Southwark palace, and I was able to send them with messages to the far reaches of Wessex. My own household troops changed horses and spread the word throughout the closest parts of East Anglia; I sent Torr ahead to Eadric of Laxfield so he could send messengers of his own to the northern part of my earldom. All were to meet me at Cambridge.

I didn't really think things were going to end badly. After all, father was the most persuasive man on Edward's council. He had always managed to talk people into agreement. Why should this time be any different?

No, I was deceiving myself. I knew the difference. For the first time we would have an army at our back. Edward would not take kindly to our actions.

I hoped father knew what he was doing.

Swegn had already joined father's growing army when I approached Beverstone. I knew they were using Swegn's castle as their gathering place, and the soldiers were camped all around the hill. Father was making the rounds in person, and I could see the relief on his face when he spotted me.

"King Edward is unsupported," he said, holding my reins while I dismounted. He turned and looked down the road that led to Gloucester. "His Witan had been called for seven days hence, so the other earls have not yet arrived."

"Then we should present our complaints while we have the advantage."

"My thoughts exactly. Painswick is halfway to Gloucester, and I think we should bring a sizeable force and meet Edward's representatives there. That way he doesn't feel personally threatened. I shall send a messenger to set up our meeting on the morrow. Ah, there you are, Swegn."

My brother was right behind me and I turned to greet him. Once again, I was struck by how subdued he had become.

"I'm glad you are here, Harold," he said. "I was just telling father about the disreputable castle built by that Frenchman Richard Fitz Scrob in my own lands of Herefordshire."

I looked questioningly at father.

"It happened while Swegn was away. Edward granted him some land and he immediately built a castle. He is known to Earl Ralph, so no objection was made."

"Except by my ceorls and villeins. Richard has been using his castle to terrorize the countryside," Swegn said bitterly. "Such deeds are done inside its impregnable walls that I shudder to think on it."

This was the first I had heard of such activities. "Surely King Edward knows nothing of this," I protested. Swegn and father seemed to think otherwise.

"If this is true, he's just as bad as Eustace and his odious countrymen," I added bitterly, filling the silence. Father nodded.

"Swegn," he said. "We will go tomorrow and present our demands. Be ready. Let us split our forces between here and Painswick. Tostig shall command the soldiers we leave here. Let us start at first light."

Obediently, Swegn nodded and moved off, collecting his followers. Father turned to me.

"I had the strangest dream last night," he said as we walked toward the castle. "A flock of ravens settled around my bedstead, and one in particular landed on my chest while I was lying there, unable to move. He looked at me in the most peculiar fashion, as though he would report my movements to Odin. He squawked and flew out the window, bidding the rest to follow."

I shrugged. I didn't believe much in the old religion.

"Nothing happened, but all day I have felt an impending sense of doom," he added.

"Well, we will have to fix that, won't we? A good meal might help."

I had never heard father talk like that before, and I was more unnerved than I would like to admit. Luckily, the following day his dark mood was gone, and we took the road to Gloucester chanting old fighting songs. Within a few hours we reached Painswick, and father climbed the hill where the abbey stood, to get a better look. He was satisfied to see a small group of men approaching our meeting point.

"Have the men set up camp," he told Swegn and me. "Let us meet Edward's messengers."

As it turned out, they were not mere messengers. As they came close enough to recognize their banners, father gave a groan.

"Oh no. Not Jumièges."

It was not unexpected, but we were hoping our old adversary, Archbishop Robert of Jumièges was far from Gloucester. But it was not meant to be. Our relationship with him had turned particularly disagreeable when King Edward overruled father's choice for the vacant seat of Canterbury. It didn't matter that the monks opposed Robert; the king forced the issue and Robert was made Archbishop. To make matters worse, Jumièges proceeded to accuse father of stealing Canterbury lands. They were still disputing the revenues when the Dover incident happened.

"This is not going to end well," father said. I did not doubt him.

As they approached, Edward's spokesmen stayed together in a little group. They did not dismount. Archbishop Robert nudged a little ahead of the rest.

"What is the meaning of this show of arms?" The disdain was unmistakable.

"I have come to request an audience with the king," father said, reasonably, "with my sons, representing three earldoms. We are ready and eager to take counsel with King Edward touching his honor and that of his people."

Archbishop Robert conferred with the others.

"I will present your request to the king," he said shortly before turning his mount around. They rode off as though pricked by a thorn bush.

We sat on our horses, watching them.

"We might as well be prepared for the worst," father said. "We will stay here and wait for their answer."

Father's old captain Eirik came up beside us. "I may need you to be my spokesman," father said to him. "I suspect King Edward will not see us in person."

I can't fathom how father knew this, but he was right. They were still setting up our big pavilion when Edward's answer came. At least he sent Earl Ralf this time rather than Archbishop Robert. He was a more welcome messenger even though he brought bad news.

Ralf and his entourage rode all the way up to our camp, dismounting. Father offered him a waterskin.

"Thank you, Earl Godwine," he said, taking a drink. "This is thirsty work, for certes." He wiped his mouth. "I suppose you know your request has been denied."

"That's a nice way of putting it," father said. "What did Edward really say?"

Ralf hesitated. "Unfortunately, Robert of Jumièges did most of the talking. By the time he was finished, the king was convinced your only object was to betray him."

Father crossed his arms, turning aside with a snort. He walked away a few steps before making up his mind what to say.

"All right. Tell the king this: I speak in the name of myself and my sons, and the men of our three earldoms. Eustace of Boulogne and the Frenchman Richard Fitz Scrob are both guilty

110

of outrageous crimes in my jurisdiction. And Swegn's. It is the king's duty to protect his countrymen, not shelter the guilty from punishment. We are the lawful Judges of our two districts, sworn to the duty the king refuses. If you, the king, prove yourself an unrighteous ruler, then it is up to your Earls to bring you to reason. Tell that to King Edward for me, and my thanks for your intercession."

Father turned and strode away, leaving Earl Ralf open-mouthed in surprise. I let out a heavy sigh. Father had just committed us to war.

Ralph looked to me for guidance. I looked at Swegn, who shrugged his shoulders. Then I looked at Eirik.

"Will you attend Earl Ralf?" I asked him. "We need a witness and we require a response. I trust you will give Eirik your safe conduct." This last was directed at Ralf, who nodded his agreement. Eirik and six men accompanied the king's party back to Gloucester.

The afternoon was drawing on, but there was still time for Eirik to do his errand and return. Meanwhile, father was pacing back and forth before the pavilion.

"I suppose you disagree with what I did?" He asked Swegn and me as we approached.

Swegn spoke first. "Whatever you decide is acceptable to me."

I was still not used to my brother's compliance. I swung my head, staring at him.

"And you, Harold?" Father's voice was cutting.

"Father, what I think no longer matters. I am with you."

He frowned, but decided not to pursue an argument. Whether or not he had intended to push Edward into a confrontation, there was no going back now.

But we were staggered by Edward's response. Eirik came back before dark, as expected. His face was glum.

"The King sat still while Archbishop Robert refused your demands," he said. "But he seemed uncertain. In the end, he silenced Robert and declared himself willing to negotiate with you, provided you and Swegn each hand over a son as hostage."

Father sat hard on a bench and put his face in his hands.

"As I was leaving," Eirik continued, "I saw a cloud of dust from the north. It was rumored in the hall that Earls Siward and Leofric were expected any minute. I doubt not that one of them was approaching."

We all knew what that meant. With added support from the other great earls, Edward's position just got stronger while ours became weaker.

"Do you want me to go to Bosham?" Eirik said gently.

Father sat up though his shoulders were still bent. "Get some rest, Eirik," he answered. "Let me think on it."

Swegn and I watched as Eirik led his horse away. My brother sat on his heels before father, a hand on his shoulder. "Edward is not one to harm our boys," he said.

"I know, I know. It's not Edward I fear."

"God forbid. You can't think the Archbishop would contemplate some evil deed!" He crossed himself.

Father seemed to recover at that. "No, Swegn. He won't harm them. But he could cause us some mischief."

I silently agreed. But it was not my sons who were demanded as hostages so I kept my mouth shut.

"I suppose we have no choice," father sighed. "We can't back down now."

As the sun was setting, the three of us stood and contemplated the valley below us.

"I grew up near here," father said, pointing. "This is where Canute won his kingdom." The broad Severn wound its way through the plains. Beyond that, range upon range of craggy hills protected our Welsh neighbors, rugged as their mountains.

I listened to the banging of pots as our men prepared their dinner, and the soft laughter as they settled around their campfires for the evening. It was all very comforting under the pink and sapphire skies.

"I love this land," father said. "We must keep it safe from the Normans."

All of a sudden I understood. Father's yearning went beyond the family and his own authority. He wanted to preserve a way of life which was receding by the day. Edward and his Norman customs were alien to us and beggared understanding. We were in danger of losing our established laws and our heritage, and this was the only way to stop it.

"Somehow, we'll make Edward understand," I tried to reassure him. Or was I reassuring myself?

WULFNOTH REMEMBERS

It's odd when looking back on our family's outlawry that events encircled me, and yet I was completely outside of them. What I mean is as a hostage, things happened because of me but I never had a chance to participate. In fact, after that exciting and terrible day when they took me away, I never saw my family again, except for Harold when he tried to rescue me from Normandy. And Tostig, after his exile. And my sister the Queen, but only at the beginning.

I was barely twelve when father's captain Eirik came to Bosham during our troubles. He told mother the king required us as hostages for our father's good faith. She started to sob and I did my best to comfort her, although I didn't have any idea what was to come. All I knew was that Hakon and I were going on an adventure. It seemed so exciting.

We each got to ride our own horse, up front with Eirik who kept looking at us to make sure we weren't crying. I was beginning to wonder whether I was supposed to cry, but Hakon kept pulling at my sleeve and pointing at every little thing on the road. Sometimes he was so annoying, but this day I was glad to have him along.

Our father was camped near Gloucester. Swegn and Harold had brought levies they raised from their earldoms. By the time we got there, I was so tired I nearly fell out of the saddle. My father gently pulled me from the horse and held me close; I was too exhausted to care. *Oh, why had I not paid more attention!* He carried me into his pavilion and laid me on his own pallet. Eirik brought Hakon and we fell asleep immediately.

The next morning, we were awakened early. Still rubbing my eyes, I came out of the pavilion and sat down to a quick breakfast. Father pulled up a box, perching on the edge.

"Son," he said. "Listen closely. There is something you must do for us, and it requires that you be very brave."

I was reaching for a piece of cheese, but something in his voice made me stop. I heard a pair of ravens nearby, croaking at each other. He turned and looked at the birds as if unwilling to go on.

"Strange, isn't it?" He murmured to himself. "Are they trying to tell us something?" He grasped the cheese and handed it to me. "Here. Fill your stomach. Do you see those men over there with Eirik?" I squinted into the sun, nodding.

"Those men are waiting to take you to the king. You and Hakon are going as my representatives. The king will keep you until we are finished negotiating. It's only for a short time," father continued hurriedly.

I smiled. "Don't worry, father. I will know what to do."

I think he choked for a second, but I couldn't be sure. "You are so grown up," he said, putting a hand on my head. "I'm sure you will do just fine."

He went over to those men, giving us time to finish our breakfast. My brother Swegn came by and placed a hand on Hakon's shoulder. As usual he had nothing to say and he moved on; I think he was ashamed and didn't know what to do about it.

I put some bread into a bag and tried to stand tall. Hakon looked longingly after his father.

"Do we have to go?" he asked so quietly nobody else heard.

"Of course," I assured him, sounding braver than I felt. "Would you want me to go alone?"

He shook his head. "No. I'm sorry."

Our horses were ready for us and father helped us up, patting our legs and stepping back. "Good bye, son," he said. "Remember what I said."

I looked around as we rode away. Father was standing with his hands on his hips, gazing at us with such a strange look on his face I remembered it to this day. Of course, had I known I would never see him again I'm sure I would have tried to run away.

Eirik accompanied us as far as the gates to Gloucester, then gave us a formal farewell. He and his men rode away and left us with the king's armored housecarls, looking fierce and stern behind the nose guard on their helmets. They split up, two in front of us and two behind us as we rode into the city. Hakon and I moved our mounts closer together.

In the king's courtyard, our guards wasted no time pulling us off the horses and ushering us up the steps to the audience chamber. I had never seen King Edward before; when he married my sister I was only five years old and I stayed at home. Hakon and I were holding hands as we were introduced to the king. The housecarls bowed and went out the door.

Edward turned and looked us up and down. The king seemed very tall from our angle, and his hair was so blond as to be almost white. His long beard matched, and it was fine and straight, just like his fingers. Suddenly he sighed, as if he was disappointed.

"Well, boys. I suppose you know why you are here."

Hakon and I were too afraid to answer.

He sighed again. "Which one of you is Wulfnoth?"

I raised my hand. His expression did not change.

"All right, Wulfnoth. Your father and I are having a disagreement. You are going to stay at court for a while, until your father comes to understand my position. I'm hoping that won't take very long."

I didn't like the way his mouth pursed after he said that, but I bowed anyway.

The King gestured to a man in episcopal robes standing behind the throne. "Archbishop Robert, take these boys under your protection."

I didn't know it at the time, but we had just been placed into the unenviable protection of our father's sworn enemy. I could see by the man's face he found King Edward's command distasteful, but he bowed to the king and put out a hand, expecting me to take it as he passed. Edward had already turned aside as if we weren't there.

What choice did we have? We obediently followed the Archbishop and sighed with relief when he turned us over to his steward. "Take these boys and feed them and find them a place to bed down. Have someone fetch their bags from the horses. Make sure they are well guarded."

I wasn't hungry but it didn't seem like a good time to argue. His steward did not speak to us but led us deep into the palace, where the servants lived. We were placed in a *dormitorium* and left to ourselves, though I noticed a man standing guard at the doorway. Hakon and I sat on our pallets, staring at each other. Neither one of us knew what to say.

In due time, someone brought us to the kitchen, where they sat us at a table in the corner and put bowls of porridge in

116

front of us. One of the scullions took pity on us and brought us some bread. "Poor boys," she said. "I'll see to it that you get some extra food. I have a son myself, and he would be happy for someone to play with."

At first I was offended that she would offer me a menial for a playmate. But I realized my status as the son of an earl didn't have much meaning here. I swallowed a spoonful of gruel. "Thank you, good missus," I forced out. "That would be very kind."

Satisfied, the woman went back to her duties. Hakon gave me a nudge. "Did you mean that?" he asked suspiciously. He always had a wary way about him.

"Until we know what they are going to do with us, we need all the friends we can get."

"Hmm." He pushed his bowl away. "I don't like it and I don't like it."

I shook my head. He wasn't going to be very helpful.

We sat for a long time at the table...so long we feared we had been forgotten. We were afraid to get up and really wouldn't have known where to go anyway. By the time our new acquaintance showed up, we were glad to see anybody.

We heard him coming before we saw him. Singing some kind of rhyme, a lanky boy with shocking red hair and freckles strode past us, swinging his shoulders and throwing an apple up in the air. He turned and tossed it to me.

"Good catch," he said approvingly. "Call me Lang."

"Wulfnoth," I said, biting into the apple. "And this is Hakon."

"Wulfnoth and Hakon. They told me to take you with me; I'm on my way to clean the stables."

And so it started. Whether we liked it or not, we were to get our first lesson at being a hostage.

It wasn't too bad at the beginning, although we were not very good at our work. Lang was a few years older than us but he didn't seem to mind our company. He laughed as we dropped

117

horse manure on our feet, but he didn't care how much we did. "They told me to keep you busy," he said, "so you don't try to run away."

I didn't like the sound of that, but it was better than being locked into a room. Or a *donjon*. I had heard stories but never took them seriously.

I found out that the king's palace was named Kingsholm, and it was large enough to accommodate a *Witenagemot* if he desired. At first, when they finally let us sit in the great hall during the king's feast we thought we would see father. But no, he was not commanded to appear. We listened to the proclamations and learned that King Edward declared they would move their *gemot* to London. He would retain father's hostages until then. That was us.

Now I knew why they had let us attend. On hearing this announcement, I had to rub my eyes to keep the tears from running down my face. I think the king took pleasure in our distress, as I saw him looking directly at me. I tried to be brave, like father said. But truly, I'd never been so frightened in my life.

HAROLD REMEMBERS

After Eirik delivered our poor hostages to the king, father sent orders for Tostig to bring the rest of his army to Painswick. There was no time to waste. Once all our forces were assembled, we marched to within sight of the walls at Gloucester then put our men in battle array. Father and sons, we sat on our horses, banners flying, and waited.

We didn't wait long. The gates were still open and Edward's three earls came forth, followed by an army pretty much the same size as our own. Earls Leofric, Siward and Ralf rode in front, fully armored as expected. As we watched, they ranged themselves opposite our shield wall. It would have been pretty to witness if it wasn't so deadly.

"I imagine Leofric savors my discomfiture," father grumbled, "as does Siward. Well, let them have their satisfaction as long as we can avoid coming to blows."

That was the first time I felt perhaps father didn't want civil war, either. I was relieved.

There were no strangers here; we all knew what was at stake. As our forces stood ready, father invited some of his greater thegns to ride by our side and we moved forward to meet the king's party in the middle. Earl Siward towered over the others, but Leofric was clearly their leader.

We stopped, facing each other.

"I don't know exactly what happened," the earl of Mercia started. "But things seem to have gotten out of control."

I could hear father taking a deep breath. "Blame it on Archbishop Robert," he growled. "He bears enough rancor toward me to sway the king."

Leofric shrugged. "That may be so, but you do have an army behind you. Edward seems unyielding. What can you offer, Earl Godwine, to soften his resistance?"

"Aside from my son?" That slipped out by accident, I thought. Leofric ignored him.

"Earl Leofric, Earl Siward, Earl Ralf," father went on, stalling for time. "We need not be hasty. I called for the miscreants Eustace of Boulogne and Richard Fitz Scrob to be brought to account for their misdeeds. Failing that, at the very least I sought to put my case before the king in person, and defend any false accusations brought against me."

"I'm afraid we've gone way beyond that," Siward broke in. "Earl Godwine, you have taken the traitor's route now, and brought hostile forces against your ruler!" His horse lurched at the harsh tone of his voice, and the army behind them started getting

119

restless. I could hear angry murmurs wash over their faceless helmets.

"Traitor! I am no traitor! I seek justice against the enemies of England!"

"And who is the enemy now?" Siward shot back. Now our own men were starting to grumble.

"Hold, hold," Leofric warned, stretching out an arm. "This is getting us nowhere. Godwine, do you really seek civil war?"

"Of course not," father spat.

"Then we must do what we can to avoid it."

We all fell silent for a moment. Father was breathing hard.

"The way I see it," Leofric continued, seeking to mollify our dispute, "We have valuable men on both sides. If we resort to civil war, many will be killed and only our enemies will benefit."

"It could be our *enemies* who are goading us, just for that purpose." I could hear a slight tremor in father's voice, but he was gaining control.

"Exactly. Why should we fight a battle to suit their schemes?"

Father nodded. The men in our army settled down.

Leofric leaned toward the others and they conferred quietly. Siward nodded and Leofric urged his mount forward a couple of steps.

"If I can persuade King Edward to submit your case to the Witan, would you agree to this?"

Father barely hesitated. "Yes. I will speak before the Witan."

"Then stay. I believe he is as unwilling to fight as you are."

With that, the king's negotiators turned back toward Gloucester. Their army parted, giving them space, but the soldiers stayed where they were. Our forces faced each other; but now, given a respite, they were content to mostly sit on the ground. Many had brought a bite to eat, and they shared a meagre meal between them.

We dismounted, though father would not stand still. Swegn held his reins while he paced. "Traitor," he mumbled to himself. "Me, a traitor. What a terrible word."

I saw Swegn grimace. He had been called that word before.

"Father," he ventured, "you did what you had to."

It was a feeble attempt to console a man backed into a corner. But apparently it was enough. Father stopped and put an arm around Swegn's shoulder.

"I don't see what I could have done differently," he sighed. "I must defend my people."

What else was there to say? Father went back and spoke to some of the soldiers while we waited for Leofric to return. I watched as men gathered around him; from their bearing I could tell they still felt great reverence for my father. Perhaps that's what he needed most.

We could see the dust before we saw the riders return. We remounted and took our former places.

Leofric was in front. "Earl Godwine," he called. His voice was not unhappy. "King Edward has agreed. Let both armies disband for now, and we will reconvene in London on September 21. The king will summon a Witan to address the issues and make a legal and binding decision."

Father nodded his agreement, but he was uneasy. "I have delivered two hostages. Who is the king sending in exchange?"

"There will be no exchange of hostages with a rebel," Earl Ralf said harshly. I was surprised at his attitude; in the past he had always seemed civil to father, if not downright friendly. Did he enjoy seeing us brought down?

"Earl Godwine," Leofric interrupted before father could respond. "Your boys will be well taken care of. I give you my word."

What could we do? The immediate crisis had been averted, which was more than we could have said that morning. Without another word, father turned us around and we left them in

121

possession of the field. We had lost the advantage and we knew it. But we had bought some time, and we needed to go back to Bosham and plan for the worst.

Edith was still there, for it had only been a few weeks since Tostig's unhappy wedding celebration. I didn't want her to bear the brunt of our family's troubles, and I needed to get her home before facing Edward and the Witan.

TOSTIG REMEMBERS

I wasn't really a part of father's thwarted rebellion, but of course I was there. Our visit to my grandfather was long forgotten, but father took the trouble to thank me for commanding his reserve forces. Alas, things did not go well. King Edward coerced father into giving up my little brother and my nephew as hostages, but none of us thought it would last past the meeting with the Witan. It didn't matter; by then there was no going back.

I think father was relieved at the delay. Just in case, he started to prepare for the worst and set about loading his treasures onto a ship. One thing he didn't anticipate: King Edward was taking advantage of the respite, too. Our men were also the king's men, and they answered to the king first. Edward commanded father's thegns to attend his royal summons. We knew we were in trouble when the first deserter presented himself at our door. They came in a small group and ignored father's offer of drink.

"Earl Godwine," their spokesman said. "The king commands us to join his force in London. We dare not disobey." He couldn't look father in the eye. Nor could any of the others.

Father was thunderstruck. Edward had given himself enough time to steal away our supporters. But, recovering himself, he stepped forward and put a hand on the man's shoulders.

"You have done an honorable thing in coming to me first. Go. You must obey the king's every decree."

We watched them scurry off; they couldn't get away fast enough.

"You should have gutted the bastard," I muttered.

Father took a deep breath. "Nay. That would have only added more brushwood to the fire. But this does not bode well for our cause. We need to get to London at the soonest."

Those men were the brave ones. Most of the rest just slunk away, shrinking our force by two-thirds.

Father, Swegn, and myself rode north and stayed in our palace at Southwark so we could wait for the summons to the king's Witan. Harold followed later after he settled his family in Nazeing.

Then we waited. We sent out messengers. We paced the floors. Finally, Earl Siward came, alone. I think he was sent by the king. Father invited him inside and closeted himself with the Dane. For some reason, he wanted no witnesses.

Their discussion didn't last long, and when Siward left, father's face was so downcast we dared not approach him. Finally he turned to us.

"Earl Siward will do what he can," he said. "I asked for a safe-conduct, for I no longer trust to our safety. It seems our enemies are declaring against us—the very men we accused of crimes against the state." He started pacing again. "We can only wait for our turn to plead our case."

Alas, the summons never came. They held the assembly without us.

This was a terrible blow to father, especially the next day as we observed Bishop Stigand's approach. We all stood at the door and watched him shuffle forward as though he had a great weight on his shoulders. Father stepped aside as Stigand came through

123

the door. He leaned on his staff and looked from my father to my oldest brother.

"Swegn," he said so quietly I had to lean forward. "I have some bad news for you."

No one expected to hear this; Swegn had been quiet for months.

"The king has declared Swegn an outlaw once again."

The room was so silent you could hear the wind blowing outside. Then everyone burst into argument.

"I do not deserve this," Swegn objected, turning his back on the Bishop.

"The king is out of his mind," I declared.

"Your Grace," started my father, trying to hold his temper. "Surely there has been some mistake."

The good Bishop shook his head. "I am sorry to say the king has been swayed by Archbishop Robert. He insists Swegn's recent participation in your uprising has caused him to forfeit his earldom..."

"That son of a whore," Swegn spat, slamming his fist on a table. "I will have his bollocks!"

Ah, the old Swegn was still there, after all. I was almost glad to see it.

"Silence," father growled before turning back to Stigand. "What about our case?"

"My Lord, it grows worse..."

At that point, the servants were setting the table for a meal and father urged the Bishop to join us. Shaking his head, he agreed but ate very little. Swegn squirmed on his bench, but father played the host and kept a light conversation going until the platters were cleared.

Finally, Stigand turned to father, wiping his mouth. "You have ever been my friend," he said, "and I will continue to support you."

Father smiled sadly at him; I could tell he was disguising his feelings. "Thank you. Your good regard has always been important to me."

Stigand took his hand. "Edward has assigned me a most unhappy task. He bids you present yourself to answer the charges brought against you by Eustace of Boulogne..."

Father waved his arm in dismissal.

"And for the death of Alfred."

"What!" Father frowned; I believe he was expecting difficulties but hoped it would not go so far. He took a deep breath. "Unjust though this is," he murmured, "I could always bring my oath-helpers to swear my innocence once again." It had happened ten years ago, in the days of Harthacnut. Father had been forced to submit to trial by compurgation; it might have been humiliating except that father's support was overwhelming and he was acquitted.

Stigand cleared his throat. "He has also denied your safe-conduct."

Father stared at the Bishop as though he did not understand. "That is a surprise. How does he expect me to appear without a safe-conduct?"

"It is a royal command." Stigand spoke with no conviction.

"It sounds like a Norman command."

"Nevertheless, it comes from the king's lips." I saw Stigand wipe a tear from his cheek.

Father pushed himself back from the table so quickly his chair fell to the ground.

"Saddle our horses. We leave for Bosham now."

I remember little of that frantic ride back to Bosham except for the arguing. Harold wanted to recall whatever forces left to us and march against the king. He was still untested, and I must say, I thought him a bit impatient. I argued on the side of caution.

125

But there was one thing we both understood: we had to stay together as a family. Harold had much more to lose than I did; his whole earldom was at stake. But to give him his due, I don't think he even once considered breaking off to save his own skin. The old Swegn business had put him at odds with father and he didn't like it; they had only recently reconciled. He told me he had spent a lot of sleepless nights worrying about putting things right. If he abandoned father's cause now, he would never be forgiven.

Fortunately, our ship was mostly prepared. Although King Edward usually gave exiles four days to leave the country, one could never be sure. As it turned out, the king did send someone to arrest us almost immediately, but somehow they managed to arrive after we were gone. I think they dawdled on purpose.

Anyway, our father called a family conference. At first, he stated that we would all take refuge in the court of Count Baldwin. It made sense; all exiles ended up there sooner or later. But Harold immediately objected. He stood up, leaning over the table.

"Are you just going to slink away, then? Like a dog that has been beaten? I cannot abide this!"

"Cannot abide!" Father tried to stare him down, but failed. "Haven't you been listening to me, son? In time, we will get it all back through diplomacy, without shedding any blood."

"And I say the time for diplomacy is at an end. We must drive the Norman invaders from our country, before it's too late. Let me go to Dublin, father, and raise a force there among the Irish Danes. They are mercenaries. They will fight for gold."

We were all shocked. Never had anybody seriously disagreed with father before, except Swegn in one of his tempers. But Harold spoke with such passion that father scratched his head, pondering. I don't know if he agreed with my brother, but he always considered all sides before making a decision. Harold bit his lower lip, clenching and unclenching his hands.

Finally, father let out a deep breath. "All right. On one condition, son. That you wait for my word before you come back.

Stay the winter in Ireland. Gather support there. But do not return prematurely, lest you destroy any progress I might have made."

Harold sat down and I could see he was relieved. I wondered if he would have moved against father's wishes if things had gone the other way.

"I will go with you, Harold," Gyrth said quickly. He really worshipped Harold.

"No," interrupted father. "I need your counsel, Gyrth. Let Leofwine go with Harold, if he so desires."

Father looked at little brother. "I need your level head to keep Harold from acting too hastily."

Of course Leofwine was flattered. I took a sly look at Harold and I swear he was blushing.

Meanwhile Swegn stirred, as if shaking off an internal debate. "Harold, I have a ship ready at Bristol. Take it; it is yours."

This was certainly a day full of surprises. Swegn and Harold had always shared a mutual dislike, and nothing more. "I have no need of it where I am going," he added mysteriously.

"Why do you have a ship?" Harold asked suspiciously.

"To be honest, I never knew when Edward would reverse his sentence. I wanted to be ready to flee if need be."

"Then it is settled," Harold said definitely. "Leofwine and I will sail from Bristol to Ireland. We will leave after a good night's sleep. I think we will be safe until then, don't you, father?"

Father nodded distractedly. "Then the rest of us—I, your mother, Swegn, Tostig and Judith, and Gyrth—will go to Flanders. We'll send the girls to Queen Emma. Yes, I think it is a good plan."

Once the king decided to return to London, we were hustled along like livestock and placed on a wagon. The trip was uncomfortable and we were very hungry by then, but luckily for us our new friend Lang was part of the baggage train and he made sure to bring us his mother's meat pies. It turns out his whole family was in the Archbishop's employ and traveled with him wherever he went. I still remember those meat pies to this day.

But once in London, Hakon and I were locked in a room somewhere in the Archbishop's wing of King Edward's palace. For many days we had to content ourselves with staring out the window that overlooked the Thames. There was a lot of activity back and forth across the river, and I knew that on the other side, in Southwark, my father owned an estate. I didn't know exactly where it was, and I wondered if anyone was there.

Finally one morning our door opened and we had a most unexpected visitor. My sister, the Queen, threw open her arms and we both ran to greet her. I was ecstatic; I hadn't seen her since she went off to wed the king.

I was almost out of breath with excitement. "Are we going home now?" I tugged at her hand, wanting to go out the door.

But she didn't budge. She pulled us to a bench and made us sit on either side of her.

"Hush," she said quietly. "You must be brave."

I didn't like the sound of her voice. "That's what father said to us," I said. "I don't want to be brave."

My sister frowned. "You must. I have some bad news for you. For all of us. You are not going home. Not yet. I'm afraid there is no home for you to go to."

We stared at her, perplexed.

"What are you saying?" I think my voice broke.

"Wulfnoth, the king has outlawed our father. Our family has gone into exile."

I don't think her words made any sense to me. But Hakon started to cry.

"Archbishop Robert has turned the king against us," she said more quietly. "The king commanded father to answer...certain charges. He refused to give him safe-conduct."

Even I knew what that meant. Father would end up in prison, like us. Or worse.

"I will do what I can for you." She tried to sound reassuring.

We both stared at her. Hakon was hiccoughing. "You are the king's hostages now," she said. "He won't hurt you. It's father he wants, not you."

After being locked up the past week, I wasn't so sure. I started crying too, then all three of us were crying.

"What will happen to us?" I finally asked.

"I'm sure you will become part of the household. Do whatever they tell you. Do not complain or give them reason to separate you. Eventually they will learn to trust you."

She got up. "I must leave. Remember what I said. Don't get it into your heads to escape. That will just make it worse for you."

I tried to keep her from leaving, but she was insistent. That was the last time I saw her.

Had I known what was going to happen, I would have tried to arrange things better for poor Wulfnoth. Alas, Edward had gotten the bit in his mouth and was determined to be rid of me as well. If Robert of Jumièges had had his way the king would have divorced me. Luckily, Edward was content with sending me to Wilton abbey, where I had spent much of my youth. He didn't even give me the opportunity to say farewell to my brother...Editha

That same day after my sister left, the Archbishop came in accompanied by some men who treated him with deference. He was not as abrupt as that first day; in fact, he seemed quite satisfied as he looked at us. No wonder...he had just humiliated my father.

"I'm afraid you will be staying with us a little longer," he said, not being afraid at all. "As you are in my care, I intend to take charge of your education. You will be instructed as befits your rank and you will need to become fluent in French as this is the king's primary language."

I was so relieved my knees almost gave out. I was afraid we would be imprisoned. It wasn't until later I realized the Archbishop was contemplating a very, very long stay.

Chapter 4

LEOFWINE REMEMBERS

The morning after we got to Bosham, Harold and I and thirty of his hearth troops rode hard to Bristol, taking ship to Dublin. This was my first trip over the sea, and I was so excited I nearly forgot the gravity of the situation. It was also the first time I had Harold all to myself, and at the beginning I didn't really know how to act with him. He was so much older than me I don't think he took me seriously. After all, I was only 16 and he was almost 30.

At first, my brother was busy getting familiar with the crew and he said very little to me. I watched him thumping seamen on the shoulder and offering swigs of mead. He didn't have much else to do as Swegn had kept the ship in readiness to leave at a moment's notice. We sailed around Land's End and north into the Irish Sea before he took any notice of me. Finally, he came along with a loaf of bread and a round of cheese. I suddenly realized I was hungry and gratefully accepted a piece he cut off with his knife. He took a bite of bread and turned forward.

"Well, little brother. I imagine we'll be spending some time together. I think we should get something settled right now. I give orders and you take them."

I knew he was vexed about father's comment. I gulped my cheese and started to object when he slapped me on the shoulder and moved away. I wanted to run after him but restrained myself. There would be plenty of time to prove myself to him later.

But I did take father's instructions seriously. I knew Harold was impetuous. I also knew he was charming, charismatic, and decisive. People like that in a leader. I had none of these qualities, but I excelled in common sense. Still, how could I tell him anything?

I determined to watch and wait. I had so much to learn.

Living up to its reputation, the Irish Sea dealt us a stormy crossing. I am not ashamed to admit I was terrified, and clung to the main mast as though my life depended on it. I watched Harold work tirelessly alongside the ship's crew, lashing things down and even bailing when necessary. He even took the trouble to tie me to the mast so I felt safer. He made sure I was all right before going back to work.

In time the storm settled down and we sailed into Dublin on a misty chilly morning. Of course we were all soaked to the bone, but my brother made sure we were presentable before we disembarked. As we tied up, Harold liberally distributed silver pennies to all those who seemed to matter.

I could see this was an active trading post. Our boat bobbed next to ships from Scotland, the Mediterranean, and even the Middle East. Men walked fearlessly down narrow planks, carrying bundles on their shoulders. Shipmasters shouted commands, sailors were tying things off with ropes; prosperous merchants weaved around stacks of merchandise, arguing about price. Pretty much everybody ignored us as we passed through the crowd.

We made our way through the main gate of the timber walled embankment surrounding the town. Just on the inside, the road was lined with market stalls. I saw slaves being auctioned, furs, casks of wine, walrus tusks and even silks from Bagdad flung over a wooden stand. Still, everything had a rustic, muddy look about it that contrasted strongly with Winchester, or even Bosham. But no wonder; Dublin had been settled by the

Norsemen only 100 years or so ago; our towns went back almost 1000 years. The wooden huts all had thatched roofs and were spaced closely together on tiny low-fenced lots, though the streets were laid out in order. The hut walls were made of wattle and daub and only reached up to my shoulders; I soon learned that the roofs were supported by posts inside.

I was looking to the right and left and backwards until I noticed that my brother ignored all the activity as if he was master here. Taking hold of my sword hilt, I tried to imitate his manner. We shouldered our way through the market and asked directions to the king's palace. Well, there was no palace. Diarmaid Mac Mael-na-mbo, who had recently declared himself King, lived in a hut similar to the others but larger, near the center of the town down a wooden walk.

I was worried about introducing ourselves, but we didn't have any problems. The name of Godwine had spread well beyond the borders of England, and King Diarmaid welcomed us as cherished guests. He bade us enter his humble abode and join him at his feast. I could see servants scrambling to set up extra trestle tables for us. It was crowded, but we didn't care. We were tired and eager for real food and drink. Harold warned his men not to overindulge in alcohol, then he bade me to attend him at head table.

The King of the Irish was a clever man, else he never would have risen above the other chieftains. Harold sat beside him and I stood behind them, a little unsure what to do. I had no training as a servant, but I think my brother wanted me near and of course I didn't have the rank to sit at his table. I helped where I could and watched.

Actually, I found the Irish king to be an interesting study. He was quick to smile but his eyes were shielded. He seemed to take personal interest in what my brother was saying, and never took his eyes from Harold's. I swear he didn't blink while my brother was talking. Diarmaid was blond, mustached and good looking. Harold liked him at once. Both of them ignored me but that was fine.

"You have come a long way," the Irish King said carelessly, finally releasing Harold from his gaze and prodding a chicken leg with his knife.

My brother cleared his throat. "I fear we have had some trouble back home...those god-forsaken Normans."

"Hmm." Diarmaid sat back in his throne, taking a bite. "And what have the Normans to do with you?"

"Too much!" Harold gestured for me to pour him some ale. "They seek to rule the kingdom through Edward. Already they have started building their cursed stone keeps on the borders. They seem to feel they can terrorize the countryside at will."

The Irish King stared at him again. "Do they, now?"

"And Edward encourages them. In return, they have turned him against my kin."

"And driven you from England? What of the other Great Earls?"

Harold paused, cup halfway to his mouth. I could see the muscles stiffen in his back. I wondered if Diarmaid knew more than we thought and was goading my brother.

"As you suspect, King Diarmaid. They acted in their own best interests. Still, once they see what England is like without my father, they may decide their best interests lay with us. May we stay with you for a while? I have more than enough funds to pay our way, and I would like to raise a little support before returning home."

I held my breath, but the king seemed pleased with the idea. I could see my brother relax, and he told me to sit down and feed myself. I was glad to obey and found a place farther down the table.

Diarmaid was more than generous and we were given a building all our own, just big enough to hold our whole contingent. I set up my bed next to Harold, for I could see he

134

would be needing me for his servant. In our haste we brought none with us, and I knew he was used to giving orders. Well, I would learn quickly enough. Why not make myself useful to him? It started with little errands, then before long I was taking care of his weapons, keeping the household in order, finding solutions to the everyday problems encountered when away from home.

We didn't know how long we were going to stay, but Diarmaid took that in stride. He took my brother with him when he rode out, every day until winter set in. After that, the freezing temperatures drove us to the main hall, where a roaring fire pit in the center of the room almost kept us comfortable. I hated being so cold, but Harold never admitted to any discomfort. In public, that is. Nay, he wouldn't even be seen shrugging into a fur. Of course at night he often asked me to warm up a stone by the fire and wrap it in cloths to put under our blanket. I didn't mind, since it helped keep me warm too.

Life in exile contains many days of boredom that turn into weeks of sameness. As the months wore on, Diarmaid seemed eager to introduce his mercenary fighters to Harold, which offered some diversion; I got the impression he was trying to get rid of them. By spring, my brother was negotiating with father's money to hire more ships to take back with us. In June, when we finally got the long-awaited message from father, we had fully outfitted eight ships plus our own.

TOSTIG REMEMBERS

Father's preparations saved us. By the time we got back to Bosham his treasures were fully loaded onto two ships. Mother must have suspected the worst, for she and Judith had been busy

135

packing our clothing, foodstuffs, and weapons; she had also made arrangements with local ceorls to take care of our livestock.

When we arrived at our manor, all sorts of people gathered around us for the news. Father dismounted and handed his reins to Eirik. He shook his head as the villagers started murmuring amongst themselves. He and mother exchanged a knowing look as she came up to him, giving him a quick kiss on the cheek.

"The tidings are not good," he said, turning to the crowd. "The king refuses to hear my case."

Mother put a hand to her mouth. Judith came up behind her.

"My cause is lost, for now," father went on. "We will take sail to Flanders. I do not know what will happen in my absence, but this estate does not belong to the king. You should not see any change in your status."

The murmuring died down very little. Father's fate concerned everyone, and they needed reassurance. "The king will not wage war on his people," he said in an even voice. It was hard not to believe him. "I still have plenty of supporters, be assured. When the time is right, I will return."

He gestured for my brothers and me to follow him, putting an arm around mother's shoulders. I kissed Judith and handed her my cloak. "I am so sorry to drag you into this."

She smiled. "I am part of your family now. Your concerns are mine."

I hugged her and we followed father as the little crowd dispersed. Back in the same room where it all started, father turned to us, arms crossed.

"We cannot spare even one more day. We will board at first light and sail to Count Baldwin's land. Leave nothing of value behind. Gytha, I suspect you have arranged our affairs perfectly."

"All is ready. There is no need for delay."

"You knew," he said, softly.

"I expected the worst. That is all. It would have been easy to undo my efforts."

As we sailed away from our homeland, it was obvious that father was perfectly miserable, and his sudden exile weighed heavily on his shoulders. He spoke to no one, refused food, and stared dully back at England as if for the last time. It was terrible; I never saw him like this. Even mother was at a loss.

But by the time we docked at the harbor in Bruges, father was pretty much resigned to our new status. He girded his belt and climbed from our ship very much in charge again, making sure his housecarls kept our treasure well-guarded until he returned. After all, Baldwin wasn't exactly expecting us.

For once in my life I had the advantage. Of all my family, I alone had been there before—and of course, because of Judith I was welcome there. She had no doubt her brother was ready for anything, and so it proved.

"Tostig," father said as I helped my wife from the ship, "could you go ahead and announce our arrival? I am not used to being a supplicant." Despite himself, he grimaced.

"A wonderful idea," Judith agreed. "While we wait, I can show you the Oudeburg marketplace, which links the castle with the harbor."

And so it was settled. I threw on my best cloak, kissed Judith's hand, and beckoned a pair of father's housecarls to attend me. For a moment I watched my family huddle together like lost sheep, but Judith took the matter in hand and cheerfully led them toward the market.

It was not far to the castle but I hated to walk like a commoner; still, there was no helping the situation. Luckily, I was recognized and announced very quickly, and Count Baldwin came forward, hands outstretched in welcome.

"Tostig, good brother," he called, emphasizing the last word. "What a surprise to see you! Have you come alone?"

"No. I bring my father and my mother and my brothers. And Judith."

Baldwin was an open-handed host and I never saw him turn away a guest. "Splendid!" He looked around to see where they were.

"Father sent me ahead since we came rather unexpectedly. All is not well in King Edward's court..." I knew Baldwin didn't mind giving Edward a nasty poke whenever possible, so this wasn't bad news for him.

"Indeed! What happened?"

"Edward's new Archbishop finally got the upper hand. There was a disturbance at Dover and Eustace of Boulogne's men took a bit of a thrashing. Father refused to discipline his own people without investigating the situation first, and before we knew it we were at odds with the court and all the north."

"And you were forced to leave the country? That Eustace is nothing but trouble. Well, we must set things to rights. So you will be here for a long stay?" His voice ended as a question.

"It may be," I nodded. It probably would be, but one thing at a time.

"Then we must not let your family stand outside while we prepare for them! Where are they?"

"Judith is with them, in the marketplace."

"Ah. I shall greet them as becomes the great Earl of Wessex."

And at that, he started giving out orders to his stewards and servants who lingered nearby expectantly. "And have the grooms bring out the horses. We shall show Earl Godwine how the Count of Flanders welcomes his guests!"

Servants were running back and forth, and one of them brought a magnificent surcoat which he slipped over the Count's head, fastening it with a gem-studded baldric. He was lucky the elegant robes drew attention away from his face, for he was none too impressive with that bulbous nose and double chin.

138

In a short time, the grooms brought up our mounts even though I had just walked the distance from Oudeburg to the castle. But I admit I loved the clatter of our hoof beats on the stones in his new road, which bounced off the walls of nearby buildings. Citizens moved aside as our horns announced the approach of the Count and his courtiers. We rode in great splendor to receive my fellow travelers, banners flying and coins being tossed. Father was quite gratified, and all awkwardness was thus relieved.

The Count pulled rein and his horse pranced a bit. Father bowed.

"Count Baldwin," he called, his voice strong. "My family and I bring greetings and beg your hospitality."

Baldwin dismounted and ceremoniously kissed father on both cheeks. "I welcome you and your followers. We are all kin now and I would get to know you better!" He kissed Judith's hand and turned to mother.

"Lady Gytha, you are more beautiful than ever I had learned." Of course, mother was as gracious as always and acknowledged him with a nod of her head.

More high-sounding greetings followed before we were finally escorted to the Castle; I suspect Baldwin needed more time to prepare a welcome. But his show of generosity was all we could have hoped for.

Count Baldwin installed us in a grand palace on the hill— the same one he gave to Queen Emma during her exile back in 1037. There was easy passage between the palace and the Castle, and Baldwin bade us attend his feast that very evening, for there was sure to be entertainment.

We soon fell into an easy routine, broken by the occasional missive from England describing some outrage or other perpetrated by the king's Norman court. These messages never failed to cheer father, who nonetheless insisted we wait for the right moment. He couldn't survive another failure.

Not long after we were comfortably housed, Judith and I attended church with Matilda, Baldwin's only surviving daughter, and her ladies. Matilda was a tiny thing, but a spirited little bundle of energy nonetheless, and very pretty. She would have fit under Judith's chin. But she was the pride and joy of her parents, well-educated and very conscious of her lineage; her mother was the king of France's sister, and Baldwin's ancestors have ruled Flanders since the ninth century.

It had been raining that day and the sun was just peeking from the clouds as we finished the services in the church of St. Donation, which stood only about 400 meters from the castle. As we were leaving, Matilda led her little procession; I was far back in the crowd when the commotion began. Women were screaming, arms were waving, and people were pushing into each other trying to fall back. By the time I elbowed my way through the door, craning my neck to see over all the heads, Matilda was lying face-down in a puddle of mud. She was sobbing for all the world like she had just taken a beating. The poor girl was covered from head to toe with muck, and her beautiful dress was ruined. As she pushed herself up by the arms, I shook the girl next to me.

"What happened?"

"It was him," she sobbed, pointing. Looking up, I saw a somewhat disheveled man riding away. There was no time to catch up with him—not with poor Matilda in need of assistance. I ran to her side and rolled her into my arms, picking the unresisting girl up like she was a child. She put her arms around my neck, smearing mud and tears all over my tunic.

"Take...take me home," she coughed between sobs. She didn't need to tell me that!

By now we had drawn a crowd, but they all parted respectfully as I carried Bruges' favorite daughter back to her father's castle. I heard the murmurs as we passed by.

"William the Bastard," said somebody.

"The Duke," said another. "He must be punished."

140

"Poor girl," said a third. "He just grabbed her by the back of the neck and threw her in the mud."

"He beat her!"

"No, he kicked her!"

"He rolled her in the mud then got on his horse."

I was shocked. *That was the Duke of Normandy?*

Murmuring words of encouragement, I carried Matilda up the hill to the castle. We passed between rows of soldiers and into the citadel where her ladies ran ahead of me to prepare her chamber. I laid Matilda on a pile of covers and she rolled on her side, hiding her face. Her father rushed in the door and knelt by her bedside.

"Oh my poor child. What happened?"

At that, she sat up and threw her arms around Baldwin's neck, covering him with mud, too. After a few moments of sobbing, she pulled herself together.

"Oh father. It was Duke William. He was waiting for me at the church. When I came out, he accused me of humiliating him! I told him I would not lower myself to marry a mere bastard, when he grabbed me and threw me into the mud. He pushed me back and forth until I was totally covered then got on his horse and rode away."

She took a cloth from one of her ladies and blew her nose in it.

"Outrageous!" spit the Count. "I will have his head for this!"

Turning Matilda over to her women, he rose and tried to look dignified. But he was all bespattered like myself, and decided to leave the room, taking the witnesses with him. He put an arm around my shoulder.

"Thank you, Tostig. Poor girl." He tried to straighten out his tunic then gave up. "Right before you came to Flanders, Duke William sent an embassy asking for Matilda's hand in marriage. You can imagine how quickly she sent them packing. William

141

was beneath her station, and a bastard on top of everything else. She is not shy, my little Matilda!" He laughed briefly. "But we weren't expecting this!"

The more he thought about it, his face became redder and redder.

"How dare he shame my little girl! Come, Tostig. We cannot let this go unavenged!"

There is one thing I can say about Count Baldwin; he is a very decisive man. He wasted no time in calling together his scribes and composing letters to his knights and captains. He summoned his household steward and demanded an accounting of all supplies. He called for his banker so he could determine how many funds he could raise. He worked long into the night.

There wasn't much I could do but watch and learn. After all, although I had been granted a bit of land to live on in Wessex, I didn't have an earldom to rule. Things were a little different on the continent, but the act of ruling was the same. Father's earldom was peaceful and ran very smoothly. I rarely got to see preparations for war, except for the last time which was very chaotic.

But the following day, as Baldwin was busily giving orders, Matilda walked into the great hall, trailing her women. There were no signs of the previous afternoon's dishevelment; in fact, she had regained her proud bearing. Everyone stopped what they were doing and stared at her.

"Father, I have made a decision," she said evenly. "You may stop preparations for war. I have decided I will marry Duke William of Normandy."

You could have heard a feather drop in the room. We were all stunned into silence.

"You what?" her father finally muttered.

"I will have no one else."

Apparently used to Matilda's strange behavior, her father leaned back and put the quill down.

"And what has brought about this change of mind?" He crossed his arms over his chest.

She appeared to think for a moment. "It must be a brave and powerful man who would dare do such a thing, right in the middle of your territory." A brief smile flicked across her face. "I understand him better, now."

Baldwin looked around at his courtiers. "There you have it. Cancel our preparations." I detected a bit of sarcasm in his voice, but he was quickly obeyed. He held out a hand to Matilda.

"Come, my child. Sit beside me."

Someone brought a chair and Matilda obliged, taking her father's hand.

"Are you sure you want to do this?" he said gently. "He may prove to be a dangerous husband."

"I will manage him. After all, he really didn't hurt me."

Baldwin didn't even try to reason with her. Given time, he told me later, she might change her mind again.

A few weeks afterwards, William came in person. Matilda most certainly did not change her mind, and her father had begun preparations for the wedding. He was resigned; after all, it was not a terrible thing to secure the friendship of this turbulent duke, especially when one might need help against the king of France. There were few stronger bonds between rulers than marriage.

In contrast to the raucous suitor of the last time, William showed up in his best clothes, brushed and clean, gold rings on every finger and a circlet around his head. He didn't exactly look handsome, but he exuded power and a little danger, which I think Matilda liked. He gave his betrothed all the courtesy she could have wished, putting her father at ease.

Luckily he didn't stay long; he made most of us uncomfortable—even my father. By then, winter was drawing on and we were getting restless, though no closer to returning home.

One of those fall evenings, I discovered my brother Swegn sitting on a stone wall overlooking the harbor. He was just staring into the distance, and for once I actually thought I would have a talk with him. He had been so quiet lately, I was beginning to change my unchristian attitude toward him.

I sat beside my brother, swinging my legs over the edge. He knew I was there but didn't say anything. So I was content to sit quietly for a while; there was a warm breeze that brought the salty smell of the ocean with it. I have always loved that smell, slightly fishy and full of moisture.

"A fine tangle we have got ourselves into," he finally said. "Tostig, I feel responsible."

He surprised me once again. "Oh, I don't know..." My voice trailed off. Actually, he *was* responsible for most of our problems. Why deny it?

"I know it. I cannot make amends," he said flatly. "I see what father has become. He is lost."

"Hmm." I looked at his profile, noticing how gaunt his cheeks had become. "You are beginning to look like a hermit. You are certainly acting like one."

Swegn suddenly looked directly at me as though shocked.

"A hermit." He pursed his lips.

"I meant no insult," I said hastily, but he was shaking his head, looking at the horizon again.

"No, no. You are right. A hermit."

That was the end of our conversation. There was no talking to Swegn. There never was.

But I was to remember that exchange come Yuletide, when Swegn suddenly announced he was going on pilgrimage to Jerusalem. He picked one of the stormiest nights of the year, and father could not talk him out of his decision. Pleading with him, using reason, then emotion, father finally broke into tears and cried like a child. Everyone in the room stopped and stared. Father had his arms around Swegn and my brother just stood there,

144

embarrassed, patting him on the back. He left that very night and my parents broke into a terrible argument that lasted for weeks. They had never fought so bitterly before.

Leave it to Swegn to cause distress even when he was trying to make amends. He never did understand how to act. But this time, it was beginning to look like he was a true penitent. Maybe God forgave him in the end.

Nonetheless, we were all glad to be rid of him. Except father, of course.

I thought he'd be back but he never returned, and as spring came along so did the ships bearing messages. Good messages. Encouraging messages. They needed us. Exiles started to appear at Baldwin's court, evicted by grasping Normans, or merely goaded by unjust decrees. Edward was totally under the control of his foreign courtiers.

Or was he? Was he merely exercising his freedom from father? Well, no matter. He needed someone to explain how things were done in England. We were not Frenchmen to be ruled by an autocrat. The people had a voice and Edward needed to be reminded.

It was finally time.

Chapter 5

LEOFWINE REMEMBERS

I remember that day in Dublin, when my brother was sitting with the Irish King, bent over a game board. Suddenly, one of father's housecarls burst into the room, waving a parchment over his head. Harold leaned back in his chair, calm as a summer morn, and nodded at the king. "It is time," he said simply, ignoring the sudden hubbub all around him. We were anxious to hear the news, but he acted like the welcome announcement was nothing special; in fact, he put the missive to the side and picked up a playing piece, moving it across the board. It was all I could do to keep from grabbing the message myself.

Of course, back in our barracks he read father's letter out loud. "The people are with us," Harold called, holding up the note in triumph. He brought the letter close to his face. "Here is what my father says: Every day I get visitors from England begging me to come back and put things to rights. The Normans are making enemies by their heavy-handed behavior. The time is right for you to come."

There was cheering in the room and Harold waited before continuing. "I need your strength. Return with your men and we will meet near the Isle of Wight." Everyone talked at once as Harold handed the letter to me with a glance that told me there was more. Then he started a fuss over his companions, laughing and making jokes.

"Ready for home?" He nudged the fellow next to him, practically knocking a drinking bowl from his hand. "What are we waiting for? We should leave the day after tomorrow." He gave orders to gather the mercenaries as he moved to the door, knowing I would take care of his things. Burning to read the letter, I stuffed it in my belt and retired to our end of the room.

Pretending to pack, I smoothed out the parchment and placed it on my bedding. I ignored the laughing and chatter behind me, bending down to see the writing in the dim light. There was a further sentence from my father, added as if written in haste. "Be prepared for resistance," it read. "I do not know the temper of the men in Somerset and Dorset. They are ruled this day by Earl Odda." *King Edward's kinsman*, I thought. *Will Odda try to stop us?*

Harold was in high spirits, and the Irish and Danish mercenaries were ready for adventure. We were loaded and off in good time, and I felt great relief as I watched the coast of Ireland recede. I never wanted to see that place again.

My brother, of course, spent most of his day in the bow, looking toward England. This was the first time he would be in charge of a fighting force, and I think he strained to test his courage. To tell the truth, I think he was looking for a confrontation. Up until now, there was little need for me to speak up. But I kept remembering our father's parting words and I finally decided to approach him.

"Ah, little brother," he welcomed me with an arm around my shoulders. "Almost home now." That didn't help me any. Despite myself, I still craved his attention.

I cleared my throat. "Where are we going to land?"

He had already planned our course. "We will need to put in for supplies. Somewhere in the Bristol Channel, I think."

I was afraid of that. This was where Earl Odda ruled...just the spot father warned us about. It used to be part of Swegn's earldom, but who knows how the populace felt after my eldest brother's antics?

"Do we have to stop there?" I pursued, cringing at the sound of my own voice. I meant to challenge him, but my words came out as more of a whine. "Wouldn't it be better to find a friendlier port?"

I could feel Harold stiffen beside me. He removed his arm. "We do not know who is friendly, if you remember," he retorted. "We barely have enough supplies to get this far. Now leave it be."

The tone of his voice was final. I dared not say more.

As the sun started to go down, the sky grew ugly and a terrible storm blew in from the east. It wasn't long before we were forced to take shelter in the first local bay we could find. Harold paced the deck, heedless of the stinging rain.

"I hope father didn't get caught in this," he shouted when I finally ventured to his side. "This storm could prove fatal to our cause."

I was so miserable I hadn't thought past my own discomfort. Harold was right; a storm like this could destroy a fleet. Father could be right in the middle of the Channel.

But there was no helping him now. I went back to find a more sheltered spot on the deck and pulled a sealskin over my head. There was no going to sleep this night.

The storm raged for almost a full day, and we resolved to wait until the following morning to resume our course.

Harold's determination hadn't changed; we continued toward the Bristol Channel where the high green cliffs, rugged and dramatic, towered over us. As we passed from the sea into the Channel, I saw fire beacons lit along the headlands, announcing our arrival.

Ignoring the threat, my brother proceeded toward the town of Porlock on the southern stretch of the sound. All of our ships drew up side-by-side on the beach. A large local contingent, fully armed, began to line up on the hilltop.

148

Harold's troops armed for battle. He had already decided that I would stay on board the ship; he didn't want his little brother getting in the way. "Father would never forgive me if I let you get hurt," he said, a little sarcastically. I didn't care. I wasn't ready to fight my first battle, anyway.

Harold sent one of his housecarls forward with a request for supplies. At least he went that far! But our request was swiftly rebuffed, and my brother immediately shouted the attack.

We were not a friendly sight; the bristling Irish mercenaries spilled onto the shore in a loose line. They charged the local contingent with spears, swords, and axes, shrieking like fiends from hell. The defenders surpassed them in number, but their weapons were clearly inferior and they were farmers, not fighters. They seemed to hesitate before plunging forward.

Harold was surrounded by his hearth troops but he didn't seem to need any protection; he laid about with his axe in a broad arc, sweeping aside any man who singled him out. I could see his prowess encouraged the others, and I would hear a howl of support every time he made contact with a poor devil. Even I could tell the local troops were in deep trouble. In a very short time, they were being pushed back, and when they broke and fled the real slaughter began.

Well, maybe I am exaggerating. Yes, there was plenty of carnage. I later learned that more than thirty thegns from the surrounding shires were killed. But the Irish mercenaries wanted plunder, and slaves were valuable. While Harold's men were herding cattle and carting supplies to the ships, the Irish and Danes were rounding up our unfortunate countrymen and women for foreign markets. They surged into Porlock and returned, arms laden with anything they could carry, while dragging their poor hostages along tied by the hands to a long rope.

Harold boarded our ship with a little more swagger than before. He was covered with blood, but it didn't seem that any was his own. He wiped a hand on his tunic and gestured toward

149

me, clearly wanting something to drink. I dipped a ladle into the beer cask and he emptied it greedily, spilling much of the ale down his beard. I moved closer to him.

"They are taking our own people for slaves," I said softly in his ear.

My brother turned briefly to look at the other ships, then shrugged his shoulders. "They *used* to be our people. Now they are Odda's people," he replied in that way of his which brooked no argument. "My allies need to be paid somehow."

This was my first real lesson in warfare, and one I never forgot.

My second lesson came shortly thereafter. Once we were supplied we sailed around Pembrokeshire and skirted the coast, looking for father. By then, the surf had settled and we searched hard for any signs of debris. There was nothing on the horizon—neither flotsam nor ships of any kind. That is, until we reached Portland, a little island sticking into the channel west of Wight.

As our little fleet pulled up in the natural harbor, Harold broke into a big grin. There was father's ship, perfectly safe, bobbing alongside a score of other boats.

We disembarked, and my stomach churned as I recognized that father's force was doing what Harold had just done, without the battle. It was obvious he was taking what he needed from the countryside. As we approached, my father was standing on a small hill watching a pillar of smoke; it rose from a settlement about a half mile away. *So this is how it is done.*

Hearing our footsteps, father turned and a look of joy spread across his face. "At last," he cried, raising his arms in greeting. Harold and I threw ourselves into his embrace.

"I feared for your fleet," Harold said. "Did you miss the storm?"

"It blew us back to Flanders, but Edward's ships didn't fare as well. I believe they are dispersed."

150

He looked over his shoulder at the burning settlement then sent some more men down to hasten the removal of supplies. He turned back to us, apparently satisfied. But I could see in his face that something was not right.

Harold must have noticed too. "You don't look well."

Father tried and failed to smile. "Swegn left us at Christmas. He went on a pilgrimage to Jerusalem."

One of Harold's eyebrows went up; Swegn, a pilgrim?

"He should have reached his goal by now, if he hasn't perished," father added quietly.

"Don't say that. Swegn won't give up so easily." Harold didn't sound very reassuring, but it seemed to be enough.

"I don't know, son. Either way, I have to go on. But it hasn't been easy."

He turned to me, looking me up and down. I wasn't comfortable with his scrutiny and squirmed a little.

"All will go better, now that we are back together," I said lamely, then looked around. "Where are Tostig and Gyrth?"

"In Flanders."

Harold and I both blinked at him. We fully expected our brothers to come along.

"I can't risk all of you," he said defensively, "They can join us later."

As father turned to give some orders, Harold and I looked at each other. *What had this exile done to our family?*

Nonetheless, our return seemed to have put some color back into father's face, and when our combined fleets turned back east, there was no more plundering—at least, not by us. I think some of Harold's mercenaries strayed off course, but we knew nothing about that until later.

As we moved east the mood of the populace improved and we were offered as much as we needed. Boats of all sizes joined our fleet. As we passed the forelands and headed toward the

151

Thames, the sea was covered with ships. London was ready to take us back!

HAROLD REMEMBERS

If I had any doubts about father's popularity, events surrounding our return from exile put them to rest. By the time we located father, word had spread across Wessex that the Godwines were back. Originally, the Isle of Wight was held by Earl Odda, the king's man, and father met with some resistance there. But as soon as Edward's broken-up fleet retreated back to London our supporters came out of hiding. There were more and more of them as we started to move east along the coast, and they soon joined their boats to our flotilla.

Leofwine and I joined father on his ship, and I watched him swell with pride as people on the shore waved and shouted our names. As we passed Pevensey we were a hundred strong, and growing. I could see he was still worried, but there was no reason for us to turn back now.

At Dover, we gained our biggest surge yet. They remembered what father had done for them, and the price he paid. Entering the Thames estuary, I looked back and marveled at the forest of masts behind us. But even so, it would do us no good to be overconfident.

Nearing London, we were obliged to drop anchor and wait for the tide to come in.

"Harold," father said, "it is not yet time for me to show myself. We shall send messages to the burghers of London and determine their mood."

I agreed with him and knew just who to send. Climbing into a little boat we were towing behind us, I rowed to my own ship and called for Tor, who was at the helm.

"Tor, my friend. We need to discover if the burghers and citizens of London are with us."

He turned around and summoned a sturdy pair of housecarls. They bent over the gunnel to hear me better.

"One of our fishermen should be able to ferry you across. You will need to requisition some horses; I hope these people are friendly to our cause."

They belted on their swords and axes and joined me in the boat. "No worry," Torr said as he took an oar. "This is a great day for your family. I do not doubt that the people will welcome us."

I let out a short laugh. "Father does not share your conviction. But I think you are right."

Torr and his men climbed onto one of the larger boats and I watched them cross the river. I would have liked to have joined them, but I felt that father needed me on hand. It was bound to be a long night.

Well, it was a long night for father. I had no trouble finding a place to sleep, but every time I woke up I saw him leaning against the gunnel, staring into the fog. We heard the occasional slap of water against the hull and the splash of a fish now and then, but for the rest it felt like the whole world was waiting with us.

Yet even this night came to an end, and as the fog was lifting we heard the hoof beats. Torr nearly dashed into the river from the other side, then stood up in his stirrups.

"Earl Godwine," he shouted. "They are with us!"

Father threw out his arms as the men cheered, and the ovation spread from one ship to the next. From a heavy silence the air was suddenly full of voices. You could hear banging and the slapping of ropes as men readied their ships for the next stage of our victorious return. The tide was coming in, and we would ride it all the way to London.

At first we were taken aback by the crush of people cramming the bridge and lining both shores. But it was soon apparent that there was no hostility. The drawbridge was soon raised; men and women started cheering and even threw flowers down on us as we passed. "Godwine, Godwine," they shouted over and over again.

"I wish your mother could see this," father said, putting an arm around my shoulders. "She would be so proud."

It was a good moment for him and I hope he had the time to savor it. How many people rose from bitter outlawry to total adulation?

But still, we were not clear of danger. Our fleet sailed past central London, but we knew that the king and his army was upstream at Westminster. As we neared our destination, we were cautious because a small force stood in ordered ranks on the north side of the river. At the same time, a crowd of men was forming on the south bank and as yet we didn't know who they were.

But we learned soon enough. "Godwine, Godwine!" The name started quietly enough, but spread from one man to another on the Lambeth side. They were ours, all right, and had assembled on their own without a man to lead them. Smiling broadly, father raised his arms again as our ship dropped anchor across from Edward's great palace.

There was a little harbor on the Lambeth side, and he disembarked, instantly surrounded by well-wishers. For a time I stayed on the deck and watched his moment of glory. He embraced his countrymen whole-heartedly, laughing and whooping with happiness, forgetting all his uncertainty. He was the Earl of Wessex once again, in fact if not yet in name.

After things settled down for a moment, he summoned me forth; men were starting to insist we attack the king's housecarls. This is not what father wanted.

"We do not want to start a civil war," he spoke firmly, though I'm not sure how many heard. "I say we send one more time to King Edward, and demand that he restore our rights and properties."

I repeated his words to the crowd and moved into their midst, reminding them we were here in peace. Finally the others started nodding in agreement. They were here to support father; that should be enough.

We re-embarked on the ship and ferried a messenger across to the king. His answer was not long in coming. As we watched, the remnants of Edward's fleet moved to block our way.

"The King does not give up easily," father murmured. "But we shall put things to rights."

He summoned our pilot to come closer. "Signal the other boats," he said. "Let us surround the king's mighty fleet."

Of course, Edward's little fleet was far from mighty, and we encircled them in a very short time. Apparently they were not terribly interested in fighting, for they did nothing to stop us.

I turned to father. "What now?"

"Let us drop anchor. We wait."

Our pilot maneuvered our ship to the north shore in full sight of Edward's housecarls. Putting my hands on the gunnel, I had to squint a little in the bright sun as I studied them. The soldiers stood straight and still, though they were supported by fyrdmen who had no such discipline. We could hear angry murmuring from the growing crowd, for not everyone wanted us back. I knew Earl Aelfgar had been given my own East Anglia, and I wondered how many of these men were his.

Once again, like in my early days, I determined that a strong move on my part should take away some of their spleen.

Unchecked, the angry grumbling started to grow in volume, matched by a rumbling on the south shore.

155

"Patience," father shouted at them, though he knew as well as I that they couldn't hear. He gestured with his hands as if pushing them down with his will. I almost noticed a lessening.

Luckily, we saw movement in the king's host and the crowd parted, allowing Bishop Stigand and his fellow monks to pass. Father let out his breath in an explosive laugh.

"Let down a plank for the good Bishop," he cried, striding across the deck.

Stigand waited, looking at the sky, while a board was laid for him. Then he climbed up, grabbing outstretched hands for support. Puffing a bit, he faced father. He was so welcome I could have kissed him.

"I am so glad you are well," father said, clasping his hand. Stigand drew him into an embrace. "*All* will be well," I heard him whisper.

Pulling back, father cocked his head. "Is Edward ready to concede my demands?"

Stigand laughed, shaking his head. "You are an impetuous man, Godwine. One step at a time. The King has to get used to the idea, you know."

"You mean he is delaying...buying time."

"I mean no such thing. Already he has agreed to a truce, until all are gathered at a Witenagemot on the morrow. You are free for now to return to Southwark."

All our men within hearing began to talk excitedly.

"There will be no trouble?" father persisted, dubious.

"Do you trust me, Godwine? There is more happening than I am free to disclose."

My family was experienced enough in politics to stop there. We watched Stigand return the way he came, and I desperately wanted to follow him. I moved over to father, taking his arm.

"Father, there is something I would do." He nodded, though he still watched the Bishop's progress. I don't think he was listening.

156

"I will venture among them and judge for myself the disposition of these people."

Startled, he jerked his head around. "Don't, please." I could see the panic in his eyes.

"We must be sure there is no danger; it could be another trick. I will be less threatened than you." I didn't want him to know my suspicions about Aelfgar. I had to do this for myself.

"Yes, go, Harold. But be careful."

I started to go then turned around, giving him a second look. That was almost too easy.

But he had moved away from me and I couldn't see his face. Shrugging my shoulders, I climbed down to the shore. Father had plenty to occupy him.

I landed in the knee-deep water and waded slowly toward the jetty, keeping my hands clearly away from my sword. The first two rows of housecarls were probably the king's men; I didn't recognize any of them. The soldiers nearest me watched my progress, but nobody moved. I could hear the sea gulls squawking behind me and a low murmuring in front of me.

Warily, I passed through their ranks, looking for a leader. They didn't feel exactly hostile, but a quick order could put me in a bad situation. Suddenly, I heard a voice exclaim, "Long Live Earl Harold!"

I knew that voice! Turning, I saw a helmeted man raising his spear. It was Eadric of Laxfield! My former adversary turned rescuer! He was nudging some of his companions and I could hear him exhorting them: "It's our Earl! Come back to us! The Godwines are back!"

There they were in the rear ranks—my own East Anglian supporters. They started talking all at once, pushing their way toward me. Eadric slapped me on the shoulder and laughed uproariously, as if we were sharing a mutual jest. And I suppose we were; from where we started, I don't think I would have been happier to see any other man alive.

This was enough for the other warriors. I don't think anyone wanted a fight, especially with a horde of supporters ready to defend my father to the death. They all began to relax and mix together, and soon they started cheering in relief. It was a good feeling to be among them, and I made contact with as many as I could, while still keeping Eadric by my side. I could imagine King Edward cringing at our welcome.

"The last person I expected to see was you," I shouted, trying to be overheard.

"Earl Aelfgar sent us to confer with the king," he said into my ear. "He wanted help putting down some disruptions in the earldom."

I pulled back, blinking.

"Earl Harold, I came to appreciate you more and more after you left!" He laughed again and I joined him this time. It really was a good jest.

As the clamor diminished, I heard someone ordering the troops back into the city to put down a disturbance. Sharply, the housecarls fell into ranks again and followed their chieftain. My East Anglians stayed behind, for they were under no direct orders.

"How goes it in my earldom?"

Eadric made a face. "From the very first Aelfgar lorded it over us like he was the king himself. He put his own men in charge and pushed many of my people out of office. It will take another year to recover, once you come back."

"I hope to come back at the soonest," I said, looking over my shoulder at the ships. It was time I went back; but before I broke away, I clasped Eadric by the shoulders.

"Edith?"

"She was obliged to return to Nazeing, though she wanted to come home to Hinton."

"Was she...threatened?"

"Oh, no. I wouldn't have allowed that. But Aelfgar resented her presence in his city and tried to take some privileges away

158

from her. I took care of that." He frowned. "But I think she was happier away from the soldiers. I was in favor of the move though I miss the boys."

I heard screaming coming from the streets but couldn't see anything from this vantage point. I was torn between running to help and going back to father.

"We will go," Eadric said, pushing me toward the ship. "You have done enough for now."

I should have gone with him, for maybe I could have stopped what was happening. But it was not the will of *wyrd*. Instead, I chose to return to father, for I knew he was worried. It took a while for the mayhem to settle, and it wasn't until much later we discovered we were hearing the Normans fleeing the court like the rats they were.

WULFNOTH REMEMBERS

When one is young, I assume it's easier to adapt to new circumstances. The first couple of months at Edward's court were difficult, I remember, but we fell into a routine fairly quickly. As the weeks passed, we saw little of the Archbishop or the king, but we were assigned a tutor who gave us lessons in the morning then turned us over to a weapons instructor in the afternoon. Lang took it upon himself to show us how to care for the horses, which helped pass some time. We were pretty much allowed to go where we wanted, provided we didn't make a nuisance of ourselves. If we wanted to leave the palace, we always had to bring Lang with us. He was more of a companion than a guard, but we knew he would be in deep trouble if we tried to escape. Where would we go, anyway?

A year passed thus. We felt completely forgotten. Of course, since our family was in exile we couldn't expect to get any letters. Hakon adapted better than I did. Even though he was raised in our household, I don't think he ever felt like he belonged. I was finally beginning to understand what it felt to be an outsider.

Then, at the end of summer, all of a sudden the king's palace was in turmoil. People were running back and forth, armored men were gathering in the courtyard, everyone was shouting. Hakon and I were watching from our window when two strange guards came into our room and flanked the doorway. We looked at each other; we were prisoners again.

Archbishop Robert stepped into the room.

"Get your things ready," he growled. "I will be back for you."

What did that mean? We did as we were told, but as I was still stuffing my few belongings into a sack, Hakon made a noise that sounded like a shout he was trying to choke back.

"Come here. Look!"

I climbed up to the window sill; our view was restricted but we could see the river from a distance. The Thames was always busy, but today it was covered with boats of all sizes, coming our way. And the foremost ship bore my father's flag!

We grabbed each other, barely able to contain our excitement. We couldn't see what was happening, and the moments seemed like hours while we strained to listen. A crowd was building fast and they didn't sound too hostile. After a very long time, they started to cheer.

I can hardly bear to remember what happened next. Suddenly the door slammed open and a handful of soldiers burst into the room, grabbing us roughly and shoving us before them. For a moment, Hakon tried to break free and run, but they grasped his arm and boxed his ears to quiet him down. They dragged us out of the building and shoved us onto horses, ignoring our struggling as though we were children. All around us the Normans

160

were pulling their mounts out of the stables, and Archbishop Robert rode up, pushed his beast against mine and grabbed the reins.

"Stay close," he shouted. "Allons!"

As a unit our tight little group bolted forward and through the gates. The streets were crowded with people who saw us coming, and the lucky ones threw themselves against the walls. The unlucky ones were trampled underfoot, or thrust away with a bloody sword. Our guards were driven like devils, slashing at everything in their way. We left behind an uproar, and not a few tried to chase us. But we were moving very fast and they fell behind.

As we neared the gates of the city, a last group of housecarls tried to stop our way. I thought they were father's men and I shouted for help. But they were not mounted and our horses broke through their ranks, scattering the brave men who tried to strike us as we passed. I doubt they heard my voice.

It was a long ride to one of Archbishop Robert's abbeys, but he wanted to make sure we were not followed. I feared father did not know we had been abducted, and this proved to be the case. The English were well rid of us and saw no need to pursue the Normans. Robert made straight for the coast then loaded us onto a broken-down ship, and before we knew it we were across the Channel.

I remember little of the next couple of days. I was prostrate with grief, for I knew I was lost. I was the youngest son, and that made me expendable. Once again, it was Hakon who taught me how to cope.

"Look," he said as I lay on my pallet staring at the ceiling of yet another abbey. "We have no control over our destiny, but we probably have value as hostages."

I turned my head away, wiping my nose.

"Acting like this will not help you any," he pursued. "You had better get used to it. Like I did."

161

I knew he was right. I sat up and put on my shoes. "All right. Let me find some food."

Food always made me feel better. By the following day, I was resigned to my situation, and by the time we arrived at Duke William's court, I was almost interested in my surroundings.

The Duke was residing at Falaise, said to be the place where he was born. The castle was perched on a manmade hill, later to be known in England as motte and bailey. Of course, I knew nothing of that and I was amazed at the view of the countryside before we entered the big gates. The Duke's keep was built all of stone and was a massive block. There was a lot of activity and I could see that the soldiers, armorers and supporting trades were all crunched together inside of the fortified walls. No one paid much attention to Hakon and me as we dismounted, and Archbishop Robert gave orders as if it was his castle instead of the Duke's.

By the time we entered the keep, it was evident that the Archbishop was glad to be rid of us. He made sure Hakon and I were given a bath and new clothes, then impatiently led us into the great hall. Apparently we were expected, because Duke William was on his throne surrounded by fine-looking men, beardless and with their hair cut short in the back. Despite myself, I put my hand to my long hair.

The Duke turned carelessly to us as we knelt before him. He was a brute of a man: large, stocky with a squared-off chin and heavy brows. He looked at us curiously for a moment before turning to the Archbishop.

Robert bowed deeply then stood in his best officious pose.

"I bring a message from King Edward of England," be began in a sonorous voice. "In gratitude to this country for giving him refuge most of his adult life, King Edward has offered to make Duke William his heir."

I gasped, but everyone ignored me.

"This offer comes with the assent of the English nobility, namely Earl Godwine, Earl Leofric of Mercia, and Earl Siward of Northumbria. King Edward has sent these two hostages, son and grandson of Earl Godwine, to guarantee the agreement."

I almost fainted while Duke William's Norman friends congratulated him on his good fortune. What could I do? There was no way my father would assent to such a thing. I knew Robert was lying, but who would believe me?

"So these are my hostages, eh?" He gestured for us to get up. "Son of Earl Godwine and who? Which is which? Speak up boy." He spoke in French and I was glad for my recent lessons.

As William looked directly at me, I kept my eyes on the floor. "My name is Wulfnoth Godwineson, Lord. This is Hakon, son of my brother Swegn."

"Hmm. All right. For now, put them with the other boys."

He stood from his throne. "I accept King Edward's offer and thank you, Archbishop Robert, for bringing me this important proclamation. And for delivering the hostages."

Robert bowed again, and as they were taking us away, I saw a look of triumph on his face. He may have been outlawed from England, but he was surely having his revenge.

As for our situation, it wasn't as bad as I feared. On the continent, it was the habit of noblemen to raise sons of their retainers to keep the fathers from rebelling. It was an amazingly simple concept that seemed to work. We found ourselves in the midst of other boys who were hostages like us. We took lessons together, ate together, spent all our time together, and we were even trained to wait upon the great ones like squires. I soon gave up worrying about going home. Like Hakon said, we might as well get used to it. Things will happen at their own pace.

We decided to take Bishop Stigand's advice and retire back to Southwark for the night. Our fleet found anchorage as best as they could, and father's makeshift army camped where they were. No one was taking any chances that the king might change his mind.

As for father, he was looking forward to seeing his old palace in Southwark; I think it was his favorite residence after Bosham. It had lain vacant the last year, except for the few loyal servants who kept up repairs and watched for intruders. They stood in a little group at the door, holding torches and watching our approach in silence.

Father paused and held out his arms in greeting.

"A welcome sight for my tired eyes," he called.

As one, the little group knelt before us. A couple of them were wiping their eyes; I knew they loved my father and they were almost like family.

"Come, come. You have served me well and I am truly grateful. I have missed my home and I missed all of you. I am so happy you are here. Come, let's see what the inside of my dear *heimr* looks like."

He bent down and helped the oldest man to his feet. "You have grown a few more white hairs this year," he joked, as the other nodded his head.

I hung back for a moment, watching this little domestic scene. I suddenly wanted to see my Edith and my babes so badly I wished I could just ride away and bury my head in her lovely embrace. *Was I always to give matters of state first precedence?*

Yes, I needed to do so for at least one more day; the Witenagemot would reinstate father and me to our old earldoms and return all that was taken from us. King Edward made the best of it and submitted to the old ceremony, taking up the axe father laid at his feet and returning it to his old defender. It was a long day. A lot of promises were made—something father excelled at. Alliances needed to be ensured once again and old bonds needed strengthening. I admit I only contributed half-heartedly to father's efforts, and as soon as I felt able I was on my horse and galloping to Nazeing. To my beloved Edith.

It had been a long year, and only two letters reached me in Ireland. When Edward outlawed us so suddenly, I had no chance to warn her. We were long gone before she even received my first hastily scrawled note, which I barely had time to send before sailing from Bristol.

And now, she was going to be equally unprepared for my return. I was in such a hurry I rode alone—which was foolish, I know. So when I thundered through the gates at her estate, her startled guardsmen nearly rode me down before they recognized me.

"*Holla!*" cried one of them "It's Earl Harold!" They drew rein at that and waved as I rode past.

A few servants were around as I threw myself from the saddle and grasped the door handle. They chuckled to themselves as they caught the reins of my poor sweating horse. I turned for a second, a little embarrassed, then burst into the house.

Startled, an infant in a cradle began wailing while my little Edmund stood in a doorway watching me and sucking his thumb. Hearing the child, Edith came up behind Edmund clucking endearments.

Then she saw me. In no time she was tight in my arms, crying as though to wash away a year's worth of worry. The baby screamed even louder.

In her everyday dress, Edith looked even more beautiful than I remembered. I kissed her all over her hair and her face and her mouth until she pulled away, gasping for breath. I pushed a strand of hair out of her eye.

"My lady," I murmured, kissing her on the nose. She put a hand on my cheek and sighed.

"All is well?" she said quietly. I nodded. "Then I can bear to hear about it."

She turned to Edmund who was tugging at her skirt. "It's your father, dear. He's come back to us."

I went down on one knee and held out my arms. He peeked from around his mother's legs until his brother Godwine ran past him and jumped onto my chest, squealing his joy. Not to be left out, Edmund joined him.

"That's better," I laughed. "My boys! You are so big!"

All shyness forgotten, both of them started talking at once while their mother retrieved the baby from its cradle. She stood quietly, soothing the child until it subsided into hiccoughs.

"Who is that?" I asked Godwine, pointing at the baby.

"My little brother Magnus," he said. "He is always crying!"

Edith held out the bundle to me. I took him gingerly. "I didn't know..."

"Neither did I," she said, "until you were long gone. You must not have gotten my letter."

I smiled crookedly. "Dublin is a backwater," I started, but the child screamed for his mother. The wet-nurse hurried in and took him away. That was a relief!

We stood and stared at each other; I felt a comfort lacking for many, many months. I finally took her hand and kissed it. "Come," I said, nodding toward the private chamber. "I have much to talk with you about."

Taking a moment to lead my protesting boys to the care of her other servants, Edith drew me into the dusky room and lit a candle. She drew a curtain across the doorway and I grabbed her around the waist, pulling her onto the bed.

"I couldn't stand another minute away from you," I murmured, kissing her neck and working my way up to her ear.

166

"I feared for you, my love." She closed those beautiful blue eyes and arched her back. My fingers found her laces and started pulling them loose, though was I soon hopelessly entangled. With a sultry laugh she helped herself out of her dress and I lay back, running a finger down her arm.

Well, that was the slow part. It didn't take long before our limbs were just as entangled as her laces!

By the next day, my entourage had caught up with me, led by the indomitable Eadric. I had told Edith about his timely intervention in London, and we both greeted him warmly. I think he was a little embarrassed by our attention, but all that went away when he saw the boys. Little Godwine and Edmund came rushing into the room, squealing with joy. He went down on one knee and both of them threw themselves into his arms. He kissed first one then the other while they dug into his pouch, pulling out two wooden soldiers. Holding the toys over their heads, my sons shouted with glee and started shoving each other.

Eadric looked up at me, embarrassed. And well he should have been: he got the greeting I expected from my children. What a difference a year could make!

Trying to get past the awkward moment, he quickly moved on to the news.

"It's not good," he warned me. "Those cursed Normans."

That got my attention. "Is there trouble?" My hand went for my sword but I had removed my belt.

"No, not like you think. It's too late for us to do anything."

He handed me a note from my father but I didn't open it. "What happened?"

"When you arrived...do you remember the disturbance in town?"

"You went to help, I remember."

167

He nodded. "It was the Normans, led by that knave, Robert of Jumièges. As soon as they saw that King Edward was not going to help them, they stole the king's horses and flew out of London in every direction, knocking down any poor citizen that blocked their way. They were so violent and unexpected, we were only able to stop two of them before they were gone."

I started pacing the room, itching to go after them. But then I saw Eadric was hesitating. Edith and I looked at each other then back at him.

"There's something else, my Lord," he said more slowly. "They took the hostages with them."

I stopped. The hostages. My brother. Did I ever find the time to think about his plight?

"Wulfnoth," I said. My poor little brother.

"King Edward did not try to stop them," Eadric said bitterly. "I wonder if he was glad to see your father suffer."

I put a hand to my head. Of course. Another blow to father. I sighed.

"You could be right, Eadric. Edward never should have kept them in the first place."

"Most certainly not," Edith broke in. I think she sensed my regret. "Your father gave hostages in good faith, and the king did not honor his side of the truce!" Her voice trailed off. My outlawry was too fresh to begin speaking against the king, no matter how justified.

I put an arm around her shoulders. "I shall have to do something about it," I muttered, though I didn't know what. Wulfnoth's fate was in God's hands, at least for now.

It took a couple of days before Edith was satisfied that our belongings were properly packed for the trip to Cambridge. She didn't want to leave Nazeing, but I had to get back and take control of my earldom again. I was afraid Aelfgar might be up to some mischief before relinquishing his post.

I was none too soon. As my little retinue approached the city, I could see strange soldiers patrolling the road. I turned to Eadric.

"Yes, those are Aelfgar's men," he assured me. "Probably posted to warn him of our coming."

Giving orders for my household troops to branch off and take my family to Hinton, I spurred my horse forward and Eadric followed with a few men. As we sped past Aelfgar's watchmen, I could see them branch off and ride toward the Council House. Of course, by then it didn't matter who got there first.

We drew rein in the city square and the townspeople broke off their activities, gathering around me and cheering their greetings. I sat upon my horse and addressed those closest to me. I liked this noisy welcome and I liked sitting high above the crowd. As expected, the noise drew Aelfgar out to the top step of the building.

For just a moment our eyes met. Aelfgar was younger than me and not as experienced; he had a difficult time suppressing his bitterness. He was not the tallest man in the world, nor did he have any particular command about him, so already I felt I had the advantage. My first inclination was to ask why he was still there, but my common sense won the day; a man's fortune could turn in an instant, and I knew what it meant to be on the other side.

He leaned slightly back and crossed his arms, then broke away with a gesture of dismissal, turning and reentering the building. That put me into an interesting position. Should I follow Aelfgar like an intruder? I didn't like that.

I called to Eadric. "Reeve Laxfield, I think it's high time you escorted the former Earl from my hall. Take as many men as you need, but be as gracious as possible. Within reason. You can find me portside, inspecting my ships."

169

Eadric looked satisfied. He had no problem carrying out my orders. I hoped Aelfgar would leave quietly and save us both a confrontation.

It took longer than I expected, but in due time I heard a large contingent exit from the western gate. When Eadric found me, he looked like a cat that had just caught a bird.

"It is accomplished," he said, bowing. I was amused.

"Was he prepared to go?"

A smile tried to break across his face but he fought it back. "Oh, he was prepared all right. He was just finishing packing our treasure into his war chest."

"Ha. I expected as much." Eadric really was a valuable henchman. "I'm sure he didn't want to relinquish a *penningr*."

"No, but he took one look at my sturdy thegns and told me he was just putting his collected revenues all together for Earl Harold. What he hadn't already squandered, I would assume."

"Well, it can't be helped. At least you were in good time. Come, I would inspect the damage."

We were a smug little contingent as we trooped back to the Council House. The excitement was over; it was already business as usual with the townspeople. As I passed through, a few locals greeted me before going back to their haggling. I turned for a moment and watched them. It was a bit of a revelation, really; it didn't matter to them who was in charge as long as it didn't affect their trade.

Eadric stopped and followed my gaze. He made a little grunt.

"Just look at them," he said. "Totally unmindful that their former Earl has just slipped out of town."

"Is that what happened when I left?"

"Hmm." He looked at me sideways. "That was a very confusing time. Your fyrd came back leaderless, and they just went home. It was a while before we realized you weren't coming back.

"So there was a bit of disorder at first," he went on, scratching his beard, "Until Aelfgar suddenly appeared. He was not benevolent. But there was no question he was our new Earl, the bastard."

I was unhappy to discover that Aelfgar had taken over my own castle in town. This was my father's property, but when one is an outlaw the lines blur between ownership and possession. Luckily, he hadn't had time to do any serious damage, so I was able to settle in pretty quickly.

As it turned out, I was only destined to rule in East Anglia another year. And during most of that year I made several trips to Wessex. Swegn had died on his way back from Jerusalem, having redeemed himself as a penitent of the highest order. The news came only a couple of months after our reinstatement, and father was visibly broken by his death. He needed my support both physically and emotionally. It seems that the realization of having wasted all his efforts—and our family's good name—on an undeserving son disturbed my father's peace of mind. He was never the same after that, and our family watched him turn into an old man before our eyes.

But none of us were prepared for his last. It was during the Easter feast that the king held at Winchester. In the middle of the meal, father suddenly collapsed; we had to carry him out of the hall and put him into a bed in the king's palace. For five days he lay there unconscious, and ironically the moment the king entered the room, he opened his eyes and died. Just like that.

There was some rumor of Edward driving him into an admission of guilt regarding the death of Alfred, but I heard none of that. What I do remember is the look of triumph on the king's face when he straightened from the bed and stated that father had quit breathing. There's no doubt he chose the wrong witnesses for this show of bile. We all stared at him accusingly.

171

Edward seemed to catch himself. Removing father's ring, he held it over my finger.

"It is a heavy burden, but I think you can bear it," he said, trying to look stern. "As second Earl of Wessex, you will be my chief support in the kingdom. Are you willing to take on the responsibility?"

I should have expected this, but it was all so soon. I looked down at father, so shrunken and pathetic. But, strange to say, his face looked more content than I had ever seen it.

My first inclination was to dash from the room. But my father's words kept coming back, uttered months before and never referred to again: *Shepherd him carefully. Find a way to succeed Edward.* In a thousand years, could I ever think of a more fitting justice?

Maybe father would have the last word after all. I looked Edward in the eyes, controlling my emotions. Grief would have to come later; now was the time for decision. I was head of the family now. It was all up to me.

"I will do it," I said finally.

"Good," Edward answered, pushing the ring on my finger. It was a perfect fit.

This is an interesting revelation. I always wondered when Harold started to think of himself as possible heir, but I didn't realize father put the idea into his head. Did Edward see my brother as his heir? Alas, he always kept his own counsel, and he never gave me the slightest idea what he had in mind, except that we raised Eadgar Aetheling as the closest blood-relation...Editha

The women in our household washed and prepared father's body for burial. I made arrangements for the horses and funeral bier that would carry him in state to his resting place at the

Old Minster in Winchester. I sent out messages far and wide, notifying all the important earls and lords in all of Britain; I did not forget Aelfgar, for I suspected he would return to East Anglia and we needed to stay on friendly terms. I also sent letters to mayors and reeves of all the towns in Wessex, for they would surely want to send representatives.

Father was to be laid next to Canute and Beorn, so he would be in good company while waiting for the Last Judgment. But in the space between his death and the funeral, we would keep watch over his body, arrayed in his robes of office at King Edward's old palace. This is where Emma had lived in seclusion, though the great hall was amply sized for the throng of visitors we expected.

Dear father would have appreciated the great number of mourners that showed up for his funeral procession. It seemed half of Wessex was there. Mother greeted every single person that showed up for the viewing until I practically carried her off to bed. I don't think she slept for a couple of days. My sister Editha stayed to help, as she had been present at the Lenten festivities.

Even the king made an appearance. He decided to call a Witenagemot after the funeral, since it seemed that everyone of importance would be present anyway. This would give him the opportunity to announce my new appointment.

I spent most of the days next to father's bier. The platform was draped in black and trimmed with purple silk ribbon; he wore his coronet and held his staff of office across his chest. In death his face had relaxed, giving him the benign expression I remembered for most of my life. Before the troubles. It gave me comfort to look at him, and I did my best to forget those last terrible months of watching him diminish before my eyes.

When it came time for the funeral procession, we moved his bier onto a wagon, draped in more black cloth and drawn by four black horses. The streets were lined with a hushed crowd of onlookers, while many more hung from windows that lined the

173

route. We took a slow and stately walk to the great Minster, and people threw flowers into the road before our horses' hooves. The most important dignitaries were already in the church, and as we lifted the bier and carried it though the great doors the roof echoed with the *De profundis*, chanted by a choir of oblates.

The funeral services were solemn and long, and I admit I fell asleep from exhaustion before they were over. Gyrth shook me awake just before the family was bid forward to pay our last respects. I leaned on him a little bit as we moved to the altar, but when I saw how devastated mother was I forgot my own exhaustion. Gyrth and I flanked her and held her arms as she knelt beside father's stone coffin.

"I offer a benevolence to the Church for the repose of my dear husband's soul," she said in a clear voice, raising her hands as we let go. "I offer the lordships of Bleadon and Crowcombe and the rents of all their lands into the keeping of our good fathers of Winchester."

This was a substantial gift to the church, and her gesture seemed to open a floodgate of emotions. As the priests bowed in recognition, grown men started crying and carrying on as though they had lost a father. Ah, so had I, and suddenly I felt the tears run down my face. Not only was he my father, but he watched over his earldom like a protector of the innocents. Once again I was reminded just how deep the national feeling had run for this powerful man who in many ways had always been a stranger to me.

And now, I must follow in his footsteps.

174

Chapter 6

TOSTIG REMEMBERS

I don't think it would be an exaggeration to say the death of our father shocked the whole nation. It's too bad his glorious return from exile was marred by my brother Swegn. It was always Swegn with him. Even in his absence Swegn had an undue influence on father, who rarely smiled that last year and aged visibly before our eyes. When word came back that Swegn had died on his pilgrimage, well that was the end of father, too. Or rather, the beginning of the end.

But in some ways, father's passing was a bit of a blessing for us, because King Edward needed Harold and me more than ever. And for some reason, the king chose to let his ill feelings die with our father. I always wondered whether he felt some guilt over the way he treated our family. It was very foolish to send us into exile, although he could never admit it. A king doesn't ask anyone for forgiveness.

Nonetheless, he made Harold Earl of Wessex at once, and because it was Easter he convened the Witan to confirm his appointment. I thought there might be some grumbling about Harold's new status, but the king took care of that. He gave Harold's vacant East Anglian earldom to Aelfgar, Leofric's son.

The only person disappointed was me! But nobody cared about my feelings. Harold, who was overwhelmed by his new honors, never thought to champion his little brother.

Though I admit, Aelfgar was given the earldom during our family's exile, and he lost it again when Harold returned. I always wondered how he felt about that. I know I would have stirred things up if it had been me! But I suppose it was only proper for the king to give it back to him and keep the peace.

So I bided my time. Since I had no earldom to keep me busy, I brought my wife to court and made myself useful to King Edward. My sweet Judith is a godly woman, and the king couldn't help but love her. She often attended mass in his company, and spent many hours with my sister Editha; her needlework is exquisite, and the Queen often asked her help with the most difficult pieces.

Harold's wife, on the other hand, was distasteful to the king. They were never properly married by the Church, and Edward couldn't abide that. I don't think the king liked Harold all that much, but my brother proved himself an able administrator and he kept his earldom in good order. There was no rancor between them, but I noticed Harold spent much of his time while in London at his own chancery, located near but separate from the king's palace. He was rarely seen at the king's side unless he had specific business.

King Edward loved to hunt, and I went with him almost every time he ventured out. I think his pleasure during those heady days even exceeded his religious fervor. He always got the kill, and the rest of us stepped back, never interfering unless he looked like he was in danger.

On the evenings after the hunt he was always in a happy mood, calling for more stories when the bard was in good fettle. He would reward the entertainers with silver—never gold—and fill my cup with the finest mead reserved for his own use. Luckily, he was not a great drinker because I don't like to overindulge; at least he usually slowed down before I felt sated. On quiet evenings I knew how to amuse him with board games, and always found ways to keep his restless spirit occupied.

176

The king loved Tostig and kept my brother at his side as much as possible. There were times when Edward seemed despondent, and Tostig was the only one who could cheer him up; he always seemed to know the right thing to say. And, I admit, sometimes I thought Tostig was my only friend, too... Editha

It was during the following year that I met young Malcolm, prince of Scotland. Earl Siward of Northumbria came south with a small force, bringing his nephew in tow. They were a colorful army, more show than force, and camped in a meadow outside the city walls. I liked Siward; he was a powerful man, towering over everyone in the room. Like his Danish forefathers, he wore his hair and beard long and braided, and he still liked to wear animal skins sewn together. They said it was colder in the north, so there was probably good reason for his preference.

King Edward hosted a grand feast for the earl, as they were planning a new campaign directed at Scotland: Siward wanted to put his nephew Malcolm on the throne, usurped by Macbeth. That was many years before, but perhaps by now Malcolm was grown enough to hold what would be won by the sword.

Harold was there, too, the great Earl of Wessex. I was still getting used to it, I admit. There were times I caught myself expecting to see father walk through the door, and I got my brother instead. What was it about Harold these days? Ever since becoming Earl of Wessex...well, he just wasn't the same. He had grown somewhat in stature, which was to be expected, I suppose. He wanted to be everyone's friend. He seemed to be wisdom itself, at least for those whose understanding was slight.

Watching his vanity drove me to distraction, but he never noticed. It was just as well; it was easy for me to walk away.

177

Edward invited us to stand behind him as we waited for the Dane to be announced. Siward and his household entered the great hall with a blast of trumpets and stomping of feet. Edward welcomed his guests warmly. The Earl of Northumbria bowed deeply to the king and gestured to his nephew, who bowed in turn.

Edward stood. "Welcome, my dear Earl. It has been too long."

Siward glanced quickly at Harold before starting his prepared speech. I think I knew why; he always had a cautious rivalry with our father, and I suspect he wondered if it was passed on to the sons. I, for one, had no interest in continuing any dissension. I was soon to learn that Harold was of the same mind; if anything, he seemed eager to spread a mantle of harmony over his fellow earls.

Once Siward's ceremonial greeting was finished, he brought Malcolm over to meet us. From the first, I liked this bluff, welcoming Scot. He was tall, like myself, with dark hair and beard and a strong body like mine. Harold gave him a quick warm welcome then let Siward pull him off to the side. I preferred the nephew. From his grin, I assumed he felt the same way about me.

"And what is this all about?" I asked my new acquaintance, pointing out a sideboard where we could pour ourselves some ale.

"Ah, my uncle means to help me get my inheritance back," he said amiably. "I have been his dependent too long." He took a deep draught and poured another.

"I heard Macbeth went on pilgrimage to Rome not long ago," I mused. Malcolm looked surprised. "Oh, King Edward knows about these things," I assured him. "Macbeth must have felt pretty secure to leave the kingdom."

That gave the prince pause, but not for long. "I fear that's about to change," he said, smiling again. "Now that Siward the Strong has shown an interest. He hopes to persuade King Edward to lend additional troops to his army."

178

I had suspected as much. "Many Normans have found their way north," I added, testing him.

Malcolm scratched his beard. "With their cavalry." It was simply said. Then he shrugged his shoulders. "It should be a good fight!"

As Siward came back and swept Malcolm away for more introductions, Harold paused by my side. "He means to ask Edward for aid," he said quietly. "And me. He offers great plunder."

Oh yes, plunder. That always pricked up the ears of a good soldier. They've been back and forth over the borders for generations looking for booty. Few mercenaries could resist its allure.

"Is it worth the effort?" I asked. Scotland was so far away.

Harold sighed. "Well, it will keep my men in good fighting mettle. If Edward approves, then I must also."

There was no real doubt. King Edward agreed with Siward that a friendly King of Scotland should help keep the northern part of Northumbria secure. Perhaps as a neighbor Siward could guide his nephew while he learned how to rule.

Harold went right to work summoning his select fyrd; this was volunteer duty only, but as Malcolm said, it would be a good fight. However, my brother was putting together another Welsh campaign and couldn't free himself for a trip to the north. He was studying a new *mappe* when I came up behind him and threw my sword dramatically on his table. Of course, he didn't jump in surprise; he never did.

"I have an idea," I said, "Why don't I go in your place?" He straightened and looked askance at me, then he shook his head. "No Tostig. I need you here, not on some fool's errand. The King wants you to inspect the construction works at his Cinque Ports."

I frowned. This is the first I heard of such a task.

179

"He told me this morning," he added, turning back to his table. "With your experience, you'll know what to look for. You have a good eye for such things."

Normally I would have chafed at his order, but I was a little flattered by the compliment. I nodded my agreement, but Harold was already too busy to notice.

"Very well, then. I shall speak with the king." I raised my voice since Harold had turned his back to me. He put up a hand in acknowledgement, then pointed with a quill at his *mappe*, speaking to one of his captains. I was dismissed.

I grabbed my sword, making sure to knock some papers from the table, but nobody noticed.

A few days later Prince Malcolm and I met at a local public house, for I was bored with waiting and he, too, was restless. Many of Harold's housecarls were already deep in their cups when the Scot came in, bringing a companion. He was a young man with smoldering eyes and a sharp way of looking about him.

"This is Walter, a countryman of mine," Malcolm said, sitting on a bench across from me and pulling a pitcher of ale toward him. He looked at his friend and the other nodded, holding forth a mug with a grin. "In fact, he is in your brother's service, but Harold has let him travel with us."

I was intrigued and thrust my head forward, taking a good luck at him. "If I didn't know better, I would say you were Welsh by your bearing and the cut of your hair," I said.

The other smiled. "I was raised in Wales," he said. "Which is why your brother finds me so useful. But my father was a Scot."

"And an old friend of mine, he was." Malcolm added, slapping Walter on the back.

"Ah." I sat back. "I see." Of course I understood Harold's interest. But what Malcolm wanted with the boy I didn't see at all. Not that it mattered to me.

"Oh, I am anxious to see my homeland again," the prince sighed, with a faraway look in his eyes. He was a little rough but he seemed to have the heart of a skald.

Then he shook his head. "We will trap that murderer in his lair and put him out of his misery. He has triumphed long enough. Eh, Walter?" He pulled out the biggest *knifr* I ever saw and drove its point into the table.

"I would have some food," he shouted to the nearest serving wench. She nodded at him.

"I will be there anon," she called. He turned back, satisfied.

"My uncle has planned to attack Macbeth by land and by sea. We will gather reinforcements as we march through Northumbria."

The woman came back with steaming platters. Malcolm slapped her on the rump and grabbed a bowl and a spoon. Not to be outdone, I did the same and we were happily filling our bellies when a new group came in the door, making even more noise than the noisy room around us. Their leaders were a pair of young nobles who seemed to enjoy pushing around their companions. Malcolm turned and looked at them then swung back, ignoring their shouts. A few mentioned his name but none of them spoke directly to us.

"Who are they?"

He grimaced. "Osbeorn, Siward's son and his cousin Neils. Well, they are my cousins too but I am an exile and an outsider." His mouth twitched, and there was more malice than merriment in his expression. "It's all right. I stay out of their way. I don't need their approval. If all goes well, I shall be a king and Osbeorn hopes to become an earl. Regardless, I shall outrank him!" He raised his mug and emptied it.

181

"But for now, I am nothing but a supplicant. It's a bitter draught, Tostig. I hope you never experience it."

Of course I experienced it. Our outlawry was too recent to forget. But Malcolm's had lasted fourteen years. I don't know how he tolerated it.

King Edward did his best to gratify Siward. He was in the habit of using Siward and Leofric to counter-balance my father, but now that Harold was Earl of Wessex it didn't seem necessary anymore. I don't think Siward thought much of my brother at all, though if he had been paying attention he would have seen that Harold wielded more power than father ever did. He was just quiet about it. More and more, Edward let Harold take on the burdens of governing, while the king concentrated on his favorite new project, Westminster Abbey.

The Earl's forces were finally gathered together. On the day of their departure, Edward had commissioned a great triumphal arch to be erected at Bishopsgate, bedecked with flowers and banners. Never mind that a triumph was for afterwards; everyone knew that Siward would win the day. The roadway was lined with cheering Londoners, for everyone loved a good demonstration. The great earl did not let them down. He was riding a large dappled horse with braided mane and tail, wearing his coronet and holding a long spear wrapped with flapping ribbons. Osbeorn and Malcolm rode behind him, then ranks and ranks of housecarls. Northumbrian soldiers followed Wessex in tightly ordered rows, waving to the pretty girls and occasionally bending over for a kiss. It was all very festive.

Edward had a little platform erected next to the arch and stood with my brother Harold; he held up his hand as though blessing the army while Siward rode past. The great earl nodded his head and continued without stopping. When Siward was safely out of sight, Harold brought a folding throne for the king. Edward

182

sat gratefully, watching the rest of the assemblage pass and acknowledging their cheers. Standing behind the king, my brother waved as well. I wondered whether the cheers were for Edward or for Harold? It was kind of hard to tell.

As expected, Siward's expedition to Scotland was a great success. The King's army returned loaded with plunder. Macbeth had fled the battlefield and Malcolm was declared victor, though he couldn't be crowned king as long as his predecessor still lived. However, he was installed in Lothian and ruled the south of Scotland, the most important territory anyway. Those Picts in the north were ungovernable, I had heard many times. Who needs the trouble?

Unfortunately for Siward, his son Osbeorn was killed in the battle, though I suspect Malcolm was secretly gratified to get rid of that snake. But the poor old earl had a weakness for his son, and he never recovered from Osbeorn's death. For the next year it is said he slowly failed, and I couldn't help but think of my father after Swegn's untimely demise. In the end, Siward had to die in bed; "like a cow" he is known to have said. This went against his Viking ethic, poor sot, so he had his people dress him in armor and give him an axe. That way he might trick his way into Valhalla. For his sake, I hope he succeeded. I had nothing against him.

His death left the earldom vacant. Siward had one surviving son, Waltheof, who was only ten. That would have been a disaster with all those vicious Norsemen angling for control. No, Waltheof was passed over and Edward saw fit to award the earldom to me. Finally! The king judged, rightly, that if he appointed an earl from within Northumbria he would cause a civil war. But I knew it was going to be a challenge. I was more Saxon than Danish and on top of that, a southerner. But I was up to the task. Nobody was going to push me around!

Especially that fool-born Aelfgar. I did not say a thing when he was made Earl of East Anglia. Nobody asked how I felt about it; I kept my disappointment to myself. But when it was finally my turn, the man went into a frenzy. I remember that day well. Why should he think he deserved the earldom more than me? I was next in line, and I think I'm the better man for the job.

King Edward had called a Witenagemot in Gloucester to announce my new appointment. As we were gathering in the hall, everything started pretty quiet. I had collected a group of retainers around me and we were waiting for the king to appear. Suddenly, we heard shouting from the back of the hall. Of course, we all turned to see what it was, and there was Aelfgar striding forward, pushing people out of the way.

Aelfgar was like a badger when he was angry. His father Leofric was short-legged and stout, and, although Aelfgar was taller than his sire, his body was long and his legs were still short. His blond beard bristled about his red face, making him look rather ugly. I think he had been drinking.

He stopped far behind me and shouted from a distance.

"Don't think this is going to be so easy. We don't need another Godwineson telling us what to do!"

The other earls, great and small, were so startled they fell silent. Then they all started arguing with each other.

Aelfgar wasn't finished. "They will rule over us all, I tell you! Why reward the man who went into exile? Why HIM instead of me?"

He was attacking me personally! I had nothing to do with my family's exile. It was quite unfair and I was trying to think of something fitting to say when Harold stepped out from behind the king's throne. He was shouting to be overheard, but at first no one listened. I wanted to go after Aelfgar but Harold put a hand on my arm. He strode forward instead, shouldering his way through the crowd. He stepped on a bench, towering over Aelfgar.

"How dare you disturb the king's court?" my brother bellowed.

That stopped Aelfgar for a moment, but he was too blinded by his rage.

"And YOU!" the badger shouted. "You think that just because you are the Earl of Wessex, you can step into your father's shoes? I spit on you!"

And he did. Harold made a fist but restrained himself.

"I spit on your whole family," Aelfgar continued, fighting off the hands trying to restrain him. "You made the king your thrall."

He jumped forward and tried to pull Harold off the bench. From all sides men were dragging them apart. Earl Leofric was shoving his way through the crowd but could not reach his son. I watched a couple of men run toward the door. The King's door. There was a lot of scuffling and then Harold and Aelfgar stood breathing heavily, straining toward each other. The place was in an uproar.

Suddenly the king's door flew open and Edward stepped through, in a righteous rage. It was obvious someone told him what Aelfgar said. The hall fell silent as we all bowed. Edward sat on his throne, gripping the arms.

"Earl Aelfgar, come forward."

Aelfgar had to straighten his tunic first. He looked a fright. I never saw a man so pale. Taking a deep breath, he advanced to the throne and went down on one knee.

"Sire," he breathed. "I misspoke myself. I was not in control."

No matter what he said, I don't think it would have made a difference.

"Aelfgar Leofricson I declare you a traitor!" Edward growled, pointing at the fool. I almost felt sorry for him. "You have shamed your father and your earldom! I give you four days to leave this country!"

Aelfgar stood up, hanging his head. Everybody backed away as his father pushed through and grabbed him by the arm.

"Go. Now." The King seemed suddenly tired.

Leofric led his submissive son away. Well, submissive isn't the right word. Stunned is more like it. Aelfgar would never submit to anyone. Men turned and watched as they made their way to the rear of the hall, then out. Neither father nor son looked back.

Edward sat for a few minutes and no one dared speak. Finally, he held out his hand to Harold, who gave him the chain of office he had been carrying. The king took the chain and beckoned me forward. I knelt as he leaned toward me.

"I'm sorry, Tostig," he said quietly. "It wasn't supposed to happen this way."

I really didn't care. I was never one for a big display.

The king put a hand on my shoulder then stood. "It is my wish that Tostig Godwineson rule as Earl of Northumbria. Are you with me?"

"Aye. Aye. Aye." I don't think they were unanimous, but I also don't think anyone dared object. Perhaps Aelfgar did me a favor after all.

If anyone doubted Aelfgar was a traitor, it wasn't long before he showed his true colors. Once he left the country, Aelfgar went right over to Dublin, just like my brother Harold, and took refuge with Diarmaid Mac Mael-na-mbo. He raised eighteen ships to raid England! Unlike my brother, who only used the mercenary fleet to reestablish himself, Aelfgar used his hired ships to join forces with our enemy, Gruffydd ap Llewelyn, Prince of Wales. Together they started to raid our borders, seizing wagonsful of plunder, burning towns, taking slaves. Gruffydd and Aelfgar attacked and killed the Prince's rival in South Wales, making Gruffydd sole ruler. Then they headed for Hereford.

186

Hereford is a very important border town. It was under the charge of Earl Ralf, the nephew of King Edward. Ralf was an odd fellow; he wasn't difficult to get along with, considering he was a Norman. But he insisted we bring in cavalry and retrain our own people to fight on horseback. This was something we just don't do unless we have to. But he would have his way and the king refused to interfere.

Ralf wouldn't listen to any of us when we insisted that the best way for Saxons to fight was on foot, shoulder to shoulder, shield to shield, presenting a solid front to the enemy. Oh, no. Ralf was too civilized for that. Didn't he realize that, broken down into individual fighting units—man and horse—each mounted warrior was exposed on all sides? How can they defend each other?

What happened was even worse than I would have imagined. Earl Ralf dutifully lined up his cavalry on the field outside of Hereford, waiting for the Welsh to come. And when they did come...what a disaster! Those barbarians ran forward, screaming and throwing their spears and waving their swords, and the horses took one look, turned tail, and ran. They bolted in the opposite direction, taking Earl Ralph with them. It was a rout, pure and simple. There never was a fight, except for all the defenders getting slaughtered when the Welsh caught up with them.

Those devils knew what to do, and were very efficient. Poor Hereford didn't stand a chance. Over four hundred good Saxons were killed, and not one of the enemy! It was a disgrace. Then the Welsh overran the town, killing the poor priests who tried to defend the church. They looted the relics, the vestments, and the treasures before burning the church to the ground. My heart breaks just to tell of it. Such a sacrilege.

After the destruction of Hereford, Earl Ralf was deemed unfit to defend such an important marcher town—what was left of it. Now they call him Ralph the Timid. He was deprived of his earldom, formerly ruled by my even more unfit brother Swegn.

King Edward commanded Harold to take over and rebuild the defenses. It was a good choice; Harold knew what to do and set about it with his usual energy.

HAROLD REMEMBERS

Ever since I was a boy I heard of October as the blood month, but I never gave the name much thought until I had an earldom to rule. I always assumed it had something to do with slaughtering the animals for winter. But now I reckon it means that once the harvest is in, men start to think about plundering someone else's barn. And so it proved in October 1055 when the Welsh and Irish Danes raided over the border into England.

Aelfgar started it all. East Anglia wasn't enough for him; when Tostig was appointed Earl of Northumbria he lost his head over it and made such an outcry that Edward exiled him. Looking back, I suppose Edward's reaction could have been too severe, but at the time it seemed justified. Aelfgar's own father couldn't control him, and he certainly couldn't control himself. Once free from restraint, he raised a force of mercenaries and went over to our enemy, the Prince of Wales.

Gruffydd ap Llewelyn was always looking for an excuse to expand his borders. No, that's not right. He didn't need an excuse. He took advantage of an opportunity and fell on Hereford like a bear going after a honey hive. King Edward's nephew Ralph was the wrong man for Hereford's defense, and Gruffydd knew it. Ralph spent so much time and gold building his palace of stone he never paid attention to the town's crumbling walls.

The English were badly served that day, for Ralph is accused of being the first to flee the enemy. I don't know if that's true, but it is certain he left the town undefended, and was either beaten or in hiding when the raiders overran and plundered poor Hereford.

Word soon reached Gloucester, where I was in attendance on the king along with many of my peers. We were witnessing charters that day, a favorite task of Edward's which invariably put him in a good mood. Alas, he needed a strong frame of mind to face the events that were to come.

An old soldier was announced into the hall; he was not of my acquaintance but the king seemed to know him. Edward quickly exchanged glances with me before putting down his quill and beckoning the man forward.

When the news is good, you can tell right away. When the news is bad, you can tell even quicker. The man must have ridden hard, because he was limping and, more to the point, he was dirty. He dropped rather than knelt before the king and bowed his head, waiting for permission to speak.

"Go on," Edward said, solemnly.

"Sire, there has been a terrible massacre."

"Massacre?" Everyone in the room stepped forward at that word.

"Hereford..." Something caught in the man's throat and he took a ragged breath. "Hereford was set upon by a large force of Welsh, Danes, and Irish, led by Gruffydd ap Llewelyn." He raised his head to stare at Earl Leofric, who had slipped forward between two burly Cheshire men. "And Aelfgar Leofricson."

I could see by the stricken look on Leofric's face he had no suspicion of his son's activities. I almost felt sorry for him when the king whirled around in anger.

"Your son is responsible for this!" he rasped. Then he whirled back.

"How serious is the damage?" Edward was bending over the man and looked like a priest giving benediction.

"Sire, the town was burned to the ground. The church... They murdered the priests who were defending the doors and

189

plundered the building before setting it on fire." He had to stop, because Edward was swaying on his feet. I rushed forward and caught the king before he crumpled to the floor. Many hands helped me place him gently on his throne, and someone thrust a cup of wine into his face. I took the cup and held it until he grasped it with trembling hands.

The old soldier stayed on one knee all this time, waiting to finish. Edward handed the wine back to me and slumped in his chair.

"What happened to Earl Ralph?"

The man grimaced. "He was seen fleeing from the Welsh, along with his precious cavalry. They were the first to turn and run, leaving the rest of us leaderless. We fought as best as we could, but they were like devils! Once they smelled our blood they came after us with such lust in their eyes. Lust for slaughter!" He finally broke down and put his face in his hands, shoulders shaking.

"Sire, it was terrible. They overran the town, murdering poor citizens, pulling down doors and grabbing whatever they could carry before setting fire to the houses. Women and children were screaming as they dragged them away to make slaves of them, or worse. I cannot tell you more. I was wounded in the leg and decided I would be of better use coming to you here."

"You have done enough," Edward sighed, putting a hand to his forehead. "Go. Take care of your wounds."

I nodded to Torr who helped the man away. It seemed he had used up the last of his strength relating the disaster.

The room was silent; I don't think I was the only man holding his breath. Finally Edward raised his head, looking around.

"Where is Leofric?"

We looked to where the Earl had been standing. He was not there now.

"Harold." The King leaned toward me though his eyes were still searching for Leofric. "Raise an army. Now. Go after them before it's too late. Raise a force from all of England. The Welsh must be stopped."

I bowed and left the room, followed by my retainers. I had no idea what I had just taken on.

I tarried at Gloucester as long as I could, waiting for the fyrd to answer my summons. When I determined that my host was big enough, we marched over the border into Wales, heavily armed and expecting a ferocious battle. Camping in the marcher district of Straddele, I sent out scouts in search of Gruffydd's army. They returned in some confusion, unable to locate a single man, even outriders. I had to make a choice: should I penetrate farther into enemy territory, or give up for the season?

Already the weather was starting to turn ugly. We had not come prepared for an extended campaign, and my men only had food for a few days. To make matters worse there were no roads, no paths through the forest, and very little water. For a day and a half we made a desultory advance heading south until one of my scouts returned with the first bit of news. He had found the remains of a camp, but it had been deserted for some time. Apparently my enemy had moved into south Wales.

This was pointless. I was wasting time and resources. I looked at my men whose faces told me everything. They wanted to go home.

"All right," I announced. "All of you who are not from my Wessex, return to your homes but be prepared if I have to call you suddenly. Until I know where Gruffydd and Aelfgar are heading, we are all still in danger. But understand this: we are not finished with them. If we don't fight this year, we will be back in force."

I don't think they cared about the future. My sub-commanders gave their orders and they started to disperse without even camping for the night. I didn't blame them.

I ordered my scouts to keep looking for the enemy forces; many of them lived nearby and had an interest in keeping their homes safe. The rest of my men came with me. I had yet to see what was left of Hereford.

Yes, I was expecting the worst. But it was so much more appalling than I imagined. As we rode toward Edward's important border town, even the outlying houses were burned. I passed bent figures still picking through their ruined belongings, carrying burnt timbers and throwing them onto waste piles. Some were attempting to salvage what was left of a ruined crop. But other buildings were desolate, without a human or animal in sight. A newly dug mound was all I needed to guess the fate of their owners.

The town was in even worse condition. A few broken-down old men held out a hand for a piece of bread. More remnants of houses were being carted away. Some structures retained partial walls, and people were weaving wattle and daub partitions to create a new shelter. I didn't see any children though I did notice a few women staring carefully at me from a safe distance.

We made our way to the church, still partially intact. One of the walls had fallen away, but part of the roof survived. Two priests came out as I dismounted.

"Bishop Aethelstan?" I asked, dreading their response. I knew he was old and blind, and his long tenure was legendary.

"He lives still," one of the clerics assured me. "Abed in the sacristy of the church."

I followed them inside. Light was coming in through big gaps in the roof. Luckily, the sacristy was tucked behind the altar and its door had already been repaired. The little room provided a bit of shelter for the Archbishop.

The poor man tried to sit up as I entered, but I hastened to his bed, encouraging him to lay down again. After a brief struggle he gave up and fell back, gasping for breath. I sat on the edge of his pallet, taking his hand.

"Rest, your Grace. We need you to stay with us."

He turned his head toward me. "I fear my work is finished, Earl Harold," he said weakly. "My flock is dispersed." A tear worked its way down his cheek.

"Not all of them." I tried to sound reassuring. "And we will rebuild.

"It was terrible," he muttered. I had to move my ear close to his lips. "I tried to summon the wrath of God, but they laughed at me. We are being punished for our sins."

I crossed myself. It was not my place to correct an Archbishop. Getting up, I ceded my place to one of the monks who knelt with a cup of broth.

What I needed was to work. Nothing else was going to help. Stepping from the building, I looked around me. The church doors had been torn asunder; there was wreckage everywhere. Silently I pointed up the hill where I expected to see Ralph's castle.

"They tore it down," one of the priests said. "Stone by stone they dismantled the castle. It is all rubble."

I blinked. Rubble. "Building material," I muttered. "We need walls around this town."

Luckily I had brought a good number of men with me, for we were going to need every available set of hands. Men were relieved to be given direction, so I started a work crew to clear a space in the village center. We set up a common kitchen. We repaired the stables, for we would soon replenish the stock. I sent to King Edward for more help, then we went to work building some temporary structures to get us through the winter. Since the populace was greatly reduced in numbers, sadly we didn't need that many houses.

193

But Hereford was too important to let languish. It would be repopulated in time, and from now on it would be properly protected.

Once new recruits showed up, we started the difficult but necessary task of building a perimeter wall. We dug a large ditch all the way around and flung the dirt on the inside edge. Soon we had a dike we strengthened with the rubble from Ralph's useless castle. Later on we would build a proper wall, but the earthwork would serve for now. We left four openings for gates, which would be fortified by wooden entryways.

The residents were cheered by having a task to work on, and rebuilding progressed at a good pace. It was my town now, and I added my own labor to my men's efforts, which seemed to make everybody work even harder. We built a wooden longhouse for the community, which served us well during the winter. By then, a few of my housecarls seemed willing to settle here themselves, since they had made Hereford their own.

I wasn't to know until later, but Herefordshire would become attached to Wessex, which made it mine in fact rather than just a royal command. I established a permanent garrison and enlisted one of my men who had been raised in that god-forsaken country to give them training in the Welsh manner. Next time, we would be better prepared to fight Gruffydd on his own terms.

But I couldn't stay on as long as I wanted. My scouts had finally discovered the whereabouts of Aelfgar, who apparently had separated from the Prince of Wales. Actually, I think the disgraced earl was ready to be found. I was beginning to think he would be less trouble under the watchful eye of the king rather than running loose with our enemies. I rode to Gloucester and confided my thoughts to Edward. It turned out he agreed with me—especially after having words with Earl Leofric.

"Our Earl of Mercia has shown himself most anxious to make amends," Edward said to me over a cup of warmed cider.

"His son humiliated him and he swore to bring him back to the fold. If he can ever find him."

I cleared my throat. "That's why I have come, Sire. I think my men have done that very thing. Much as I hate to pardon him..."

I paused, thinking about how hard it was for my own family to return from outlawry. And here I was facing the king, the author of that misadventure. I shook my head, ridding myself of such an unworthy thought.

"He could cause us much more mischief running loose in Wales," I finished.

"I know. I fear you are right. If we offered him his earldom back..."

It was Edward's time to pause. I think he remembered that East Anglia was my old earldom, more than Aelfgar's.

"With your permission, I will offer him terms," I said, hating the thought.

"Do as you see fit," Edward concluded. My sister was coming into the room and she kissed me on the cheek.

"Harold," she said warmly. "Are you staying?"

"No, dear. He must return at once to Hereford," the king answered in my stead. I would have liked to have stayed the night, but Edward took care of that. Bowing, I left the room. I don't think the king liked me very much, though he certainly found me useful.

Returning to Hereford in the rain, I was chilled to the bone as I made my way to the fire pit in the center of the longhouse. Servants were on hand to strip off my dripping clothes and wrap me in a blanket. I soon began to relax as I spooned some steaming gruel down my throat. Exhaustion soon caught up with me and I fell asleep right on the bench. It was the best sleep I had in weeks.

The following day, I went in search of my Welsh trainer Walter. I knew he and Aelfgar were distant kin—and Gruffydd too—though I knew precious little else about him. Who would be better than he to speak directly with our errant earl?

I found him at the archery butts, demonstrating to a desultory group of volunteers. They didn't look very promising. No matter...I beckoned him over and he hung his bow on a tree branch.

"They need much practice," I said, having trouble starting the conversation. Even though it was my idea, I hated having to go to Aelfgar and I couldn't get used to it.

Following my gaze, Walter looked over at his men doubtfully. "Their hearts are not in it, I'm afraid. They still view the bow as a serf's weapon, or at best, to be used only for hunting. They still don't realize how important this skill is against the Welsh. But we will keep at it."

"Ahem. Good. Meanwhile, Walter," I said, putting an arm around his shoulders, "there is something I would ask you to do. You are under no obligation, of course. But I think we can get Aelfgar to parley with us. I know where he is right now; he is separated from Gruffydd. Have you ever met him?"

Walter shook his head. That was too bad.

"No matter. Whatever it takes, if you can get Aelfgar alone...perhaps we can persuade him to abandon his worthless cause."

"It may not be worthless to him."

"Ravaging English land? Can you really justify that?" I couldn't stop myself. Walter wasn't making this any easier for me.

"It is not for me to justify anything," he said calmly. "You seek to deal with Aelfgar, remember. What do you want me to do?"

"Talk to him, argue with him. You can see what I am getting at, surely!"

"Oh, I see. When you said 'we', I thought you were coming along."

This was maddening. "Of course not. It would be too dangerous to place myself in his power."

"But less dangerous to me..."

"As kin, Walter! He will not harm you."

Considering this, he reluctantly agreed. I let out my breath.

"I think you will find yourself a welcome guest," I added, regaining my confidence. "King Edward has authorized me to offer Aelfgar back his earldom. And total forgiveness. Losing his position is what angered him in the first place. I doubt he'll refuse."

I had been so certain that Walter would agree I had already outfitted a horse for him. His guide was standing by as well—another Welshman. I hoped they would get along well enough.

Walter was riding into danger and he knew it. But, having committed himself to my plan, he went willingly enough. I stood at the gate and watched them melt into the forest.

As I suspected, Aelfgar was more than ready to accept King Edward's terms. He immediately disbanded his troop of mercenaries and returned to Mercia. I understand his allies took ship to Chester and waited to get paid; where the money came from, I didn't have the will to ask. At the Christmas gemot Edward reinstated Aelfgar in his earldom and all was as before. With the exception of poor Hereford. And Gruffydd, of course.

Did the Prince of Wales expect a gift in his turn? Deserted by his ally Aelfgar, once again he started his same old raids across the border. Before long, he was making stabbing attempts at Herefordshire. Probably the only thing that saved my town from another attack was the fact that nothing was left to plunder. Still, I feared for the safety of our borders. My other duties weighed heavily on my mind, and I determined to appoint someone in my place to keep building Hereford's defenses.

197

I had just the person in mind: my own chaplain, the vigorous Leofgar. Well-trained in the military disciplines, he had chosen the way of the church instead. But I knew how efficient he was and I had him appointed Bishop of Hereford. "Be vigilant," I told him. "The Welsh are treacherous people. I could not catch them when I went after them. We must concentrate on strengthening our defenses. There will be time to deal with them later."

Leofgar went off in great pomp while I stayed in Chester with the king. Looking back, I wish I had been firmer with my instructions, for only three months later he took it upon himself to attack Gruffydd at the first sign of trouble. The fool took his priests, my good sheriff Aelfnoth, and many volunteers I could not afford to spare. The Welsh must have given them a merry chase, for they were ambushed in the valley of Machfwy, many miles from the border. Leofgar was killed with his mace in his hand and a great gash to his head, his long moustaches covered with mud. Such a terrible waste.

By now I had gotten the measure of these troublesome people. You can't fight them on their own ground; they just melt away, using paths and crevices they have walked since childhood. If an army tries to follow them, the Welsh will ambush by day and raid by night, rather than stand and fight. They would wear an enemy down from exhaustion. My army tried a half-hearted chase just to avenge Leofgar, but I soon recalled them. There must be a better way.

King Edward was still in Chester and called a Witenagemot to discuss the Welsh problem. Bishop Ealdred was in attendance, freshly returned from the continent. Now they called him Ealdred the Peacemaker. He was the same man who brought Swegn back from his outlawry because he needed help ruling Herefordshire. It was in my mind to ask him to take Leofgar's place, since he had governed there before. The man had more strength of will than anyone I ever met.

Earl Leofric was already at the gemot, since Chester was in his earldom. Apparently he was still making amends, for I could see he was very attentive to the king. Aelfgar, of course, stayed away.

I could see Edward was in one of his petulant moods; he was often this way when things went awry. The king tapped impatiently on the book he was holding as the other thegns and vassals filled the hall. I saw Tostig come in, but I couldn't catch his eye.

"This so-called Prince of Wales," the king finally started. He practically spit the words. "This Gruffydd has been a thorn in my side. How do you propose we shall deal with him?"

He looked directly at me; I knew I had to be careful with how I answered. I stepped forward, stood below his throne and faced the room. "Gruffydd ap Llewelyn has been raiding across the border again," I started slowly, looking at the faces before me. Most of them were unhappy but not hostile. "He moves quickly and his aim seems to be plunder. He is difficult to confront."

"We must put an end to his depredations!" Edward shouted over my words.

I took a deep breath, waiting for the uproar to settle down. Bishop Ealdred stepped up beside me.

"I suggest we negotiate with the Prince of Wales," he said loudly. "No need to waste more precious lives."

Even Edward paused. Ealdred had that effect on people. But the king wasn't ready to give up his temper.

"Make peace with that traitor and oath-breaker? I would rather send him to the depths of hell!"

I certainly understood how he felt; how humiliating to give in to such a man as him. On the other hand, we did give Aelfgar back his earldom after Hereford. There wasn't much difference between them.

"We can reason with him," Ealdred continued. "Surely he has no more to gain with his ceaseless raiding."

199

Aside from more plunder, I thought. I was a little doubtful about the whole thing, but it was worth a try. I decided to join my voice to Bishop Ealdred's. "I agree. Let us send a messenger to arrange a meeting."

Edward leaned over and consulted with his Norman advisors. Then he stood.

"Very well. Earl Leofric, you are my most effective negotiator. I would have you bring your skills to bear."

Leofric stood as well, surprised and not very enthusiastic. He bowed. "As you wish, sire."

Now, this presented both of us with a dilemma. Edward was well aware of the deep division between both our houses. Perhaps we needed Ealdred's peacemaking skills to keep us from tearing each other apart.

We soon had the opportunity to find out. Surprisingly, Gruffydd agreed to a peace conference and in a short time we were on our way to him. Taking a small retinue, Leofric, Ealdred and I set out from Gloucester to meet the Prince of Wales. At first the old earl avoided me, but by the second evening he sat down beside me as I enjoyed my meal at a makeshift camp table. I poured some wine into his cup.

"Thank you, Earl Harold." He took a sip, deep in thought, then looked at me. "Perhaps I have been mistaken about you."

That was a surprise! His gesture demanded a response.

"Earl Leofric. You are most generous."

He grimaced, though I attributed it to the wine. "I do this because I am commanded to," he continued. "But also to make amends for the foolishness of my son." He looked me in the eye, nodding as though willing me to understand. "You do this because it is your duty, and I respect you for this."

He said nothing more, but I appreciated his gesture.

Ealdred came up behind me. "Leofric is an important man," he said quietly. "Peace between our great earls is best for our country. Do not waste this gift."

I was willing, and for the rest of the trip we traveled side-by-side. We didn't have much to say to each other, but I found comfort in knowing we had common cause. To get through this parley we were sure to need all the goodwill we could summon up.

We met the Prince of Wales not far from Chester, on the Welsh side of the border in a territory he had illegally appropriated from England. Of course this added to the insult, but we needed something to bargain with and this land was just the answer. If Edward awarded the territory to Gruffydd officially, perhaps this would give him incentive to compromise.

As we approached Gruffydd's encampment, we all dismounted and stood at a distance, willing him to meet us halfway. Alas, he was too clever for that and sent a representative to greet us. Three representatives, actually. They were short and wiry men—as were many of their race—but bore themselves proudly. Their spokesman gave us a partial bow.

"My King sends his greetings." I winced at his words, knowing Gruffydd claimed the title after Aelfgar helped him destroy his rival. But it took more than brute force to make a king.

"King Gruffydd ap Llewelyn ap Seislit is prepared to welcome King Edward's representatives and has sent me to lead you. If you would come this way..." He gestured toward Gruffydd's encampment.

I heard Leofric grunt beside me. "The king's representatives, indeed," he growled. "I have half a mind to put him in his place..."

"Before he puts us in ours," I finished. "We can give him this little triumph, I think, rather than fail at our mission."

"As long as we keep our arms," he mumbled under his breath. I remembered that Gruffydd had killed Leofric's brother about fifteen years before. Trust was not foremost in the old earl's mind.

"Then we shall not give them a chance to disarm us." I strode forward and the others followed close behind. Luckily, the Welsh didn't ask us to give up our arms.

Gruffydd ap Llewelyn was sitting in a throne under a striped linen canopy, flanked by two warriors who stood stiff and straight with long lances angled forward. The so-called King of Wales was a large man with a thick red beard and a shock of red hair, swarthy cheeks and fiery eyes.

Bishop Ealdred was the one who stepped forward. "Prince Gruffydd," he said. "Your people and our people on the borders suffer greatly. I propose we find a mutually acceptable solution to our disagreements."

Gruffydd shrugged. "And what do you propose, exactly?"

"King Edward has authorized us to set up a meeting between you and him. If you would swear to be a faithful under-king, he is prepared to grant you full possession of the disputed border territories."

"Which I own already," Gruffydd snapped.

Ealdred dismissed him with a wave of his hand. "Truly not. Otherwise they would not be disputed."

"Hmm. And what more can he offer?"

"A cessation of hostilities would be desired by God."

"Hmm. Your King Edward does not present much of an argument."

Leofric stepped forward. He was a short man but carried himself with his chest thrust out, giving him an air of command. "Prince Gruffydd," he said, trying to sound respectful. "Surely you have no more to gain and much to lose by continuing your invasions."

"Oh, and how is that?" Gruffydd's eyes rested on Leofric's sword. His hands unconsciously curled into fists and I could see his lower arms bulge.

"England is a wealthy country," Leofric continued, ignoring Gruffydd's marital stance. "We have many, many more
202

warriors we can bring into Edward's service. Earl Harold is training them to fight as we speak. You are not a rich country. You have few warriors and cannot resupply. If we put our minds to it, we can overturn your advantage. It's just a matter of time and effort."

Leofric spoke a thinly veiled threat but Gruffydd saw the logic in it. The earl was right; we had the advantage. Gruffydd shifted in his seat.

"Very well. I agree to meet with King Edward at a place of his choosing."

I bowed my head to show my relief. Earl Leofric had done it again.

In due time, there was a meeting between Gruffydd and King Edward. Promises were made, treaties signed, territory ceded. As we broke up the meeting, Edward seemed satisfied enough but I don't think any of us were fooled. We had bought a brief peace, during which I would continue to train our men and rebuild Hereford.

TOSTIG REMEMBERS

Harold went after the Prince of Wales with a single-minded determination that would be hard for anybody to withstand. Nonetheless, Gruffydd was a formidable man. Tall and strong, he commanded almost suicidal loyalty—until Harold and I came along, that is. Before Gruffydd's rule, his country was fractured into little pieces, each one controlled by its own territorial prince. He brought them all together, north and south, finally killing his rival with the help of Aelfgar. That was right before Hereford. I would have admired him, if he wasn't my enemy.

I remember the time afterwards when King Edward met him from across the Severn River, which bordered on his territory. Both of those rulers stared at each other from opposite banks without moving, because neither one wanted to give up the advantage by making the first gesture. It went on for several minutes like that, until Gruffydd got impatient and just strode into the water. It wasn't all that deep, mind you, but he was a prince after all, and it was most undignified.

But Edward was so impressed that he got into a boat and met Gruffydd halfway. Then Gruffydd embraced the boat and plucked Edward out of it like he was a piece of wood, and settled him on his broad shoulders. I wish I could have seen the look on Edward's face while he was being carried to the far shore, but of course his back was to me at that point. It's just as well: none of us could help but laugh, he looked so absurd.

It turned out to be a wise gesture on Gruffydd's part, because Edward was probably more cooperative than he otherwise would have been. As it turned out, the whole treaty was wasted, because as we saw, Gruffydd broke it at his first opportunity.

Chapter 7

TOSTIG REMEMBERS

Although King Edward was occupied with Wales, I had my own new earldom to think about. Northumbria hadn't been visited by an English King since Canute's early days. They have been left alone for decades, and even old Siward—Dane that he was—was considered an outsider.

For many years, the eastern half of my earldom was divided into two provinces: Northumberland to the north and Yorkshire to the south. A large mountain range separates east from west, leaving precious little lowlands for farming. In the west, Siward had recently annexed Scottish Cumbria and Cumberland—absorbing the old kingdom of Strathclyde as well— so he could control the invasion routes through the Tyne Gap and Stainmoor. Where once there were two rulers in Northumbria and the king of Scotland in Strathclyde, now there was a mighty earldom extending from the North Sea to the Irish Sea, and from the Tweed to the Humber. Finally, a worthy challenge!

Siward had built a palace at York, in a district called Earlsburh; his residence crowned a hilltop next to the church of St. Olaf which he built and where he was buried. Thither I determined to go since it was probably the most defensible spot in York. Judith insisted on accompanying me, and although I feared for her safety the dear girl didn't want to be parted from me again. So we determined to travel with our whole household, wagons, furnishings and all. Why delay? My entourage consisted of a substantial force of retainers, guards, and mercenaries; I reckoned we were too numerous to be attacked. I reckoned wrongly, as it turned out.

As we left the familiarity of East Anglia, we soon noticed that the population dwindled. Villages sat farther and farther apart, ancient forests closed in on us; I was glad of the old Roman road, still in passable condition. Occasionally we spotted a stealthy group of ruffians, who looked willing enough to attack us except for our numbers. I noted how they followed us, sometimes for miles. But we did not relax our vigilance, not for a moment.

This was going to be the first task I would undertake, I vowed. No one should have to fear for their life just to travel from place to place.

We stopped at many of the homesteads along the way, welcoming a drink of water or a basket of fresh eggs and leaving a donation behind. I tried to question them, but for the most part they would not confide in me, for they couldn't recognize I was their new earl. Well, that would come in time.

After we had been on the road for a week, there were no more villages for us to stay in and we were obliged to set up our tents along the highway. The non-combatants were lodged in the center and the rest of us ranged ourselves around them, as far as the edge of the forest would allow.

It was Freya's day. We were still erecting shelters for the night when I turned, hearing a sharp crack; someone had stepped on a branch in the gloomy forest. I suppose the need for silence had been broken as well, for the most alarming shrieks assailed our ears. A horde of villains burst out of the forest with murder on their faces. We were not prepared to fight, but most of us wore our swords out of habit and we barely drew our blades when they were upon us.

The man next to me was down in an instant with an arrow in his shoulder. I didn't even have the chance to help him before

206

two of the attackers ran at me. I blocked the sword of the first and followed through with a wild slash at the second which luckily connected. He turned away, howling. I couldn't recover quickly, though, and expected to be struck at any moment when the first man fell on top of me, a sword sticking out of his back. My defender pulled out his blade and shoved the dead man aside, giving me a hand. I scrambled to my feet with just enough time to stop my other attacker who apparently came back for more. Striking aside his blade, I sank my sword deep into his thigh. He wasn't getting away this time.

The fight was over as quickly as it started. Some of the outlaws were escaping into the forest, but others were squirming on the ground and a few had thrown their weapons down in surrender. Unfortunately, I lost five men in my own company. I was outraged.

"Tie the bastards up," I shouted, and my men were not loth to obey. Kneeling down, I helped my prone companion sit up. He grimaced and looked down at the arrow. "We need a surgeon," I hollered, tearing his garment from the wound. Our healer came up and together we laid the man back down again; I held him firmly while the other pulled the arrow from his shoulder. Fortunately it came out cleanly and I left him to tend the wound.

I had to find Judith. I ran toward what I thought was our wagon. No Judith. Then I stumbled toward the cooking area. She was not there. Turning around, I frantically shouted her name. A couple of women shook their heads, then I heard her calling me. She was bent over one of our servants, tying up a wound. I knelt next to my wife, gathering her into my arms.

"I'm all right, my dear." She kissed me on the cheek then turned back to her work. She was so brave.

That was all I needed to know. By the time I returned to the prisoners, my guards had shoved the captives, healthy and wounded, into a tight little group. Some were sitting on the ground, others stood up boldly, arms crossed. I strode over to the meanest looking rogue who scowled at me.

"Do you know who I am?" I growled.

He spat on the ground. "No."

"Who is your leader?"

"We have no leader."

I punched him as hard as I could in the mouth. His head snapped back but he faced me again.

"Who is your master?"

This time he spat out a tooth. I hit him again.

"Who do you serve?" I pulled out my sword and placed the tip below his chin.

He seemed to think better of his arrogance, because he glanced down. I waited.

"Gamel son of Orm sent us," he mumbled, wiping his mouth with the back of a bloody hand. That gave me an idea.

"Outlaws, all of them," I said, raising my voice. "They would have killed us if they could and deserve to die." I watched as my men eagerly grabbed them by the arms. "But wait. Cut off their hands instead, so they can spread the word that Earl Tostig Godwineson has come to claim Northumbria." I gestured to the edge of the field. "That boulder should serve."

For a moment everyone stared at me in surprise. Then two of my retainers dragged the man I had first selected over to the boulder. By now he was struggling, but one of my men kicked the feet from under him. A third helped heave him over to the rock, pulling his arms tight while a fourth man swung an axe. The blade struck his wrist with a sickening thud—drowned out by a horrible scream—followed by the second wrist. By then, the next prisoner was being tugged forward, struggling and begging for mercy though they would have certainly shown us none. His hands were struck off and he was shoved aside to make room for the next.

They were fourteen in all, and we served our rough justice efficiently and quickly. I stood and watched until every villain had been dealt with, then together we turned our backs on them, leaving a pile of bloody hands as our retribution. They were no threat to us now, so we let them go.

It was too late in the day to move our camp away from this ugly scene, but we still had enough time to bury our own dead. It was only fitting that their fallen be left to the wolves; there were enough corpses to provide a good meal. We posted extra guards that night, though no further trouble came from Gamel son of Orm and his hired killers. At least not that day. I don't think any of us slept well, and we were off extra early in the morning. As we rode slowly past yesterday's battlefield, the ravens rose into the air, squawking at us. But they didn't fly any great distance before settling down to resume their meal.

I brought my horse next to Judith's wagon. She was understandably restrained, and even looked a little pale. I reached over and took her hand.

"This is a harsh earldom," she said quietly. "I am not used to so much violence."

I restrained myself from reminding her I had suggested she stay behind. That wouldn't help now.

"Look what they made you do." She rested her brown eyes on me; her sad face almost broke my heart.

"We must match the punishment to the crimes," I said, looking forward. "I will make these roads safe if I have to kill every outlaw in the north."

For a few minutes we rode in silence. "There is no other way," I pursued. "This is the only justice they understand."

She reached behind her and tucked a blanket around our wounded servant.

"They would have killed us all," I reminded her. I felt like I was making excuses. "Judith, I wonder if they knew who I was and tried to stop me."

209

She turned back, surprised. I don't think she considered this possibility.

"I am an outsider, and a southerner. This will not be easy for us. I may already have more enemies than I know."

"You will know what to do," she finally said. I knew she would support me no matter what happened.

The night before we reached York, we rested in Tadcaster on the River Wharfe. This was a sizeable market town with a river ford, and we were all able to acquire lodging for the night. By now, word of our approach had preceded us and the local residents treated me with the respect I deserved.

I instructed my followers to rub down the horses, clean the wagons, put on their best clothing in the morning. My warriors were ordered to don their chain maille. We needed to look our best as we entered my capital city, and I especially wanted to be seen as a formidable leader. Judith was to ride beside me as befitted their countess. I wanted people to understand that I was a man to be reckoned with. And I was here to stay.

I wasn't exactly expecting a joyful greeting, but neither was I expecting to be snubbed. What we encountered was indifference. Passing through Micklegate bar, I took note of the crumbling Roman walls that the Danes had fortified with mounds of earth topped by a wooden palisade. The city seemed secure enough, at least from the south. Timbered houses lined both sides of the street, leaning together like I remembered from London. We crossed the River Ouse on the wooden bridge and entered the old part of the city. We rode in ordered ranks, myself and my lady in the front followed by my housecarls, my liveried retainers, my train...all the rest. There were a few citizens watching from the side of the road, but many others paid us no mind at all.

This was my first time to York, so I didn't really know where to go and I certainly couldn't ask for directions! But I could

210

see the spires of the great Minster so we followed Ousegate into the heart of the city. A sturdy building near the cathedral looked like it could have been the Guildhall, and we paused in the marketplace and dismounted. Finally, a group of nobles filed out of the building and made their obeisance. It wasn't much, but I was somewhat mollified. This was not the most auspicious beginning.

A few of the thegns introduced themselves; there was an Orm among them which got my attention; was this the father of Gamel who ambushed us? I determined to learn more about him later. I was too tired to remember the other names, but finally a young man stepped forward and introduced himself as Thegn Copsig. I saw the others sneered at him—indeed, a few of them walked away—so I liked him already.

"I have prepared the palace for your homecoming," he said, smiling. "We are ready to welcome you and your household."

Despite myself I let out a sigh of relief; this Copsig must be an administrator, so I didn't have to prove anything to him. For once, I was glad to relax.

"I am most grateful," I said, remounting. "Please lead the way."

Gesturing to a group of attendants standing off to the side, Copsig took us through another merchant row and out of the western gate. He walked between me and Judith, casually describing the area.

"We are on Bootham Road, and this market is held by the monks of St. Olaf's church. This stone gateway goes all the way back to the Roman times."

Despite myself I was impressed, but I was sorry we were leaving the safety of the city walls. As if he read my mind, Copsig said: "I believe Earl Siward chose to stay closer to the docks when he built his Galmanho estate. See how he arranged for many ships to tie up under his palace."

He pointed at a grand edifice built into the hill facing the river. It was nestled inside its own fortified walls. People were busily transferring goods from the ships to the palace. It did look very efficient.

This stretch of the Ouse was lined with docks and was crawling with activity. Next door, the church had been built along the road which led from Bootham to the river, and served as the entrance to the palace court.

"You will see," he continued, "that Earl Siward used his residence for business as well. There is much back and forth between here and the city."

"Did you serve him?"

Copsig looked up at me. "I served him for years. I would serve you as well, if you would have me."

"You will be my first man," I said decisively, enjoying the flush of pleasure on his face. My early uneasiness was fading away.

Siward had lived in great luxury for a rustic northerner. His palace had a good view of the river and was carefully thought out. The barracks and stables were ample and close, well placed for quick defense. The *garth* was clean and swept, the curtain walls were in good repair and a well stood in the center of the court.

I helped Judith dismount and Copsig escorted us through a large double door; Judith looked around at the high ceiling of the great hall and gave me a nod.

"We will be very comfortable here," she said. It was like a blessing on our house.

My servants knew what to do. As we explored our new home, our goods were being carried in, furniture put in place, chests brought up to our sleeping quarters. Other servants belonging to the house were laying down rushes, stacking firewood, bringing food to the outside kitchen. I remembered I was hungry.

I don't know if it was Copsig's doing, but my household was well fed that evening, just as though I was returning home after a long journey. I was satisfied.

Early the next morning, Judith was in motion. Although the servants were busy putting things away, she kept interrupting them to help her with her veil, tug her laces even tighter, and all those women things I didn't quite understand. I leaned against a post, watching. Judith had kept her trim figure, and I was proud to have her by my side. Turning, she made a clucking noise at me.

"Come Tostig. You must look your best. We have to pay a visit to the archbishop at the earliest."

I couldn't help but smile. "All right. Why don't you help me?"

It never took me long to prepare. I didn't have many tunics to choose from. After a little fussing, Judith declared she was content. We brought a small retinue and decided to proceed on foot. I wanted a closer look at York.

First we visited our own church of St. Olaf, only a few steps away. It was a small stone building, newly sanctified I had heard. The clerics bowed respectfully; they were well aware that I was to be their new patron. Near the altar, the high priest was waiting for us. Judith held out a hand to him.

"Father, we thank you for your welcome."

The priest smiled, flattered. "Whatever we can do to make you comfortable, please let me know."

"Yes there is, father. I would attend mass every morning at the first hour of the day."

"At Prime." He looked a little surprised; he was soon to find that Judith was very devout. "That would fit in with our observances perfectly."

I looked around the church. It had a square tower and few windows.

"Would you like to see Earl Siward's sepulcher?" The priest was watching me closely.

213

"Why, yes. That would please us very much."

The curate led us to a little niche built into the wall with an altar and a stone coffin underneath. The stone mason, whoever he was, had little skill and there was a rough cross carved into its side. But the altar was draped with a fine linen cloth; a real wax candle flickered atop a marble pedestal, imparting a soft glow to an otherwise dreary space.

"The flame never goes out," the priest said proudly. "And we pray for his soul daily."

I wondered how much Siward concerned himself about prayers to the Christian god. But perhaps, since he did not die in battle, Siward wanted to make sure he was welcomed somewhere. A man can't be too careful about these things.

I kept my thoughts to myself. The day was still young and Judith was anxious to see the great cathedral. It was not far, and occupied a large area inside the Roman walls to the north of Bootham road. Next to the church stood the Archbishop's palace, nearly as grand. We decided to visit the palace first.

As it turned out, Archbishop Cynesige was leaving for Rome to collect his pallium. This was a good thing, since we technically hadn't had an archbishop in England since that rogue Robert fled to Normandy in 1052. Stigand served at Canterbury, but the pope would not award him a pallium; all this time his tenure was considered illegal. That was too bad, since Stigand had always served my family well.

But I liked this Cynesige. He was a humble man, but firm in his beliefs. He took time away from his preparations to show Judith and me around the cathedral precinct. I was glad we had arrived in time to give him a sizeable donation for his voyage; I made sure he was favorably disposed toward my new office.

As my little retinue accompanied me around York, I couldn't help but notice the dark looks directed my way by the wealthier citizens. I had always heard that these northerners were different, but I never realized how much. First of all, I could barely understand what they were saying. Secondly, they seemed to cling to their outdated fashions which we had given up many years ago at court. Even their hair and beards were worn longer. I tried to converse with some of the merchants, but they merely grunted like I was an unwelcome visitor. Well, I may be unwelcome but I was no visitor. They would come to see that I would make their sordid lives better, despite themselves.

My first business was to summon the high-reeves, thegns, and sheriffs of my earldom to an old-fashioned folkmoot; we could have our assembly in the outdoors, just like their Norse ancestors. I had already identified a hill outside the city walls. Perhaps this concession to northern customs would soften up their attitude toward me. I hoped so, for my patience had a limit.

With Copsig's help, we sent out messages far and wide. I ordered extra supplies and food to be brought in, for I intended to impress them with my prosperity. I would host a grand feast and show magnanimity to one and all; I had no favorites here. Everyone was equal until proven guilty. And then, once we were assembled, I would reveal my plan to bring law and order back to Northumbria.

Meanwhile, there was so much for me to learn. Earl Siward had kept his business to himself. How did he rule? Edward didn't seem to know. I don't think the king understood Siward at all, and he seemed content to leave things alone as long as the north was quiet. I was soon to learn there was a reason it was so quiet: Siward had burned and plundered his way through Northumbria until all resistance was crushed. Maybe that's what was needed.

Already Copsig had become invaluable to me, so I kept prodding him for more information.

"Copsig," I started, putting my quill aside. "Who are the leading families I must know about?"

He sat back. "That is as good a place to start as any. In Northumberland, where all the trouble comes from, you have the house of Bamburgh. Their chieftain Uhtred was murdered way back in King Canute's early days by Thurbrand of York; Thurbrand was a Dane and supported Canute. There has been trouble between our people ever since, and much feuding. The only surviving heir to the house of Bamburgh is Gospatrick, youngest son of Uhtred."

"And where is this Gospatrick now?"

"When Siward conquered Cumberland," Copsig went on slowly, trying to keep things straight, "He made Gospatrick his sheriff there. This was to compensate him, I suppose, for the loss of his earldom. For by then Northumberland was absorbed into Northumbria and Siward ruled over all of it. I suppose he hoped to legitimize his position by marrying Gospatrick's niece. But I don't think it worked."

Already I was scratching my head. "So Gospatrick probably considers himself the true Earl of Northumberland?"

"I imagine so. Wouldn't you?"

"Hmm. What should we do about him?"

"Leave him alone, for now. You have plenty of other things to worry about."

I sighed. This was going to be a long day.

"All right. So we have the house of Bamburgh in Northumberland and the Danes in Yorkshire. And they don't trust each other."

"That's right. In Yorkshire, you have Orm son of Gamel, Ulf son of Dolf, Thored, Osbert..."

"Wait, wait. I won't remember all these names. Later, as I meet them, you can remind me. For now, let's go back to the west. Cumberland, you said, is governed by Gospatrick."

"Yes. For now, Cumberland is quiet. We need to establish your rule in the east. Our best plan will be to keep the Northumbrian nobles and the Yorkshire Danes at each other's throats. This won't be hard to do! If they are kept busy quarreling with each other, they won't have time to give you any trouble."

I wasn't excited about his suggestion but I understood what he was getting at.

"Also, Siward had over 200 housecarls," Copsig went on. "You will need the same."

"And who pays for that?"

"King Edward granted Siward the southern shires of Huntingdon and Northamptonshire to cover the costs. I believe these shires will be conveyed to you as well. I have seen no evidence to the contrary."

It seemed there was very little Copsig did not know. He spent the remainder of that day filling my head with details, though I don't know how much I remembered. But I absorbed the important things: ruling Northumbria was going to be very complicated.

As the day of our assembly drew near, York started filling up with nobles and their retainers; my small contingent of housecarls were hard put to keep order in the city, but they managed.

I waited in my new palace for the important chieftains to present themselves to me. I saw now why Siward preferred his center of government outside the city walls: it put him in a position of power to be the one who is sought out. He was removed from day-to-day business. I liked that.

But on the other hand, what if they did not come? I could see my hall was not filled with big men of dignified bearing. Oh, there were a few lesser thegns who paid their homage to me, and I went to great lengths to make them feel appreciated. But where were the important men? The landed thegns who commanded thegns of their own? I kept asking Copsig, but he was as baffled as myself. I think.

But as I had summoned nobody directly to my palace, no one had disobeyed me. No one had done anything wrong, yet. But that didn't keep me from being disgruntled. The days passed thus, and by the time we progressed to the meeting place, I was thoroughly annoyed. Copsig had erected a platform for me to stand on and I waited, arms crossed, as my subjects slowly gathered below me.

Copsig had a list of the thegns who had been summoned and he made notes as he greeted all and sundry. Some were marked off, many were not. Too many. Some of the great thegns sent their underlings with excuses; it seemed everyone was ill that day.

I suppose I should have expected this, but I did not. It was an unpleasant reality that many of my chieftains thought themselves above me. Above my rule. Outside the law. We would see about that.

But in the meantime, there was no choice but to proceed. Once it looked like everyone had pretty much arrived, I stepped forward.

"I thank you for coming," I started. "For those who have never met me, I am Tostig Godwineson, appointed by King Edward as your new earl. There are a few matters of import I would like to make known."

The more I spoke, the bolder I felt.

"First," I continued, looking directly at some of those standing nearest, "my retinue was attacked while on my way north. Many were killed. I don't know whether the attackers were outlaws or ambushers. I understand it was in Gamel's territory." I looked at Copsig and he shook his head. Gamel was not present.

"I cannot allow such lawlessness in my earldom! It is not acceptable that even a group of 20, and especially 50 armed retainers, cannot travel safely. How are we to prosper if men cannot deliver goods to our markets? I make it your charge to patrol your shires, and serve justice to lawless predators. And if you cannot perform this task, I will send my own housecarls to

218

impose order." I was practically shouting by now and had to control my temper. I took a deep breath.

"If you see beggars with no hands," I continued in a menacing voice, "ask them if they attacked Earl Tostig and his company." There, that was better. My onlookers were starting to squirm.

"All right," I went on. "Let it be known that Thegn Copsig will be my seneschal. He will be taking care of the normal business in this earldom." No one objected, nor did they comment. "I understand Earl Siward left a few charters unsigned. I hope to get matters moving forward as soon as possible. If any of you have issues or problems, I will meet with you after this assembly."

More business of that sort went on, but I had made my main points. As promised, after the meeting I sat down at a table and looked at a long line of petitioners. Copsig sat beside me and started taking notes. Many of the complaints were border disputes, some were about cattle raids, and a few actually offered me their services. I was keen to increase my household, so we gave the latter special attention.

Once my household troops were sufficiently strengthened, I intended to visit my recalcitrant thegns. They knew who they were.

But before I dealt with them, I was interested in my northern border. What would be the best way to keep the Scots quiet? Make friends, I reckoned. I already liked Malcolm. It wouldn't take much to persuade me to pay a visit to Scotland's new king.

All right, I get ahead of myself. As I said, he really wasn't the king of Scotland yet. But he was close. Macbeth was still around and Malcolm needed help in getting rid of him. In reality, Siward's campaign of 1054 was never finished. From what King Edward told me, the old Dane had every intention of following up once Malcolm had established himself. Macbeth was still lurking around in the north of Scotland, though his presence was more

219

annoying than dangerous. Still, Malcolm couldn't be more than a petty king while his rival lived.

King Edward's position in relation to Scotland had not changed. So far, it seemed Malcolm felt enough gratitude toward Edward to keep his borders quiet. I intended to see that his goodwill stayed intact. And of course, it wouldn't hurt if I took Siward's place in his estimation, even though he wasn't bound to me by blood.

So it seemed like a good idea to find a way to put Malcolm in my debt. As far as I knew, no English monarch had ventured so far north—not even the great Canute. I felt some exhilaration to be the one representing the king and spreading his influence. I took 50 housecarls with me and left Copsig in York to take care of things.

The farther north we went, the sparser the population. I suppose the outlaws would have had a hard time making a living, for we saw few strangers along the way.

What surprised me most was the great beauty of the scenery, and I began to understand why my Northumbrian subjects were so wild and untamed. They suited the countryside perfectly. By the time we reached the Cheviot Hills, rolling and green with lush valleys and streams...well, I was more than happy to have been awarded this remote earldom. This was my new home and I embraced it.

We continued north to Edinburgh, a little town perched atop a rugged cliff; Dun Edin it was called in the old days, as in Hill Fort. Malcolm had a small palace there, and came out to greet us as we announced ourselves.

He put his hands on his hips and leaned a little backwards, grinning and laughing, then put an arm around my shoulders and led me over the bridge to the palace.

Once inside the hall, he called for food and ale, and his servants scrambled about as my men found places at the trestle tables. We had a grand old feast, and Malcolm leaned back in his throne, draping a leg over the chair-arm as he picked the last shreds of chicken from a leg-bone.

"So, Earl Tostig of Northumbria. I drink to your good fortune. My uncle Siward was a great man and I will miss him. But it seems he has a worthy successor." He raised an ale horn to me.

Looking sideways at him, I wondered whether his words were genuine. But there was no evidence of sarcasm.

"Prince Malcolm," I replied, using my most charming voice. I had carefully prepared a little speech. "I came here to preserve the good-will between my earldom and your kingdom. I think we would be stronger as friends than friendly strangers. I would open my hearth to you. I would offer assistance to you in your struggle against Macbeth, just as your uncle did."

That certainly got his attention. He sat up in his throne, looking surprised. I doubted it; why else would I have come? Of course, we both knew my army would probably gather some plunder along the way, but that was to be expected. They had to be paid somehow.

"Earl Tostig. My Friend!" he said, refilling my horn. "Stay with me for a while so we can get to know each other better."

And so it was all arranged. My men and I stayed a fortnight, hunting by day, drinking by night. Malcolm was a shrewd judge of character and apparently liked what he saw in me. We laid out some preliminary plans and he determined to track Macbeth, who was always on the move. I liked this Malcolm more and more; we had similar viewpoints and he always laughed at my humor.

But there was a darker side to him, too. When we spoke of his uncle Siward, he actually grimaced at one point, though I don't think he knew I was watching.

"He was a clever one," he said, reaching over to pour himself some ale. Malcolm loved his drink. "I wasn't the only refugee, you know. My uncle Maldred, my father's brother, appeared shortly after Siward took me in. He came along with his son Cospatric. My cousin. There were plenty of others and the old fox took them all in. Siward dangled my uncle and me in front of Macbeth's face whenever he thought the Scots were getting restive. Maldred had a better claim to the Scottish throne than I, but *I* was the heir to the kingdom of Cumbria. That is, until Siward took it from me in exchange for the Dunsinane campaign."

That was a surprise to me. "What happened to Maldred?" I asked.

"Oh, he was killed back in 1046. Siward led an army into Scotland that year, you know."

"No, I didn't."

"Ah. Yes, he drove Macbeth from the throne and put Maldred in his place. Then he went home; I suppose he thought his job was done. Unfortunately, once he was gone, Macbeth came back and killed my uncle."

He fell silent. I needed to know more.

"Then you had another death to avenge," I ventured.

"Yes. Yes I did. That's why I gave up Cumbria, though I shouldn't have. I didn't know Siward would have campaigned anyway. He had a lot to gain in plunder, as it turned out." He frowned. "He waited until I was old enough to claim the crown and... Well, you know the rest. Once he had his hands on my Cumbria, he just kept moving south, swallowing up more and more land until Cumbria was absorbed into all of Cumberland. And it all belonged to his earldom."

I swear he gave me the strangest look.

"I understand why he needed Cumberland," Malcolm added, trying to make light of it. "He wanted to protect the mountain passes to Northumbria. It was a wise choice..." His voice trailed off.

"And who is this Gospatrick who rules Cumberland?" I pursued. He gave me another odd look.

222

"Gospatrick. Oh yes, he is the youngest son of Uhtred of Bamburgh who was killed by Canute. Or so it is said. They tell me Gospatrick feels he ceded too much territory. He wanted Bamburgh, I'm sure. But Siward wanted it more. In recompense, Siward appointed him governor of Cumberland. It kept him out of Northumberland, and kept him busy. Yes, my uncle was a clever man. And now you benefit from it."

That last sentence made me uncomfortable, but Malcolm quickly changed the subject. We talked of lighter things, then I announced it was time to return to Northumbria. I had a lot to think about. So did he.

I was sorry to leave but I had much to do. When I returned to England he loaded me with gifts.

On my way south, I decided to take the coastal route; it had a bigger population, and I needed to be seen. We crossed the Tweed and I sent a messenger ahead to Bamburgh, announcing our intent to spend the night. I was anxious to see this castle that I had kept hearing about.

This was one of Siward's great strongholds, and of course it was mine now. And what a stronghold! Perched high on a ridge, it commanded a view that went on for miles. On the ocean side, grass-covered dunes stood in the shadow of the castle, sloping to a beautiful beach.

As my little company approached Bamburgh, I was a little unhappy that no one came out to greet us. But I was getting used to discourtesy, so it came as no surprise. But when we approached the stronghold, I saw men-at-arms standing guard along the battlements and the portal was firmly closed. This was unacceptable! We stood in front of the gates and I had one of my housecarls sound the horn.

We waited. Nothing.

"Your Earl Tostig stands before you," I shouted. "Where is our welcome?"

My horse shifted from right to left and I jerked the reins. "I demand entrance!"

I don't know what would have happened if they ignored me; we were too few to attack. But after another couple of minutes, the gate cracked open and a man came forward. I supposed he was the castle steward.

"What brings you here, my lord?" He almost squeaked and I could see he was nervous.

"I sent a messenger ahead. Did you not see him?"

The man shook his head. "We saw no messenger."

I let out my breath in an impatient gust. "We will investigate that later. Who is your master here?"

"Cospatric, son of Maldred, Reeve of Northumberland."

"Where is this Cospatric?"

"He stands before you," came another voice as a young man stepped through the gate. He was dressed so beautifully he must have needed extra time before presenting himself. Running a hand through his black hair, he stepped forward, extending the same hand in welcome.

"Earl Tostig," he said smoothly. "Had I known you were coming I would have given you a better greeting. Please forgive me; these are lawless times."

He turned, commanding his men to open the gates. Somewhat mollified, I urged my mount forward. Cospatric walked beside me.

"What brings you so far north?" he asked conversationally.

"I have just visited the king of Scotland."

"Ah, King Malcolm my cousin."

I looked down at my host, who swung his shoulders slightly as he walked.

"Your father Maldred..."

"Was the younger brother of King Duncan, Malcolm's father. Yes. My father married the daughter of the great Earl

224

Uhtred which is why I am here. Like Malcolm, I was raised in exile by Earl Siward."

"And he made you reeve of this castle."

"Well, yes. I was his reeve."

We had reached his thatched hall and I dismounted, gesturing for my men to do the same. I felt we were in no danger, and truly I was tired from the journey. Cospatric showed us where the bath house was, and he made arrangements for my men to stay throughout the settlement. For myself, Cospatric insisted I take his chamber and he would sleep in the hall with his household troops.

But before I could relax, I wanted to know what happened to my messenger.

"You came from the north?" Cospatric scratched his ear. "He would have followed the main road. In the morning I will send some soldiers out to see if they can find him." He looked concerned. I think I believed he was genuine. I wanted to trust somebody in this cursed land!

They fed us well enough, and Cospatric's skald kept my men entertained. He and I pulled apart from the rest, for I had much to ask him.

"Did you not receive my summons to the assembly?" This was my first question though I didn't really know if his name was on the list or not.

He twirled his cup in his hand, thinking. "I did," he finally answered, as if he had won an argument with himself. "But by the time it got here there were not enough days left for me to reach you before it was over."

I nodded. It was possible. At least he knew who I was, or he might have killed me in front of his gate. "But you did not send a message," I pursued.

"Would it have mattered? I am a busy man."

I decided to let that pass. He, on the other hand, wasn't finished with me.

"Earl Tostig," he pursued. "I was busy in your service."

225

Oh, he was a clever one. I turned my whole body, facing him.

"Are you in my service?"

"Of that there is no doubt. My family has lived here for generations. We collect your rents, keep your peace..."

"And with your cousin as neighbor, I trust there will be peace on your borders."

"There you have it. Malcolm and I are on the best of terms."

He smiled at me—that kind of smile which implied an accord between us. I couldn't help it. I found him interesting.

"Tell me more about your kin."

And he did. He was from the younger branch of the family and always feared...no, I think he hated his uncle Gospatrick, who threatened to come back to Bamburgh and take over the earldom.

"Why he thinks he can do that, with you in charge, I do not understand," he assured me. "He is a brutal man, and he should be happy with what he has. His people in Cumberland fear him. That should make him happy enough. He bears watching, that one."

I had suspected as much. Another nobleman to beware of.

At least Cospatric seemed tractable enough. He knew—as well as I did—he was so far north that as long as his revenues came in, I had no reason to concern myself with him. Actually, I liked his company.

The following day, his men came back carrying my messenger on a litter. The man had died a violent death, for his face was bloodied and his throat had been cut. He had been robbed and left on the side of the road. I don't know how we missed him.

Cospatric was obviously angered by this, or maybe he just pretended so. I don't know. I was furious and paced back and forth as they wrapped him for burial.

"This seems to be rampant throughout the earldom," I fumed. "No one is safe to travel the roads."

226

He shrugged his shoulders. "It has been like this for years."

"Well it has to stop!" I exclaimed. "If you need more men-at-arms, I will send them to you."

Cospatric looked shocked. "No, no. That will not be necessary..."

"Look. You must punish the offenders. Hang them, or if not, cut off their hands."

I could see he was uncomfortable. "This is not a request," I reminded him. "It is my command. If you don't make your roads safe, then I will."

It was too bad. This exchange damaged any geniality between us. But this situation could not continue. I had just lost a good man, for no good reason.

When I rode out the following day, Cospatric watched glumly from his fortress walls. I had a feeling he did not plan to obey me in the least. Well, I would be back next year and we should see.

The following year, I was as good as my word. Supported by five hundred eager fighters, mostly of Danish stock, I passed through Northumberland and joined Malcolm for his final campaign against Macbeth. The old king had been greatly weakened by Siward's invasion in 1054, and I don't think there was much doubt as to the issue of this new offensive. Prince Malcolm was reportedly a fearsome fighter, and he still felt the need to avenge the death of his father at Macbeth's hand.

Did Cospatric patrol his roads and reduce the number of outlaws? I couldn't tell. We were too many to be challenged. The few villages we passed were deserted, and I assumed they fled from our approach. I gave orders not to destroy their crops or ransack their homes; we had our own supplies and these peasants

227

were my people. By the time we reached Scotland, it was up to Malcolm to provide for our needs.

He met us along the road as we crossed into Lothian, accompanied by a small force. We fell in with them and the king slapped me on the back as he turned his horse around.

"What a happy day this is," he said, looking about. "I feel so certain that we will win." His eyes were glittering with triumph. "Tostig, nothing can stop us."

I was glad to be on his side of this argument. Woe betide Malcolm's enemy now that the exile had become a full-grown man. I could see he had the makings of a formidable ruler.

Malcolm ferried us across the Firth of Forth just above Edinburgh; although it took all day, it was still faster than marching all the way to Stirling. Once across, we were joined by the rest of his troops—several hundred more men. He took us past a pretty little town named Dunfermline, a few miles north of the ferry. Pointing to a rocky outcrop between two streams, he told me he was planning to build a palace there after he became King. I liked that kind of optimism.

Malcolm had reports that Macbeth was in Aberdeenshire. This was not easy countryside to get around in! A large range of mountains stretched before us called The Mounths. Malcolm told us these mountains formed a natural barrier between the highlands of northeast Scotland and the lowlands. Luckily, Malcolm's scouts knew where to lead us, and from one of the high vantage points we spotted our quarry with about five hundred mounted warriors, heading north.

"I know where he is going," Malcolm said smoothly. "He is headed toward the old Roman Cairn O'Mounth Pass. If we hurry, we might stop him there."

Hurrying was something we knew how to do, but the going was rough and we sent up a dust cloud announcing our presence. Pretty soon, Macbeth's force gained momentum, and they were through the pass before we reached it. By then, the sun had gone well past mid-day, and Malcolm suggested we set up camp before crossing through.

"Macbeth has nowhere to go," he assured me, dismounting from his horse. "I trust he will be anxious to meet us tomorrow. If not, too bad for him!" He handed his mount to a groom. "I intend to make sure he does not see the end of the day."

Prince Malcolm knew his enemy. By the time we made it through the pass, we saw Macbeth lined up in battle formation, in front of a little fortified motte near the town of Lumphanan. Macbeth's men were a little fresher than ours, but we outnumbered them almost two-to-one. Both of our forces dismounted, and we were barely in battle array when Malcolm raised his sword above his head and shouted the attack.

The Prince was in the front ranks and his well-trained fighters formed a tight wedge behind him, holding their shields before their bodies. Most were armed with long-handled battle axes, and when they crashed into Macbeth's shield wall they went right through, bringing the rest of us with them. It was obvious Macbeth's men were not very encouraged and they did not fight well. Many broke and ran, and the rest fell under our blades. It was a slaughter.

The fight was over in a couple of hours. We searched under the biggest pile of bodies and found Macbeth still clutching his sword. He had many wounds, and I could see that more than one were fatal. I thought Malcolm used great restraint by allowing his supporters to take away the corpse.

It was a great victory for Malcolm, and he was very appreciative of my support, even though he probably didn't need it. Unfortunately for him, Macbeth's step-son Lulach was crowned a month later, so he had to be dealt with before Malcolm could take the crown for himself. That took about six months, and Malcolm didn't need my help.

It's just as well, because at the same time, Earl Leofric breathed his last. The year 1057 was one of many changes, but his death was the most significant for our family.

GYRTH REMEMBERS

When Earl Leofric died, King Edward did not hesitate to give Mercia over to his son Aelfgar. This was not a hereditary post, so many of us were surprised, considering Aelfgar had recently turned traitor and raided Hereford with Gruffydd ap Llewelyn. Mercia bordered Wales, so we thought it was dangerous to put those two troublemakers side-by-side.

At least Harold was firmly in charge of Hereford by then. There was nobody more suitable to protect that vital place, and King Edward knew it. Earl Ralf, who had made such a mess of things with his cavalry, also died in 1057. If Aelfgar thought Herefordshire was going to be attached to Mercia, he must have been sorely disappointed. There was no way he could be trusted.

So Aelfgar's move to Mercia opened up East Anglia. Leofwine and I were honored when King Edward split the earldom between us. I was 25 years old by then but did not have much experience in government. Once in a while father had brought me with him when traveling across his earldom. I would watch and learn while he witnessed charters, made laws and presided in trials. But watching and doing were two different things.

Harold was more than helpful and decided to accompany me to Cambridge, where I would start my tenure. Leofwine came with us, for he wanted to see how I settled in before attempting to do the same. We started out in good spirits, but by the time we reached Bishop's Stortford, about halfway to our destination, it was pouring rain and we were miserable.

By then, the local inn looked very inviting; Leofwine and I were wringing out our cloaks when Harold sat down beside us, carrying three mugs of ale. His hair and beard were dripping but he had a big smile on his face and seemed oblivious to any discomfort. That's how I remembered him when I was a child; he was always laughing when we were crying, making fun of us when we complained—especially when he was going away. Tonight, I think he was smiling for pure joy.

"Father would be so proud," he said. "He always wanted this for you."

Leofwine and I looked at each other. We never really thought about that.

"Do you realize that we will rule every earldom except Mercia?"

Of course we knew this, but it couldn't hurt to hear it spoken out loud.

"And the way Aelfgar has been acting, Mercia might be up for spoils, too."

"Oh?" I realized I needed to start paying more attention. "What has he done now?"

"He has gone and married his daughter Ealdgyth to that old fox, Gruffydd ap Llewelyn. I knew we were too lenient after Hereford, and now we are paying the price."

I was surprised. Even for Aelfgar this seemed a little too disloyal.

"They share a long border, don't they?" I ventured.

Harold looked disturbed. "They do. This alliance is not in England's interest, that's for certes."

"And the king's reaction?" Leofwine asked.

"You can imagine. I just don't know what he is going to do about it. If they remain quiet, perhaps he will do nothing. But I doubt that will last long." He frowned, then pulled himself back with an effort.

231

"But tonight is no time to be talking about Aelfgar. Tell me, Gyrth. What have you learned about East Anglia?"

What was I supposed to know? "The Fens and the Wash dominate the northern end, and the river Stout is on the southern end..."

"Good. That's more than I knew when I started. And Leofwine, although your new earldom does not include London, you do have control of Sandwich and Dover. Except for the profits of Justice, which belong to them. Still, these are our most important ports and needed to be tended carefully."

Leofwine looked a little uncomfortable though I knew that would pass. We had much to learn, but Harold would be there for us. He knew more about ruling than King Edward. In fact, he started instructing us that very evening, and we paid close attention. That is, until we were too exhausted to think.

The weather had cleared by morning and we were on our way at first light. We rode hard, for we wanted to be in Cambridge by nightfall. The closer we came, the more animated Harold got.

"I love this town," he told me. "I think I've always been happiest here. Of course, it reminds me of the time I wooed Edith. You know, I fell in love with her the day I met her. She was so lovely. Not that she isn't now," he laughed. "Even after five children she is like a willow.

"And because she loves her manor at Hinton, we will be visiting regularly and I can keep an eye on you!" He laughed again and I joined in, less enthusiastically. I didn't exactly like the sound of that.

When we entered the town, Harold was acting like the earl and I felt like his servant. We kept stopping to greet people, who shouted their welcome and bandied words with him. I could see he was still very popular, especially as people kept saying they were glad to be rid of that wretch, Aelfgar. Apparently Aelfgar had not proved a worthy successor to my brother. Would I do any better?

I noticed Harold didn't take the time to introduce me. But as I was always more shy than my charismatic brother, I satisfied myself with an occasional smile and nod. No one seemed particularly curious about me anyway. I dropped back to ride beside Leofwine.

"This comes as no surprise," I assured him.

Actually, I think I was reassuring myself. "How could they not love our brother?"

Leofwine understood all too well. "Don't worry," he said. "After Harold has gone, your time will come."

We rode up to the council house, where a group of thegns were waiting at the top of the stairway. Harold told me later that he was originally greeted the same way, though I suspect he knew just what to do.

We dismounted and Harold led us up the stairs. He went right up to the leader of the men and they embraced heartily. Harold held him at arm's length, treating him almost like an equal. He turned to me, an arm around the man's shoulder.

"Gyrth," he said, "I owe much to this man. Eadric of Laxfield, meet my brother and your new earl, Gyrth Godwineson."

Eadric bowed slightly to me and I looked at him nervously. He was almost old enough to be my father. Would he try to dominate me, too? But when he looked into my eyes, I could see something closer to affection. Maybe his friendship toward my brother would rub off onto me.

Harold hadn't let go of his old friend yet.

"Reeve Laxfield has had the charge of these shires for many, many years. He knows everything about the law, about the finances, and about the rule of these lands. I leave you in good hands, Gyrth."

Well, that much was final. I was not to disturb anything.

"I wish Aelfgar had understood as much," Eadric assured Harold. "Everything is out of order. Our coffers are poorer for his rule."

Harold frowned. He hated to hear such things. He finally let go of Eadric and took my arm, pulling me up beside him.

"By order of the king, I am here to see that our change of leadership goes smoothly," he announced. I think he made up the king's order, but no one seemed to object. "I instruct you to aid him as readily as you can."

I was glad he stopped there. Apparently he was satisfied, and the others stepped aside as we strode through the double doors and into the great hall. As the sun was beginning to set, the room was full of shadows already. Servants were lighting torches while others were setting trestle tables for a small feast. I could see we would have no time to rest.

"Come, Gyrth," my brother urged. "Take the high chair. Let your thegns meet you. It is important to gain their good will."

I duly obeyed my brother and tried to stay alert while man after man introduced himself to me. Harold stood by my side and greeted each by name after they rose from their knees and moved on. It was all very proper, and I felt a little easier as I made my way to the head table and took a long draught of wine. At least I would eat well. Leofwine sat with me and piled food on his trencher. But Harold seemed unable to relax, as he moved around and bent over people's shoulders while we feasted. I don't think he took a bite.

Finally it was all over and we moved to the castle by the river. My household servants had spent the last few hours preparing it for me, and Harold showed me where the sleeping chamber was.

"No, you take it," I said. "You are my honored guest."

"Nonsense. You are the master here. It will give me pleasure to bed down with the household troops. I rarely have a chance to do so."

I was a little uncertain, but too tired to argue. Falling on the bed, I was asleep before I knew it. But I soon woke up, unused to the noises in my new home. I lay still for a while then got up to explore.

The moon was full and cast a soothing light through the few window openings. This part of the castle was built of wood, and I ran my hand along the wall as I slowly took the stairs down to the main floor. I nearly stumbled off the last step but paused, recognizing Harold's voice. I didn't want to disturb anyone, so I moved slowly toward the open door, listening.

"I never trusted that Aelfgar, especially with East Anglia. How much damage did he do?"

"More than enough." I recognized the voice of Reeve Eadric. "But I managed to keep some funds in reserve, out of his hands. Aelfgar was never one to pay much attention to keeping records."

Harold grunted. "I must get Oxfordshire out of his hands and into Gyrth's. Edward favors Oxford and increasingly uses it for his Witan. We must put it into trustworthy hands. In fact," he lowered his voice and I had to strain to hear, "I intend to limit Aelfgar's authority as much as possible. Starting with Herefordshire. Now that Earl Ralph is dead, I must leave as soon as possible to secure its borders. He cannot be allowed anywhere near there."

"Knowing Aelfgar, he will object most strenuously," Eadric replied.

"Once King Edward learns Aelfgar married his daughter to the Welsh Prince, I doubt our foolish friend will have any influence at all. In fact, he may see himself outlawed again."

It was Eadric's turn to grunt. "You are running out of brothers." He gave a brief laugh.

It took Harold a long time to answer. "There is poor Wulfnoth," he said, and I detected a note of regret in his voice. "I must free him somehow from his prison."

235

After another pause, his voice picked up. "But for now, I put Gyrth in your charge. He is very dear to me. Don't let any harm come to him."

There it was again. My big brother protecting the child. I was ready to interrupt but thought better of it; he wasn't finished yet.

"If King Edward dies without a direct heir, now that Edward Aetheling has passed on, I may need Gyrth's support. And Leofwine's. We must get them ready for governance." He lowered his voice again. "Young Eadgar is only a child, after all. He may be Aetheling, but he won't be strong enough to rule for a long, long time."

"Aye, though I believe you won't face much opposition... except from the house of Leofric, I suppose. Do not worry; Gyrth shows great promise. He will be ready when the time comes."

They were moving away and I leaned back against the wall. What were they saying? Harold as king? It took my breath away.

TOSTIG REMEMBERS

Ruling Northumbria was like trying to tame a pack of wolves. No matter if I used fair words, reasoned with them, or even bullied them, one man would bare his teeth at me while another snapped at my heels. In those early years I was often on the move, leaving Copsig to oversee the government in York. A large band of seasoned warriors accompanied me, for the roads hadn't been safe for generations as far as I could tell. I got used to a cold welcome from my thegns, but they knew better than deny me a night's lodging. After my experience with Bamburgh, I sent ahead not one but six messengers to announce my approach. That seemed to be a good number, for my men were bristling with arms and looked ferocious enough.

I had a few comital manors that came with my earldom, but they were often poorly maintained and under provisioned so I rarely stopped there. Besides, I needed to know who were my most troublesome chieftains, so I paid them a visit, one and all. Alas, I didn't find one I could trust with my back turned.

Typically, when I called a meeting with local thegns and sheriffs, they grumbled when I complained about the lawlessness, and refused to answer any direct questions unless forced to. They were a miserable bunch, and I saw why Siward had to deal with them so harshly. But it gave me a lot of satisfaction to recruit their younger sons into my household troops. All were looking for advancement, and it seemed a good way to ensure the cooperation of their fathers. So my entourage swelled as I made my way across the earldom. And it was a good thing, too, I was soon to discover.

It was finally time to get the measure of this Gospatrick who claimed the rule of Cumberland and possibly Northumbria. He had been quiet so far, even though he ignored my original summons. Still, I would be content to leave him at his post as long as he gave me his proper respect.

Our obvious route followed the old Roman wall through the Tyne Gap. It was beautiful to look at. The hills were long and low, and the stone wall clung to the crests like a ridge of bones. For many stretches, the land fell sharply off to the north, providing a natural defense. I believe some Emperor built this astonishing wall as the northern end of the Roman Empire; at least this was what my tutor told me. It was tall as a man in places— maybe taller—and originally extended all the way across the country. Seeing this marvel in reality was a lesson in man's ability to do whatever he wants. That is, if he is willing to work hard enough.

Every so often there was a stone fortress, and we took time out to crawl over the crumbling walls and explore the nooks and crannies. It was a welcome change from all that riding, and we even broke our fast and leaned back against the sheltering stones, though the sun did not warm us and the winds never ceased to blow. But soon it all started to look the same, and we rode west in earnest.

The Roman wall passed near the old town of Carlisle, which was my destination. Rich and verdant farmland spread before my eyes, a welcome sight after all those high peaks. Placed near the Solway Firth and at the juncture of three rivers, Carlisle looked like it originally supported a large Roman settlement. Now it appeared like it had been overrun a few too many times. Nonetheless, from here Gospatrick controlled access to the north and the south, and of course the invasion route to the east.

We approached a low-lying timber fortress with a stout wall, and Gospatrick's men were on hand to escort us inside. That was a good start. It was a large fortification; there was enough room to shelter my men. Aside from the main hall, I saw a separate kitchen and a larder. We walked past a pen full of goats as I was brought to meet my host. I gestured for a few of my men to accompany me; the rest could prepare the camp. I wished Copsig was here; he always knew what to do.

Gospatrick was pacing the floor as I entered the great hall. He pretended not to see me. There was no place for me to sit, so for a moment I contented myself with looking around the room. Beautiful carved trusses supported the roof and even the posts were decorated. Woven tapestries hung from the wall. This was a hall fit for a king.

"Is this how you greeted Earl Siward?" I asked. I tried to sound detached.

He turned, not bothering to show surprise. He gestured for someone to bring two chairs. We sat, facing each other like a pair of stags.

"That's much better." I nodded, trying to relax. "Now we can see eye to eye."

I waited for him to respond, but like all the rest of his countrymen he stayed silent. I noticed he was gripping his pommel. Good. I made him nervous.

No, on reflection, it was too bad, really. He was about the age of my father, and Gospatrick even reminded me him, the way he sat and the turn of his head. He had ponderous shoulders, a thick neck and strong legs. But the resemblance stopped there. Father always knew how to behave toward a guest, no matter how unwelcome.

I tried to smile but received no encouragement. I sighed.

"Thegn Gospatrick," I ventured, not knowing exactly what title to use. "I hope we can come to understand one another. Earl Siward gave you the rule of Cumberland, and I see that you are well placed to defend my people."

Nothing. I think he objected to my last few words.

"We shall convene a royal court, for King Edward would extend his hand of justice to all the corners of his kingdom. He instructs me to represent him."

Gospatrick jumped to his feet. I was surprised at how fast he moved.

"Come." He waved for me to follow and I obeyed, feeling a little awkward. But I was also curious about his settlement. It seemed he was a man of action, and was ill at ease unless he was moving around. That was all right, because as he showed me his fortification he finally started to talk. We climbed the parapet wall and looked at the valley below.

"We command the River Eden and the arm of the sea," he said, pointing toward the Solway Firth. "My ships are scatted up and down the coast," he added proudly. "We watch for the Norsemen, who often raid from the Isle of Man. But I am ready for them." His voice rose in anger, as though I had something to do with it.

239

"What are you going to do about the Scots?"

I stared at him. What was he talking about?

"The Scots," he repeated as though I was hard of hearing. "There have been incursions from the north. In Cumbria. They are coming over the border, man!"

I admit it; he had me at a disadvantage. I hadn't heard about any incursion from the Scots.

"It's your responsibility to protect our borders," he added triumphantly.

"No, it's *your* responsibility," I retorted angrily. "That's why you are here."

We glared at each other, then I shook my head. This wasn't what I wanted.

"Come," I said, trying to sound conciliatory. "We are on the same side. Let us help each other."

Gospatrick grunted. He turned and I followed him again. How was I going to learn more about the border raids without seeming so uninformed? Damn that Malcolm!

Later that evening, Gospatrick laid out a feast I envied despite myself. When his servants put down a platter heaped with salmon, I nearly groaned with anticipation. All we had in the east was herring, herring, herring. To sink my teeth into salmon almost made this unpleasant stay worthwhile. I spooned a little sauce over the delectable pink meat and closed my eyes, enjoying my first bite. When I opened them again, Gospatrick was studying me.

I put down my knife. "I would travel north and see what damage the Scots have wrought," I ventured. "And discover who has led them."

My host shrugged his shoulders. "You will never discover their leader," he said scornfully. "They strike fast and disappear, leaving us much the poorer."

"Can we guard the passes?"

"There are too many of them." He put another piece of salmon on my trencher. "It's like trying to stop a waterfall."

"Perhaps we should raid across their border in reprisal."

He shook his head. "There are never enough troops. I can spare no men."

This sort of discussion went on for a long time. I probed, he deflected. At no point could we agree on anything.

But I wasn't ready to give up. As planned, I established a local court for all the people to bring their suits, their requests, even to grant a charter or two in the king's name. There were many attendees, and I was kept busy handing down judgments to respectful supplicants.

But in the middle of the third day, a rider burst into the hall, breathless and agitated. He spotted me and moved hurriedly forward, falling to one knee.

"I have come to bring news that Earl Aelfgar has joined forces with Gruffydd ap Llewelyn. They bring fire and rapine over the border."

I leaped to my feet, knocking my chair over. "Earl Aelfgar? Why?"

"He has been outlawed by the king," the man gasped. "He raids to gain revenge!"

Hereford all over again. This time he was farther north.

"There's more," the man added, catching his breath. "They have joined forces with the Norsemen, who are raiding the coast."

I started running for the door. "We must find Lord Gospatrick," I shouted over my shoulder.

But the Reeve had already heard. As I headed across the bailey, my host was already shouting his orders. He turned as I approached.

"Looks like we must fight together after all," he said. "I have sent out summonses to my fyrdmen. We must deal with the Norsemen first."

241

"Do you know who their leader is?"

"Magnus himself, son of King Harald Hardrada. He is formidable like his father."

"What has he to do with Aelfgar?"

"Convenience, I would reckon. Maybe you can find out, *Earl* Tostig." He emphasized the word earl. His sarcasm was not lost on me and I swore to myself I would deal with him when the time came. But for now, we had to face one, possibly two invasions.

We were on our way north that very day, with my housecarls and Gospatrick's household troops. The fyrd would follow as soon as they had gathered. All of us were mounted so we thundered across the lowlands at a very good pace. Fortunately, we didn't see any evidence of damage for many leagues. Then we saw a spire of smoke on the horizon. Gospatrick spurred his horse angrily and we all followed.

As we neared our destination, we adjusted our pace and gathered closer together.

"That is one of my coastal towns," he growled. "They have been raided before."

Getting near as we dared, we dismounted, drawing our swords. So far we didn't see any Norsemen, but we could hear shouting and fighting from the other side of a tall ridge. Gospatrick's men doubled their pace and my men followed, holding our shields before us.

Rounding some boulders, we charged forward, taking some of the raiders by surprise in their killing frenzy. They turned to face us and barely paused before raising their weapons and shouting a challenge.

"Shield wall," Gospatrick shouted and we were right there, overlapping our shields with a satisfying clang. The Norsemen were not organized and they hesitated, for we were many and they were few. As one we moved forward and our adversaries fell back, calling for help. We were confident and strong, but more and more joined them until their numbers started to match ours. I saw three sleek Viking ships in the bay, and thanked my stars there weren't more of them.

As soon as the Norsemen had recovered they charged our shield wall, bristling with spears and long-handled axes. Some of their shorter axes came hurtling over our shields and the man next to me howled with pain as he went down, blood spurting from his scalp. We tightened up, stepping over the poor man as we pushed forward.

The Norsemen tried to shove through our defenses and hook their axes into the edges of our shields, tugging and stabbing. We responded equal viciousness, now hacking at their heads and again thrusting upwards from beneath our shields, aimed at their guts. Back and forth our lines flowed, and our shield wall soon lost its definition. We were fighting man to man, but we were defending our own and I think our anger was more powerful than their greed. Step by step the Norsemen retreated toward their ships.

The buildings were fiercely ablaze by now. The roar of the fire added to the confusion of screaming, clanging, and shouting until there was no telling what was happening. But apparently the invaders were interested in easier prey and soon swarmed onto their ships, abandoning the fight by some unspoken agreement. We stopped at the town's edge. Gospatrick was more interested in helping the wounded than chasing the Norsemen; our enemy was dangerous in retreat, and we couldn't afford further losses.

He helped a man to his feet, then propped another up against a wall. In these simple actions Gospatrick seemed more human than ever before, but as soon as he straightened and scowled at me, the old wolf came right back.

"See what I have to deal with?" Once again, he seemed to be blaming me for his misfortunes. I ignored him and tended to my own men.

243

We did our best to put fires out, but our efforts were pretty useless. Most of the buildings were already caving in. The raiders were very efficient at stripping all food and valuables from the poor townspeople, and I heard Gospatrick assure the few survivors that he would send supplies to get them through the winter. He ignored me while we gathered the dead and dug a mass grave for their burial. The next day, we were on our way north again.

It seemed like every place we stopped, we were too late. The Norsemen were so much faster than us by sea, and now that they were aware of our presence they knew not to get caught again.

Gospatrick was all for returning to his fortress and joining up with his fyrd. I wanted to go north and see what the Scottish raids were all about.

"Go yourself," he retorted. "Go, waste your time. I have more important things to worry about."

I had to go on. Otherwise, I would have looked weak and foolish. Nonetheless, we were unprovisioned, so we were obliged to return with Gospatrick and prepare for the next part of my journey. He was more than happy to get rid of us and even gave us extra mounts to carry our supplies. He made sure to be away the day we departed. But it didn't matter. I had figured him out.

There were few roads through Cumbria, but we were able to make progress by following the ridges of low hills. I stopped in villages along the way and the occasional estate; everywhere I asked for news, the story was the same: Scots came down across the border, stealing cattle and sheep for the most part. When warned of their approach, the local population fled to the mountains and forests. When caught by surprise, my hapless ceorls were captured and dragged back to Scotland as slaves. It disturbed me that the raids were sporadic; the Scots were getting bolder and bolder. Surely Malcolm didn't know about it. Surely he wouldn't condone such a thing.

No sooner did I return to York than I immediately prepared for a visit to King Edward. Earl Siward had attended the royal court at least once a year, and now I understood why; it was so easy to lose contact with the real world way up in the north.

I was determined to call Northumbria home and did my best to appreciate it. But in truth it was a cold, unfriendly place that only someone born and raised there could love. Judith was anxious to return south with me, and we attended Edward's Christmas Court at Gloucester that year. We traveled slowly due to the bad weather, but we were so happy to go home that every step closer made our hearts lighter.

By the time we reached the court my whole entourage was feeling festive. Many guests had arrived before us, including my brother Harold and his lovely lady Edith.

People were wandering around the great hall, carrying their food and drink; minstrels played their silly stringed instruments, raising their voices above the steady murmur. My sister the queen seemed to be looking for me, because as soon as I saw her she flew across the room. I picked her up in a most unqueenly embrace. Oh, it was so good to see her.

"My dearest, most favorite sister," I laughed, kissing her on the forehead. She reached up and tugged at my earlobe, her favorite gesture.

"I thought you'd never get here," she said. "Come, Edward has been asking after you. Judith! Come, come my dear. I have so much to talk with you about."

Regaining her dignity, my sister led us through the crowd. Edward, sitting quietly on his throne, visibly brightened when he saw me. I was very gratified.

"Tostig, you shouldn't stay away so long," he called, holding out his hand to me. "A chair, a chair! Come, sit." I waited for a servant to place a chair next to the king.

"How goes it, Tostig? How are your unruly subjects?"

I sighed. Did he want to know the truth?

"I manage," I said finally. "It is a large earldom and divided by its mountains."

"How is the hunting there?"

Ah, a safer discussion. We spoke at length about Edward's favorite past time, and he pretended that he would like to come north and give it a try. Edward in the north... I suddenly got an idea.

"Sire," I ventured, seeing his attention wander. "There is something I would suggest."

"Oh?" He turned to face me fully.

"It's about Prince Malcolm."

"Ah, our young exile. I understand he is still chasing Macbeth's son across the country."

That was an interesting observation. He was better informed than I thought. "Yes, but that won't last long. The pup is no challenge, even if they did crown him king. A puppet king."

"And once he is taken care of, Malcolm becomes king in his own right. And he will be free to challenge you."

"Yes." I loved Edward's mind. He was quick. "I think he has started that already. In Cumberland."

"Ah. If I recall, Malcolm was Prince of Cumberland at one time...and would be again."

"Yes. I had hoped to bind him closer to me by helping him track down and destroy Macbeth..."

"And how much can we depend on his gratitude? Siward seemed to think we could. And you carried on his policy." He put his hands together and placed his fingers against his lips.

"We have been very friendly," I added, encouraged by Edward's interest. "If you were to come to Yorkshire—to hunt— perhaps I can persuade Malcolm to pay us a visit."

"And give him a chance to thank me for my support."

246

"Quite right!" I sat back, nodding. "And while he is feeling grateful, perhaps we can find a way to bind him closer to us."

"And keep him quiet!" Edward ended with a flourish. "Yes, Tostig. That is a fine idea. Perhaps we can solicit the help of Archbishop Cynesige, since I will make York our meeting place. I have long desired to see the Cathedral there."

And so it was settled. Already I was glad I had visited the Christmas court. I was content to sit beside King Edward and entertain him with my usual banter. Eventually, of course, Harold came up to see what we were talking about. I think he was jealous of all the attention I was getting.

Edward called for another chair and my brother joined us. I think he had grown in self-importance since I saw him last, and he sat down next to the king as though they were equals. Edward must have been used to my brother's behavior because he paid him no mind.

We exchanged the usual pleasantries about wives and children, but the Viking question was heavy on my mind. I looked around the hall.

"I see Aelfgar has not yet returned to favor," I ventured.

King Edward frowned. "He continues to ravage my borders," he said. "Without cease. He and Gruffydd ap Llewelyn have formed a devil's alliance."

I was waiting for Harold to say something, but he just watched Edward with interest.

"And the Norsemen? Is that an alliance also?"

"Ah, Magnus." Harold spat the name. "As far as we can tell, Magnus was acting on his own until Gruffydd started his raiding. They formed some sort of partnership."

"At my expense." I tried not to sound bitter. "They are raiding up and down my west coast."

"Tostig." Harold paused, putting together his thoughts. "There will come a time when we will give Gruffydd his just

247

retribution. We must find a way to get him apart from Aelfgar. His son-in-law."

Edward made a derogatory sound and turned his head.

"Sire," Harold pursued, "I don't see where we have much of a choice. Just like before, Aelfgar is easier to contain as Earl of Mercia rather than a dangerous outlaw procuring unfriendly allies."

I couldn't help but notice that Edward didn't want to talk about it. This looked like an ongoing discussion.

"Look at what happened to Northumbria," my brother urged. "Tostig can ill-afford such raids."

Since when did he care about me? What did he have in mind?

"I understand," Edward conceded. "But mind you, Harold. The last time, he was quiet for only a short while. It didn't last. Why should this time be any different?"

We both looked at Harold, waiting for an answer. He shrugged. "I can't think of a better solution. He's already been accused of treason and outlawed. That didn't work."

"Hmm." *Murder was an option.* I kept my mouth shut.

"In any event," Harold went on, "it shouldn't be difficult bringing him back to the fold. Provided he sends the Norsemen away."

"There's not much left for them to raid," I muttered.

Harold ignored me and we were fortunately interrupted when Edward's steward whispered in his ear.

"Ah," the king said, "they are bringing in the trestle tables. We shall have a grand feast."

And indeed it was. Edward invited my brother and me to sit at head table with our wives and the Bishops Stigand and Ealdred and a few Frenchmen I didn't know. King Edward was not a big eater, but he was generous with his table. The feast started with a peacock whose skin and feathers were reapplied to seem like the bird was ready to fly off its platter. But that was just

248

for show. As we drank copious amounts of wine, the servants carried in full carcasses of beef, partridges, pigs, does, geese, and plenty of bread with cheese. Harold was his usual jovial self and constantly asked questions about my earldom and the differences between north and south. I found myself enjoying the conversation, and even King Edward started to pay attention. Later, as Gyrth and Leofwine arrived at court bringing mother, it almost felt like the good old days.

As we celebrated Twelfth Night, the snow was coming down fast and hard and Edward insisted we stay until spring. It didn't take much to convince us! Judith and Editha were like sisters, and I loved to sit with them while they were working on a new cope for the Archbishop of Canterbury. Their conversation was lively and often turned to ecclesiastic studies; they were both so well educated I could barely follow their rapid exchanges. Edward sometimes joined us, which only enhanced the discussion as he was a great scholar in his own right.

But soon enough, we were on our way back to York; I carried letters from the king in my traveling bags announcing his intent to visit. I was anxious to return, for this was my longest absence since becoming earl. It was hard to hold back and accommodate my household and our supplies, but I was conscious that the roads were no safer than the last time I traveled this way. These were the first routes I would have to patrol for King Edward's visit to the north. I had much to do.

After the last snows had melted, I persuaded Archbishop Cynesige and Aethelwine, Bishop of Durham to accompany me on a state visit to Malcolm. We needed to bring him back to York with us to parley with the king. I thought I would require all their eloquence to persuade the Scot to come to Edward rather than the other way around. I don't think I realized how bad Cynesige's health really was, else I wouldn't have asked him to come, but

Edward's letter was most adamant and he dared not disobey. So we fitted a wagon with extra seat cushions and blankets; Cynesige was greatly cheered when we picked up Aethelwine on our way. The two ecclesiastics amused themselves with debating the great schism of the church, as the eastern and western patriarchs were still busy excommunicating each other. I soon tired of their discussion and rode in the front with my less argumentative housecarls.

Malcolm turned out to be a gracious host and gave my churchmen every consideration. He even invited the Bishop of St. Andrews to join us, though there was some stress between the three bishops because the Scots leaned toward the Celtic interpretation of our faith. Nonetheless, they apparently decided to put their differences aside for a time and we were able to get down to business.

Malcolm dressed in his best kyrtle and wore a simple gold circlet that accented his thick black hair. He really did look every bit the Scottish king.

"So what brings you so far north, Archbishop Cynesige?"

The old man was wheezing a bit, and he had to clear his throat before answering. But once he rid himself of all his phlegm, his voice was surprisingly robust.

"King Edward has sent us to meet you and bid you ride forth to greet him," he said, nodding benignly. "He travels to York and desires to see my congregation, for this is his first visit to the north. He wishes to greet you officially now you have regained your throne and are no longer an exile."

"Hmm." Malcolm stroked his beard. "King Edward was very good to me." He looked sideways at me but I tried not to betray any anxiousness. If he refused to come, Edward would certainly be wroth with me. I set my mouth and stared at Cynesige.

"Well, I am impressed by the dignity of your embassy. I know Edward is a powerful king, celebrated far and wide for his wisdom and piety."

The Bishops nodded enthusiastically.

"I'm not sure what he wants with me," Malcolm muttered, and I think I was the only one who heard him. He looked at me again.

"We spoke about you at the Christmas court," I assured him. "And he voiced an especial desire to see you. After all, you never had the opportunity to thank him for his aid."

"Ah. You are right, Tostig. I should and I shall pay that debt." He clapped his hands, once. "That settles it. I will come back with you to York. Let me summon an appropriate retinue and we shall greet Edward in the manner he deserves."

More talk of this kind went back and forth, and the churchmen prepared themselves for an extended stay. We would be ready to leave in a fortnight, which gave me time to send messages to Copsig. His task was to summon as many thegns and chieftains as possible to meet the king. I hoped more would show up for Edward than for my own pathetic assembly.

But I was not to worry. Having the king visit Yorkshire was an important event, not to be missed. Many had petitions they wanted to present; others sought to establish ownership of debated lands; still others hoped to obtain the king's goodwill by presenting him with gifts. I hoped to impress Malcolm with a substantial showing.

We rode together much of the way south. As always, Malcolm was a good companion and regaled me with amusing tales, mostly at the expense of his exasperating subjects.

At one point, he interrupted his own story. Turning in his saddle, he asked me, "What does Edward really want?"

I was expecting that. Trying to sound reasonable, I shrugged. "He wants peace in his kingdom, especially on the borders."

251

"Ah, my borders."

"*All* your borders," I said, hoping I didn't sound accusatory. "East and west."

We rode in silence for a moment.

"Since we are all friends," he considered, "and your people own land in Scotland, while my people own land in England, our borders blur a bit, don't they?"

Malcolm wasn't fooling me. He knew every inch of his border and wanted to push it south.

"Since the days of my grandfather, the English kings have tried to subdue us, or worse, force us to swear fealty as underkings." I detected a little anger in his voice, but this was better than deceit.

"I hope Edward doesn't try the same. Let us understand one another, Tostig. We have both been held down and kept from our destiny. I see how your brother lords it over the other earls, yourself included. You and I together...let's just say, protect my back and I will protect yours."

That was an interesting approach.

"You would resist Edward..."

"Only if he seeks to make demands!" His voice was booming when he let go. He looked around, hoping the churchmen weren't listening. Luckily, they were too far behind us.

"Tostig, you are far from Edward's government. Northumbria must look to its own. But Cumbria...our old kingdom of Strathclyde. Sometimes I think Cumbria must take care of itself, too."

"And we should watch over it together?" I tried to sound jovial though he troubled me. I remembered that he ceded Cumbria to Siward and resented it.

Still, Malcolm laughed. "What use has Edward for this poor country? There is very little revenue to be had."

Especially after his raiding. I kept my thoughts to myself.

"We shall see what he has planned," Malcolm conceded. "Believe it or not, I look forward to seeing him again."

That was going to have to be good enough, for Malcolm was skillful at keeping his own council. By the time we reached York, I had my hands full getting everyone settled. Thegns and sheriffs and nobles of all kinds were arriving daily, and most of them expected the best quarters. It was all I could do to keep fighting from breaking out between these stubborn louts, for I was still learning who was allied with whom and who were bitter enemies. Luckily, Copsig was on hand to ease the stress somewhat. But he was only one man, after all, and was busy making the city presentable for the king.

Cospatric came from Bamburgh, to Malcolm's delight. Those two had much to talk about, which made me happy. I wanted Malcolm to stay occupied but didn't have much time to spend with him. They both looked for Gospatrick, but the slippery earl had apparently decided to stay away.

The day finally came when Copsig's rider rode back with the good news that King Edward was one day away. I was ready, and sent messages to my guests to meet me at the Council building at first light. From there, we would progress south and welcome the king with all our splendor, for I knew he loved a colorful spectacle.

Even Malcolm looked grander than usual; his white stallion was fitted with copper bridle fittings and tassels hanging from his reins. His stirrup-straps were tooled in the Norse style, his gloves were studded with jewels, and his crown was so shiny the sun glinted off when he turned his head. I felt a little diminished beside him; but after all, I reminded myself, he was a king and I was only an earl. My own thegns fell in behind us as we started off, and I raised my hand in greeting to the small crowd that had gathered to watch us. There were about forty of us plus our wives and priests. We rode with pennons tied to our spear tips, horse manes and tails braided with ribbons, and we even brought along our falcons to remind Edward of the great hunting ahead.

Even the weather cooperated that day. The sky was a beautiful blue and I sniffed the air, enjoying the heavy scent of linden trees. I was determined to make a good impression, and I think we did.

Edward came lumbering north with a great retinue; it looked like he brought half of Wessex with him! The king commanded his trumpeters to announce his presence, like we didn't know it already. But it sounded impressive enough, though I could see some of the horses lurch in surprise. Nonetheless, they were brought under control quickly enough, and we were entertained by a little demonstration of riding skill as some of the younger *cnihts* spurred their mounts and encircled each other in a pretty display of gallantry.

As the king neared, my sister the queen waved to me, and I was filled with the joy I always felt when greeting Editha. The smile she gave belonged to me alone. Edward pulled rein and I leaped from my horse, throwing out my arms. Then I saw Harold. For a moment I was frozen in surprise but soon caught myself. Why wouldn't my brother come? He was often involved with the king's business.

I noticed Tostig's reaction that day, when he saw Harold in Edward's retinue. For a moment I felt sorry for him; this was his moment, and he didn't want to be eclipsed by his big brother. I don't think Harold realized his effect on Tostig; he was so self-composed it never would have occurred to him that Tostig might be subdued by him...Editha

"We bid you welcome, King Edward," I called, and my companions followed my lead. Even Malcolm dismounted, though
254

he was not in a hurry. Edward sat on his horse and observed the Scot curiously.

"Well, King Malcolm," he said, genially. "I am happy to see you in such fine fettle. You wear your crown well."

Malcolm grinned. "I have come a very long way since we last met," he said, taking Edward's rein from a groom. I took his own horse's rein and we all turned, falling in with Edward's companions.

Harold kicked his mount and rode beside me. "Well, brother. You seem to be very friendly with our Scottish friend."

I looked at Malcolm and shrugged my shoulders. "I hope King Edward finds a way to bind him even closer. I have enough trouble with my own earldom. I don't need to be worrying about Scotland, too."

"Ah, so you do," he agreed. I wondered what he meant by that and looked askance at him. I never knew what he was thinking.

"They view me as an outsider," I shrugged. There was no point in denying anything. "They resist any thing I say or do."

"Hmm. Well, that's one thing we need to talk about. It's time the north understood they are English subjects like the rest of us. This earldom has been under assessed for generations. Edward needs more revenue. So do you, if you require a larger force of hiredmen to keep the peace. We are reviewing the royal household, and believe me it requires much reform."

"Give me time, Harold! I'm not even settled yet."

"Of course, brother. As you say, in good time." He turned to the other side as Editha spoke to him.

"My apologies. You two have much to say to each other." He pulled back momentarily and let Editha take his place at my side. Harold was right; we started chattering like the old days, and talked all the way back to York.

Fortunately, we didn't have far to walk. By the time we reached the gates of the city, Malcolm and Edward were happily
255

exchanging pleasantries like they were old friends. The crowd of onlookers had grown tremendously and the king seemed pleased as rose petals and flowers were thrown before his horse's hooves. It was all very festive and I was proud as we approached the cathedral where the archbishops were waiting. Edward dismounted and climbed the steps with his cluster of priests and we all hung back, watching him greet the prelates with his usual dignity.

Malcolm took his reins. "We can make this work," he said. "I think he likes me."

The whole *sennight* went well. We managed three hunting trips, giving the king an opportunity to enjoy the scenery and taste some unusual wild meat. Finally, Edward was ready to do some business. He held court and greeted my thegns warmly, listening to their petitions, handing out judgments, accepting gifts, signing charters. Harold and I sat by his side almost the whole time.

Some of the local chieftains complained about the severity of my rule, though few of them dared look at me. While protesting their innocence, they inadvertently exposed their own rapacity; those of them who couldn't get what they wanted from their own socmen resorted to highway robbery. When I first took office I warned them all I would enforce the law myself if they didn't perform their duty, and it became clear that most of them refused to take me seriously. Surely I was within my own rights to fine them if they broke the law. Edward seemed to agree, for he usually found in my favor. Wise king that he was, Edward would smooth their ruffled feathers with an appropriate gift. Nonetheless, I had Copsig record all the transactions for future reference.

Finally it was Malcolm's turn. He approached the king flanked by his top advisors, all very tall and somewhat intimidating. Edward pretended not to notice, though I saw him grip his arm with his other hand.

"I thank you for coming all this way to meet me," he said. "King Malcolm, I hope we can agree on a treaty that will benefit both our countries."

That seemed like a good start. Malcolm nodded his head.

"Sire, it is my wish as well. But I would also remind you that Cumberland, which my uncle Siward guarded during my minority, is mine by inheritance. I am prepared to resume control of my patrimony."

Edward made a face, quickly squelched. "We will talk on this later," he said quietly. "For now, I am prepared to confirm your overlordship of Lothian."

This was safer grounds. Lothian, although under loose jurisdiction of England, had long ago reverted to Scotland in reality. However, Malcolm greedily jumped at the chance to get a firm treaty, and the argument about Cumberland was forgotten for the moment.

There was much back and forth discussion about the exact wording of Edward's documents, for the king loved this sort of exercise. But finally, when both of them seemed satisfied, I stood up and made my own request.

"Sire," I said, bowing to both, "I hope to strengthen our treaty by becoming sworn brother to King Malcolm."

I could see from Malcolm's hearty grin he approved of my gesture. I stepped forward, holding up my right hand.

"Let each of us hold up his hand to the other," I said, looking at King Edward as witness. "And each of us become the other's brother." He held up his hand likewise, bending his elbow, and we placed our forearms together, entwining our fingers. "With this hand-transfer I plight my troth and swear to be your faithful brother."

"And I swear to our brotherhood as well," Malcolm responded. He gave my hand a squeeze before letting go and giving me a hug.

King Edward stood up and applauded; after a moment Harold did the same. The others in the hall added their support to the general hubbub, while Edward gestured for one of his servants to come forward. The man apparently had been waiting for the right moment, for he bore gifts in his arms. One by one Edward studied each gift before presenting it to Malcolm, who passed them on to his followers. It all seemed very spontaneous, and by the time we were finished our little crowd moved into the feasting hall. I couldn't have planned it better.

Harold sat beside me at the feast, and congratulated me on my clever strategy. "I hope Malcolm proves a better brother than Swegn," he muttered, taking a bite from a leg of chicken. "If he respects your borders, you can concentrate on other things."

"Such as?"

"Taxation, as I mentioned earlier. I've been studying the assessments for Northumbria. It seems they pay a quarter of the taxes as compared to Wessex."

I felt my hand contracting into a fist. "Of course, Harold. This is a much poorer earldom, in case you didn't notice."

"Yes, yes. I know that."

"And much less populated." I think my irritation came from Harold's insistence on minding my business. I was having trouble keeping my voice even.

"Tostig, this is for your own good," he cajoled. "We need not move too quickly on this. But I speak for the king when I remind you he put you here for that reason."

This wasn't helping any. I wondered if it was true.

Chapter 8

GYRTH REMEMBERS

     Settling in as earl of East Anglia was easier than I feared. With Harold's help and Reeve Laxfield's steady hand, I was able to step into my brother's shoes. Many of the tenants were glad to see the last of Aelfgar and they gave me every consideration. My earldom was so quiet that I resolved to accompany Tostig on a pilgrimage to Rome.

     It all came about because Archbishop Cynesige died and our good friend bishop Ealdred was promoted in his place. He had been serving at Hereford these last six years and also Worcester, but York was second only to Canterbury and he was the best man for the job. Ealdred needed to travel to Rome to receive the pallium from the Pope. Tostig thought this would be a perfect opportunity to go on a pilgrimage, and I was more than happy to accompany them. Judith came as well, and we brought several young noblemen to keep their kinsmen quiet while we were absent. There were few objections; the hostages were our guests and all were well accommodated.

     Tostig insisted we stop at every shrine and leave a donation. We traveled through Saxony and I got to see the Rhine Valley. When we reached Rome, Pope Nicholas II greeted us almost as if we were royalty. Our visit corresponded with Easter and the Pope hosted a Synod, during which he insisted that Tostig sit by his side. My brother was impressed, and showed up in his best robes, looking every bit as regal as a king. His gold fillet rested lightly on his head, and his long blond hair almost glowed in the light. When he smiled, you couldn't help but notice his perfect teeth and his blue eyes. He towered over the Pope even when sitting. He almost looked as handsome as Harold.

At first the synod went well, and Nicholas consecrated two other English bishops that had preceded us. But when it came to Ealdred's turn, once it was discovered he held Worcester in plurality, the Pope denied his pallium. In fact, he demoted our Archbishop which was completely absurd; there were enough precedents to support Ealdred's position.

Tostig knew the Pope was trying to establish himself as a church reformer, and it looked like he was making an example of Ealdred, calling him an empire-builder. That didn't stop my brother from arguing the point both in private and in public. He refused to leave until he could be convinced that our cause was lost.

Weeks dragged into the second month, and by then Rome was becoming uncomfortably hot. Animal and human waste lined the streets, giving off a foul vapor, intensified by the stench from the Tiber. Tostig decided to send Judith home while he continued to negotiate with the Pope. Clearly relieved, she agreed and set off on the return journey accompanied by King Edward's royal escort and most of my brother's housecarls. Luckily for her, she had an uneventful trip back, unlike our own!

As the summer drew to an end we decided to return home, even though our mission was unsuccessful. All three Bishops were in our embassy, and we felt their status would help safeguard our greatly reduced numbers. But it was not meant to be. The very first day of our journey as the city walls had barely receded on the horizon, a large group of armored horsemen came from the trees. The lined up across the road before us. Turning, we saw an equally imposing group block our way back to the city.

The leader of the robbers, as they turned out to be, pushed his horse forward.

"My name is Gerard, Count of Galeria," he said proudly. We had heard of him; he was the leader of the party opposing the Pope. "Which one of you is Earl Tostig?"

Before my brother could say a word, one of his young retainers spurred his horse forward; it was Cospatric from Bamburgh, the fellow who always dressed in a manner to outshine the rest of us. He had been the object of many jests, but always took our comments in good spirit. "I am Earl Tostig," he declared with a warning glance at my brother.

I could tell Tostig was not pleased, but could see the sense in what Cospatric was doing. It was a risk, but Cospatric was giving us the opportunity to get away.

Count Gerard held out his hand. "I would have you surrender your arms," he ordered, and waited while Cospatric pulled his sword sheath from his belt. Meanwhile, the rest of the band insisted we dismount, and we were shamefully relieved of our weapons, our horses, and our wagons. They took everything, leaving us like paupers, and rode away with Cospatric, pulling the reins of his horse.

It was well that they robbed us so close to Rome, for we were forced to walk back the way we had come. Tostig was furious but kept his words to himself. We entered the city gates and immediately drew a crowd who escorted us to the papal palace.

Pope Nicholas met us at the portico, a look of shock on his face.

"How distressing," he clucked like a mother hen. "Come in, come in. You must be exhausted."

We were all tired and hungry, and spent the rest of that day attending to our own comforts, much as they were. Somehow, the papal delegates found enough clothing for us all, so at least we

261

could attend that evening's repast with a semblance of dignity. Tostig ate quietly, speaking to no one.

But the following morning, he insisted the Pope meet with us in state. I could see he had come to some sort of resolution; I recognized the way he held his chin up and arched his shoulders. He always acted like that when he confronted Harold.

"Holy Father," he started in a strong voice. "I am distraught at the way we were accosted almost under your very walls."

I could see that the Pope almost cringed.

"They knew we were coming and asked for me personally." His voice was rising in anger. "Someone here must have told them we were leaving." He glared at the Pope, who squirmed in his seat.

"One of my companions put himself in my place. He sacrificed himself for me! Who knows what they have done with him?"

Pope Nicholas stood from his throne but Tostig had much more to say. "They have taken everything from us! I know they stole over £1000 of our goods and treasures. You are fierce enough toward your supplicants, but you are powerless against your own rebels!"

Nicholas put out a hand. "I intend to excommunicate him!"

Tostig made a gesture of disdain. "Why should anybody care? For that matter, why should the English pay any attention to your censures against Ealdred! Even your own people ignore you! I shall take care that King Edward learns the truth about these matters. Considering how we have been humiliated, I would not be surprised if he withdraws all his tributes to the Episcopal See! Perhaps he will come to applaud the sentiments of your rebellious subjects."

Pope Nicholas sat down on his throne, breathless. He leaned to the side, listening as three cardinals whispered in his ear. Tostig stood with his arms crossed and one foot on a step above the other. He waited patiently as the Pope came to a decision.

Nicholas sat up, pursing his lips. "My dear Earl, and Archbishop Ealdred." His voice was almost caressing. "We are deeply troubled at the mistreatment you have undergone at the hands of our contemptible countrymen. I vow to replace all your losses out of the papal treasury."

He leaned aside again, nodding his head. "And Archbishop Ealdred, I have reconsidered your position and will willingly invest you with the pallium, provided you resign the See of Worcester."

Ealdred bowed, trying to hide his amazement. Tostig had accomplished his mission after all, through his brazen rhetoric. No wonder he had been so quiet.

As our delegation was leaving the following day, we were delighted to encounter Cospatric, astride his own horse and none the worse for the experience. Tostig gave him a great hug in front of everyone.

"How did you manage to get away?" my brother asked in wonder.

Cospatric gave him a broad smile. "Once you were safely far away, I told them they had the wrong man. At first, I feared I would come to some harm. But once they got over the shock, they admired my pluck and gave me back my sword and all my money." Tostig slapped his back, only slightly annoyed that they kept our goods. The Pope had more than made up for our losses.

Tostig's trip to Rome had done wonders for our church in England. Archbishop Ealdred was our great friend, and the Pope's stubborn refusal to give him his pallium would have caused resentment on our side of the Channel. Fortunately, Tostig

263

was quick to react and saved Ealdred much embarrassment...
Editha

TOSTIG REMEMBERS

Our experience in Rome brought Cospatric and me closer together than I ever anticipated. I already liked him, which is why I invited him to join our pilgrimage. But his courage inspired me with a new sense of loyalty. Alas, I was soon to discover I owed him much more than friendship, for his absence nearly beggared him.

The Pope sent us home in high style, even though I was annoyed that he also sent along two of his cardinals to make sure we complied with his demands. Nonetheless, Archbishop Ealdred graciously entertained them. When we landed in England I was glad for their presence because I needed all the prayers I could get. For everything had gone all wrong.

I wasn't aware of the depredations until I entered York. My city was too far south to experience any border raids, but there had been an influx of displaced landowners who filled my council halls with pleas for help and retribution. Copsig was harried but relieved to see me, and I was soon surrounded by shouting men.

There were so many complaints it took me a while to sort it out. Yes, it was Malcolm. My sworn brother. He took advantage of my absence and came blazing across the border, almost all the way to Durham. He even ravaged Lindisfarne, much to my disgust. Then, turning west, his army pushed through the Tyne Gap and occupied Cumberland. Malcolm had recaptured his inheritance.

My first inclination was to put together an army and go after them. But much to my annoyance, the call to arms was largely ignored by my faithless Northumbrians. Those most directly affected were too concerned with their own problems to respond to my summons. The Yorkshire men felt no impulse to support their neighbors to the north.

Determined to deal with my recalcitrant nobles later, I took my household troops and moved out to investigate the destruction. At the very least, I intended to confront Malcolm in person and demand an explanation.

Cospatric and his retainers were anxious to return home, and they planned to accompany us as far as Bamburgh. The farther north we went, the grimmer the surroundings. One after another we passed burnt-out farmsteads, broken-up wagons, the occasional carcass picked clean. Cospatric spoke little, but I could see the distress on his face. I felt responsible; I thought the north was secure, else I never would have left the country.

"Shall we accompany you to Bamburgh?" I ventured, not sure how he would react. But his shoulders immediately dropped and he sighed with relief.

"I would like that very much, Earl Tostig. I don't know what to expect."

I didn't need to voice my opinion. We passed through the Cheviot Hills, but this time they had no charm for me. I kept thinking about the Scots raiding my poor towns and dragging the survivors off to slavery. I'm sure Cospatric was torturing himself with much the same thoughts.

As we finally entered the last valley before Bamburgh, our way was blocked by a force of men who had apparently been warned of our approach. At first I thought there was some mistake, but suddenly my companion groaned.

"I know those men," he muttered. I turned in my saddle.

"Who are they?"

"Their leaders are Gamel son of Orm and Ulf son of Dolphin. They support my cousin Gospatrick."

"Gospatrick? What has he to do with us?"

I kicked my mount forward; they sat on their horses, passively waiting. Cospatric came up behind me.

"Gamel son of Orm," I said scornfully. "Every time I hear your name, something violent seems to be happening."

I could tell by the sneer which man answered to that name.

"Go back the way you came," Gamel said.

It was my turn to bristle. "Do you know who I am?"

"We know who you are. Take you and the pup and get thee gone."

My retainers moved to my side and we faced our opponents. Our numbers were about equal. I drew my sword with a long, slow rasping noise. I loved that sound.

"Would you care to explain yourselves?" Even I was impressed with the threat in my voice.

They drew their swords as well. Then, at a sudden disturbance, another score of warriors appeared from behind a large rock outcropping. The men facing us parted and their commander kicked his steed forward. Cospatric gasped.

"Uncle," he said quietly. The man ignored him and spurred his mount toward me, almost colliding with my horse. I ground my teeth as I recognized the harsh features of Gospatrick. Why did the very sight of him always make me want to break something?

"Since you left your earldom undefended," he said insolently, "Malcolm of Scotland saw fit to push me out of Cumberland. MY Cumberland, under my rule these past twenty years. As you know. I did not have the force to resist him. Nor do you, I see." Those last words came out with scorn. The fact that he was right didn't help my temper any.

But Gospatrick wasn't finished gloating yet. "As I am the rightful Earl of Northumberland, it was only fitting that I take back my castle at Bamburgh. The earldom is mine, and I am telling you to depart from my lands!"

266

Poor Cospatric was furious, but his uncle was a powerful man and I could see he was afraid of him. "What about my men?" he managed to ask.

"Oh, don't worry about them. They serve me now."

This was maddening. But I dared not start a battle with such poor odds. I had no allies here, nor were we adequately armed for serious fighting. I sheathed my sword and nodded for my men to do likewise.

Gospatrick wasted no time and turned his horse away. The man was so offensive I wished I could sink an arrow into his back. Gamel and Ulf watched us impassively, and I decided to deal with them later.

"Come," I said to my men. "Let us leave this place."

Cospatric was none too happy and spoke not a word for many miles. I risked an occasional look in his direction, but it wasn't until we were back on the old Roman road that I decided to speak.

"Come with me to Scotland," I said. "Cospatric, I would have you be my *gesith,* my companion and advisor. I will grant you lands in Yorkshire to keep forever, even after I restore you to Northumberland."

These were not empty words. I had come to appreciate my young companion and sincerely wanted him to stay with me. After all, he probably saved my life and I trusted him. And it was my fault he lost his earldom. I could feel his bitter regret.

But what choice did Cospatric have? His uncle was from the senior branch of his family; Gospatrick was the direct descendant of Earl Uhtred. In effect, poor Cospatric had been holding Bamburgh against the time his uncle would reassert his claim. But it shouldn't have been so easy.

For now, there was nothing I could do. I needed to regain my strength, and reestablish my authority. I could not offer Cospatric enough to compensate him for the loss of Bamburgh, but at least I could raise him up and give him a place of honor in

267

my administration. And it was only a matter of time before I dealt with Gospatrick and his insults. The man was a fool to underestimate a son of Godwine.

We continued unopposed to Scotland. Malcolm was at his new tower at Dunfermline, and by the time we arrived he was well informed of our presence. I wasn't sure what I was going to say to him, but it seemed best to act in a neutral manner, at least for now. He was master here, sworn brother or not. He possessed all the advantages of the situation.

Malcolm chose to wait for me in Dunfermline, and sent out a retinue to meet us. They would accompany me and my companions through his lands. His small party approached leisurely enough; we did not feel threatened.

The king greeted us in his full regalia. I approached his throne and he finally rose to meet me, grabbing my shoulders in a brotherly embrace and kissing both cheeks very ceremoniously. I presented him with gifts and he offered me a seat beside him on a lower chair. His court was mostly informal and people started milling around, ignoring us for the most part. Malcolm removed his crown and handed it off to a page.

He took a drink of wine and looked hard at me over the edge of the chalice. I knew he was waiting for me to speak first. I took a deep breath.

"What happened to our brotherhood?" I ventured, trying not to sound hostile. Indeed, I was disappointed and I think it showed.

"Why, nothing," he said quietly.

I frowned. "You devastate my lands and call it nothing?"

"Ah, your lands. Mmm, that is debatable."

"What?"

"Tostig, I only took back what is mine."

"Yours." This was not going well. "While I was out of the country."

"And hence, I did not break our oath. You were not there, so I did not fight against you."

He gave me one of his charming smiles. I wondered how long it took him to think up that line of reasoning. I looked away, annoyed. He was so clever.

"And what about Cospatric?"

At least Malcolm had the decency to look embarrassed. He glanced at his cousin who returned his look impassively.

"I am sorry about that. Truly I am. These marcher territories change hands so many times one can depend on nothing. I wasn't expecting Gospatrick to take such action. How can I make it up to you?"

"I'll take care of that," I interrupted. I didn't want Cospatric to go with Malcolm. The king shrugged his shoulders.

"As you wish. Look, Tostig. I swear to you. I have no interest in land farther south. I reclaimed my own and from now on, until you or I leave this earth, there will be peace on our borders."

On our borders. Our borders with a new borderline. Malcolm sat back in his throne and draped a leg over its arm. I don't think he was expecting a response.

And what could I do? Like Cospatric, I was cut adrift without support. I had already seen that my own thegns were reluctant to pursue any policy against the Scots at this time. Even if they were willing, it would be expensive and probably not worth the effort.

Malcolm was a strong young king, and a bold one. The loss of Cumberland was troublesome, but of all the territory this was the county he truly claimed by inheritance. He had tried to get Edward to return it, and that went nowhere. So he took matters into his own hands.

And what of the lands north of Durham? Maybe I should let Gospatrick break his head against the rock of Malcolm's greed. If he wants it so bad, maybe I should leave it to him...and all its troubles.

It was a bitter tonic to swallow, but in the end I went back home with nothing accomplished except a promise from Malcolm that it would never happen again. As ever, he was so convincing I actually believed him. Perhaps it was my fault for having neglected to extract such an oath in my more trusting days before the invasion.

GYRTH REMEMBERS

While we were in Rome, Harold had been busy rebuilding Hereford and training his local force to fight in the Welsh manner. They needed to relinquish their heavy chain maille hauberks and travel lightly, striking and retreating. He was destined to use this new training earlier than he anticipated.

In 1062, King Edward held his Christmas court in Gloucester as usual. All of us were expected to attend, and it happened that Harold and I met in Oxford and traveled there together, along with his growing family. The days were crisp and clear and we were feeling very cheerful as we approached Kingsholm, Edward's favorite palace. As we dismounted in the courtyard, the children were laughing and I watched Harold pull Edith by the waist from her horse, kissing her hair as he placed her feet on the ground.

"Come, brother," he turned to me. "Let us see who else is here."

We were relative latecomers and the hall was full already. I saw Leofwine speaking to our sister, and there was our mother looking radiant as usual. She came over to us and kissed Harold on the cheek before giving me a hug.

"I understand you and Tostig had quite a tour," she laughed. "Archbishop Ealdred tells me he saved the day." Mother turned and put an arm around Edith. "My dear, I am so glad to see you..."

They fell into women's talk and I wandered off, looking for something to drink. The festivities hadn't started in earnest yet, and I moved through the small crowd, looking for familiar faces. I wasn't surprised that Tostig hadn't yet arrived, but I certainly expected to see Aelfgar. It wasn't long before I discovered why he hadn't come.

I happened to be standing near the king when a messanger came forward, kneeling before the throne.

"Sire," he said loudly enough for many of us to hear. "I bring sorrowful news. Earl Aelfgar is dead."

The men around me stopped mid-speech. The Earl of Mercia was a young man; he was not much over 30. The King crossed himself.

"What did he die from?" he asked the messenger.

"My Lord, he was sick for many weeks. I believe he had an ailment of the lungs. His breathing was noisy and not very deep."

King Edward directed his steward to reward the man, then made a comment to my sister. I don't think he was too fond of Aelfgar. Deep in thought, I was watching him when suddenly Harold put his arm through mine, pulling me to the edge of the hall without pausing in his haste.

"Here is our golden moment," he said in my ear, looking to see that no one heard us. "We will never have a better chance."

I'm sorry to say I wasn't following him. I looked at him questioningly.

"That Welsh fox! Gruffydd!" he said impatiently. "We can catch him in his den before he learns of Aelfgar's death."

I sucked in my breath. It was a daring idea.

"If we put together a small and mobile force, we can be upon him while he is celebrating his Christmas festivities. We will easily be back before the New Year. We will pass right through Hereford on the way to the Prince's palace at Rhuddlan. There I can gather my new recruits."

I was flattered that he wanted to include me in his plans, but I felt sorry for Edith. Once Harold made up his mind, there was no changing it. His wife was going to spend Christmas without him.

"We must keep our movements a secret, lest word gets out. Alas, I'm sure I will be missed. Gyrth, notify my hearth-troops of my new plans. Tell them to meet us in the palace courtyard at first light." He put a hand on my shoulder. "I am going to tell the king of my plans."

He started away then turned back with a half-grin on his face. "And tell them not to drink too much."

I watched for a moment as Harold approached King Edward and bent over his ear. At first the king pulled back in surprise, then a slow smile covered his face. I imagine he didn't want Harold to miss the Christmas activities, but Gruffydd was a thorn in his side. Harold would be doing him a great favor.

Then my brother went to find his wife. I turned away, suspecting her beautiful face would crumple with disappointment and not wanting to see it. I would prefer the company of Harold's housecarls anyway, and went to carry them the news.

It was about 10 leagues to Hereford, and it was fortunate we got an early start, because we were on the road all day. It was much farther than that to Rhuddlan, so Harold would be anxious to be on our way as soon as possible. However, no one at Hereford knew we were coming, and it took some time before his little force could prepare for our lightning journey. The likelihood of our living off the land in winter was very slim.

This was the first time I ever traveled with him in a military capacity. I knew Harold was an organized administrator, but I never saw him do so many things at one time. He could effortlessly switch from ordering food to gathering weapons to outfitting the horses to cajoling his men, then take a short spell of sleep and be right back again. I don't think anyone could have moved faster.

We were soon back on our horses, and I was glad we were keeping a good pace because it was the best way to stay warm. Even so, there were times when the road disappeared and we had to pick our way through the forest. It seemed like the wind never stopped, but at least the trees slowed it down. We tried to stay on even ground, and we kept the mountains to the west of us. We camped at night under the stars, for there were no towns or monasteries along the way to give us shelter. It was a miserable time, and I hope never to do it again. But no matter how uncomfortable we were, Harold was right there with us, urging us along. He had vowed to put an end to Gruffydd ap Llewelyn, and there was no stopping him.

I knew we were getting close when the air started smelling salty. Rhuddlan was on the northern coast of Wales, up against the river Clwyd. That's all I knew about it. As we neared the palace, we all dismounted so as to approach silently. Harold waited impatiently while we gathered in a tight group behind him.

"You know what we must do," he reminded us. "There is plenty of dry wood available. Let us gather as much as we can. I will go ahead and observe his defenses, and discover how far along they are in their cups. If they are lax, like I imagine, we can pile our wood against the building and set fire to it in the Norse manner. We can kill the men as they run out of the burning hall."

As we started gathering wood, Harold stood at the edge of the forest and waited, listening. It seemed that nobody was alerted to our presence, and no wonder: we had arrived on Christmas night, and surely everyone was celebrating the Yule. The moon was behind the clouds; and the only other sound we heard was the rustling of the trees. I moved next to Harold, determined to go with him. Then suddenly we heard the unmistakable sound of an oar splash; noises can travel in the strangest ways on a night like this. Harold looked at me, his face covered with shock. Then he growled, "Something is not right. Let us take a few men and get a closer look."

I quickly picked our best fighters and we followed right behind him, having trouble keeping pace. We flattened ourselves against the wooden palisade and edged toward the river. The palace spanned the Clwyd, leaving space for boat mooring. But tonight, there were too few boats.

The moon was coming out from behind the clouds, and to our astonished eyes we saw a small group of ships moving away from the shore. Harold gripped my arm and I knew there was nothing to say. Someone had gotten here first, and this whole expedition was for naught.

"Have someone go back for the rest of our men, and bring the firewood," he growled. "Looks like we no longer need stealth, but I will tell Gruffydd that Harold was here." He drew his sword, stomping toward the palisade gate.

I did as instructed then we stormed the gate, which gave way before our determined axes. There were a few frightened people scurrying away from us and Harold pointed to them. Nothing loth, our men scattered and started what we came for. "Remember Hereford!" they were shouting, as if to justify the slaughter about to begin.

Harold made straight for the feasting hall, kicking the doors in and charging with his sword upraised. There was no need: the tables were empty, with platters knocked over and thrown on the floor, food strewn everywhere while the dogs devoured the Christmas feast. My brother swing around and shouted, "Fire this place." Then he shouldered his way out the door and looked for a vantage point from which he could watch the boats.

"Remove the figurehead from Gruffydd's flagship. We'll take it back with us. Then burn the rest of his fleet."

274

It wasn't long before the others came, carrying bundles of wood and kindling. They quickly set fire to the palace then gleefully joined the plundering. The poor villagers were screaming, some were trying to defend themselves while others were killed running away. This was my first taste of warfare, and I was horrified. Thatched roof huts went up in flame, animals were running wild, and Harold just stood there, arms crossed. The look of fury on his face was enough to keep me silent.

"It's a paltry revenge," he finally said to me. "But Gruffydd has not seen the last of me."

We stood there while the palace blazed behind us, and we could only imagine what the Prince of Wales was thinking, out there in his chilly boat. Did he feel relief, I wonder? Or did he wish he could have perished along with his people? I never forgot the terror of those pitiful, abandoned serfs.

TOSTIG REMEMBERS

I would guess the high point of Harold's early career came when he conducted his Welsh campaign against Gruffydd ap Llewelyn. It was an altogether different kind of offensive: fighting against wild men who didn't understand the first thing about real warfare. Harold would have had a difficult time of it, if I wasn't there to help him.

This took place in 1063, the year following his Christmas fiasco. By then, King Edward had come to depend on Harold as his right hand, so to speak. The King preferred to spend all his time at prayer—as he does now—or at the hunt, leaving the government in Harold's capable hands. My brother was always good at that sort of thing, and he governed England in much the same way as his earldom of Wessex. Still, I was beginning to think he was getting a little too arrogant.

After Harold failed to catch the Welsh Prince at his Christmas court, he was back in Gloucester in time for Twelfth Night. Empty-handed. On his ride back to the king's court, he must have had plenty to think about, because he had already decided to try again in the spring. I know. I was there.

The holiday feasting was still going strong. The evening after his return, Harold got up from his place next to the king and made his way over to me. I was not at head table this day; I was sitting nearby at a trestle table with Judith, Cospatric, and my brothers. Harold asked Leofwine to cede his place next to me and my little brother obliged, putting a piece of bread in his mouth and reaching for his wine. I handed it over.

Harold sat down with a grunt. "My rump still hurts from the saddle," he complained conversationally. I knew better.

"We haven't settled our grievances against that so-called King of Wales," he added, clearing a space in front of him on the table. A servant placed a fresh trencher before he even asked.

I let out a short laugh. "I suspect Gruffydd has his own grievances, now."

"No matter. He is a dead man."

I raised my eyebrows. "Aren't you a little ahead of yourself?"

"Not if I have your help." He leaned forward and spoke to Judith briefly. Now, this was the first time Harold ever asked me for anything. Imagine, the great Earl of Wessex needing help from his little brother! After complimenting Judith on her lovely embroidered veil, he turned back to me.

"We still have that unfinished business about the Norse invasion of Cumberland."

Harold knew as well as I that Cumberland was no longer my concern. But he also knew I was exposed to attack from the west. As long as Gruffydd was around, my earldom was not safe.

276

But more than that, he knew I held grudges for a long time.

"Of course, your men will have their share of plunder," he added. I doubted there would be much of that, but promising it should dig up some enthusiastic response.

My participation was almost to be expected; how could I refuse my brother?

As I suspected, I had no problem raising an army. There might have been no profit marching north through lands already devastated, but this was new territory and my people had an innate dislike for the Welsh.

By the end of May I was ready. I marched my troops due west across England and followed the northern coast of Wales before reaching our meeting point at the Isle of Anglesey. We even passed the burnt-out palace at Rhuddlan—and what a devastation Harold wreaked. Although we were instructed to pillage all we wanted, there was not much further damage we could inflict where Harold had already been.

I was the first to reach Anglesey, and we set up camp on the mainland. Harold showed up a few days later, having transported his troops along the coast by boat, so he could catch Gruffydd if the Prince had attempted to escape by sea.

The idea of this campaign was to capture Gruffydd in a trap by systematically ravaging the country north to south until he couldn't run away anymore. This meant we would have to cross the mountains of Snowdonia on foot, trying to march in some semblance of order. It sounded impractical to me but, looking back, I can see there was no other way.

Of course, at the time I didn't know that. I was expecting some real fighting; I didn't have the benefit of Harold's experience with the Welsh. Harold instructed all of us to dispense with our heavy weaponry and instead to bring javelins and bows to fight with, and of course our swords. We were to exchange our usual chain maille for leather scale armor. Our numbers were smaller, too, else Harold would never have managed to commandeer enough ships.

We were all rather dubious about his instructions at first, but events proved him right. Harold ran us a merry chase into the mountains, and with our usual gear we would have bogged down in a hurry.

But I'm getting ahead of myself. When my brother came into sight on his ships, I lined up my troops to meet him. Harold made the most of his moment, finding it necessary to create a ceremony out of a simple disembarkation. But I had to admire his bearing. My brother stood at the prow of his great dragon-ship, looking every bit the Viking warrior. His long brown hair blew away from his face, and that strong jaw cut a stark silhouette against the grey sky. He looked better without a beard, which he had gotten rid of last year. He seemed taller than usual, more filled out, though I suppose it must have been the effect of the moment.

Harold stood for a long time, looking out over my troops. It was as though he was their leader rather than myself, which irked me a bit. Sometimes I wonder if even then he was contemplating taking the throne for himself. He seemed to enjoy the power he could command over men's hearts.

Then his eyes settled on me, and a smile broke over his face that made me forget all of my annoyance. He leaped gracefully from the ship and waded through the water, embracing me in front of everyone. It was all very ceremonious, yet at the same time he held my gaze in that private way brothers do, silently communicating his satisfaction that everything was working as planned.

Then Harold put his arm through mine and led me to my own tent, dispensing with ceremony and getting right to the point. "The locals tell me Gruffydd has fled to into the mountains, like we expected," he said, pouring for himself a cupful of my ale. He forgot to offer some to me.

"As I rounded the coast of South Wales, the chieftains were waiting at each and every port. They fell all over each other trying to make treaties with me, the treacherous bastards."

Like it or not, I'm sure Harold signed every treaty. "So Gruffydd has no allies in the south," I asked.

"None." Harold looked at me, hungry for action. "We will chase him into the mountains until he can run no further. By then, his people will be so sick of warfare that they will gladly surrender him to me."

I wasn't so sure I agreed, but I kept quiet. I knew better than to argue with Harold.

"We will devastate the land as we pass. I want these people to know they are conquered."

I sighed, disappointed. A plundering expedition, nothing more. Is this what I came hundreds of miles for? My dissatisfaction must have shown on my face, because he took an unusually long time explaining matters to me.

"I know you expected to fight. But I know what I am doing, Tostig. These Welsh are smart enough to realize they will lose a pitched battle. They don't fight that way. Their strength is in retreat, which is why they excel in attacking and running. You will see. They pour out of mountains that only a goat should find a foothold on. And before you know it, you have an arrow in your back. I lost many a good man that way."

Watching his face, it was then I realized that Harold's first priority was revenge. This nation of Welshmen had made a fool of him. Trying to fight them was the only time Harold had failed; he was taking all of this personally.

"But I'm still not sure I completely understand," I pursued. "If your men were injured wearing heavier armor, why will lighter armor benefit us?"

"We cannot travel far so heavily burdened. My men began taking off their hauberks so they could move faster. It was then that the Welsh would attack, as if they were watching for just such a moment. Oh, they are sly, Tostig. This time, the men will live in their leather armor, night and day. We will find a way to crawl into those mountains if we have to wear our fingers to the bone, gripping the rocks for a hold."

He turned to the distant peaks, taking a long look as though to memorize every line. Indeed, that's what I think he was doing.

"So you think we can beat them with their own tactics?" I asked.

Harold did not take his eyes away from the horizon. "There are more of us. If they destroy this army, I will return with another, then another, until the Welsh are defeated. Time is on my side."

Even knowing Harold as I did, I was appalled at his reckless single-mindedness. Something had changed about him in the last few years. He had become full of his own importance, and I dare say was beginning to think of himself as invincible.

On the other hand, this humor of his was infectious. Even I felt it a little, and I know the men did; we tramped into Snowdonia ready for anything. Side by side my troops marched with his, and nothing could stand before us. Shepherds fled with their flocks but we caught them, took what we wanted and killed the rest. We had no lack of food this campaign. There were few homesteads to burn, and little else to occupy ourselves with but marching and climbing, marching and climbing.

At first, we encountered no opposing force of any kind. It was as if this cursed land had emptied at the first word of an English army. But then, when we were just beginning to believe this was going to be an easy campaign, the Welsh leaped out of nowhere and assailed our men. There were hundreds of them. It was just as Harold had warned. They were quick and efficient, startling us, then striving to hurl our murdered souls to hell with blood-curdling screams.

I'm ashamed to say, but we were totally unprepared for their onslaught, and the first few bloody minutes went very badly for us. We were stumbling around in confusion, fighting a defensive battle, though I will say that when we connected, a Welshman fell dead to the ground. They were poorly armed, those fighters; some were even attacking us with sharpened stones tied to sticks. Of course their protection was minimal. But they made up for this by the most agile movements I have ever seen. These men weaved in and out of range as though by magic—and I have heard tell that they practice the black arts—so just as I attacked another, he was gone without a trace.

And I can't begin to express the havoc the Welsh wreaked with their long bows. I thought Harold was mad to insist that we bring ours. But each Welshman brought down his mark cleanly with every feathered shaft, and from such a distance that he could safely escape. They shot backwards as they ran away, with accuracy that put all of us to shame.

So at first we were confused and frightened. Yes, I'm not ashamed to admit it. A man would be mad not to fear that kind of death. But just when we were ready to break and run, Harold dove into their midst, teeth gnashing in a berserker frenzy. I have never seen him like that! My brother seemed impervious to attack; their blades glanced harmlessly off his armor.

Harold inspired us with his example, and we gathered together and rushed forward as a unit, pushing the Welsh before us like so many cattle. We were glad of our leather armor now, as it permitted us to charge without exhausting ourselves.

For a few minutes the Welsh turned at bay, facing us with the ferocity of a mother bear defending its cub. Then, responding to some secret signal, they all turned and ran, shooting at us again in their flight. At least this time we had the foresight to raise our small shields. Then they were gone, and the hills were silent. We looked at our dead, somewhat comforted by the knowledge that we killed nearly two for every one of our losses.

Harold came up to me, breathing hard. "Did you see him?"

"See who?" I couldn't distinguish one of those caitiffs from the others.

"Gruffydd. The large red-headed man with the axe."

I shook my head. "I barely remember what he looks like."

"Well, he was among them," Harold growled at me, though I don't know why he was so irritated. "I tried to reach him, but he was too well guarded."

"Point him out to me next time," I said.

Harold looked at me, exasperated. "You don't even know who you are fighting?"

I had almost forgotten. This campaign was Harold's private revenge; he probably dreamed about Gruffydd at night. "If I had killed him for you, I would have taken your glory away." I couldn't help the sneer that entered my voice; it was an old habit. Bracing myself for retaliation, I was surprised when nothing came. Harold stood in thought.

"You know, Tostig, you could be right. I might not appreciate seeing Gruffydd killed by anyone else. But ending the campaign would be more important than my pride." He looked at me with those clear blue eyes, silently asking for confirmation. Harold wanted everyone to love him, even me.

"I'm sure you would remember that, in the end," I said, putting my arm around him. He was so weary he actually leaned against me. But when people started coming up to him and asking questions, Harold straightened up like he wasn't the least bit tired.

"I think we will show them how much we have learned," he said, rubbing his chin. "This soil is too rocky to bury our own dead, so let us make a funeral pyre. As for the Welsh..." I swear, his eyes sparkled here. "As for the Welsh, cut off their heads and make a pile of them. There, on the roadside."

282

Harold's men stared at him like he had lost his mind. He reddened. "It is their own custom," he said defensively. "It's time we showed them how it feels. They are your enemies, don't you remember?"

The men knew better than to argue. Frowning, they started off. "Oh, and something else," he called. "On our stack of heads we shall hang a sign, saying...yes, that's it: 'HERE HAROLD CONQUERED'. There will be no doubt in their minds as to who they are dealing with."

How like Harold to assume that just because he was in possession of the field, he had won a victory. He, most of all, should have realized that the Welsh ran away not because they were vanquished, but rather to fight another day.

But no, my brother insisted on building a grisly cairn at every site—and there were many of them, for the Welsh attacked us nearly every day. It was tiring work, but Harold insisted it was terrible for the Welsh morale. I suppose he was right in the end. The men became accustomed to chopping off Welsh heads, and even made a gruesome game of it, tossing those trophies to each other rather than walking them over to the pile.

The worst times for us were the nights. I don't think I managed to get a full night's sleep the whole campaign, what with nocturnal raids and the weird noises coming out of the darkness. Didn't the Welsh ever rest? I think they enjoyed sitting on their frigid rocks and howling at the moon, just to aggravate us to death.

One night I leaped out of my blankets just in time to avoid a huge blade that slammed into the ground where my head had been; it even made sparks when it hit. The sword's owner didn't live to repeat his treachery; I awoke knife in hand and drove it into his belly.

It took a couple of minutes kneeling and listening to his dying gasps before my body stopped shaking. I was lucky the man came alone, else another would have found me easy prey. It was

283

the closest I ever came to death, and it was the more terrifying that it was so unexpected.

After I thanked all the Gods for my deliverance, I looked up to see Harold running, holding a sword. "Are you all right?" he cried, and his concern erased any thoughts I might have had of his treachery. He threw his arms around me and held me close.

I derived a lot of comfort from his embrace; it was the only time he ever hugged me.

But this brotherly moment did not last long. "Where was our guard?" I asked, pulling away. I was a little embarrassed by it all.

By now most of us had woken up, and people were running about, searching for more assassins. Someone came up to Harold. "Two of the guards were found dead, their throats cut," he said.

Harold stared at me, his eyes moist. "That could have been you. I wonder if they singled you out."

My thoughts exactly. It was not a pleasant thing to dwell on. But it never happened again. At least, not like that.

The rest of the summer passed in pretty much the same way, blurring together in a series of skirmishes, all with the same results. We steadily moved south through the mountains, systematically burning and destroying whatever we could find. We searched long and hard for Gruffydd's camp, and we often found where he had holed up for a time. But it was always too late; the site would be abandoned at first sign of our approach. That was one disadvantage to our type of expedition; the smoke from our pillaging gave us away.

However, it became evident we were making progress; the forces attacking us got smaller and smaller, and fought for shorter stretches before retreating. Perhaps we were finally wearing them down; they certainly had that effect on us.

Finally, one day, we burst upon a camp freshly abandoned; the fires were still burning, and breakfast was merrily cooking on a spit. Harold was so provoked by the sight he spewed a whole string of oaths, and commanded his men to find the refugees. I tried to stop him but he shook me off angrily, telling me to mind my own business.

Imagine that. If this wasn't my business, what was I doing there?

Of course, I was right and he was wrong. We were so scattered that the Welsh turned on our men and slaughtered them, once again magically appearing out of nowhere. They even charged us in camp, where Harold and I were nearly overwhelmed. I think this last attack was made out of desperation rather than any deliberate plan, but it nearly finished us. If I hadn't taken a moment to blow on my horn, it would have been all over. As it was, this signal nearly cost me my arm. I killed the man who attacked me, but the wound aches to this day.

Harold and I stood back to back, and the handful with us made a circle, protecting us as best as they could. I looked for Gruffydd this time, but without success; he must have preferred safety to revenge. Of course, there were enough opponents to occupy me, and I hacked and slashed with my sword, trying to ignore the pain in my left arm. I think all those frantic movements forced me to shed more blood.

After what seemed like hours—though I'm sure it was only minutes—our men poured into camp in response to my call. The Welsh found themselves surrounded for once, and fought like animals trying to break loose. Never once did they attempt to surrender; I suppose they don't know the meaning of the word. Nor am I at all certain that Harold would have spared them—he was so angry.

This was the end of their resistance that day, and the ground was littered with corpses. This time, too many of them were ours. I was so mad at Harold I nearly punched him. But he was too full of himself to notice me; he realized he had been a fool, and he was more embarrassed by his blunder than upset by the loss of men.

Harold sat down in the middle of all that carnage, looking around. He threw his sword on the ground. "That's it," he groaned, putting hands over his face. "We must find another way."

I still don't understand why he admitted defeat, so close to the end. Oh, I suppose he was not really admitting defeat, but that's how I saw it. I almost forgot about what he said until later that night, when Harold summoned me to his tent. This was a most unusual occurrence and I went right away, intensely curious. When I parted the door, I was greeted with a bizarre sight. There was my brother, as calm as could be, sharing his dinner with two wild, mangy Welshmen. The hairs on the back of my neck bristled, but I fought back my natural reaction. It was obvious my brother was up to something.

"Oh, there you are," Harold said, pointing at a cushion by his side. "Come, join us."

Fortunately, I had already eaten, so I could politely refuse to share their table; it almost made me sick, anyway. Harold frowned at me but merely said, "Tostig, this is Bleddynn and Rhiwallon, half-brothers to Gruffydd ap Llewelyn."

I nodded briefly, wondering how he had managed to contact the enemy so soon. Perhaps they had been communicating for some time.

"They are here to negotiate with us. It seems the Welsh are sick of warfare, and desire peace at any cost." Harold's tone sent shivers down my spine; I recognized it immediately. He spoke like this whenever he wanted something badly and would not take "no" for an answer.

The bigger stranger shifted his weight, clearing his throat. "You see, Earl Harold, Earl Tostig," he said with a tolerable grasp of our language, "Prince Gruffydd stubbornly refuses to listen to reason. He witnesses the destruction of our land and people, yet his only thought is to evade your grasp." He spit on the ground. "He cares nothing for our misery. But his force shrinks day by day. Soon he will be fighting alone." As if to emphasize this

286

statement, the man shoved a drumstick into his mouth. I dare say he would have eaten the bones if he could.

Meanwhile, Harold was watching him with flickering eyes. How could this Welshman talk so freely? It was as if he didn't notice Harold's scrutiny at all.

"So you say his force is dissolving?" my brother finally asked.

The other nodded, swallowing a half-chewed mouthful. "The campaign is a disaster. Gruffydd is the only one who doesn't realize it. My brother and I have decided to take matters into our own hands..." He looked at his companion, as though to smother any objection. "Gruffydd is obviously unfit to rule. We propose to end this senseless war. We put ourselves forward as his successors."

For a split second, a greedy smile broke through the man's studied respect. I know Harold saw it too; he sighed, disappointed. In my brother's personal version of honor, betrayal for one's country is all right, but betrayal for personal gain is despicable. Then again, that didn't stop him from using any advantage that presented itself.

"Just how are you going to end this war?" he sighed.

"Leave that to us. You will know when all is over."

"I need positive proof," Harold emphasized, leaning forward.

The other seemed unconcerned. "Do not worry. You will have it." Grabbing a last handful of food, he stood, gesturing for his brother to do the same. "Do we have your countenance?"

My brother nodded wearily. The Welshman bowed, almost mockingly, then was gone, taking his vile odor with him.

Harold's shoulders slumped. "I would there was another way," he said. He was a picture of tragedy.

By now, I had begun to lose patience with him. "What is the matter with you?" I said. "You got what you wanted, didn't you?"

287

"Wanted? I didn't want it this way...through treachery. Oh, you wouldn't understand."

That did it. I leaped to my feet, enraged. "Wouldn't understand? Just what do you call a surprise raid on Rhuddlan during Christmas festivities, when men should be thinking of peace, and God? You weren't concerned with treachery then, were you?"

By now Harold was on his feet, forgetting his distress. "Since when did you get so pious?"

If I hadn't been so angry about the other subject, I would have taken offense. My faith was genuine, but I wasn't sure about his. Though I doubt he meant what he said; Harold was angry because I saw through his pretense.

"I just know that you could not care less how Gruffydd was betrayed, so long as you earned glory out of the campaign. Let's not fool each other."

Harold turned a dozen shades of red, but it seems he was speechless. Maybe that's why we never got along; I couldn't keep my mouth shut about the truth.

Just as suddenly, his face fell. "Is that how you really see me?" he asked. Of all the reactions, this is one I least expected. It was my turn to be speechless.

"Then why did you help me?" he added with a small voice.

That was a good question. I knew there would be no glory in it for me. "Because you're my brother," I managed to say before pushing my way out of the tent. I didn't want him to see my face.

I think I woke up a few men while stumbling back to my tent; I may have even kicked one or two. I don't really remember. At the time I was too busy cursing myself for giving in to Harold so easily. He was a master of manipulation; when it looked like he would lose an argument, he would fall back on that old strategy of appealing to my brotherly instinct. He caught me off guard, and won again. How could I be so gullible?

The next day Harold carried on like there had been no argument, but I was still angry. I refused to talk to him all that day and the next, and didn't bother to ask him why we hadn't moved. Of course, the reason soon became evident. At the end of the second day, I saw a Welshman sneak into camp, and I followed him to Harold's tent. Evidently, my brother had been expecting someone, because he came out personally to greet him. But first his eyes settled on me.

"Come, Tostig. You should hear this, too."

I followed the stranger into the tent, determined to keep silence. Harold sat, letting the messenger stand. I backed into a corner, preferring to watch from a distance.

The Welshman looked around as though expecting an assassin to leap on his back. "My master instructed me to tell you that all is prepared. Gruffydd is camped at Rhaeadr Ewynnol, which we call the foamy white falls on the river Llugwy. If you send some men at dawn tomorrow, you will find he has no guard. You may take him at your pleasure."

Harold set his mouth, considering. "And where will your master be?"

"He will have departed. He and his brother feel safer that way. They will contact you after the deed is done."

"How will I find this place?"

The messenger hesitated; evidently he had not anticipated this problem. Then his eyes began to gleam; it seems that greed is a common vice of this race. "I could show you...for a price."

Harold frowned. He found this very distasteful. But I was enjoying myself.

"And what is your price?"

The man only hesitated for a moment. "Two hundred...no, three hundred head of cattle. That will be sufficient."

I nearly gasped. That was a king's fortune! But Harold had his head about him. "A mighty sum for so small a deed," he said.

The other shrugged. "When weighed against the cost of how many lives? How great a sum could it be? I will even wield the blade, if that is your desire."

Harold considered this for a moment. "What is your name?"

"Madog Min."

"All right Madog Min. Be here an hour before dawn. Now be gone." Harold made no attempt to hide his disgust.

After Madog slinked out of the tent, Harold turned to me. At that moment he gave me such a strange look, I guess he thought I contemplated murder as well. Maybe he had a guilty conscience.

"Well, there we have it," he said finally.

With a wrench I pulled myself out of the corner, unfolding my arms. "Now what?"

Harold turned away from me. "This is not what I expected."

"I know." He had expected Gruffydd's brothers to take care of things, themselves. Then he could sit back with his hands clean. It doesn't really matter; in warfare there are no rules, I always said. But I wonder whether Harold really thought he was less tainted because he didn't witness the deed.

He paced back and forth, waiting for me to offer my services. I know that's what he was doing, and I was tempted to let him stew in his own muck. But eventually I ran out of patience.

"I suppose you want me to lead our little foray," I said, exasperated.

He looked so relieved I wanted to slap him. "I would be in your debt, Tostig."

He certainly would. I'd make sure of that! But it was just as well; with me in charge we could finish the task and be back at camp without a fuss.

Madog Min was back at dawn like he promised, looking every bit the assassin. He leaned against a tree while we got ready, happily engrossed in cleaning his fingernails with the tip of his knife.

I summoned my picked men and we followed the Welshman into the forest. There were thirty of us altogether; it was a good number, our guide said. I could tell that we were disturbing him, sounding like a whole herd of elk in our advance; we were not trained for stealth.

It took about an hour of steady marching before I heard running water and knew we had reached the river. At that moment, Madog turned with a finger on his lips. "If you value your mission," he whispered, "you will all move silently."

We looked shamefacedly at each other and followed as carefully as possible. As it turned out, there were no guards, no sentries, only Gruffydd and his wife, abandoned by everyone. We saw a couple of people run away at our approach; such was the last remnant of his army.

It was a pitiful sight. The Prince of Wales sat hunched over his uneaten breakfast, staring off into nothingness, while his wife was hanging up a wet chemise she had obviously just washed by herself. She was trying to talk some spirit back into him, but she was wasting her breath.

What a shame. I could tell she was once a vigorous woman, but war and hardship had taken its toll. Long soiled hair hung limply down her back, as though she had no reason to tie it up. She was Aelfgar's daughter, remember, though she bore little physical resemblance to him. At least she had that to recommend her.

As if he was reading my thoughts, Madog Min leered at me and nodded toward them. Then he slipped quietly out of the trees while I ordered one of my men to take the woman.

It all happened very quickly. My man had a hand on the princess's mouth and had spun her around—just in time to get showered by blood spurting from Gruffydd's neck. Even before I knew it had happened, Madog Min had severed his head with a clean sweep of a sword, and the body slumped forward, jerking a few times before it knew it was dead. Gruffydd's head came to a

291

stop at my feet, staring at me in almost comic surprise. At least his wife had fainted before she saw everything.

"Take her," I said shortly, while pulling a sack from my belt and putting the head into it 'ere the thing put the evil eye on me. My man picked up the widow and flung her over his shoulder. I would have preferred that he carry her more respectfully, but we were in a hurry. She didn't regain consciousness until we reached camp, anyway.

Harold was pacing the ground, waiting for us. He was so anxious he nearly grabbed the bag from my hands. I couldn't help it; he irked me so much I made sure to smear blood on his tunic, though he hardly noticed.

"Ahh," he purred, raising the ghastly head by its hair. "King Edward will be most pleased." He presented the face to me, as if I hadn't already seen it. "Do you realize, Tostig, that we can go home now?"

What did he think I was...a dullard? However, whatever sarcastic comment I was going to make was cut short by a groan from the princess. She was just waking up.

"Who do you have there?" he asked, just discovering her presence. "Why, it's Ealdgyth."

Yes, that was her name; it was on the tip of my tongue. Someone had laid her on a blanket by my brother's tent, and she put out a hand, as if looking for support. Then Ealdgyth opened her eyes and stared at us, without saying a word.

Harold crouched by her side. "Do you remember us? This is my brother Tostig and I am Harold."

She didn't respond. She merely looked scornfully at him.

"You are safe here," he said uncomfortably. "I will not hurt you."

Her mouth curled into a sneer. I could read it in her face: we had already hurt her as much as it was possible. Harold straightened up and looked at me for help.

I had something for him to do. "Madog Min awaits your pleasure," I said, emphasizing the last word. At the name, Ealdgyth came up on her elbows.

"Madog Min?" she said. "Now I understand." She laid back down and put a hand before her eyes.

Harold was not happy. He frowned at me and stomped off, though I knew he was relieved to get away. He took out his shame on Madog, anyway. Instead of the three hundred head of cattle, the traitor got a kick in the ass and two days to leave the country. He left, too, on a ship to Dublin that sank and drowned him. So much for my brother's honor.

When we were alone, Ealdgyth looked at me again, and the tears finally came. I think she couldn't cry in front of my brother; she could see that this was his campaign, not mine.

I felt awkward, but this wasn't the time to walk away and leave her alone. Rummaging around, I found some wine and bread and gave it to her. She accepted the food so greedily I could tell she was starved. I watched her eat, thinking how I admired the way she carried herself—especially now, at her most vulnerable. She would be just fine with a rest and some clean clothes.

After she had drained the wine and wiped the tears away, Ealdgyth shook herself as though preparing for the worst. She faced me squarely. For a moment we just stared at each other; but something in my face seemed to inspire her with trust. Her mouth quivered a little bit, and her shoulders relaxed.

"What happens next?"

I blinked, expecting some sort of recrimination. "Ealdgyth, we are tired and sore and ready to go home."

"Home!" She exclaimed, almost hysterically, and clapped a hand before her mouth. "What am I to go home to?"

That question was a little too direct. I couldn't meet her eye. "Did you like it in this savage country?"

"Like it? No, I do not suppose I liked it," she said, releasing me from her perilous gaze. "They always treated me like an outsider, here. But I'll tell you one thing, Tostig." Her voice became bitter. "Your people murdered one of the most extraordinary men that ever lived. Of course, you will never know that, now." She wiped her eyes again. "The golden age of Wales is over. This country will soon deteriorate into clusters of tribes forever squabbling."

I felt sorry for her. The very thing she condemned was exactly what we were striving for; it was the easiest way to control these people.

Just then Harold came back, watching us. As soon as she saw him, Ealdgyth stiffened and stopped talking. My brother let out his breath in a deep sigh. "You might as well relax," he said. "You are going to be with us for some time."

"Oh? And just what are you going to do with me?"

"I'm not yet sure. Since your father died, I've had to deal with your brothers Edwin and Morcar. That's not as easy as it sounds."

"I know." She shook her head. "If they are my only hope, I'm better off fending for myself."

I couldn't help but agree with her. King Edward gave Edwin the earldom of Mercia, and younger Morcar was waiting his turn which was bound to come sooner or later. Between the two of them they had the sense of a mule, and the stubbornness as well. It goes without saying they hated our house.

Ealdgyth put up no resistance when Harold assigned a guard to watch her; but she asked me quietly to keep her company whenever possible. This, I did most willingly. I'm not ashamed to say that my heart went out to her.

We were soon on our way back to England, bearing Gruffydd's head as a gift to the king. It bounced unnaturally in its leather sack behind Harold's saddle, for my brother would trust no one with such a valuable prize. I noticed that Ealdgyth pointedly avoided looking in my brother's direction.

The rest of us followed him glumly, disappointed to return empty-handed after such a difficult campaign. These Welsh owned nothing of value, except for an occasional musical instrument, no use to us. We didn't pass through one single city, and the towns we plundered were already stripped of everything but the walls and furniture. There was no glory for anyone but Harold.

We passed through the town of Chester on the way back. Harold went to a lot of trouble to outfit one of the wagons to carry Ealdgyth in comfort. She was so exhausted and weakened she barely knew what was happening, and my brother spent a lot of time riding next to her, looking in and bringing little food offerings. At first I didn't understand this unusual behavior, but it suddenly came to me. Of course! It wouldn't look good if we delivered her to the earl of Mercia in a terrible state.

Nonetheless, as we had no servants at our disposal she didn't get the care she deserved. However, she rallied somewhat and was sitting by the time we entered the gates at Chester. We found our way to her brother's dwelling and announced our presence to his guards. Edwin came running out to see us, looking very undignified. He seemed surprised to see Ealdgyth in our company and ignored Harold and me while he called for help and picked her up as if she was a child. She put her arms around his neck and wept.

Even Harold looked uncomfortable, but we had no choice except to follow Edwin as he handed his sister to some women. Then the earl seemed to recover himself and bade us welcome. He offered food and drink to us and our captains. My fighting men had already dispersed into the city, looking for some well-earned diversions.

Edwin toyed with his food, apparently searching for some way to start. His face looked like he had taken a draught of spoiled ale.

295

"Well, Harold," he said finally, scratching his neck. "I must assume your venture was successful?"

My brother was quick to recover his shrewdness. "The King had granted me the power to raise a force and destroy the overweening Welsh prince. I have done so. It was a long and arduous campaign, but I ran him to the ground and his people all deserted him."

I was waiting for Harold to acknowledge my help, but I was destined to be disappointed. He was warming up now, and started giving some more glorious details that ended up making him look like a brilliant commander. I admit he was a formidable warrior, but he didn't do it alone! I couldn't help but notice that Edwin never once looked in my direction. I think he was carrying on his father's resentments.

I think Harold forgot that Edwin had lost a potential ally. But the earl endured his blustering, and after listening for a suitable stretch of time he called for the servants to clear the tables. "My hall is yours for the night if you would all like to make yourselves comfortable." His voice trailed off uncertainly.

But Harold demurred, probably not trusting our host with his life.

"My thanks to you, Earl Edwin. But my men are setting up camp outside the city walls and we plan to leave in the morning."

Edwin stood up and bowed, looking relieved. As our company prepared to leave, Ealdgyth walked slowly into the hall, leaning on a maid. She had been bathed and clothed in a gown more fitting to her rank, and I could see color in her cheeks already. Her brother kissed her hand then protectively put an arm around her shoulders. But she gave him a little push and came up to Harold.

"I thank you, my Lord, for returning me to my brother." Then she turned to me. "And you, Tostig, for taking care of me."

I think I blushed. My brother cleared his throat. "Lady Ealdgyth," he said, trying not to sound annoyed. He hated when

296

someone showed me more favor than him. "Your safety was our primary concern."

He gave me a little nudge and we brushed past Gruffydd's widow, who bowed her head slightly. Her brother moved between us protectively. "I believe the king is at Gloucester," he said. "Please relay my good wishes."

We were glad to get away. Edwin's welcome left much to be desired.

The morning was wasted gathering together our scattered troops, but by afternoon we were on our way. I only took a small force with me and sent the rest home; they were glad to go. I thought it would be best to accompany Harold so he wouldn't take all the glory for himself. The scene with Earl Edwin had been most instructive, and I would have to make sure it didn't happen again.

King Edward greeted Harold with enthusiasm, and this gentle, saintly man triumphantly held Gruffydd's head up by the hair for all to see. The thing was rather ripe by then, but Edward didn't seem to notice. The man never ceased to surprise me. I thought he would gingerly push the bag away without opening it.

Edward made a fuss over Harold and me, and my brother's immediate reward was the addition of Hereford to his earldom of Wessex. He was effectively ruling it by then anyway, so the royal proclamation was more of a formality. That is, if you discount Edwin and his potential expectations.

My reward was...nothing. Well, Edward really started treating me as his favorite, which was flattering but did little to fill my empty coffers. The expedition had cost me much more than I anticipated, and the plunder was practically non-existent. This was something I needed to consider when I got home.

CHAPTER 9

HAROLD REMEMBERS

The end of the Welsh campaign ushered in a quiet time. I needed it. There were so many things I wanted to do. I was determined to build a new church at Waltham. I wanted to spend some time with my family. Gyrth and Leofwine required looking after. And then there was the nagging question of Wulfnoth. He didn't deserve to be forgotten; no one else could free him from William's bondage. I had to do something for my poor little brother.

Now I understood why father never seemed to be at home. Wessex was such a large earldom that there were parts of it I'd never even visited. This time, I decided to take Edith and my children on a tour of my estates so I could remind my sokemen and my tenants and my thegns who their master was.

Actually, it's not really fair to call all of my children...children. My eldest son Godwine had just tuned fifteen; at his age, I thought of myself as a man. Strange to say, he still seemed like a boy to me, though I admit his voice was starting to slip into a deeper pitch. And he was serious like a man, probably because he was the eldest. Edmund was just a year younger, and I think he still had more of the boy about him. He was prone to laughter and loved to tease his little sisters. But if I think on it, my father started our training at their age, and I determined I would take those two with me when I visited my tenants.

And so we passed an uneventful but happy spring. There were no catastrophes, no rebellions, no invasions. I took them to see the ancient standing stones on Salisbury plain. It is said they were originally brought from Africa to Ireland by giants then moved to Britain by the magician Merlin to serve as King Arthur's grave. I don't know how true that story is, but I don't see how else they could have been moved. Then we went to visit my sister Queen Editha at Bath where she was staying at her manor near the cathedral. Bath was one of her dower lands and I think she loved it the most. She showed us the famous hot springs where we could still see Roman ruins and even take a steaming bath. After that, I showed my boys the harbor at Bristol on the Severn, while I carefully explained to them why this port was so important to our defenses. We liked the coastal lands and made our way back east, following the route I took after our outlawry back in '52, though I was reluctant to talk about it. Fortunately, it was an old story and not of much interest to my children.

By the time we reached Bosham, I was beginning to get impatient with our slow progress. I think my family was ready for a long rest. Mother greeted us enthusiastically, and of course the children loved their grandmother. Edith and mother got along well together, and watching them I decided it was a good time to broach the subject of Wulfnoth's captivity.

"Mother," I ventured, sitting beside her. She handed me a rope of yarn to hold so she could wind it into a ball. I smiled despite myself, for we spent many hours just so when I was a boy.

"What's on your mind, Harold?"

"Wulfnoth."

Edith looked up quickly but didn't say anything. She knew how I felt.

"Poor child. Do you think you can do anything for him?"

"Not from here. But things are so quiet, I think it's a good time to visit Duke William."

Mother sighed. "You'll need permission from King Edward, I would think."

"Yes. I understand he is in Winchester right now. I would leave Edith and the children with you, if that's all right."

"Is that all right with you?" The question was directed at my wife. She glanced at me quickly before returning to her needlework.

"Whatever Harold thinks is necessary," she said quietly.

"After visiting Edward, I will return here," I assured them. "I don't know how long this will take. Edith, I will leave some troops to escort you home, whenever you wish."

They knew I had already made up my mind. My duties weighed heavily on my conscience.

What surprised me was Edward's reaction. The king was in Winchester, as I thought, and granted me a private audience. He frowned when I told him of my plans.

"Harold, think hard on this," he said. "Duke William is a wily fox and he may well outsmart you."

I stood up and paced the room; I didn't think the king knew William very well. After all, Normandy's duke was only fourteen years old when Edward returned from exile and took the crown. I had heard that William visited England when our family was outlawed, but other than that, there was no other contact between the two of them that I knew of. Could Edward have other motives to keep me from Normandy?

I knelt before his throne, bowing my head.

"Sire, what possible reason could William have to keep my brother captive? He has your friendship. The Danes are quiet. I would persuade the duke to return Wulfnoth, and I will be prepared to pay a ransom if need be."

Edward nodded slowly. He bade me sit beside him.

"I do not know," he said, "but I fear there may be consequences if you put yourself into his power."

"I'm willing to take my chances. Do I have your permission to go?"

"Yes, but be careful. You may be entering the Lion's Den."

I was deeply disturbed by Edward's warning, but my resolve was firm. Duke William would be bound by the obligations of a host. If he tried to harm me, all of Europe would know. If I let fear keep me from my duty, I would never forgive myself. Father would never have forgiven me. No, I must go and do what I could to gain Wulfnoth's freedom.

On the way back to Bosham, I stopped at two of my manors along the way, gathering the company of my favorite thegns and household troops. Taking my hawk and hunting dogs, I resolved to make this voyage as unthreatening as possible. I would present myself as nothing more than a nobleman at leisure, on a hunting trip to the continent. William should welcome me as a traveler, and in the course of my visit I would ransom my brother.

The day before our departure, I hosted a great feast for my fellow travelers and for those I was leaving behind. We served many of the catches from our own waters, as well as meat I had hunted on the way back from Winchester. Edith was quiet, but she tried to put on a good face and succeeded in looking beautiful and graceful. Mother was the perfect host, for she had years of practice when father was alive. I think she welcomed the opportunity to play the great countess once again. My two eldest sons were given places at the table, though they were disappointed I was not taking them with me.

That night, Edith snuggled in my arms and I kissed her tears away.

"What is it, my love? I have left many times before."

She wrapped her arm around my neck and pulled a lock of my hair forward, kissing it.

"I cannot tell you why, but I fear for you."

I let out a brief grunt. "You sound like Edward."

"Oh?" She pulled away, sitting up and wrapping both arms around her knees. "Edward said the same thing?"

"In his own way, yes. But I don't understand it. I felt like he knew something I didn't know."

"We cannot pretend to understand the king," she muttered. "Especially as he was no friend to your father."

"Hmm." I knew she had the rights of it. "He can't be harboring evil thoughts against me."

"God forfend!" She crossed herself. "No, I don't believe so. But he could be communicating with Duke William by letter and you wouldn't ever know of it."

It was my turn to sit up. "As any good monarch would do." I pulled her toward me. "Come, my dear. This serves us nothing. Put your fears to rest. I will be well guarded. Everything will be fine."

Edith allowed herself to be gentled, as I had a great need for her that night and I think her desire was as strong as mine. She put aside her tears and kissed me fervently, almost as though for the last time. I was glad, for those kisses were destined to stay with me a long time.

The following morning we boarded three ships, tucking our tunics into our belts and wading out to the boats, carrying my hunting dogs under our arms. It was a glorious day and my men were singing sailors' songs, pulling out the oars and arranging our trunks for us to sit upon. I had so many companions there was no room for horses but we made sure to bring extra provisions, and of course enough money to live comfortably. We waved farewell to my family and friends gathered by the quayside and made our way into the harbor and out to sea, where we unfurled the sails and headed for Normandy.

Alas, my luck wasn't with me. As the sun was just past its mid-point in the sky, ugly black clouds rolled in and we furled our sail as quickly as possible. It was almost too late; the wind came up from nowhere and buffeted our little ships. We almost had a

302

collision and then worse happened; we lost sight of the third boat. Hard stinging rain followed, waves crashed over the sides and we frantically tied down what we could while bailing for our lives.

As always, the storm seemed to last forever and by the time it cleared we were left shivering and cursing and lost. One thing it did do was push us closer to the continent, though we did not recognize the shoreline. By then, we didn't care where we landed as long as we could step on dry soil.

My ship master discovered a little harbor and we headed for it, gratefully. Alas, our relief soon turned to dismay, for shortly after we landed we were surrounded by an armed guard. And they were most unfriendly.

My men were still wading to shore as I drew myself up to my full height and faced our challengers. I felt rather helpless in front of mounted antagonists. My clothes were still clinging to me, my hair was wet and stringy, making me look more like a beggar than an earl.

"Where are we and why do you threaten us?" I tried to sound challenging.

"You are on the coast of Ponthieu, and you are my prisoner," said one of my captors.

"Prisoners! You see we have no hostile intent!"

"That is not the question, here. You and your men shall accompany me to my castle of Beaurain. We will await the horses, which are coming from the settlement." He pointed his finger, indicating a little town by the mouth of the river.

"And who are you that insists on taking me prisoner?"

"I thought you understood. I am Count Guy of Ponthieu. Now, please hand me your sword." The man held out his hand.

I was tempted to draw the sword and cut his arm off, but I knew that was foolish. And it would surely be my death. I gave him my sword, gesturing for my companions to do the same. But I was even more upset when he ordered one of his men to take my hawk. The bird flapped and snapped at the Count as he raised his hand up, pulling his head back for safety. Oh, how I wish that hawk could break its bonds! But Count Guy seemed to think twice about stealing my bird, and he quickly passed it over to me and pulled his mount away. I spoke softly to the ruffled creature, trying to calm it. I wasn't calm, so it jumped around on my hand until I forced myself to relax. I knew just how it felt.

In due time, spare horses were brought up and we had no choice but to mount. We were surrounded and led like children to the Count's stronghold.

Guy's castle was an impressive stone fortification with a dry moat and a drawbridge. The clacking of our horses' hooves over the bridge sounded like the knells of doom to me. I glanced worriedly over my shoulder, hoping this was not my last view of the sun. The Count's servants scurried forward as we entered the bailey, taking our horses. I was obliged to surrender my hawk once again, but I remonstrated with the man to take good care of him.

My bird was the least of my problems. County Guy took his place on a high throne and his men actually shoved me forward and pushed me onto my knees. I took a deep breath to calm myself.

"What is your name?" the Count asked.

"I am Harold Godwineson, Earl of Wessex and envoy of King Edward of England," I retorted. Surely he knew who I was.

"Harold Godwineson," he said slowly, savoring his power over me. "And what made you think you could land in my territory?"

"You know we were blown off course," I growled, having trouble controlling my temper. "I was planning to visit Duke William."

"Oh, William. Well, we shall see about that." He nodded to one of his henchmen, who moved away from the wall. The others followed and grabbed me and my companions none too gently. I tried to pull away and turned to Count Guy.

"I apologize for my hasty accommodations," he snarled. "It's the best I could do for now."

My guard wrestled me around and pushed me forward. I thought about my sword, safe in the Count's hands.

We were led down a flight of stairs and shoved into a row of cells with straw on the floor and bars on the window openings. I suppose it could have been worse; there was a bit of light and the cells were dry. But as my guard turned the key in the lock, I swore that Count Guy would not be rid of me so easily.

We spent a long night in those cells. My men called to each other, comforted by the knowledge that we were still together. I had little to say, fretting over my ships and the small treasure the Count most certainly had already confiscated. My ransom would have to come from England. Guy neglected to feed us that night, but his surly guards did pass some ale to my men.

The sun was high in the sky before our captors showed up the next morning. Much to our surprise, they opened our cells and escorted us back to the great hall, laid out with tables and food. We fell to eating without much ado. When a man is hungry, pride usually has to wait.

Finally Count Guy came into the hall and walked up to me, carrying my sword.

"I return this to you, Earl Harold," he said. He frowned as I took it back.

I'm sure he didn't expect any answer nor did I say what was on my mind as I strapped on the belt.

"It seems Duke William values your friendship," he went on, "and is coming to meet you."

He stepped back and crossed his arms. I think I detected slight fear in his eyes.

"I hope you will forgive our little misunderstanding." He looked to the side as someone spoke in his ear.

"That depends on whether you left my ships unmolested," I said.

"I have given orders to guard your possessions from the townspeople." He started away.

"And from your men?" I called out.

He nodded. I would have to see for myself. But for now, I would have to wait.

WULFNOTH REMEMBERS

I had been a hostage at Duke William's court for over eleven years when help finally came, in the guise of my brother Harold. I had already given up on being rescued, especially after father died. It wasn't such a bad life; I had been here so long I was the senior member of our little household of squires. Oh yes, Duke William made me a squire and treated me affably, as much as he was capable of, for such a strict man.

Once I learned how troubled his own childhood was, I found myself better able to understand. His father went off on crusade when he was young and never came back. Although the nobles had sworn to recognize William as the next Duke, as soon as the father was dead they tried to do away with the son. William had survived more assassination attempts than I can count, and even his protectors were slain. No wonder he was so harsh with his people. Yet inside his privy chambers, he was more relaxed. He would even play at chess with some of us from time to time.

Shortly after I first arrived here, Duke William married the daughter of Count Baldwin of Flanders, who was the niece of Tostig's wife Judith. Matilda was very pretty and very sweet, and often remembered to send special things to eat and drink to the household squires. When we served the nobles at their feast, she always made sure we had plenty to eat afterwards. Every one of us would have defended her with our life.

306

So I was resigned to my fate, and I am almost sorry that Harold came to negotiate my release. All he did was raise my hopes again, only to see them terribly dashed. And the repercussions for him were infinitely worse, though I must say I didn't think anyone really gave much credence to Duke William's designs for the English crown. Except maybe for Duke William, who kept his thoughts to himself. I don't believe Harold even had a suspicion, or he probably never would have come near this side of the Channel. After all, I am certain that Archbishop Robert made up the whole King Edward promise to satisfy his own sense of revenge, may God curse his immortal soul.

But of course, Harold never consulted me before he came— or ever, for that matter. Duke William never gave me his or anyone else's letters. I thought I was dead to my family. So I was all the more surprised when the Duke summoned Hakon and me to saddle up and attend him.

"Wulfnoth," he said, gesturing for me to tighten a strap on his saddlebag. "We are going to rescue your brother Harold from the indignity of Ponthieu's dungeon. I thought you would like to meet him."

I was shocked, but tried not to show it. I'm not sure I was more surprised at Harold's presence or William's thoughtfulness. It wasn't until later I concluded that William was using me as for his own purposes, as ever.

"It seems that the Earl of Wessex foolishly landed on the shores of Ponthieu and was immediately taken prisoner. Maybe he was blown off course. I don't really know. But I think he'll be much happier as my guest than Guy's captive. Don't you?"

He didn't really care about my answer so I kept silent.

"We shall see whether Count Guy puts up an argument or not. I've sent my envoys ahead to prepare the Count for my arrival." He waved me away, having said all I needed to know.

Walking back to my horse, I was surprised at how my heart was pounding. Could it be? Why him and why now, after all these
307

years? Of all my brothers, I knew Harold the least, after Swegn. I was still a boy when he was made Earl of East Anglia, and I don't think he ever paid any attention to me. But now, we were both men and could talk like adults. I almost forgot how desperate I was to hear news of my family. Would he know me? Probably not. Would I recognize him? I wasn't sure.

Hakon came up to see what the Duke had wanted. I turned to him, hiding my emotions. "My brother Harold is here, at Ponthieu. We are going to see him."

He caught his breath. Although he had adjusted to our situation better than I, we were both homesick.

"Don't get your hopes up," I said bitterly. "Why would Duke William let us go home?"

I didn't want to believe my own words, but I was too bitter to let myself hope. Not yet.

Four other squires came with us and we rode behind William and his tight-knit group of knights who thundered across the terrain with a frightening clamor. Our destination was Guy of Ponthieu's castle Beaurain, close to the sea. As we approached along a wide dirt road, we could see that the Count was ready for us. He and his knights were blocking our way. They sat on their horses, looking ahead, spears pointed up in the air. At their head sat the Count in his armor with no helmet. He dismounted before Duke William but did not go down on one knee. I could see he was a proud man, and jealous of his dignity.

William wasted no time. "You know why I am here," he said harshly. "You may not make that man your prisoner."

Even I could see that Count Guy was restraining his anger. "And why not?"

"As I am your lord, I demand you turn the Earl of Wessex over to me. I am prepared to compensate you."

For a moment the other grasped his hilt, but thought better of it and bowed slightly. "As you wish," he conceded. "Earl Harold is in the great hall."

He remounted and turned his stallion, leading us the rest of the way to the castle. I could hardly contain my excitement.

We entered the great hall, only to see the restless group of Englishmen sitting in various positions around trestle tables. Some were straddling the bench, others seemed ready to fall asleep on their arms. The table was spread with a modest selection of breads, fruit and cheeses. All around the edge of the hall stood Guy's guards looking fierce and annoyed. Perhaps we were spoiling their fun. I scanned the prisoners, hoping to identify my brother.

Oh, there he was. I couldn't miss him. He hadn't changed that much, except now he sprouted a mustache. He still had a full head of hair, and when he briefly smiled at our entrance, I thought he looked even handsomer than I remembered. Alas, his eyes passed over me without recognition.

Taking his time, Harold stood and actually sauntered over to Duke William, who crossed his arms, amused. Count Guy stood next to him, scowling. I could see that Harold was savoring the moment.

He knelt before the Duke. "My lord, I place myself under your protection."

William made little clucking noises, pulling Harold to his feet. "Not my protection, Earl Harold. My honored guest. Count Guy has graciously offered to accompany us partway back to my domain."

Count Guy's scowl became even deeper, if that was possible.

William was clearly enjoying himself. "Oh, and I have a surprise for you, Harold. I have brought your brother and nephew with me."

It was gratifying to see Harold's face light up with joy. He looked quickly around, trying to find us. I held my breath. Had I changed that much?

309

William gave him a minute, pretending not to notice Harold's frustration. Then he pushed me forward. "Here he is, Harold. He's grown some since you last saw him."

Harold cocked his head, looked hard at me, and then threw his arms wide. I ran into his embrace, not the least embarrassed. I was never so glad to see anybody in my life.

He put me at arm's length, biting his lip. "You look like father," he said wonderingly. I didn't realize that. "I should have recognized you instantly."

I smiled and would have responded, but Hakon came up from behind and Harold greeted him too, though a little less enthusiastically. William didn't want to waste an instant and he was already ordering us to depart. Harold put an arm around my shoulders as though he wouldn't be separated from me. We were surrounded by bustling servants and warriors, and he kept me with him when we went outside even as they returned his hunting dogs and hawk. I wanted to say something but words failed me.

"Come," Duke William ordered, riding up to us. "You can get reacquainted later. We must go while we have daylight. Come, Harold. Ride with me."

My brother gave me an encouraging smile and mounted his horse. Hakon and I fell back with the rest of the squires. I hoped nobody noticed me wiping away a tear.

Count Guy was obliged to accompany Harold's men to their ships, and launch his own vessels. William wanted him to escort my brother's crew down the coast to the Seine and all the way upriver to Rouen. Only that way would Harold be sure his belongings were safe.

Over the next couple of weeks the Duke treated my brother like royalty. Harold started to relax, letting down his guard. William could be very gracious when he wanted to be, though I don't think he did anything without calculating it first. However, Harold didn't know him so he might not see any duplicity.

At first, I had very little opportunity to see my brother alone, because William occupied all his time. It seemed they got along very well together and went hunting almost every day. During the evening repast Harold always sat at high table. I was given permission to serve him, so at least I was comforted in that respect.

Finally one day, William needed to pay a visit to one of his vassals and left Harold behind. My brother suggested I go riding with him and I gladly accepted. I knew a wonderful vantage point and led him there, just the two of us. We tethered our horses and climbed onto an outcrop that overlooked a lovely valley. Harold leaned back on the rock, stretching his neck as we were warmed by the sun. A flock of ducks flew overhead, squawking at each other.

I had waited so long to talk with him, and now I was afraid of ruining our perfect moment. Harold was relaxed and didn't seem particularly interested in breaking the silence. But I had to know why he had come.

"Harold," I ventured.

"Hmm?" His eyes were closed.

"Harold, did you come to take me away from here?"

His eyes slowly opened and he looked at me, pursing his lips. For a moment I didn't think he was going to respond.

"Yes, Wulfnoth, that was my intention. My earldom has been quiet since I dealt with Gruffydd ap Llewelyn, and I thought this was a good time to make things right."

I didn't know what he was talking about, but the Gruffydd story could wait. "You must be very careful with the Duke," I warned. "He is a clever and unscrupulous man."

He looked back at the sky again, putting an arm behind his head. "I'm beginning to see this, Wulfnoth. In fact, I'm beginning to wonder if I am his prisoner, too."

311

That thought had already occurred to me, but I hadn't wanted to say anything. "Has he done anything suspicious?" I asked.

"Noooo. But I haven't tried to leave yet, either. I see I am going to have to play his game a little longer before I make any suggestions about you. If I ask too soon, a refusal could be final."

I took a deep breath, willing myself to make the best of it. But he wasn't finished.

"Wulfnoth, I am prepared to pay a ransom for you and Hakon. Never fear that. However much he asks, it doesn't matter."

Unless he doesn't ask, I thought. I knew my value as a hostage, and it wasn't necessarily in money.

"Harold, there is more." This was so hard for me...I wished it was as easy as a ransom. "Do you know why Duke William is keeping me here?"

Harold sat up, puzzled. I don't think he knew.

"He means to become King of England," I said quietly.

My brother drew in his breath through clenched teeth. His mind moved very quickly; he could see as well as I what kind of trap he had fallen into.

"How do you know this?" His voice shook a little.

"Archbishop Robert. When he...abducted us. He told Duke William that King Edward wanted him to be his heir. He said he was Edward's messenger! And we were surety for King Edward's promise. I think he made it up to avenge himself on father!" My voice was rising and I brought myself under control. "Of course Duke William believed him."

Harold was watching me closely. Then he put an arm around my shoulders.

"That is a grievous thing to carry around all these years," he said.

I almost cried, though from relief or from sadness I cannot say.

312

"I would think this hardly seems likely," he said, "since our King made Edward the Exile his heir many years ago. Too bad the man died soon afterwards, but his son Eadgar is next in line. Provided he is grown when the time comes."

I had heard something of this, but they kept news away from me as best as they could. I felt somewhat better. Harold seemed a little distracted, but I didn't want to waste any more precious time worrying about things I had no control over.

"Tell me about mother. And has Leofwine finally learned how to whistle?"

He laughed, happy to be on solid footing. He pulled open our little lunch bag and told me all about home. About Bosham.

We spent all afternoon on that rock outcrop, and the following day we went hunting. Hakon came along, and we had a great time, singing and joking and testing our skills. It seemed Harold would go nowhere without his hunting animals; I never saw someone so skilled with a bird of prey. My brother spoke to it as though it was a lover.

By the time we got back, Duke William had returned and immediately entreated Harold to join him. Shrugging his shoulders at me, my brother obliged and spent the rest of the evening eating and drinking at the Duke's side. Duchess Matilda sat at her husband's other elbow, and she kept leaning over and pouring wine into Harold's cup. When she wasn't looking, he would add more water.

This particular evening, William retired early, declaring he was exhausted from his travels and bidding the others to stay. As soon as he had disappeared, Matilda moved over to his throne and leaned toward Harold. I stood behind them in case they had need of me.

"I was wondering about my aunt Judith," she said, waving for the servants to clear the table. "I haven't seen her since she married Tostig."

Harold smiled at her and I swear she fluttered her eyes at him. Reaching for a fig out of a bowl, he took a bite while thinking. "Let me see," he said. "It has been many years. Your aunt has made a most splendid Countess of Northumbria. Everyone speaks of her piety." He looked sidelong with a mischievous smirk. "And her inquisitiveness."

Matilda straightened out her skirt, looking away. "Well, she is certainly a lively woman. But what do they mean by inquisitiveness?"

"It has to do with St. Cuthbert and his church at Durham. I would call him a patron saint of Northumbria. You know your aunt is very devout and is known for her many donations to the church." Matilda nodded wisely. She was known for the same thing.

"It seems Cuthbert ruled that no woman was permitted to set foot in the cathedral housing his relics. I certainly don't understand that, since I think women are admirable." He picked up her hand from the throne's arm and kissed it. "Judith wanted to worship at his tomb and sent in one of her maidens with an offering, to test if there were any consequences breaking the Saint's decree. Alas for the maiden! When she into the churchyard, a fierce gust wind dashed her against the wall and she took such a blow to the head that she expired shortly thereafter."

Matilda gasped.

"As you can imagine, Judith was terribly ashamed. She sought forgiveness by donating to St. Cuthbert a magnificent silver crucifix, wrought with splendid decorations. It must have worked, for she has fared very well since then."

The Duchess shook her head. "I do not blame Judith for resisting Cuthbert's shameful decree. She had every right as a man to worship."

Harold turned around to me, asking for more water. I don't think he wanted her to see his expression of scorn. He made some neutral comment and told her of his last visit to Flanders. That lightened things up.

This was the beginning of their nightly conversations after the Duke went early to bed, as was his wont. It seemed that Matilda was starved for conversation of the less-militant kind, and Harold was as cultured as he was warlike. Nonetheless, I noticed they often sat with their heads together, and I dare say my brother was smitten with her beauty.

One evening, she seemed uncomfortable and withdrawn, and I noticed that William did not speak to her. After he went to bed and Harold took his accustomed place by her side, Matilda started wiping her eyes. He leaned close.

"What is the matter?" He was most consoling. Standing behind them I rolled my eyes, hoping nobody would notice.

"Someone told my husband about us; he is terribly jealous. No, he is furious. He wants to know what we are talking about all the time."

Harold sat back in thought. "Then we shall tell him what we are talking about. At the soonest."

Matilda looked questioningly at him but he didn't say anything more.

The following day, my brother asked Duke William to speak with him in the throne room. He wanted witnesses. Of course William was curious and gladly assented. Harold bid me to follow, and when we entered the room Matilda was sitting beside her husband.

"Your Grace," he started, bowing slightly. "There is something I would to speak with you about. I have it in my mind that I would like to marry your daughter Adeliza. This was what Matilda and I have been discussing late into the evenings. I understand Adeliza is too young and needs to stay at your court until she is of an age."

315

I knew he had made this story up, and I admired the grace with which Matilda accepted his deception. William was clearly startled, then his face broke into a large grin.

"I am delighted," he nodded. "It is an honor to be joined to your house."

Tragedy averted. Matilda was forgiven and Harold was even closer to Duke William, if that was possible.

Not long afterwards, Duke William made an announcement that he had been challenged to meet the Breton Count Conan, who was laying siege to the city of Dol. I could see Harold's eyes shine at the opportunity to go on campaign with the famous Norman.

"May I take Wulfnoth along as my squire?" Harold asked. The Duke carelessly waved his assent, and there I was at my brother's side, anxious to see why his legend was already so big. He brought all his household knights with him and of course Harold rode up front with the Duke of Normandy, banners unfurled, fully armored and holding their spears. William furnished all our mounts, but his white stallion was the biggest and burliest, just like his rider, while Harold's was strong but sinewy and somewhat shorter. My brother didn't seem to mind; he looked every bit as warlike and formidable as his host.

I was rarely permitted to travel far, so for me this was a grand adventure. I had been given plenty of training in the yards but had never seen combat, so I was grateful for this opportunity to witness the very best in action.

As we approached the border of Brittany, the magnificent abbey of Mont Saint Michel rose from the horizon, tall and craggy. I had heard of this place but couldn't imagine it, emerging like a magical vision from the flat, swampy quagmire. Of course, that was at low tide. At high tide it was even more incredible, an island in a sapphire blue sea. Our army needed to pass below this imposing edifice across a vast expanse of sand, but first Duke William had to hire a guide who knew the firmest paths through the shifting mud flats. It was daunting. One man could be standing

316

in just a few inches of water, and the man right next to him could be up to his thighs.

"Follow carefully," the guide stressed, as though we needed to be told. And even so, as we were nearly past the mount, two of William's soldiers cried out in terror and we could see they were sinking into the quicksand.

"Poor bastards," the man next to me murmured. I shifted on my horse uncomfortably. The men were flailing their arms, which only served to make matters worse for them. I could see that William was frowning at the situation, but he didn't move. Suddenly, Harold slipped from his horse and sort of skated purposely toward the foundering soldiers. William made a move as though to stop him but thought better of it. We all watched, holding our breath.

As he approached the men he threw off his chain-maille hauberk to lighten his weight. Then he slowed his steps, taking care as the water started to move slowly up his leg. "Quiet down" he shouted at the men, and his words seemed to have an effect on them. It seemed to me that time slowed to a crawl as I watched my brother take the closest man by the arm with one hand. With muscles straining in his neck, Harold wasted no effort but concentrated on pulling the soldier's arm. He gritted his teeth but did not move any other part of his body. At first, nothing seemed to happen and I feared the worst. But Harold didn't stop, and suddenly with what must have been a great sucking noise, the quicksand lessened its grip on the man's legs and Harold pulled him onto firmer sand. The solder landed on hands and knees, coughing and gagging.

My brother ignored the man and concentrated on the second one, who had sunk even deeper in the interim. By then I had regained my courage and approached my brother on the sand.

"Bring my hauberk, Wulfnoth", he demanded. "I can stand on it and distribute my weight."

317

I did as he said and we both placed the chain maille on the ground. It sunk a bit into the water but held. He put his feet far apart and grabbed the man under both arms. There was no way I could get in there, but I stood by, waiting. Harold's strength was enormous, and I could see he was determined to save this man who was in so deep I would have given up. But as I watched, little by little the man's body inched from the muck. Finally, with a big grunt Harold pulled him all the way out, almost dropping him onto firmer ground. The men all around us were cheering.

As Harold bent over to retrieve his muddy chain maille, he shot me a weary smile. "That should give William something to think about," he said. I glanced over at the Duke and smiled, despite myself. He face was a mask of concentration.

Once we were off the sand flats, the men surrounded Harold, pounding him on the back. My brother responded genially, giving everyone a smile and appearing to enjoy himself. He looked for me and handed over his dripping hauberk, then gratefully accepted a wineskin from one of his housecarls. He was clearly the hero of the day. When Duke William approached us, it seemed to me that Harold was expecting some sort of acknowledgement. And indeed, he was not disappointed.

William had on his regal expression, and held out a hand to one of his squires. The youth passed a chain-mail hauberk to him and William held it up, showing everyone how finely made it was.

"I would not have you wear mail armor that has been damaged by the quicksand. Please accept this gift as recognition of your great feat." As Harold bowed, William started manipulating the hauberk, obviously intending to put it over my brother's head. Harold obliged, raising his arms. The Duke slid the chain-mail over his head and adjusted it, as if he were the squire and Harold the knight. William was a genius at showmanship, and men were still talking about him as we set up camp that night. He almost stole the moment from Harold. Almost.

We were safely across the border into Brittany, and to tell true, I have never seen a flatter landscape. However, we certainly made good time. We were already nearing a large outcrop that had a great view of the surrounding land, and on it was our destination, the town of Dol. Our force must have looked formidable, because once Conan saw us coming he abandoned his siege.

Duke William drew rein as the happy villagers poured out of the fortress doors, welcoming us as their saviors. He pointed at the empty encampment. "Conan has left some of his pavilions for us. Wasn't that kind of him? We will rest here," he commanded, "and await my good countryman, Count Alain le Rouge."

We were weary and happy to oblige. But we were surprised as one week turned into two before Count Alain and his army approached. Alain le Rouge was as good as his name; he had a shock of red hair and beard you could see from far away. Duke William welcomed him graciously, but didn't seem in a hurry to leave. We stayed in front of Dol for a whole month before the city's mayor came out to our encampment, bowing prodigiously, first to William, then to Harold.

"My name is Rhiwallon," he said respectfully. "We are grateful to you, my Duke, for your timely intervention. But I must report that Count Conan's siege had already reduced our resources to nothing. My Lord..."

He paused, and I could see he was gathering his courage. "I ask you this. What does it matter to us if we are plundered by our friends or our enemies? The result is the same."

Having made this bold statement, the man stood with bowed head, as though he expected William to strike him. But the Duke seemed to admire his courage. He turned a wry smile to Harold. "The man is right. We are doing no honorable deed, here. All right, then. We will march in the morning."

Obviously relieved, Rhiwallon backed away.

"Wait!"

The mayor froze.

"Never use such an attitude with me again, or I will burn this town to the ground myself."

For a moment the man looked at William with disbelief. But seeing the Duke's expression, he scurried from the tent.

Even Harold was a bit shocked, but William's face quickly relaxed, and he even smiled. "That man will never cause me trouble, I assure you," he said in answer to Harold's questioning glance. "There are times when a simple reminder is enough. Besides, he is right. We have spent enough time here. Sufficient scouts have returned to assure me that Conan is headed back toward his town of Dinan. We can take him there."

We had been packed and ready to go for some time. Everyone was a bit restive and we were moving at first light. Dinan was only one day's ride away, and as we neared the town we saw that our road was blocked by a ditch with sharpened stakes and a mound of dirt behind it. The ditch was flanked by a forest on both sides. Conan had taken advantage of his month's reprieve. His little army faced us behind the mound, about eight deep.

William didn't seem the least bothered. From the way he commanded his troops, it looked like this was going to be a straightforward battle. First, the archers came forward and shot into the air; the arrows slowed then dropped to earth at an amazing speed. I could hear the screams of the unprotected. While this was going on, he sent his infantry into the ditch and they busied themselves breaking up the stakes, while the archers harried anyone brave enough to inch forward with a spear.

While this was going on, William gave the order to his cavalry to penetrate the forest where they could outflank Conan's army.

Harold and his men all dismounted, as was our habit. I stayed beside him as best as I could and they ran forward with their shields held before them. My brother was in front and we climbed down into the ditch and up again in fairly good formation. Conan's soldiers resisted bravely, but my brother was at his best, and men fell before him right and left. Some were only wounded and I finished off a few of the ones who looked like they intended to keep attacking him. I didn't like it, but I had been well trained and I seemed to know what to do.

Suddenly, the cavalry broke from the forest and Conan's army took to their heels, running back to the safety of the city walls. Many of them didn't make it. But that was the end of our participation. Putting the point of his shield on the ground, Harold leaned upon it, breathing heavily. Duke William came up, as fresh as if he had just taken a little ride. Of course, he was splattered with blood, which told another story.

"The bodies lie thickest around you and your men," the Duke said, looking around. "I wish I could have watched you closer."

Harold bowed slightly. "We are not used to fighting on horseback," he said. "I would not have been at my best if I had fought by your side."

William looked at him for a moment then pulled his stallion around, riding away. "He wants to get your measure," I mused.

Harold looked at me concernedly. "We have learned much about each other. He will not underestimate me, nor I him. I hope to God he doesn't use this knowledge against me."

That was worrisome. What was Harold referring to?

Dinan was a small town built on another one of those odd hills overlooking the plain. It was topped with a traditional motte and bailey castle made of timber with a wooden palisade. As we prepared to lay siege to this new town, I saw that Duke William sent a herald to demand Conan's surrender. The man was soon driven back with rocks and clods of dirt.

The day was late for fighting and William gave orders to set up camp for the night. I was making a fire for Harold's dinner when the Duke came by, in the company of his red-headed Count.

321

"This will not last more than a day or two," William said. "I have been away long enough. If Conan does not want to parley, I will simply burn down his fortress. What say you, Alain?"

The Count scratched his beard. "That man is trouble, and we would be better off if you showed him the pointed end of your spear."

"Now, now, Alain. When you have to deal with as many rebellions as I have, you learn that if you killed every one of the instigators, there would be no one left to rule." He laughed at his own joke and moved on. Harold shook his head.

"Odd man," he said. "Strange mix of wisdom and heartlessness."

The next morning, William gave Conan one more chance, but the herald's challenge met with silence. The Duke gestured at his men to bring forward the kindling and wood. As they were piling the brush against the walls, a score of archers started shooting fire arrows into the fortress. Soon little flames licked up the palisade.

It didn't take long for William's tactic to work. Tall flames began to shoot up from clouds of black smoke. Before long, the gates opened a crack and a spear was thrust forth, the city key dangling from its tip. William gestured for Count Alain to retrieve it.

Harold and I were standing off to the side with his housecarls, watching the fire as Alain rode forward and ceremoniously plucked the keys off the spear. He held the key over his head and turned his horse around; immediately afterwards, the gates flew open and the errant Conan strode out. The conquered supplicant kneeled proudly before the Duke and bowed his head in submission. I wondered whether he expected to be killed.

William stood with his arms crossed, apparently enjoying the moment. Finally, he spoke. "You have learned your lesson, I think. For your act of aggression, I will be content to receive your forfeited lands, including this Dinan and the town of Dol. Make sure this never happens again!"

That was all. Conan went away and soon the refugees were pouring out of the fortress, leading their livestock, some pulling carts. William pushed his way through them and came up to my brother.

"Harold Godwineson, you have fought most bravely and shown that you are a mighty knight. Kneel, my friend."

Harold quickly glanced at me before going down on one knee. Without wasting a moment, William drew his blade and tapped my brother on both shoulders while the fire raged behind us.

"I dub thee Sir Harold." William put his sword back in its sheath then removed his belt. The Duke gestured for me to unbuckle Harold's sword so William could replace it with his own.

I think my brother was surprised. William stepped back for a moment before knighting a couple of other Normans. We stood quietly a long time, then Harold's men surrounded him with congratulations when William moved away. Harold smiled and nodded and spoke quietly, then suggested we all get ready to depart. I sensed that he was uncomfortable, and I thought I knew why.

"Duke William has made you his man," I said quietly. "And I guess now he is your Lord."

"And I am to put his needs before my own," he added. "Oh, Waltheof, I fear where this will lead us."

For many years afterwards, I remembered his face at that moment. I think Harold already suspected that terrible thing I knew nothing about. Yet.

By the time we were back in Bayeux, Harold was restive and I saw that he was ready to return home. But how to accomplish his mission? I was so nervous that I nearly made myself ill. As ever, my brother was very perceptive and he took me aside one afternoon. We walked to the kennels so he could look at a new litter of hunting dogs.

"Look, Wulfnoth," he coughed. "I can't put it off any longer. I am going to ask William to release you and Hakon. I hope we have come to an understanding."

He played with one of the puppies and wouldn't look at me.

"I don't know what will happen," Harold continued. "I fear William has something wicked planned for me. It would not be like him just to let me go. He will try to extract something from me, I am sure. I hope I can afford it."

My stomach sank. My brother no longer sounded confident. He was letting me see how bad things could become.

He stood up, sighing. "Well, we shall make the best of it. Come, before I lose my resolve."

Once again my brother requested a formal meeting with the Duke. Hakon and I were permitted to attend, as well as some of Harold's housecarls.

As we watched the Duke take his place on the throne, I was thinking about that day he made Harold a knight. They weren't equals any more. William was his Lord, at least on the Continent. He leaned forward.

"Yes, Harold. I understand you want to take your leave. How may I assist you?"

That sounded promising. Harold's face was totally expressionless.

"Your Grace," he started. Duke William always liked that. "My earldom needs me. I have been away too long."

William nodded, encouraging him to continue.

"I would return with my brother and my nephew. They would see their homeland again."

I held my breath. I could feel Hakon stiffen at my side.

William looked at Harold a long time in silence.

"I am sorry you feel the need to leave me," he said, almost sounding sincere. "Let me think on this. You may prepare to leave, and in one week's time we shall meet in my great hall accompanied by my lords and ecclesiastics. This will give my countrymen sufficient opportunity to bid you a proper farewell."

Harold turned to me, crestfallen. William's plan was not encouraging.

Nonetheless, we all resolved to act like nothing was amiss and that Hakon and I would be going home. Harold had much to pack, and William had graciously restored his ships; the hulls were patched and sanded, the masts had been replaced and the sails repaired. They looked seaworthy enough to get us across the channel.

The important day dawned bright and cheerful, and Harold put on his brown linen tunic and gold armbands, looking every bit the Danish Earl of Wessex. I was proud to walk beside him. But when we entered the great hall, William's guards made Hakon and I wait by the door, and they directed Harold to stand before the Duke. Giving my shoulder a squeeze, Harold obliged.

Once William and Matilda were seated, the Duke pointed to the table in the center of the hall. One of the Bishops was placing a Bible on the table. Leather-bound, it looked very old and worn on top of the delicate lace.

"Go, my friend, and take your place by the Bible."

My heart went out to Harold as he calmly stepped down and put his hand on the Bible. I knew how uncomfortable he was, but one could never tell to look at his face. He gazed at William impassively.

"My friends and nobles," said William, getting up and pacing before the assembly. "Earl Harold would return to England, despite my protests. But ere he leaves, I have asked him to swear an oath, before my assembled Lords." He turned to face Harold, who had already broken into a sweat. No mention of an oath was ever made in my presence.

"I would have you swear, my Lord Harold, that you will espouse my daughter Adeliza as soon as she is of marriageable age."

That was all right; he had offered to do so. After a moment, Harold said, "I swear."

"Secondly, I would have you swear to give up to me, this day, your castle at Dover, so that I may garrison it with Norman soldiers." The corner of William's mouth turned up into an almost unnoticeable sneer. He must have known this was impossible. Even if he would, Harold had not the power to give up a royal castle.

Harold looked up at the ceiling, sighing. "To this also I swear," he said evenly.

"And thirdly, lastly, I would have you be my man in England, and uphold my claim to the throne of my friend King Edward upon his demise. In return for this, I swear to give you all the highest honors in England, and allow you to retain your earldom."

So William hadn't given up on his design for the English Crown. I was glad I had warned my brother. He stood silent for a long while. I don't think anyone really expected Harold to keep this promise. But if he didn't, he would damned as an oath breaker.

"Swear," shouted William, filling the room with his voice.

I hated Duke William at this moment, with all my heart. Shaking his head, my brother obeyed. "I swear," he said quietly.

"Speak the words, Harold."

"I swear to be your man in England, and speak up in your support. Now let me go."

Harold started to walk toward me when William called "Wait" in a harsh voice. My brother stopped and waited.

Suddenly, Duke William summoned a man forward who was sitting next to Count Alain le Rouge. I didn't know him, but as Harold whirled around I could see from his shocked expression that he knew the man very well.

"Walter, pull the linen from the table, and bid your countryman to come forward."

Harold walked slowly back to the table. I know he was dreading a wretched surprise.

Hands shaking, that other man obeyed then turned away, burying his face in the cloth. My poor brother sank to one knee. William turned triumphantly to the assembly.

"See the holy relics of the Saints of Normandy," William blared. "Earl Harold has sworn his oath on their bones. Take heed, all of you!"

The game was over for the Duke. He stood proudly, arms crossed over his chest. Matilda had turned her head the other way; I could see she was crying.

I dared not move but waited as the other man helped Harold to his feet. He led my brother over to me; Hakon and I could barely support him for a moment.

"Don't let him gloat over you," I whispered in my brother's ear.

Harold heard me. He regained his resolution and straightened up.

"Come, let us go before it's too late," he muttered.

Nothing loth, we picked up our pace. Outside, we were joined by his remaining housecarls and we strode purposefully toward the waiting horses. Harold was mounting when suddenly ten of William's soldiers converged upon us. Harold's housecarls pulled their swords, surrounding their Earl.

But the Normans weren't intent on stopping Harold. They surrounded me, pushing Hakon toward my brother.

"Take him and go," their leader said, pointing his sword at Hakon. "Wulfnoth stays here as surety for your oath."

Harold sat astride his horse, his face awash with misery. If he tried to fight for me, they might imprison him for real. I struggled with the guards and they released my arms. All of us knew I wasn't going anywhere.

327

I raised my hand in farewell. I couldn't speak but managed to nod my head. Harold nodded back then turned his horse, applying his spurs. He couldn't get away fast enough. Hakon mounted his horse and took one last look before following my brother.

I thought I had felt alone when Archbishop Robert dragged us away from England. But at least I had Hakon. Now I had no one. I watched my brother disappear then sighed heavily, trying to make the best of my situation. At least Harold had gotten away safely. He wasn't likely to come for a visit again.

END OF PART 2

AUTHOR'S NOTE

I made the decision to write this book in first person because it struck me that the inside story of 1066 is still open to interpretation. So many things happened that don't make logical sense, like the murder of Beorn or the Northumbrian insurrection after ten years of relative quiet. I think a lot of the story can be inferred by looking at the relationship between the brothers.

Like Judas Iscariot, Tostig Godwineson has gone down in history as the ultimate traitor. Yes, he did invade England with Harald Hardrada, but was it his idea or Harald's? There is no agreement on this. But even if he was the one responsible for Stamford Bridge, it's certainly possible that his side of the story is more complicated than we are usually told.

I believe that, although Tostig and Harold apparently got along up until the Rebellion of 1065, there may have been friction between them from the beginning. After all, Harold was said to be his mother's favorite just like Swegn was their father's favorite. That left the rest of the boys to garner attention as best as they could. Did Tostig resent his elder brother?

Harold is history's darling, or even a martyr if we take sides, Norman vs. Saxon. He seems larger than life to us, a perfect representation of the doomed Anglo-Saxon hero. But there were sides to Harold that even his most valiant defender could be puzzled about. Even Edward A. Freeman, Harold's faithful apologist, admits to one single error when Harold raided his homeland and killed 30+ thegns after his exile in Ireland. But I think there are other moments when we might wonder about his motives: what about his refusal to return Swegn's earldom after his brother's aborted restoration? Why didn't Tostig get any credit for his participation in the Welsh campaign?

And then we have the ultimate question, which I will tackle in volume three: FATAL RIVALRY. Did Harold let Tostig down

329

when negotiating with the Northumbrian rebels? Did he turn his back on his brother? Did he really have any choice? Could he have offered Tostig any compensation for the loss of Northumbria? Why did Tostig accuse Harold of fomenting the rebellion? I think the answers to these questions have a lot to do with their early relationship. Perhaps the rift between them was so deep that Tostig's subsequent actions were inevitable.

The younger brothers, Gyrth, Leofwine, and Wulfnoth are often sketched in as appendages to the Harold Godwineson story. But they, too, have stories to tell, and give us their perspectives on Harold's activities. Gyrth and Leofwine are the most neutral of all the siblings, though they are somewhat in awe of their big brother. I think that Wulfnoth, in particular, has been given short shrift by history. Of all the Godwinesons, he alone survived Hastings and in fact lived to the ripe old age of 58. In volume three, it is Wulfnoth who carries on with Editha's chronicle, for he survives her by almost 20 years.

And what about Edith Swanneck? Once again, we have very little to go on. We think she was a rich East Anglian heiress, and Harold may have married her to gain favor with a local powerful chieftain. But so much emphasis has been made on her wealth, I wondered how she would have been prosperous as a daughter? Then I ran across the suggestion that she might have been a rich widow, and that helped inspire my Eadric of Laxfield subplot. Oh yes, there was an Eadric of Laxfield, one of the richest men in East Anglia, who was outlawed for some unspecified offense, then pardoned by the king. He was also said to have been a supporter of Harold at the Battle of Hastings. The rest of his tale is my own making.

Would you like to learn more about Gruffydd ap Llewelyn? Gruffydd is the grandfather of my protagonist in HEIR TO A PROPHECY, and much more of his story, including the timely warning Gruffydd receives on Christmas night of 1062, is covered in that novel. Walter made cameo appearances in this volume,

330

when Tostig met him in Malcolm's company before Dunsinane (I cover the battle of Dunsinane in depth, as well, in HEIR TO A PROPHECY) and when Harold sends him to parley with Aelfgar.

I believe it is the job of the historical novelist to connect the dots, so to speak, and fill in gaps left by history in the most credible way possible. We try to explain things that don't make sense at face value, and flesh out characters that often seem two-dimensional. When writing about events that happened almost 1000 years ago, many of our "facts" are conflicting, and often even our sources contradict each other. My interpretations may not agree with the next person's conclusions, but I hope at least they might make sense in the world I have painted.

Don't Miss

FATAL RIVALRY

Part Three of The Last Great Saxon Earls

CHAPTER 1

HAROLD REMEMBERS

Fate has dealt me a mortal blow. I know it. Never in my life have I done anything I am destined to regret more. William the Bastard has gotten the better of me, and has forced me to give an oath to support his claim to the throne. He trapped me in a golden cage of my own making.

It seemed a hundred years ago when I left Bosham with my hunting dogs and my falcon. I may have pretended I was going on a hunt, but my real aim was to ransom my little brother Wulfnoth and my nephew Hakon. They had been hostages in Normandy long enough. I was so proud of myself back then—so sure I was ready for anything. And just as soon as I set foot on land, my world went to pieces. I could still be languishing in Count Guy's dungeon if it weren't for Duke William's timely intervention. And so, like Scylla and Charybdis, I was caught between the rocky shoal and the whirlpool.

For a while I became William's hostage, as sure as Wulfnoth was. How was I to know that the duke thought himself King Edward's heir, duped by that wily Robert of Jumièges? Who would have thought the archbishop would take such a far-sighted revenge on my family—no, on our whole country—because of his feud with father? I never would have ventured to Normandy if I had known about William's expectations. And once I was caught

332

in his power, I had no choice but to do his bidding. I would have done anything to get away from there.

As soon as William got what he wanted, he let me fly away. But not Wulfnoth. Poor Wulfnoth. The duke of Normandy kept my brother as surety for my wretched oath. Sick at heart for leaving Wulfnoth behind—wondering if I was doing the right thing—I watched the Norman coast recede along with my brother's hopes. What else could I have done? I listened to the boat creak and the water splash in that comforting way which tells us all is well; though in my case this was an illusion. I put my arm around my nephew Hakon's shoulders, chiding myself for wishing it was Wulfnoth standing beside me and not him. But I never had any feelings for Swegn's son and it was too late to change that now. It wasn't Hakon's fault Duke William saw fit to retain my little brother as hostage. Ironically, it was Hakon's good fortune that he had no particular value to anybody.

I should have felt some relief that my mission wasn't a total failure. But I didn't. I may have gained freedom for my nephew, but I may have lost my soul in the process. And my self-respect. How could things have gone so wrong?

No matter whom the witan elects as next king, Edward's successor will have to face Duke William and his remorseless claim. But there was something more that bothered me. Archbishop Robert was friends with King Edward. He had served the king for years, and only left the country because he was forced out of power—by my father, of course. His first act of revenge was to snatch away poor Wulfnoth and Hakon as hostages. His second act was to promise the throne to William. It's possible that he and Edward planned my family's outlawry all along; could it also be that the king really did offer the crown to Duke William? I shuddered to think on it.

And how was I going to ask him? I would have enough trouble explaining myself when I got back to England without seeming to accuse him. What would be the point? As king, Edward could do whatever he pleased. But to give away his country to a foreign ruler? I just didn't see how that was possible. Even Edward had some loyalty toward his subjects. I hope.

333

Looking back, I would say my troubles with Harold started after he returned from Normandy, back in the late summer of 1064. While Harold was gone, things were so much better. King Edward and I spent a lot of time together, and I'm proud to say he treated me like a close companion. Without my brother's presence, Edward was quite another man; he was more relaxed, he would laugh more and even jest on occasion. Anyway, when Harold returned—already stinging from the trouble his pride had brought him—he made a quiet entrance into the great hall. He took one look at the king and I, drinking together and laughing, and his face turned three shades of red. My sister the queen told me about it later, because at the time I was turned away from him. What I would have given to see my brother's face!

The king looked up and saw Harold, and the change that came over him was immediate. His smile faded, his eyes took on that old guarded expression; his manner turned formal as he stood with a hand out for Harold to kiss. "Welcome back to court," the king said sadly. "You have been sorely missed."

Everyone except Harold could tell that Edward said the exact opposite of what he meant. But of course my brother chose to take him literally. "I am relieved to be back, Sire," he said. "Although I'm sorry to say my mission was only half-accomplished."

Harold had gone to Normandy to retrieve my brother Wulfnoth and our nephew Hakon, held there as hostages for the last twelve years. Edward had advised him against going, but my brother had to play hero, no matter what the cost.

I sat up at his admission. "What happened?" I exclaimed. "Where is our brother?"

I expected some sort of retort from Harold, but he actually hung his head. "Duke William allowed me to bring back Hakon, though he insisted on keeping Wulfnoth. He wanted security against certain promises he extorted from me..."

He trailed off. I jumped to my feet, angrily. "What's that! You left Wulfnoth behind in Normandy?"

334

That got a reaction from him. "You weren't there, Tostig. I tried my best." He was angry, but something was holding him back.

"And your best wasn't good enough. Poor Wulfnoth! We'll never get him back now."

King Edward put a hand on my arm, nodding for me to contain myself. I turned away.

"Was it such a difficulty, then," he asked Harold, "getting my cousin William to cooperate?" William was more of a second or third cousin to Edward, but our king spoke of the duke with great regard.

"Sire," Harold blurted, rushing his words together, "I must speak to you alone on this matter."

My brother's manner radiated desperation. Despite myself, I watched curiously as he followed the king from the room. My sister and I exchanged glances, and she slipped out after them. Edward never excluded her from his presence—nor indeed, do I think he could have.

Tostig was right. My husband never forgave himself for exiling me to a nunnery when he banished my father back in 1051, even though I think he was glad when father died two years later. Still, there was no denying the injustice of my imprisonment, and ever since then, Edward attempted to atone by admitting me to his presence on any occasion I desired. That is how I was able to witness the emotional scene between Harold and the king, when he confessed to his foul oath to support William's claim to the English throne... Editha

My sister was gone a long time, and the great hall gradually emptied out. When Editha came back she was very pale. She sat down on the throne and I moved to her side, taking her usual chair. She put a hand to her forehead.

"Prepare yourself," she said to me. "I have some very disturbing news."

"Where's Harold?"

335

"He's gone. There is nothing more for him to say right now."

I took her hand. "Tell me."

Editha gave a great sigh. "Edward had warned him not to go. But mayhap it is better this way. At least we know."

She was trying my patience. I forced myself to stay calm. "Know what?"

"About William's designs on the throne. He sees himself as Edward's heir."

I gasped. What was she talking about?

"From what Harold just admitted, Archbishop Robert of Jumièges told him Edward promised the throne, way back after our father's exile. Robert delivered Wulfnoth and Hakon into William's hands as hostages for this promise. All this time, William has schemed for the throne of England."

I was shocked. But then I was puzzled.

"What has this to do with Harold?"

"Our brother fell into William's trap. The duke would not let him leave until he swore an oath to support William's claim. A frightful oath. An oath on the relics of Normandy's saints."

I crossed myself, twice. This was indeed dreadful news. For all of us.

"Harold was lucky to get away," she added. "Hakon was lucky to get away. William kept Wulfnoth as hostage against Harold's promise. Now our brother needs to expiate his sin, for we all know he made that oath in vain. What will happen to poor Wulfnoth?"

No wonder he couldn't face me. We could only hope that Edward would outlive William, which would make Harold's oath moot. Otherwise...well, there was nothing to be done now.

HAROLD REMEMBERS

My meeting with the king was just as distressing as I expected it to be. At least he let me tell him alone, with just my

336

sister in tow. I wasn't strong enough to confront Tostig just yet; the few words that passed between us were almost more than I could bear. He has a way of making me uneasy; ever since we were boys, he has always been on the verge of fighting with me, and his sarcasm can be biting.

Unfortunately, I wasn't feeling much better around Edward, but for different reasons. We both remembered his warning when I originally announced my plans. And now I couldn't shake the uncomfortable feeling that even back then, he knew much more than I did about William's secret ambition.

The king offered me a seat; I was glad of it, for my emotions were exhausting me. I looked at the floor, waiting for him to speak. But of course, I was the supplicant here.

"Tell me, Harold," he said finally. His voice was not friendly.

I raised my head.

"Sire, had I known William desired the throne, I never would have crossed the Channel."

That was as close as I dared to make an accusation. I waited for a reaction.

Edward was much better at hiding his feelings since our outlawry. He rubbed his cheek, looking into the distance.

"The throne," he said quietly. "What about the throne?"

Could it be possible he didn't know? I looked at my sister but she shrugged her shoulders.

"Wulfnoth told me," I went on, "that Archbishop Robert made the announcement directly after he left England. With my brother." This was shaky ground, for I don't think Edward ever forgave our victorious return from exile. Many of his Norman friends left the country and never came back. Including Robert, who died a couple of years later. I'm sure Edward was thinking about this as well, but his face betrayed no emotion. I took a deep breath.

"The archbishop told William you wanted him to be your heir. That you sent Wulfnoth and Hakon as hostages to secure your promise."

I stared at the king. He blinked back.

"Do you believe that?" he said finally.

I didn't know. I took a deep breath. "Wulfnoth said Robert told the duke that my father and the other great earls agreed. I certainly don't believe that!" His question was only half answered. I waited. He didn't move a muscle. "He said Robert made it all up to wreak revenge on us," I added.

After a moment, Edward nodded as if in agreement. "I will tell you this, Harold. When your father was in exile, Archbishop Robert and I spent a lot of time together, much of it in idle conversation."

He paused so long I thought he was finished. Editha bent over his shoulder.

"No, my dear, Harold deserves to know. You deserve to know. There was a time I mentioned William's name, more as wistful musing than any desire to act on it. I know the witan. William would not be popular in this country. He would understand your customs less than I did."

I didn't know what to say. Where was the truth in this?

"And the hostages?"

He looked away. "They were in Archbishop Robert's charge. I was not involved."

I frowned despite myself. As I suspected, Edward took no responsibility for my brother at all.

"He was so brave." My voice shook. "I hated to leave him behind."

"What exactly happened?"

It was hard to look back at those months. "William treated me well, but I was never left alone. He set guards outside my door at night. He kept me at his side nearly every day. He took me on campaign with him. He even knighted me..." Those words were hard to say and I had to swallow. "When I finally tried to take my leave, he insisted that I do so in front of a grand assembly of nobles and ecclesiastics."

The king pursed his lips but said nothing.

"Sire, he made me swear an oath that I would be his man in England and support his claim to the throne." I put my hands over my face. "He made me swear that I would give him Dover castle so he could garrison it with his own men." Edward gasped.

"There was no other way." My voice was almost pleading with him to understand. "I swore that oath on the bones of his saints, though I did not know it until too late. And I don't even know which saints!"

Edward probably crossed himself, for I heard the swish of his sleeves though I could not bear to uncover my face.

"I forswore myself to gain my freedom," I said, still trying to control my voice. "I took that oath under duress."

Those last words served to calm me, for I truly believed I could stand behind this defense. But when I finally looked at Edward, I was not reassured.

"Your actions will have grave consequences, Harold. I fear for you."

I gasped. He sounded like a reproachful prophet. Or was it my own guilt ringing in my ears?

BIBLIOGRAPHY

Barlow, Frank, THE GODWINS, The Rise and Fall of a Noble Dynasty, Pearson Education Limited, 2002

Borman, Tracy, QUEEN OF THE CONQUEROR, The Life of Matilda, Wife of William I, Bantam Books, New York, 2011

Courtship, Love and Marriage in Viking Scandinavia
http://www.vikinganswerlady.com/wedding.shtml

Fletcher, Richard, BLOODFEUD, Murder and Revenge in Anglo-Saxon England, Oxford University Press, 2003

Freeman, Edward A., THE HISTORY OF THE NORMAN CONQUEST OF ENGLAND, Oxford at the Clarendon Press, 1875

Hill, Paul, THE ROAD TO HASTINGS, The Politics of Power in Anglo-Saxon England, Tempus Publishing, Gloucestershire, 2005

Hollister, C.Warren, ANGLO-SAXON MILITARY INSTITUTIONS On the Eve of the Norman Conquest, Oxford at the Clarendon Press, 1962

Kapelle, William E., THE NORMAN CONQUEST OF THE NORTH: The Region and its Transformation, 1000-1135, Univ. of North Carolina Press, 1979

Lander, Jeremy, QUEEN EDITH, The Story of a Saxon King, his lover and a Cambridge Suburb, a short paper, 2009
http://www.frrarchitects.co.uk/wp-content/uploads/2011/07/Queen-Edith_-Jeremy-Lander.pdf

Mason, Emma, THE HOUSE OF GODWINE, The History of a Dynasty, Hambledon and London, 2004

Morris, Marc, THE NORMAN CONQUEST, The Battle of Hastings and the Fall of Anglo-Saxon England, Pegasus Books, 2012

Rex, Peter, HAROLD II, The Doomed Saxon King, Tempus Publishing LTD, Gloucestershire, 2005

Walker, Ian W., HAROLD THE LAST ANGLO-SAXON KING, Sutton Publishing, Gloucestershire, 1997

Printed in Great Britain
by Amazon

42082489R00195